SURPRISE!

Movement on the horizon caught his eye. An aircraft sped toward them.

Tanay saw it too and darted off in the opposite direction.

"Hey, wait a second, who is that?" he asked as he attempted to unencumber himself of the chute and damaged flight suit.

Tanay continued her flight as the approaching ship grew. It was not the Black Knight Satellite returning, as Cormac first suspected, but its own terrible surprise.

It looked like a flat patrol boat with an open-air canopy, yet it had boosters along the bottom allowing it to have incredible speed, and a hovering power lifting it at almost thirty feet in the air. A troop of men were aboard. Cormac shuddered in horror as he realized they were not mere men but giants, at least twelve feet tall, wearing a bizarre mismatch of archaic-looking armor and spectacular tech—such as a robotic arm where one had apparently lost a limb.

The craft landed with a great blasting of dust over the top of Cormac, and the giants disembarked.

"This one must be an escaped slave," said one to another.

"I'm no slave," Cormac shouted.

"He barks like a dog!" said the one with the cybernetic arm.

"I'm an Airman of the United States Air Force and must be treated as stated in the Geneva Convention!"

"Convention?" repeat

"Air-Man?" asked yet

"We shall see."

BAEN BOOKS by
CHRISTOPHER RUOCCHIO

Disquiet Gods (forthcoming)

BAEN BOOKS
edited by
CHRISTOPHER RUOCCHIO

Sword & Planet

WITH SEAN CW KORSGAARD
Worlds Long Lost

WITH TONY DANIEL
Star Destroyers
World Breakers

WITH HANK DAVIS
Space Pioneers
Overruled!
Cosmic Corsairs
Time Troopers

BAEN BOOKS
edited by
SEAN CW KORSGAARD

WITH HANK DAVIS
They're Here!

To purchase any of these titles in e-book form, please go to
www.baen.com.

WORLDS LONG LOST

edited by

Christopher Ruocchio

and

Sean CW Korsgaard

Copyright © 2022 by Christopher Ruocchio and Sean CW Korsgaard

"Introduction" copyright © 2022 by Christopher Ruocchio; "The Wrong Shape to Fly" © 2022 by Adam Oyebanji; "Mother of Monsters" copyright © 2022 by Christopher Ruocchio; "Rise of the Administrator" copyright © 2022 by M.A. Rothman and D.J. Butler; "Mere Passers By" copyright © 2022 by Les Johnson; "Never Ending, Ever-Growing" copyright © 2022 by Erica Ciko; "They Only Dig at Night" copyright © 2022 by Sean Patrick Hazlett; "Howlers in the Void" copyright © 2022 by Brian Trent; "The Building Will Continue" copyright © 2022 by Gray Rinehart; "re: something strange" copyright © 2022 by Jessica Cain; "The Sleepers of Tartarus" copyright © 2022 by David J. West; "Dark Eternity" copyright © 2022 by Jonathan Edelstein; "Rocking the Cradle" copyright © 2022 by Patrick Chiles; "Giving Up on the Piano" copyright © 2022 by Orson Scott Card; "Restrospective" copyright © 2022 by Griffin Barber

A Baen Books Original

Baen Publishing Enterprises
P.O. Box 1403
Riverdale, NY 10471
www.baen.com

ISBN: 978-1-9821-9311-9

Cover art by Bob Eggleton

First printing, December 2022
First mass market printing, December 2023

Distributed by Simon & Schuster
1230 Avenue of the Americas
New York, NY 10020

Library of Congress Control Number: 2022041571

Printed in the United States of America

10 9 8 7 6 5 4 3 2 1

CONTENTS

WORLDS LONG LOST

INTRODUCTION

Like most children, I was a long time learning to distinguish fiction from reality. (Indeed, some never outgrow the condition—which is one of those amusing thoughts that will hit differently for each individual reader.) I distinctly remember believing that Sherlock Holmes was a historical figure—never having heard of Sir Arthur Conan Doyle—and that Camelot could be found on a map. Leaving aside the matter that there *was* a Camulodunum and was probably some kind of Arthur, one of the more interesting ways this inability to distinguish fact from fiction manifested was in a childhood obsession with the lost continent of Atlantis. By the age of twelve or thirteen, I found myself the owner of several volumes of conspiracy-theory-rich pseudohistory on the subject. My parents, delighted that I was so interested in reading—and in "serious" reading, no less—were happy to encourage me. And so I learned all about the ringed city and crystal skulls and—more usefully—about Knossos and the Minoans, and about the way the Greeks of the misnamed "Golden Age" believed the Minoan sites were built by cyclopses (whence cometh the word "cyclopean," so beloved of H.P. Lovecraft).

1

In time, I came to learn that Atlantis was only ever a thought experiment of Plato's, and not something widely believed in by the Greek world. Unlike Camelot, there wasn't even a kernel of true history at the bottom. It was an ancient fiction, and regarded as fiction even in antiquity. I was crushed. This discovery was far worse than the discovery that my parents were acting in the role of Santa Claus at age nine, because my parents at least were creating magic for the benefit of my brothers and me. I think about how many people throughout history took the Atlantis myth seriously, about how many people went looking for it, or used the myth as the basis for their insane eugenic ideologies.

Overnight, the History Channel's *Ancient Aliens* show went from a deeply interesting and meaningful exploration of humanity's entanglement with extraterrestrial forces to a waste of time. If I wanted to watch hours of fiction devoted to ancient aliens, I was just going to watch *Stargate*, and boy, do I love *Stargate*.

Which brings us to the matter of this collection.

It doesn't matter that Atlantis never existed, or that aliens *probably* haven't visited Earth (I am pretty sure most UFOs are the result of waveguiding, but I could be convinced. Consider me agnostic on the alien visitors question), leastways for the purposes of the science fiction writer. What matters is that it makes for fertile ground in which to plant a story. As I say, I adore *Stargate*, and even *Ancient Aliens* is fun if you take it for the pseudodocumentary it is. There's still something of the old world romance in such stories, of a time when the world still had unturned stones in it.

That's part of what makes them so much fun.

But now, with the edges of Earth's map almost all filled in and the monsters painted over, we had to move our lost cities off world. If the aliens never visited us, we would have to visit them. Since there were no alien gods beneath the pyramids in Egypt or lost deep in the Yucatan, we'd have to build pyramids on Mars, or the moons of Jupiter, or about some other sun.

This is my last Baen Books anthology—at least for the foreseeable future. The last one on my docket when I resigned my job in May of 2021. Anthologies usually start from a premise. The editor says, "Hey, you know what would be fun? A sword and sorcery anthology!" and rolls with it. This one started—in suitably archaeological fashion—with a lost artifact. We were turning through old files at the Baen offices when we discovered a piece of unused art, a landscape by the great Bob Eggleton, one we'd long ago paid for the rights to use, but that had languished in some obscure folder.

"What can we use this for?" asked Toni Weisskopf, Baen's publisher—my old boss—with the air of one inquiring what the purpose of some cracked amphora might have been, unearthed in some Achaean tomb.

It depicted jagged pillars of stone rising from the barren surface of an alien world, a galaxy turning in the skies above as rockets left blue contrails against a rosy sky. Like all of Eggleton's paintings, there was a magic in it, a call to adventure.

"Ancient aliens, maybe?" I suggested, peering over her shoulder. "Like . . . xenoarchaeology stories."

"That'll do."

It's taken some time to excavate these stories from the minds of their various authors. May of 2021 was already a long time ago, and that day when we unearthed Eggleton's painting from beneath years of mounded paperwork is even further gone. There's something bittersweet in this book then. I started working for Baen in my senior year of college, in January of 2015. I was just an unpaid intern then, doing the job for college credit. They hired me about a month after I graduated, about a week after I sold *Empire of Silence* to DAW Books and became a writer.

A lot happened for me in the years since. I met my wife, got married. I published five novels (the fifth, in fact, shares a release day with this anthology), two novellas, more than a dozen short stories. I edited eight anthologies, released two of my own short story collections . . . and even quit my day job.

But this is the end, my last official task as Junior Editor for Baen Books, and I hope you will forgive this little bit of self-indulgence at the end of this intro. It's fitting, too, that Sean is coediting this one with me. He took over my seat in the Baen offices, and so I figured I should drag him along and show him the ropes.

So read on, dear Reader. Both Sean and I hope you enjoy the stories here.

And know that when you close this book at its ending, that I closed the book on a long and happy chapter of my life. I'll let Sean take it from here. He'll be the one introducing the stories in this book!

—C.R.
May, AD 2022

THE WRONG SHAPE TO FLY
Adam Oyebanji

Few questions in science fiction have been asked and answered more times and by more authors than "Are we alone in the universe?" or "Is there other intelligent life among the stars?" Many of the stories that fill the subgenre of tales about ancient aliens, ruins on other worlds, long dead progenitor races offer a grim answer to those questions: Yes, but you just missed them on the way out. Yet in a way, finding those ruins or remnants are almost as miraculous as first contact, perhaps not the answer you wanted, but an answer all the same.

This story from Adam Oyebanji explores some of the biggest things that need to occur for that miracle to happen at all. The dozens of things that can wipe out life before it can spread from the planet that spawned it. The matter of perfect timing across the vast distance of space. Recognizing something as result of an alien intelligence at all, and not just a bit of space junk or cosmic coincidence. The tragedy of had things gone just slightly differently, you might have found a civilization rather than a tomb . . . and the reflection that you just as easily could have never known they'd existed at all.

5

Perhaps it had been birthed from the nightmares of a child. A profusion of spindly, asymmetric limbs, sprouting in every direction from a gold-sheathed, polyhedral torso. A vast, blind eye protruded from its front.

There was no mouth.

"What is it?" asked Cho Abi Sorocaba, broker of planets.

His host, Ree Aba Jen, tried hard to hide her amusement, and failed.

"An embarrassment, my lord. Hiding in plain sight for many years."

"It doesn't look like an embarrassment, mistress. It looks . . . intriguing."

The object of the planet broker's attention was surrounded by a small army of construction bots. Or, more accurately, *de*-construction bots. The sculpture, trapped inside a transparent dodecahedron like an arthropod in amber, was being removed from a plinth. A truck waited nearby to take it away, engine idling under the soft light of the local sun, the name of which Cho always struggled to remember. He was a broker of planets after all, not stars.

The object was like nothing Cho had ever seen. Its ungainly dimensions were far from auspicious. The transparent casing, while no doubt necessary to protect the sculpture from the ravages of weather, also served to conform the installation's shape to the harmonious requirements of *Maidagan*. Dodecahedrons were always propitious. Combined with the elegant shape and size of the plinth, the overall presentation amounted to a powerful token of good fortune.

The bots broke the connection between dodecahedron and plinth. There was a sharp hiss of collapsing vacuum. Or perhaps it was the sound of escaping luck. Unable to stop himself, Cho made the sign of the Protector, cursing himself for his superstition. He turned away, hiding the gesture from his escort, and strode purposefully toward the gilded commercial headquarters that was his destination. He didn't have to look back to know that the object was being swung smoothly onto the bed of the truck, or that the truck would be extending the necessary arms and straps to secure it in place.

"How can a work of art be such an embarrassment as to be removed from the grounds?"

Ree chuckled.

"Because it's not merely a work of art, my lord. At least, that is not what it was sold as. My Lady Morota and the board paid several million jigu for an archeological artifact. An abstract representation of the Drekkar Supreme Deity."

Cho's response was an incredulous guffaw.

"Any fool can see that this is nothing like a Drekkar deity—or *anything* Drekkar, for that matter."

"Hence the embarrassment, my lord." Ree ushered him into the building.

It was unfortunate for Cho that his business that day required him to meet Morota face to face. He spent far too much energy fighting the urge to ask her—in front of a number of functionaries—how she could have been so foolish in her acquisition of ancient artifacts. In the end, he brokered the sale of three planets to Naiyami Corporation for rather less than he had hoped.

"Come," Morota said, clearly pleased with the day's business, "join me for a drink on the ledge. You too, Ree."

"Yes, my lady."

"And less of the 'my lady,' Ree. We are done with work for the day."

"Yes, my lady." Ree grinned. Morota made a sound of mock exasperation.

The ledge was a broad terrace that ran along the outside of the building. Cho knew better than to look over the edge. It was a long way down and there was no railing. He knew that if he stared too long, the urge to jump would become irresistible.

"I feel," Morota said, after drinks had arrived, "that you have been distracted all day. Any particular reason?" There was a twinkle in the chair's eye. Cho realized, with a sudden and crushing certainty, that he'd been played.

"The artifact," he confessed. "The one that was being removed from the grounds this morning. I couldn't understand how it could ever have been mistaken for a Drekkar."

"I thought that might be it." Morota didn't insult his intelligence by trying to hide her satisfaction. "You should have been an antiquarian rather than a broker of planets. It is, I feel, your true passion—as I have told you many times."

Cho smiled ruefully.

"Perhaps. But it does not pay the bills."

Morota laughed at that. But she, too, turned rueful.

"An appalling mistake, truly. I have already had to apologize to our people on behalf of the board. The profits of their labor should not have been wasted in such a fashion. The local media have not been kind."

"But how? I know I only saw the object briefly on my way in...."

"But for long enough," Ree chuckled.

"But for long enough," Cho agreed, smiling. "Long enough to see that it was constructed from a number of ductile alloys. It is primitive to be sure—and intriguing. But not so primitive as to be Drekkar. Ten thousand years ago, when their own sun killed them, they had only recently learned to work iron. Ductile alloys—apart from bronze—were well beyond their abilities."

"You noticed its proportions?" Ree asked. "Of the object alone, I mean, rather than the final installation?"

"Horrifying. But oddly compelling. You can't stop looking at it. Its irregularity, its unbalanced nature, its ... aggressiveness." He hesitated before adding, "It was like looking at the heart of a demon."

"Exactly. The thing is, though, there are apparently many objects on Drekkar that share similar proportions. Two, *two* chartered archaeologists certified that the ratios were so matched to other renditions of the Drekkar Supreme Deity as to be beyond coincidence."

"But the technology, mistress. How could the archaeologists have failed to notice such a thing?"

"Oh, they noticed," Morota intervened. "Not that it stopped them." She stared morosely at her empty drink; signaled the service bot for another.

"Drekkar is, as you know, a desert world, and, even

now, only partially explored," Ree said. "There are subcultures and nations that still await to be discovered. The archaeologists—"

"Charlatans, more like."

"—belonged to a school of thought that argues Drekkar was turned to desert by artificial forces, rather than a brightening sun."

"We've seen that elsewhere," Cho agreed. "Runaway heating caused by industrial pollution. On Xakas Sei, for example. But there's usually some massive chemical footprint: generally in the form of ridiculous amounts of carbon dioxide, either still in the atmosphere, or trapped in the fossil record somehow. There's none of that on Drekkar."

"This school of thought asserted that we'll find the footprint eventually, that the brightening of the Drekkar sun alone cannot account for the scale of the damage, and that there must be, somewhere on the planet, a Drekkar civilization far more advanced than any yet discovered. This object, they said, was proof of that." Ree allowed herself a wry smile. "Scholarly papers were written. Obscure academic arguments ensued."

"So, what changed your mind? Why remove a certified, one-of-a-kind Drekkar artifact from the campus?"

"Drekkar scholars, by definition, I suppose, are skilled in the analysis of extremely primitive artifacts, in iron and bronze and stone. Their arguments revolve around shape, and proportion, the Drekkar historical record, and the planetology of Drekkar itself. But then someone had the bright idea of bringing in archeologists specializing in the Bren C cultures."

"Bren C? Why? They have no connection to the Drekkar, either in time or space. They were in their heyday before the Drekkar people even evolved. They were around, what, a million-and-a-half years ago? And their sun didn't kill them, as I recall. They did that to themselves. A devastating nuclear war."

"True, my lord. But, given that they wiped themselves out with fusion bombs, they had technology. The sort of technology that was more than familiar with ductile alloys. They had *machines*, the remnants of which survive to this day, even if we have no idea what many of them were for. Bren C archaeologists spend a lot of time with machinery. If this artifact was as advanced as its proponents claimed, someone had the bright idea that it might not be a deity at all, but a machine. And who better to investigate a machine than a Bren C archaeologist?"

"And these Bren C specialists somehow settled the argument?"

"And then some," Morota said. "They reanalyzed all the original scans. Apparently, it took them less than a day to deduce that the artifact had never been anywhere near Drekkar."

"Really?"

"Really. The object's 'torso,' the gold-sheathed polyhedron in the middle of all those arms and legs, isn't solid. There are a number of devices inside. Some of which are little more than pellets of uranium two-three-eight."

"Odd."

"It gets odder. The pellets are uranium two-three-eight now, but they also contain trace amounts of plutonium two-three-nine. Everyone—*everyone*—agrees that the pellets must once have been pure plutonium, but they've decayed into uranium over a period of about a thousand years."

"So, too young to be Drekkar?"

"Precisely. About nine thousand years too young."

"And did these new archaeologists hazard a guess as to what this thing is?"

Morota smiled into her drink.

"They don't know. But one of the team thought it might be a spacecraft, or the remains of one."

Had Cho been drinking at the time he would have choked.

"Seriously?"

"Seriously."

"A tiny, ill-balanced collection of appendages with no room for passengers or cargo, no fuel tanks, no A-Grav engines, no soliton generator, with the aerodynamics of a . . . a rock, is a spacecraft?"

"In fairness," Ree jumped in, "the archaeologist said it was the best he could offer. The Bren C cultures made copious use of something called rockets. Giant tubes of explosives. The explosive force is channeled out of one end and the resultant thrust pushes the object high into the atmosphere—even to the edge of space if it's big enough."

"And these . . . *rockets*, really worked?"

"Apparently. In any event, our 'Drekkar deity' has a number of devices that look like tiny rockets. The problem is, they're so tiny that they're useless. And, as you've pointed out, the object is the wrong shape to fly, anyway.

In the end, the new team came up blank as to what it is. But they are *very* certain as to what it is not. Our certifying archaeologists had no answer to the radioactive decay problem. The Drekkar civilization is ten thousand years old, and this object is barely a thousand. They were forced to concede their error. The certificate was withdrawn, and my lady Morota had to consume large quantities of humble pie."

"Charlatans," Morota muttered again. "If they'd just *thought* about what was inside the object, this would never have happened. But they were so wedded to their advanced Drekkar subculture theory, they ignored what was right in front of them."

"And that," said Cho, smiling, "is archaeology in a nutshell: wild guesses, based mostly on personal prejudice, mutate into equally wild theories. Theories into which the guessers have poured so many hopes and dreams that they will not let them go until the evidence against becomes overwhelming. At which point the academy moves on to a slightly less wild theory, which gives way in turn to something even less wild until, after many, many years, and many, many shattered egos, something close to the truth is finally arrived at."

"Well, I wish these people's personal growth had not come at the expense of my company's balance sheet," Morota grumbled.

It was at this point that an idea, an idea as persistent as it was ridiculous, lodged itself in Cho's head. He was careful to keep his face devoid of anything beyond an expression of mild curiosity.

"What will become of the object?" he asked.

"Don't know," Morota said. "Don't care, either."

"It's being taken to a storage vault in Chosungdal City," Ree offered. "It's where we keep the items in our collection that aren't on display or loan."

"And it still has its title papers, I presume?"

"Yes, my lord. Although, *obviously*, the Drekkar claim is no longer valid."

"In that case, let me make you an offer for it."

And so, for considerably less than the price paid by Naiyami Corporation, Cho Abi Sorocaba, broker of planets, acquired an ill-proportioned object of no known purpose, and no known provenance, on the basis of an idea that was, he had to admit, about as unlikely as an iron-age civilization manufacturing plutonium.

Cho hated the cold. Unluckily for him, Braym's southern hemisphere was in deep midwinter by the time his ship, *Abstract Existence*, nestled into a berth on the outskirts of Gaiyo, the planet's largest city. Not that that was saying much. Braym, lying on the edge of trafficked space, and close to the daunting voids of the Rimward Reach, was something of a backwater. If its owners ever approached him with a view to selling, there would have to be some very hard conversations about its value.

Unless, of course, he turned out to be right.

Leaving the crew to do whatever it was the crew did in the aftermath of a landing, Cho hurried into town, mildly worried that he would be late for his appointment, but rather more concerned that he would freeze to death before he got there.

"Come in, my lord, come in."

Seo Aba Mai welcomed him across the threshold herself. She personally removed his snow-crusted cloak and handed it off to a subordinate before escorting him across the showroom to her office.

"You took a ground car, my lord?"

"I did. I didn't much fancy flying in this weather."

"A wise choice, I'm sure."

Seo's office was almost as large as her showroom. Like the showroom, it was full of carefully curated antiquities and objets d'art. For an out-of-the-way place like Braym, it was an impressive collection. Cho took time to compliment the antiquarian on her taste.

"Coming from you, my lord, those are words to treasure."

A warm beverage, delivered by a person, not a bot, materialized at Cho's side. He accepted it gratefully, taking up Seo's invitation to perch on a luxuriously upholstered bench. He didn't recognize the material. Local, presumably.

"And now, my lord, how may we be of service?" Seo didn't bother to hide her puzzlement. "What brings a collector of your stature to my humble premises? I cannot imagine what we have to offer, that you would journey so far to visit us."

"I have other business to accomplish here, mistress. But now that I am planetside, I thought it would be remiss of me not to visit." Cho's eyes flitted around the room, alighting on one of the shelves. "I have a number of first era steles from the Moan subculture of Sadako Prime. But they are large and, if I may say so, vulgar. Fine as outdoor decoration, but no more than that. I am looking for something of similar provenance, but smaller. More personal, if you understand my meaning. They are harder to find than you might think. So many antiquarians want to sell only the big, flashy pieces."

Seo followed his gaze and smiled.

"You have a good eye, my lord. I personally feel that, of all the many civilizations we have come across, those of Sadako Prime were the most artistic. Who knows what they might have achieved had they not succumbed to disease." She rose from her stool and removed the subject of their discussions from its shelf. "This is a late first era statuette of the Moan god-king, Tallamok the Second. It's fully provenanced with the title documents in order. Hard to believe it's almost half a million years old. Would you like to examine it more closely?"

"Later, perhaps. I shall most certainly want to purchase it. Assuming suitable terms, of course."

"Of course, my lord."

"But while I am here and enjoying your hospitality, I wonder if we might discuss another matter?"

"Anything you wish to discuss, my lord, would be an honor."

Cho wriggled his fingers, causing a 3-D image to materialize in the center of the room. There was a sharp breath of recognition from his host.

"Several years ago, now, you sold this object to a representative of Naiyami Corporation: an abstract representation of the Drekkar civilization's Supreme Deity."

"I did indeed, my lord. Though, as I'm sure you're aware, it now seems unlikely that this piece was from Drekkar at all. But it was certified as such by highly respected experts in the field, and we sold it to Naiyami on that basis. There was no intention to mislead."

"Of course not, mistress. I know that the archaeologists in question had a good faith, if misguided, basis for their findings. That is not why I'm here."

"No, my lord?"

"No. I'm more interested in the provenance annotation on the documents of title." Highlighted script flowed in curling ribbons around the object's holographic image. "It says here that you acquired it from one Ryo Abi Ahn, who had acquired it as, ah, *scrap* on Otai Station."

"Yes, my lord. His papers were in order, and that is the provenance described."

"This Ryo, whoever he is, is a bit of mystery. He claims to be a spacefarer of some kind, but he appears on none of the registries either now, or at the time of this sale. And how did this person, someone who almost certainly has no background in antiquities, come to know that he had a, quote-unquote, 'Drekkar' artifact on his hands? And, even if he did, how did he come to you?"

Seo favored him with a whimsical smile.

"As for your latter question, my lord, the answer is reasonably straightforward. Although it may not count for much elsewhere, my establishment is the most prestigious antiquities dealership in the whole world. It would not have taken much by way of inquiry to have learned of my existence."

She paused for a moment, blowing the heat from her beverage before drinking.

"Master Ryo, if memory serves, was an engineer on some sort of freighter. I don't remember the name of it, but if he came from Otai Station as the papers say, then it would be one of the independents. Most ships that run as far out as Otai are. The profit margins are too small for the corporations to take much interest. That's why you won't find him on any of the usual registries. I have no doubt, though, that you will find him in Otai Station's database. He retired there after the sale. Stations generally keep detailed records of who's been breathing their air."

"And was this indie engineer an expert on the Drekkar civilization?"

"Protector, no," Seo chuckled. "Although *everyone* knows something about the Drekkar. They are the only sentient beings we have ever come across who existed at the same time as us. And they lived practically next door, astronomically speaking. They were far more advanced than we were at the time, working with metals while our own ancestors were struggling to fashion hand axes from stone, but we shared the same sky. It's easy to imagine our ships meeting in orbit somewhere had the universe treated them more kindly."

Cho nodded. Trafficked space was a lonely, friendless void, scattered with the remains of long-dead cultures. That it had once been shared with the Drekkar, that they had come so tantalizingly close to becoming a sibling civilization, someone to share the galaxy with, held a powerful hold on the imagination.

And made their artifacts the most valuable in existence.

"If Master Ryo had no great expertise in the Drekkar, what made him think he had one of their artifacts when he came to you?"

"I don't think he did, not really. I think he believed it to be something else altogether, although he was too circumspect to say so out loud. But the trade guild on Otai Station had identified it as a salvaged Drekkar artifact, so when Master Ryo brought it to me, I had it appraised by two of our local academics who, somewhat to my surprise, concurred."

"I take it then, that you did not believe it to be Drekkar either?"

"Not at first. Braym is a long way from Drekkar, and Otai Station is even farther. It made no sense for a genuine Drekkar artifact to be all the way out here. And while I'm no expert on the Drekkar, it struck me as too advanced an object for them. But the academics insisted, and I suddenly found myself holding a genuine Drekkar relic. I couldn't afford the item myself, of course, it was far too valuable, but I brokered the sale."

"To Naiyami Corporation?"

"Exactly, although there was quite a lot of competition for it, as you can imagine. The first artifact from a previously undiscovered—and advanced—Drekkar culture. We were quite famous for a while."

Cho chuckled at that. His beverage finished, he rose from his seat.

"You have been more than helpful, mistress. I appreciate you taking the time."

"The pleasure was all mine, my lord."

Cho wandered toward the Moan statuette, turning it over in his hands. It was heavy with history, the scrollwork beautifully detailed, with the classic, blurred toolmarks that marked it out as being genuinely first era.

"This is a very fine piece, mistress. Very fine."

He paid her considerably more than it was worth.

The view was spectacular.

Otai Station circled a moon of the same name. The moon was a marbled blue and white that took its appearance, not from the aqua seas and swirling clouds of a habitable planet, but the rare rock formations that spoke to the mineral wealth lying just beneath the surface. Apart from the mining complexes dotted around Otai's airless craters, nothing lived down there.

Stunning though Otai was, it was by no means the only thing worth looking at through the restaurant's vast windows. The moon and its many sisters circled a massive, multicolored gas giant that, in turn, hewed close to its parent star, an orange monster that flared and spat its fury at the universe in gouts of irradiated flame. Otai Station rotated at a leisurely pace so that, in the course of one meal, a diner could take in Otai, its planet, its star, its sister moons, and deep space before starting the whole cycle once again.

"This station should think more about tourism," Cho said, taking a bite of his meal. "I can't think of another place like it in the whole of trafficked space."

Ryo Abi Ahn smiled in polite appreciation.

"Perhaps, my lord. But the journey is long, and I suspect the cuisine is not up to your lordship's usual standards."

"Who can think about food with a view like this?"

"Perhaps one who has not eaten in a while."

Cho had to laugh at that.

"If you have no love of the cuisine, and no great attachment to the view, why retire here?"

"It's my home. I was born here. My friends and family all live here. And there is, as you can see, no other place quite like it. It never occurred to me to live anywhere else. And after the sale of the artifact, I had the funds to settle down, so I did."

"I noticed from the title documents that you acquired this Drekkar artifact as scrap. How did you come across it?"

The engineer-as-was chuckled.

"I didn't 'come across it,' my lord. Well, not exactly. I knew it was scrap, and I knew where it was, so I went looking for it."

"You went looking for a Drekkar artifact? Out here?"

"You sound surprised." Ryo looked faintly amused.

"We're a long way from Drekkar."

"And yet it was certified as Drekkar. By two highly respected archaeologists."

"Of course. The documentation is entirely in order." Cho picked politely at his food. "And yet, I can't help wondering. Do *you* think it's a Drekkar piece?"

"Do you?"

Cho hid a small smile. Mistress Seo had been correct in her assessment. The retired spacer was nothing if not circumspect.

"I do not," he admitted. "In fact, I know it's not." News of the artifact's decertification did not appear to have made it to Otai Station, so Cho filled him in on the details. "You don't look surprised," he concluded, looking at Ryo. "Or even disappointed."

"I'm not, my lord. I never thought that thing was Drekkar. *Never.* Neither would you in my position."

Cho found himself leaning forward on his stool.

"Do you understand how a soliton generator works?" Ryo asked.

"Only in the vaguest sense." Cho felt like he was back in science class. "On a planet, a soliton is a standing, solitary wave in a closed body of water, like a lake, generated by some kind of resonance. They can be quite destructive when they reach shore, I understand. Up here, at the cost of a great deal of energy, you can create the same effect with space-time. You create a soliton of space-time around a ship, and let it go. The soliton folds space-time as it moves, carrying the ship with it. Because you're folding space-time as you go, you effectively travel at many times the speed of light, even though, safe inside the soliton, you're not really moving at all. Depending on the amount of energy put into the original generation, the soliton will carry you a very great distance before it fades away. At which point, you hope to be close enough to your destination for the A-Grav engines to carry you the rest of the way." Cho grimaced a little. "I'm always slightly relieved when my ship's captain tells me we've gone sub-light within range of a port beacon."

Cho expected that his small confession of weakness would elicit a smile or some other sign of amusement. It did nothing of the sort. Ryo simply nodded.

"Then you understand," he said. "Solitons require an enormous amount of energy. For that reason, we use massive in-system launchers to send ships on their way. In trafficked space, at least, shipborne generators are strictly for emergencies. And that's fine: until the launch teams screw something up."

"But the safeguards . . ."

"Don't always work. Ships have been lost that way."

Cho stared at the engineer in something approaching horror. Ryo shrugged.

"It's a fact of life. The port authorities will tell you that ships are lost in space for all sorts of reasons. A hull breach, gravitic implosion, unfavorable *Maidagan*. Maybe even the will of the Protector. But spacers know better. *I* know better."

The engineer pushed the remains of his meal away from him, as if suddenly nauseated.

"Back in the day, I was an engineer on an indie freighter, the *Nothing In Excess*. We were making a run from Braym to Otai Station. Easy enough to do. We'd done it dozens of times. No one gave it a second thought. We broke orbit from Braym, traveled to the edge of the system, and waited in line at Lishi Station for our launch window. Off we went without incident. Or so we thought. The trip was taking far too long, and that soliton just kept going and going and going."

"Couldn't you just shut it down?"

"No, my lord. That much energy? We'd have torn ourselves to pieces. We had no choice but to go wherever the soliton was taking us. It died away eventually. Dumped us in the middle of the Rimward Reach."

"No!"

"Yes. The middle of proverbial nowhere, where the stars are far apart and unexplored. No way to get help, and no easy way to get home."

"But you got home, clearly. Or else this whole meal is a figment of my imagination."

Ryo rewarded him with a quick smile.

"We shed as much extraneous mass as we could and drained every last proton and anti-proton in the tanks to make a soliton. We barely made it. Our soliton faded away so far out that it took us a year—*a year*—to get back. And even then, it was only because Otai Station finally received our distress call and sent help. We'd never have made it on our own. As it was . . ."

The engineer stared through Cho, reliving who knew what. He brought himself back to the present with a visible effort.

"Anyway, you don't want to know about that. You want to know about the artifact."

Cho nodded, but he felt small and petty as he did so.

"Solitons have a habit of picking things up as they ripple through space-time. Interstellar gases, dust, the odd meteoroid, that sort of thing. Nothing you need to worry about, usually. When the soliton fades out, the navigator will check the scopes for obstructions before firing up the A-Grav. No point head-butting a rock if you can possibly avoid it, yes?"

"Of course."

"Well, this time, we picked up something more substantial. The artifact. It must have been drifting in open space, somewhere in the Reach."

"Which is how you knew it couldn't possibly be Drekkar."

"Exactly. The Drekkar were thousands of years short of interstellar travel when their civilization collapsed.

There's no way anything Drekkar could have made it all the way out there. Protector knows, there's nothing of *ours* out there. It's beyond trafficked space."

"So, what did you think you'd found?"

Ryo lowered his voice.

"The remains of an undiscovered, dead civilization, somewhere in the Reach. An undiscovered, dead, *space-going* civilization." Taking Cho's silence for skepticism, he plunged on. "The thing is unbelievably crude, but it's *designed* for space. It's hardened against radiation and low temperatures, it had a frighteningly primitive atomic power supply, and it had little rockets to provide attitude control. A rocket is . . ."

"I know what a rocket is, Master Ryo. Enough to know that these 'little rockets' of yours could never have lifted it off a planet."

"Of course not, my lord. But something else could have lifted it off a planet. An enormous artillery piece, perhaps, or a space elevator. Maybe even a huge, giant rocket. Then they could just *cast* it into space, allowing it to drift into the Reach. They must have been a patient people, my lord, for whatever journey it was on would have taken many thousands of years."

"But in the name of the Protector, *why?*"

"Who knows? Maybe it was a religious observance, or an experiment, or a joke of some sort. What matters is that they did it, we found it, and I persuaded the captain to let me bring it in for examination."

Cho finished the last of his meal, his face thoughtful.

"So, if you knew you were looking at the relic of a dead, space-going civilization, why didn't you report it as such when you finally arrived here? That would have been *huge* news. You would have been famous. And, if you'll forgive me for saying so, even more comfortably off than you already are."

"We tried to. The captain added it to our manifest as an 'ancient space-going artifact of unknown origin.' But the authorities here thought it was a hoax—or maybe that our time in the Reach had sent us mad. Either way, they refused to process us until we either modified our manifest or waited until they could convene a panel of experts from all across the sector—which would have taken forever."

Ryo looked bitter.

"I was all for holding out, but the crew were tired, my lord. Traumatized. They wanted to go home, see their loved ones, maybe never walk a ship deck again for as long as they lived. In the end, we changed the manifest to 'salvage of unknown origin' and sold it to the Port Authority as scrap. They put it in the boneyard."

"The boneyard?"

Ryo pointed toward the vast, panoramic window.

"It's the libration point between that moon out there and the planet, where the gravitational forces are in balance. You dump something there, it stays there, pretty much forever. Wrecked ships, dead probes—all sorts of space-worthy scrap—is placed there, so that indie traders and hobbyists can scavenge them for parts. It's owned by the Port Authority, so they make money off the spread between what they pay for the salvage and what they sell it for out of the boneyard."

"And I'm guessing that, once your shipmates gave up

on it, you bought it straight back from the Port Authority?"

"Exactly. I stayed on with the captain for one more run, took it to Braym, and sold it to an antiquarian there. Made enough on the deal to retire here for life."

"By selling it as Drekkar?"

"Yes. When you buy something from the boneyard, the documentation is real easy. I bought it as salvage but went to the trade guild to get it reclassified as a Drekkar artifact. The trade guild don't care what you call it, they just need it to have a name and a registration number for transit tracking. They don't weigh in on whether the *name* you give it is accurate, so long as the description of the goods is. So it was easy to call it a Drekkar artifact and then append a scan of the actual object as its description."

"Why Drekkar?"

"Because it's...well, *Drekkar*. Most people don't understand how the trade guild labels things, so I knew I could get the attention of an antiquarian. I figured they'd bring in some archaeologist who would recognize it for what it *truly* was: a relic belonging to an undiscovered, long-dead, space-going civilization. Thing is, though, the archaeologists Mistress Seo called in decided it *was* from Drekkar; that it must have been lost in transit somewhere. Something about lines and angles and proportions. They were idiots."

Cho found himself grinning.

"So, you made millions of jigu selling something from Drekkar instead of tens of millions, maybe *hundreds* of millions for the remains of an undiscovered space-going civilization?"

"Ironic, eh? But once academics make up their minds, it's almost impossible to change them. At least, not for years and years. Mistress Seo brokered a deal that was more money than I would have seen in a lifetime, so I took it, and here I am."

"And do you know where your vessel picked it up?"

Ryo's expression became guarded.

"Possibly."

Cho smiled without rancor. He was, after all, a person of business.

"What would it take to persuade you to divulge the information?"

"A share of whatever profits you intend to reap from it."

"There may be no profit at all. Wherever this place of yours is, it must be deep within the Reach. We would need a lot of assistance to get out there, pre-positioned fuel dumps, support vessels, things like that. We'd need the resources of a corporation. I doubt their assistance will come cheaply, particularly as it would be a rather, ah, *speculative* investment for them."

"So long as I make what you make, I will be satisfied."

Cho thought long and hard before replying. He was a broker of planets. And a broker of planets was nothing if not a person of his word.

"Agreed," he said. "The notaries can draw up the details."

"In that case, when I see the details, I will hand over a detailed location. In the meantime . . ." He wriggled his fingers. A holographic representation of a gold disk, with odd-looking markings carved into it, materialized above the table. "I removed this from the artifact as a keepsake.

It was loosely attached to the main body. Meant to be removed, I think."

"What is it?"

"I'm not an archaeologist, my lord, so I have no hesitation in telling you that I don't know. It's a protective cover for a crudely grooved metal disk. I *think* the disk contains a message, but I have no idea how to retrieve it. You see this?" A small cursor appeared next to a series of lines carved into the cover. The lines radiated outward from a single point, each line a different length. The overall effect was not unlike that of the artifact itself, with its ungainly collection of differently sized limbs. "This is a pulsar map."

"A what?"

"A pulsar map. A pulsar is a very dense star, very dead, spinning very fast and blasting out radiation as it rotates. The radiation 'pulses' with each rotation. As the rotation rates differ from pulsar to pulsar, they are easy to identify, like beacons across the galaxy. If you can find three or more of them in your scopes, you can take bearings and know exactly where you are. An old technique, but invaluable when you are completely and utterly lost."

Cho nodded solemnly. Ryo and his shipmates had been stranded in the Reach. Of *course* he would recognize a pulsar map. And understand its purpose.

"And this pulsar map tells you where the artifact originated?"

"Yes."

"How can you be sure?"

"First, you can assume that, wherever this thing was

going, there'd be little point in telling the recipients where *they* were. They'd know that already."

"Makes sense. And second?"

"And second, the map correlates to the only star system in the Reach that we came close to on our way home."

Cho's heart started to beat very, very fast.

"You are becoming a creature of habit, my lord," said Ree Aba Jen with a smile. "Though I thought we might have seen you at the presentation." She settled beside him, her legs dangling off the edge of the building.

What was left of the building. Most of the walls had crumbled away, but the denizens of this particular civilization had built to last. The structure's recalcitrant spine refused to buckle. Seventy-five stories remained, scratching defiantly at the sky.

That the building was sturdy and stubborn seemed appropriate, given the appearance of its creators. The inhabitants of this place had been toweringly tall and built for strength. Their likenesses were everywhere: on statues, and friezes, and still-bright portraits in sheltered chambers. The expedition scientists had described them as aerobic, bipedal beings, more or less symmetrical (left to right) on a vertical axis, with binocular vision, and well-developed, many-fingered hands. They were probably warm-blooded with at least two sexes.

To everyone else, it was like looking in a strangely distorted mirror. Their faces, but for their massive size, were almost identical in structure; their arms and legs likewise: gigantic versions of Cho's own limbs. They must have been incredibly strong, he thought.

And as stubborn as their buildings. It would have been almost impossible for these handsome, heavy creatures to ever leave the ground.

And yet they had somehow managed it.

The planet broker's admiration was tinged with sadness.

Ree had joined him at the very top of the building. The remnants of the city's other structures, many of them achingly familiar in appearance, stretched out beneath them. A strangely green jungle hugged the foundations, taking over what must once have been bustling avenues and plazas. Beyond the city limits, the greenery stretched almost uninterrupted to the shores of a distant, whitecapped ocean. Feathered animals flew between the alien treetops. Here and there, a wide circle had been blasted through the flora, where *Abstract Reality* and the much larger Naiyami Corporation vessels had come to rest. The invasive bulk of the intruders, sunlight gleaming on their hulls, didn't seem to bother the flying animals at all. They perched carelessly on the A-Grav fins, watching the comings and goings of people and their machines with mild, otherworldly interest.

Having got no response from the broker of planets beyond an absentminded nod, Mistress Ree tried again.

"The city is magnificent, is it not? You can almost *feel* what it must have been like when the cousins were alive."

Cho favored her with a wry smile.

"Even you, Mistress Ree?"

"I'm sorry?"

"I see you've taken to calling the former inhabitants of

this world by their nickname. I don't think the 'Cousins' civilization' will sit well with the archaeologists."

"But they were *so* like us, my lord. They had two arms and two legs . . ."

"*Enormous* arms and legs, mistress. I suspect even the young could have snapped my neck like a twig."

"Well, not *exactly* like us, to be sure. But close enough that 'cousins' seems appropriate. And the buildings!" She patted the dusty floor with her hand. "If you showed anyone at home a hologram of this and told them it was one of *our* thousand-year-old ruins, no one would be any the wiser."

"Perhaps not," Cho conceded. Truth be told, the city's very familiarity fascinated him. It was why he liked to sit up here, looking down at it, imagining the "cousins" going about their business in the same way his ancestors must have done. He took a deep, reflective breath.

Trying to lift his mood, Ree said, "This has got to be the greatest archaeological discovery of all time, my lord. These people may not have been close neighbors like the Drekkar, but the Drekkar died out ten thousand years ago, while these people, *who look like us*, were still around maybe a few hundred years in the past. We were going into space at the same time. They'd started to settle other worlds in their system. We almost met each other."

Cho made an effort to match her enthusiasm.

"Your lady Morota will be pleased, no doubt."

"No doubt. This is a planet where everything is so . . . so *recent*, the archaeology is still on the surface. There are over a thousand cities like this one. You saw what it looked like from orbit: like it was still inhabited. Once we've built a station and a soliton generator, people will come from all over trafficked space to see it. The trade in artifacts alone will justify the cost of the expedition, and it is, as you can see, a beautiful world, in a system full of resources. People will settle here, and it will give us our first foothold in the Reach."

"Today the Reach, tomorrow the spiral arm," Cho said, quietly.

"Protector willing." Ree looked at him curiously. "All this is thanks to you, you know. I suspect you will become one of the most famous people who ever lived, and certainly one of the richest. And yet, if you will forgive me for saying so, you look distinctly underwhelmed."

Cho said nothing for a while, staring instead at the distant ocean. The planet turned a little quicker than he was used to, and its sun was already starting to slide from blue sky toward bluer water. Ree was right: it was a beautiful, beautiful world.

"Have you ever heard of Chuda's Paradox?" he asked.

"No, my lord."

"Meom Abi Chuda was a philosopher who lived about twelve hundred years ago, just about the time we first started to reach into space, and long after we'd been studying the stars for signs of intelligent life. People in Chuda's time knew that there were more stars in the galaxy than grains of sand on a beach, that most stars had planetary systems, that untold numbers of planets would be able to support life, and that the galaxy must be full of intelligent beings who had been around for millions, if not billions of years before our world was even born. And yet, none of these beings had ever made contact with us. None of the stars we looked at day after day, year after year, produced any signal, any sign of intelligent life. One day, chewing this over in his mind, just before he was about to give a lecture on a completely different subject, he startled his students by blurting out the following words: 'Where is everybody?'"

"But, my lord, there is no paradox. At least, not in this day and age. We know what happens. The universe is capricious, and intelligence is deeply unstable. The Drekkar civilization was wiped out by its own sun, the Bren-C cultures committed suicide by nuclear holocaust, and the inhabitants of Sadako Prime succumbed to a lethal pandemic. Planets have tilted in their orbits, civilizations have boiled themselves alive through global heating, meteors have leveled entire worlds. Intelligent beings don't survive long enough to reach space or contact others. *We* are the oddity, my lord. Thank the Protector that we exist at all, with our solitons and our A-Grav engines and our multiplicity of star systems. *That* is a genuine miracle. The odds of it happening once, never mind twice, are incalculably small."

"And yet here we are. Thank the Protector, as you say." Cho continued to look out toward the ocean. Pristine: devoid of vessels, or settlements, or power stations, but otherwise shockingly similar to the seas of his home world. "This presentation that I missed. Did we learn anything of interest?"

"Very much, my lord. The archaeologists have finally managed to decode the grooved disk: something to do with the mathematics of hydrogen, apparently. In any event, we now know that the cousins had hundreds of cultures, and a similar number of languages, but their favored name for this place appears to have been 'Earth.' It means soil, or ground, or something similar."

"And the artifact we found?"

"They called it Voyager Two. As you surmised, they cast it into space deliberately. It was a probe, once, and reported back here with its findings. But it died and drifted on, as the cousins knew it would. The disk was a message to anyone in their distant future who might find it."

"Odds about as likely as a sentient civilization making it into space, I suppose. Any clue as to how the cousins went extinct?"

"No, my lord. The grooved disk describes a civilization incapable of settling the local moon, or the fourth planet, so whatever happened took place after the Voyager Two artifact was cast adrift. From our preliminary surveys, there's no obvious physical reason, which suggests they somehow managed to do it to themselves. Or maybe the planet killed them and has since recovered. It may be years before we know for sure."

Cho couldn't stop himself from sighing.

"I apologize for being such poor company, Mistress Ree. This is, as you say, a momentous discovery. But ever since you told me that this . . . *Voyager Two* was only a thousand years old, I had hoped, I had really, really hoped that its makers were still here. That we would be hailed by their ships as we crossed the Reach. Or that we could maybe help them with their first steps into the galaxy. That we wouldn't be forever alone in the universe. That we'd have someone else to . . . to *talk* to."

"Ah," Ree said, as kindly as she could. "I grieve for your

dashed dreams." She laid a consoling hand on his wrist.
"Maybe, my lord, you will be right one day. We missed
the cousins by a few hundred to a thousand years at most.
Maybe next time, we'll arrive before it's too late."

"Maybe." He pried himself off the floor, stretching
arms that the cousins would have found to be laughably
insubstantial. "Shall we go down, mistress? I may have
missed the presentation, but I have no desire to miss the
evening meal."

And with that, he stood on the edge of the building and
hurled himself off. Broad, delicate wings, not so different
in design from those of the feathered animals in the
treetops, unfurled from his back, guiding him in a graceful
spiral down to . . . What had Ree called it?

Down to Earth.

MOTHER OF MONSTERS
Christopher Ruocchio

One of the greatest joys of following Christopher Ruocchio's time at Baen has been seeing how he manages to come up with a story that fits every theme anthology that still ties back into his sweeping Sun Eater *space opera series. No matter the theme or subgenre, he always finds a way to tell a gripping story that offers new looks and different perspectives into the universe of Hadrian Marlowe. In this particular story, we follow an unlucky soul who finds there are some corners of the universe with things far more dangerous than the Cielcin, where beings beyond our comprehension slip between the walls of reality, and where one wrong step may find you beneath the thumb of an alien god . . .*

"Do you know what a thought hazard is, M. Valen?" asked the blank-faced Imperial agent across the table, setting a cup of stiff, black coffee between them.

Risking a glance at the official, Valen shook his head. He did not dare take the cup, as much as he felt he

needed it. He had been through round after round with
the Empire's men, agents and bureaucrats from Earth-
only-knew what agency. There'd even been an inquisitor
of the Holy Terran Chantry in to see him. The woman had
put him to the Question, read his autonomic responses,
his encephalography, his breathing—everything—all to
ensure he was still *human*, to guarantee that no alien or
mechanical influence had him in thrall.

Valen wished they'd told him the answer.

"No, sir," he said at last.

"It's a piece of information so dangerous that
someone's merely knowing it is enough to make said
information a risk," the man said.

Valen risked another glance at the agent. The man was
Legion bald, scalp lasered clear of all stubble and clearly
waxed, but he wasn't dressed like any Legion man, in the
black tunic and trousers and knee-high black boots of an
officer—and he *was* an officer, or must be. He talked like
one, at any rate. All brass and polish. He had schooling,
more than Valen had. But he looked like a civilian, dressed
as he was in an unassuming gray suit of the kind favored
by civil service, high-collared and well made.

"I don't know anything like that, sir," Valen said.

"Nonsense, sirrah," the man said, strangely affable.
"You're a soldier of the Empire. An engineer, no less. You
know explosives, don't you? How to make them?"

"Yes, sir," Valen had to admit, understanding the
concept a little too late. "I suppose I do."

"Someone got a hold of you, made you talk... made
you tell them how to build a bomb... that information's
dangerous, you see?"

Valen had to admit he did see. "But I don't understand what it is I've done wrong, sir. I've told everyone everything they asked. By Holy Mother Earth, sir, I swear it."

The agent said nothing to that. After a few seconds of awful silence, Valen risked a glance up at the man, found him smiling a thin but not unfriendly smile. "You were stationed on Echidna."

It wasn't a question. It didn't need to be. If the man really was what he appeared: an agent of the Imperium— of the Imperial civil service, no less, or of the Intelligence division—he would already know Valen's whole history.

"You know I was, sir," Valen said.

"Echidna's a whole information hazard in itself," the agent said. "They warned you, before they sent you in with the survey team. Warned you there'd be no going back once the work was done. *For Earth and Empire,* you said. You and the rest of the team."

"I meant it," Valen said.

"Of course you did," the other man said, resting interlaced hands upon the tabletop. "No one questions your patriotism, M. Valen. The only question is: what is to become of you?"

Valen swallowed, found his gaze sinking toward some indeterminate place on the polished back glass of the tabletop. Ten seconds passed—perhaps—before he realized he was staring at the halo that encircled the reflected light in the ceiling above. "I was told the Echidna post would be it," he dared at length. "I'd spend the rest of the war in the Outer Perseus. Out of the way. That was the deal. Five years active on Echidna, then some border world for the rest of the war."

"The war isn't ending," the man said simply.

Valen shut his eyes. None of it seemed real, still. The fighting. The Cielcin. The Valley of Lords. Echidna itself. When he'd been a boy on Zigana, all he'd wanted was to enlist. His father had been a legionary, and his father before him. That was how they'd come to Zigana in the first place, shipped in on ice from Tiryns in the Outer Perseus. It'd been only right that he follow in their footsteps, only right he serve the Empire as they had. When he'd been a boy on Zigana, the galaxy had felt... not small, not precisely, but within his reach. Mankind had gone out and conquered sun after countless sun, had spread across the parsecs, across hundreds of thousands of habitable worlds and countless million star systems... but *conquered* was the word. The galaxy had been man's when Valen was a boy.

It was contested now. Echidna had contested it.

The Cielcin had contested it.

"Tell me what you saw," the man said.

Valen blinked at him. "I've already told... I don't know how many people, sir. They took recordings..."

"I know," the man said, tapping his folded hands on the table. "But for the Emperor, son. Tell me again."

Valen looked round the empty room, the black walls, the black mirror that doubtless hid the observation room beyond, the golden lamps in the ceiling almost buzzing—right on the edge of hearing in the stiff silence. It was like every other conference room, like every other interrogation chamber on every other Imperial starship he'd ever been aboard. Even the paper cup with its stale coffee was the same. And there was a comfort in that sameness, after the alien horrors of Echidna, even in the stale bureaucracy. He was in human hands at least...

Thinking of hands, he clenched his own beneath the table.

"I gone to Echidna with the second wave," he said. "Lord Powers had come and gone by then, took their prince back to Forum in triumph and paraded him before the Empress."

"*It*," the man corrected. "Paraded *it* before the Empress. The Cielcin don't have sexes."

"Quite right, sir," Valen said, thinking of the pale xenobites with their smooth faces, their huge, black eyes and crowns of horn. Somehow, he always thought of them as male. He'd seen the official footage, seen Lord Cassian Powers present the inhuman prince to the Empress of the known universe in chains. It had died like a man, beheaded by the White Sword. "But it was long gone by the time I arrived. There was still fighting, though. The Cielcin were dug in deep. They had tunnel cities all over the worldship, some miles deep. We were years rooting them out. Killed them to the last, like we was ordered. We heard stories there was some captured and shipped to some reservation somewhere for study—I never learned anything real about that, but...we just killed them." Valen swallowed. It was not a pleasant memory, not what he'd pictured as a boy on Zigana. But there had been no xenobites when he was a boy, no aliens.

The Cielcin had come to Cressgard in their wandering moon and burned its cities to ash. They had carried off its people by the million, used them for slaves and feed.

Remembering the bodies of men and women hanging like pigs from hooks in an abattoir sent a shiver through Valen, and he snatched the still-warm paper cup of coffee up with shaking hands.

When he taken a bitter draught, he pressed on. "Three years in we'd done it. There might have been some holdouts in the deep places, but things had gone real quiet. That was when we got orders to ship out. We were needed on the surface, up by the pole—as far from the worldship's engines as could be. Brass didn't need me collapsing tunnels anymore. Intelligence had a dig they wanted help with, and me and mine were the best sappers on Echidna, so . . . we were off." He had told this story at least a dozen times since they thawed him out last week. The words were starting to sound unreal even to him, the whole thing as rehearsed as some holograph mummer's speech.

"They called it the Valley of Lords, it was a . . . a big rift valley, near the pole, far from any of the Cielcin cities. Tor Mencius—he was director of the dig there— said it was where the Cielcin buried their kings, sealed them up in tombs in the valley. One hundred and eleven tombs, stretching back . . ." he rubbed his eyes, realizing a piece of the information hazard the agent was talking about as he said it, ". . . forty thousand years, or so old Mencius said."

Forty thousand years was more than twice the age of the Empire, nearly twice the length of all human civilization. Forty thousand years ago, man had lived in the garden, having only just crawled up from apedom in the light of Earth's Golden Sun. The Chantry taught that man was the eldest child of the stars, firstborn and destined to rule. For more than fifteen thousand years, mankind had been expanding, stretching her hands out across the galaxy, gathering in star after star. They had found other races, *lesser* races, peoples that had discovered bronze, perhaps, or steel, but none that had learned to sail the black oceans between the stars.

None until the Cielcin.

"Go on," the man said, not unkindly, but Valen thought the man guessed something of what passed in his mind. The mere fact that Cielcin had been spacefarers for so long—for longer than man had been civilized—was a hazard of the sort the man had described. A threat to the stability of Imperial order, a threat to man's place amid the suns.

"Some of the tombs were sealed tight. The doors were metal or solid stone. Some of them weighed tons," Valen said. "Our job was to dig our way in. Remove the doors if we could, but undermine them if we couldn't. It was careful work. More careful than blasting our way through the tunnels down south where the fighting was . . ."

He grew silent then, thinking of the alien cities of Echidna, the great caverns and trackless tunnel warrens where dwelt that Pale enemy of man. He'd never seen anything like it, not in all his years in the Legions. The Cielcin didn't live on planets, didn't have colonies or settlements. They hollowed out asteroids, dwarf planets, whole moons, dwelt in them like termites in the foundations of a house. The worldship Lord Powers had named *Echidna* had engines vast as continents, huge warp drives fueled by vast reservoirs of antimatter. The whole

world had sailed between the stars, its inhabitants protected
from cosmic radiation by thousands of feet of ice and stone.
They had been years plumbing those depths, rooting out
the xenobites hive by hive, township by township until not
a one remained.

Just as they had done to the men and women of
Cressgard.

No, Valen told himself. *Not just as.* The Cielcin had
eaten the people of Cressgard.

They had only killed the Cielcin in return.

"M. Valen?"

"I'm sorry," the engineer said, and took another swig
of the old coffee. "Most of the tombs were just that.
Tombs. We spent two months or so sublimating the
nitrogen ice off the doors in the east wall of the valley.
The oldest tombs. Tor Mencius, he said the Cielcin
buried their kings up on the surface because the surface
dwellings were the oldest. That they dug their way in.
That's probably true, but me . . . I think they were safest
from looters so high up. Cielcin can hack in vacuum with
just a breathing tube, but the tombs were so far from any
of their proper cities . . . I don't know. We found an old
tunnel—a highway—that connected the Valley of Lords
to the greater warrens, but Silva—he was the geologist—
he said it'd been caved in for almost ten thousand years.
Looked deliberate to me, like one of their princes
sapped the tunnel to cut the valley off."

"We found the tomb of the one who settled Echidna,
near the north end of the Valley on the east wall, just
beside the doors to the Great Tomb. Zahamara, his name
was—its name, sorry. The prince buried there. Had to get

in at it from the south side, through the wall. We lost part of a . . . a mural I guess you'd call it, only the Cielcin don't paint. Mencius said the Cielcin don't do art. It was all writing. Calligraphy, you know? Mencius was . . . less than happy with the damage, but we found the old prince's body. Almost forty thousand years old, and still there. The vacuum and the cold preserved it . . ."

He could still see the mummified xenobite's body lying in its stone bed under the lamps in the controlled environment back aboard their ship. Tor Mencius had let the diggers watch from the theater above the lab. The Cielcin prince had been nearly eight feet tall, and thin like all its kind. The Cielcin were man-shaped, with two arms and two legs; two huge, round eyes above a too-wide and lipless mouth set in a face smooth and hairless beneath a crown of tangled horns. Silver bands like rings there were about those horns, some rune-scored, some set with opals and sapphires, others with violet amethysts and emeralds like green and lidless eyes.

Its void-boiled flesh had been wrapped in silken bandages, its banded silver armor polished and arranged with care. The rope of white hair that grew from the base of its skull was still intact, and hung over its left shoulder almost to its feet. The body had been sent to the Emperor on Forum to lie in state as part of an exhibit to showcase the conquest of Echidna and the supremacy of man for all the great lords and ladies of the Empire to see.

That exhibit would be hugely redacted, Valen guessed, fictionalized for the viewing public. History was just that. A story. The truth was too much.

"What's to be done with me?" he asked, interrupting

the flow of his story. "With Silva and the others? And old Tor Mencius?"

The man in the unassuming gray suit smiled, but remained otherwise immobile. "Tell me about the Great Tomb, M. Valen."

"About the Hand?" Valen stared into the depths of his cup. "The Hand's the information hazard, isn't it? Like you were saying? Just knowing about it is dangerous. Like a bomb."

Still the bald man said nothing.

After a moment, Valen shifted in his seat, chewed his tongue as if the words were some unpleasant taste he longed to work from its surface. "The Great Tomb. The Great Tomb was at the head of the Valley. The north end, nearest the Tomb of Prince Zahamara. Nearest the pole, too. Mencius thought that was significant. I don't know why. The doors must have been three . . . four hundred cubits high? Solid stone. Mother Earth knows how heavy the damn things were. And they were *locked* tight. Silva's team, they had gravitometers in. X-rays. Sonar. Deep scan, you know? We're talking huge gears, bolts big around as you or me and solid steel, sir. And Mencius, sir, he didn't want us blasting. Not after we wrecked that mural in Zahamara's tomb. So we get to drilling. Took us more than a week to get through the west wall in beside the door and get a probe in, but once we did we found a spot that was to Tor Mencius's liking, and we brought in the plasma bore. Cut a hole big enough to crawl through.

"Once we got in, we went down. The tombs all opened on stairs that ran down into the bedrock. How long it took the xenos to cut those tunnels I don't like to think . . . but they did. Hundred steps straight down, maybe more. That was where we found them. Dozens of them. Cielcin bodies, not mummified, just . . . left there. M. Silva, he said they were probably workers the Pale sealed in the tomb, but Tor Mencius reckoned they were priests or something, to judge by the way they were dressed. He reckoned they volunteered to stay in. Leastways, that was his theory . . . after."

"After you saw . . ."

"The Hand, aye sir." Valen's own tired eyes stared up at him from the black surface of the coffee. How long had it been since he had a proper sleep? Not since they pulled him out of the ice for these interrogation sessions at least, maybe not since he left Echidna. "It was at the bottom. The stairs led to a vestibule. That was where we found their dead priests just lying there in their robes . . . but past that was this big, domed chamber. There were these stone . . . panels, I guess you'd say . . . displayed around the walls. Covered in writing. Only it wasn't Cielcin writing. Even I could see that. The Cielcin letters are all circles. Mencius said they don't write in straight lines. But these were all straight. Straight lines with little notches up and down. I didn't look at them much. The floor stepped down like an arena. Big circles. And in the middle was . . ."

"The Hand?"

Valen just nodded.

He could see it, clear as day. The sarcophagus lay at the very center of the domed chamber, at the bottom of the steps, in what had seemed to him to be the floor of the arena. Never in his life had he seen so large a coffin. Twenty cubits long it was, or so he'd guessed, and carved of a greenish stone scored with the same notched, linear writing that decorated the slabs displayed about the walls. What lid it had lay to one side, smashed into three great slabs and innumerate lesser pieces. The Cielcin dead lay all about it, some with skeletal hands—boiled by vacuum—caressing the alien stone. How clearly Valen could see them still, their six-fingered, four-phalanged hands with nails like iron claws raised up to touch the coffin.

And within?

Within there lay the bones of an enormous *hand*.

The box was no coffin, no sarcophagus as in the other tombs in the Valley of Lords. It was an ossuary, a *reliquary*, a sacred *thing*. What creature could have produced such a hand Valen still did not dare speculate—if indeed it were not itself the work of alien hands.

The Cielcin don't make art, old Tor Mencius always said, and Valen said, "The Cielcin don't make things, like I said. That's why I thought it was real from go. That's why I've been saying so, sir. To the others. When they ask. Old Tor Mencius, though, he wasn't so sure. Thought it was some . . . what'd he call it? Fetish? Like it was a religious thing. Me and Silva and the rest . . . we were always joking that the scholiasts always think its some kind of religious thing. Maybe it was. I don't know. But you could tell it was a hand at once. Had three fingers and what looked like a thumb, but it looked broken, like maybe there was some missing." He held up the requisite number of fingers best he could, finding it strangely difficult to keep just the last finger down. "They were all black, like . . . you ever seen volcano glass? I grew up on Herakos, we had it everywhere."

The bald man nodded. "Did Tor Mencius say anything about the Hand? To you or any of the others?"

Valen had emptied the coffee by then, stared at the dregs. Suddenly he missed the companionship of his own reflection in the black liquid. His reflection in the dark mirror on the wall seemed somehow far away and not himself by comparison. "I don't understand what it is you think I've done wrong, sir," he said. "Except that I had a theory different from the scholiast's."

"Done wrong?" The interrogator frowned, shook his head. "You've done nothing wrong, M. Valen. That isn't the issue. It is my duty to ascertain whatever it is you know."

"But I've spoken to . . . I don't remember how many people," Valen said. "Captain Daraen, those Legion Intelligence men, some guy from civil service . . . Chantry even came and tested me. Who's next? Lord Powers? The Empress herself?"

"You told your captain?" The bald man turned to glance at the dark mirror glass. "You left that out of your earlier reports."

"I only just remembered," Valen said. "I didn't make any official report to him. Only told him about it when we left Echidna. He cornered me when Mencius and Silva and the other higher-ups wouldn't talk. Had a right to know, he said. He was my commander. It was his ship."

"It's all right, M. Valen," the interrogator said. "Depending on what you know."

"I don't *know* anything, sir," Valen said. "Only that Mencius said the Cielcin worshipped this giant Hand . . . thing. I don't know what it is. Mencius said it was a statue, and I guess he'd know. It just seemed wrong to me. In my gut, you know? But that's all I know, by Earth and Empire."

"By Earth and Empire," the man said, almost reflexively. "I believe you, M. Valen, when you say you don't know what it is. But you know *that* it is, and that is enough."

"What is it, then?" Valen asked, sitting a little straighter.

The nameless man did not reply.

"If I'm going to be punished for knowing, sir, then I should know." Was that approval in the bald man's dark eyes? Valen cleared his throat. "It's because of the Chantry, isn't it? Because we're meant to be the oldest civilization in the galaxy? But I already know the Cielcin are older, just . . . slower to advance. I already know that."

The bald man looked at the dark window that pretended it was only a mirror. What he saw in it or through it Valen dared not guess. Presently, he shook his head, and stood with a long sigh. "You're right, M. Valen," he said, "you *should* know. But you don't, it seems. And that is as well. The Chantry's Inquisition cleared you. Your Tor Mencius was right. You saw a statue, nothing more. Do you understand?"

Valen understood. It would be a little thing for them to freeze him, to put him on ice for a thousand years if he stepped out of line, if he spoke out of turn. He'd heard tell of Special Security doing just that—and he was sure this bald man must be with Special Security—he stank of secrecy.

"Are we done, then? Can I go?"

"To a place of our choosing, yes," the man said. "You're

likely to be given some outpost in the Norman Expanse, somewhere remote, where what little you know poses no threat to Imperial security. You're not to speak of Echidna ever again, do you understand?"

Valen only nodded. A feeling of intense relief washed over him, more bolstering than any amount of bad coffee. He had been through days of this. Weeks. "I understand."

"Thank you for your time," the nameless man said, and saluted. "For Earth and Emperor."

Valen stood and beat his breast. "For Earth and Emperor," he said, a touch too late and clumsily. The relief he'd felt a moment earlier faded all at once, and Valen of Herakos felt a slick and oily disappointment spilling from his guts. He had been close to the answers, he sensed, close to whatever secret they thought he held, to some monstrous, labyrinthine complex of state secrets and secret offices. The bald man was like the tip of some impossibly vast and translucent iceberg upon whose shoulders rested much of Valen's world. If he did not speak now—ask now—he would never know.

He spoke.

"Can I ask one question, sir?"

The bald man turned, one hairless brow up-raised.

"The Hand, sir. The Cielcin have six fingers. I said the statue might have been broken. Missing fingers . . . only . . . only the Cielcin have four knuckle bones on each finger." He held up his own hand to demonstrate, pinching the phalanges of his last finger one after the next. "The statue had three. So it can't have been Cielcin. It wasn't a Cielcin hand. Mencius had to be wrong . . . it had to be real."

The bald man said nothing for a long moment, did not

even turn to regard the black mirror glass. He kept his eyes down, and seemed for a moment—or was it Valen's imagination?—to nod to himself, ever so slightly.

"Good day, M. Valen," he said at last.

The door dilated at his knock, permitting the nameless functionary his exit.

No one came for Valen then, not for a long time, not even after he hammered on the door and the mirror alike, shouting for someone to come and get him. He imagined the bureaucrats and Legion officers debating, arguing over what would be done with him, with Mencius and Silva and Captain Daraen, with every member of the dig at the Valley of Lords. The Empire had its secrets, and it would keep them—them, and those privy to them.

After what seemed an age, Valen folded his arms on the table. His memory went back to that icy moon—or perhaps he dreamed.

Echidna. Mother of Monsters, Tor Mencius had called it, said the name came from some ancient myth. The Cielcin worldship hung—half-gutted where her engines rose like mountains from shelves of ice—a white gem in the black of space. Valen could recall the first time he'd seen it, the Imperial fleet glittering about its orbit like so many polished knives. Below them hung the ruined planet, Cressgard, its cities burned, its people stolen away. Valen well remembered the anger he'd felt at that first look, thinking of the women and children carried away, of the men who died fighting. For seven years the planet had been under siege, seven years while Lord Cassian Powers assembled his fleet and launched his counter attack. It had been Lord Powers who broke the Cielcin assault, crippled their ship, captured their prince. It had been Lord Powers who sent the summons that had brought them to Echidna, soldiers and scientists, engineers and xenologists—everything humanity needed to get to know its new neighbors.

We are not alone. The first words out of Captain Daraen's mouth at the briefing had set a chill in Valen's bones that no spring had yet thawed. For over fifteen thousand years the Sollan Empire had spread the glory of mankind across the stars, unchallenged.

No more.

How well he remembered the shock of those first engagements, the tunnels and cave-cities beneath Echidna's surface. They'd been brought in not to conquer, but to pacify the alien world, to put the Cielcin down for the horrors their kind had wreaked upon Cressgard. Some of the soldiers had whispered that it had been *they* who had struck first, humanity that had fired on the alien world as it fell into orbit, that the Pale had only ever acted in self-defense.

Valen did not believe it, was not sure how any of the others could.

He had seen the butcheries, the abattoirs buried deep beneath Echidna's surface, the hell-pits where men were trussed like cattle and bled, and the blood went to feed the worms the xenobites husbanded, raised for food and silk in equal measure. He could still remember the cavern he'd found—filled with the torn bodies of women—and the all-too-human stink on the alien air.

Even if the people of Cressgard had fired first, Valen knew they had been right to do so.

Man was not alone, but perhaps things would be better if he was.

And yet the Cielcin were not mere brutes, not the demons the Chantry preached from every pulpit on every planet in every corner of the frightened Empire. Or not only demons.

He stood once more upon the frozen surface of that wretched world, staring up at the green and white face of Cressgard burned and war-scarred above, its small and narrow seas like the tracks of tears. And he remembered the Valley of Lords opening beneath him as he and the men of the expedition debarked from their shuttles when the fighting was done. Great pillars rose above the walls of the Valley, some broken, others topped with capitals of gray stone—all of them carved with the circular writing of their kind, the finest done in inlaid silver that shone in the sunlight of naked space. The great doors of the tombs glittered a hundred cubits high in places, monuments to house forgotten kings older than the memory of man.

Valen was no scholar, no scholiast like Tor Mencius, who had studied for more than a hundred years in his ivory tower, had even been a part of the team that solved the aliens' tongue after their attack. He was no great sage, but he knew enough of the enemy to respect them even through hatred and fear. They were a proud people, ancient and terrible. It was no wonder that the nameless man from the Empire should fear the very idea of them—and the very idea of the Hand.

He had heard it said that once man believed himself the center of the universe, that Mother Earth lay at the heart of all the uncreated gods had made. Until one day a scholiast—although there were no scholiasts in those early days—discovered that Earth orbited her sun. Mankind had never recovered from that shock, or so the man who'd told Valen said. That discovery had dealt mankind a mortal wound, and that mortal wound had nearly strangled her in Earth's cradle, and it had been only the sacrifice of Mother Earth herself—lost in the Foundation War that made the Empire—that had preserved mankind at all and scattered her scions across the stars.

The nameless man feared a similar wound.

A deeper wound.

Three fingers, black as volcanic glass and more than twice as long as he was tall, lay in a coffer of green stone rudely carved. Valen had stood with Lorens and Sykes at the foot of the sarcophagus, staring transfixed while old Mencius stooped over the hideous thing in his pressure suit, face lost in thought behind the darkened glass.

"It's not . . . real, is it?" Sykes had asked.

"Real?" Mencius had looked up sharply. "Whatever do you mean by that, young man? You see it, do you not?" They said scholiasts were schooled not to have emotions, but Valen did not believe that sort of thing was really possible. The old man was always so short with them, the diggers.

"I mean was it alive, do you think?" Sykes asked.

Tor Mencius had looked then long and hard at the men through his suit mask, breath misting the frosted glass. He did not answer at once—Valen had not found that strange at the time. He wondered if he should have done.

"What kind of creature had a hand this big?" Valen asked.

"Nothing, Val!" Sykes had said. "Nothing gets that big."

Lorens audibly frowned. "Inverse square law, isn't it? Thing's own weight would crush it. Doesn't make sense."

Tor Mencius spoke suddenly, in memory like a drowning man relieved to find his life line tossed across his shoulders. "Quite right, M. Lorens. Quite right. Inverse square law, indeed. This is clearly some cult-statue. A primitive fetish! But a valuable find. It's most unlike anything else in our experience. The Cielcin produce little by way of art. Architecture, yes. Music, poetry, literature. But nothing like this!"

Had he been lying? Covering for some *other* truth? Had the nameless man known that truth? Had he come to interrogate Valen specifically to know if Valen knew it himself? And did Valen know it? Or know enough? How would he know?

Do you know what a thought hazard is, M. Valen?

You know explosives, don't you? How to make them?

Almost Valen felt like an explosive himself. He could feel his forehead pressing into the flesh of his arms where they lay against the table of the interrogation room, felt the cold, black glass. Felt also the glassy blackness of the three fingers in their coffer beneath the domed vault of the Great Tomb of Echidna. They felt cold—even through the rubberized polymer of his suit gloves. Their surface was uneven, ridged, more like wood than stone. Valen ran his fingers along those lines, marveling at the dark material.

"M. Valen! Stop that!" Tor Mencius barked, voice

cracking like a whip, magnified by the speakers in the helmet of Valen's suit.

The engineer sat bolt upright—and found he was not in the interrogation room at all.

He was on a shuttle, his face pressed against the bulkhead near a round porthole. Outside, the silent stars were ever watchful, remote and deep-sunken in the black. Blearily, Valen looked round. He could not remember being moved. He had been aboard a starship, that much he knew, but not Captain Daraen's *Ecliptic*. Some other Imperial dreadnought. Now he was going . . . somewhere else.

His head swam. He must have been drugged. Had he been dreaming? Or were those memories the symptoms of interrogation?

It didn't make sense. The bald man had said they were finished, had seemed satisfied. He was supposed to go to some border world posting, as far from the fighting—as far from the Cielcin—as the Empire and galaxy would allow. They had deemed him not-a-threat to Imperial security, or so he'd thought, judged that whatever information he thought he had was no hazard to the peace and the Chantry's lie.

But he knew it was a lie.

Was that enough?

He must have grunted, or made some other noise as he stirred, for a legionnaire in full combat plate emerged from the aisle to his left, coming up from behind. The man peered down at him, his face obscured behind his ceramic face-plate, devoid of eyeslit or glass. He placed a hand on Valen's shoulder as if to check him, then signaled to some unseen presence in the rear. Bleary still, Valen tried to turn, but the crash-webbing that secured him in his seat prevented him from rising.

"Where?" was all he managed to say.

Had there been something in the coffee? No, that didn't make sense. They had been going to let him go—unless they were never going to let him go. And he had sat around for so long in that little cell, waiting for someone to come retrieve him. He could remember sitting there, face in his arms.

They must have pumped something into the air.

He could not remember anyone coming to get him. Could not remember being moved.

Why go to all this trouble?

A hand settled on the headrest just above his left shoulder, and for an instant Valen discerned the flash of a signet ring as the owner of that hand pivoted into view and seated himself on the bench opposite Valen.

Valen would not have needed the ring to tell him that here was a Lord of the Imperium, one of the palatine high-born. He knew him. Every veteran of the Battle of Echidna did. He wore an officer's dress blacks, without medal or marker of rank, silver buttons and collar tabs gleaming with the embossed image of the twelve-rayed Imperial sun. An aiguilette wrought of heavy silver chains decorated his right shoulder, marking him for a knight of the realm as surely as the unkindled hilt of the sword that hung from his shield-belt.

"Are you well, M. Valen?" the lord asked, and brushed back his untidy fringe of auburn hair with his ringed hand. "It is *just* Valen, isn't it?" His hard eyes narrowed. "Valen of . . . Herakos?"

"Where am I?" Valen asked.

The man seated before him cocked his head, reminding Valen of nothing so much as the tawny owls that lived in the rocks and dry old trees of his home. "Nowhere, I'm afraid. That's the point." He grew quiet, composed himself. "You know who I am?"

Still shaking off the haze of the drugs, Valen struggled to hold his head up straight, but he said, "You're Lord Cassian Powers."

Lord Powers smiled ever so slightly. "I am."

"What do you want with me?" Valen asked. "I . . ." Here was a great lord, a hero of the Imperium, of mankind itself. What could he possibly want with Valen of Herakos? "I'm just an engineer. A digger, for Earth's sake."

"For Earth's sake, indeed," said the Avenger of Cressgard. "M. Valen, you are one of only six people to enter the Tomb of the Monumental on Echidna. Whether or not you are aware of it, you are in possession of information that threatens Imperial order."

"Monumental?" Valen could only shake his head. "I don't understand how."

"You don't *understand*," Lord Powers said. "But someone might. You know enough to answer questions others might ask. Questions that could change *history* as men understand it."

"You mean like the Cielcin?" Valen asked. "How old they are? Their civilization?"

"Like that, yes," the lord said. "Or about the Hand."

Valen frowned, remembering his vision, his memory, the cold, glassy stone of the finger beneath his own. "Where are you taking me?"

"You work for us now, M. Valen. For me."

"Who's we?"

"*We* are Hapsis. The Emperor's Contact Division."

"Legion Intelligence?"

"*Not* Legion Intelligence. We report to the Imperial Office, you understand?"

Valen said nothing. From Powers' tone, he could already guess that he had no say in the matter. He was shanghaied, pressganged, enlisted. "Why me?"

Powers blinked at him. "You saw the Hand."

"But why *bother* with me?" he asked. "I'm just an engineer. You could have iced me, spaced me, sent me to Belusha."

Again Powers cocked his head, a thin smile on his palatine face. "Waste not, M. Valen."

"Waste not . . ." the engineer almost snarled, shaking his head. "What is it you want from me, then?"

Powers straightened. "Have a care, sir," he said, "I understand the stress you must be under, sitting through the vetting process like you did, but I am a palatine lord of the Imperium. Do not forget."

Valen hung his head. "Forgive me, lord." Angry as he was, he was still a soldier, and a citizen of the Empire besides. He knew there was no going back, had known since he first set sail for Echidna. The Empire had ordered him to serve, and serve he had. It was far too late to change his mind. The time for that had been on Herakos, before he ever enlisted. "How may I serve?"

"That remains to be seen," Lord Powers said. "That is not the purpose of this interview in any event . . ." He grew silent, turned to regard the slow and silent passage of the stars beyond the window. "I did not choose this career, either. We have the same ill luck. Do you know what it was you found in the Great Tomb?"

"A hand," Valen said tartly, and realizing his mistake, tried again. "A hand, my lord."

"It was the hand of a god, M. Valen," Lord Powers said, not waiting to allow Valen the time to process. "A god to the Cielcin, at any rate. Athos tells me you realized the hand was not—as our man Mencius tried to make you believe—the sculpted hand of a Cielcin. *That* bit of knowledge was the real hazard. *That* bit of knowledge is why you are here." Again he turned to look out the window. "The universe is so much older than we like to believe, older perhaps than we *can* believe. What you realized—whether you knew it or not—is that the Cielcin are not the only race older than our own. What you found in that tomb on Echidna belonged a creature of a kind far older than life on Earth. Than Earth itself."

"A . . . Monumental?" Valen said.

Powers said nothing.

"Why are you telling me this?"

"Because you are doomed, M. Valen," Lord Powers said. "The Empire has its enemies: not just the Cielcin, there are others. Barbarians and the like . . . any of whom would leap at the opportunity to turn this knowledge against us. Against Mother Earth and Empress, against the Holy Chantry. So we cannot allow you to fall into the wrong hands. What little you know might confirm for any of our enemies what they might already suspect."

Valen could feel his eyes narrowing, knew his mouth hung half-open. "That xenobites exist?"

"These are no mere xenobites," Powers said, leaning forward. As he did so, Valen's vision swam, and the Avenger of Cressgard seemed to double. The world seemed to double. Two lords sat on two benches, and two windows spun on the wall. "I told you. They are gods, Valen. The Monumental you found on Echidna— Echidna herself, in a sense—is not the first we have found. Hapsis was formed centuries ago, ordered by Emperor Sebastian XII after an expedition discovered the body of another such creature near galaxy's edge. That the Cielcin know about them, too, is cause for grave concern."

"But it's dead!" said another voice, so like his own.

"It was just a hand," Valen said, and put a hand to his face.

"A giant hand . . ." said the other voice.

Powers signaled for someone in the rear. Valen heard feet approaching. Two sets of feet. The bald man came into view, still in his innocuous gray suit. "He's splitting again," Powers said to him, and the bald man—whom Valen guessed must be Athos—stooped and peered into his eyes. Or did he? He seemed at once to be looking at some point to his left and into Valen's eyes at once, as though it were the trick of some funhouse mirror.

Valen heard the pneumatic hiss of an injector, felt the needle bite. Some other voice gasped in alarm, and his vision stabilized. A stimulant? It must have been. "What did you do to me?" he asked.

"We're trying to help you, Valen," Powers said, dropping the honorific. "You're very sick."

"Sick?" he asked. "What?"

"You touched it, didn't you?" Lord Powers asked, painfully intent.

"Through the suit!" Valen exclaimed, incredulous. "We were in vacuum!"

"It isn't that kind of sickness," Power said, though what kind of sickness it was he didn't say.

"It was dead!" Valen almost shouted.

"Partly," the lord allowed.

"What do you mean?"

"What your team found in the tomb was only a fragment. The creature whose...hand you and Tor Mencius uncovered on Echidna extends beyond what we ordinarily think of as space. Into...higher dimensions."

"Higher dimensions?" Valen suppressed a sneer. "You're crazy, lord."

"Crazy?" Powers looked round, his gaze settling on bald Athos. The doctor made no sign. "That may be. But I tell you: there are parts of that *thing* you found that still live, and it is for *that* reason that the knowledge you possess is so dangerous. There may be more of them, scattered across the galaxy. The Cielcin surely are aware of them, and may use them in their war on us. Our other enemies may try."

"Use them?" the other voice asked. "Use them how?"

Lord Powers turned his head, a frown creasing his owlish face.

"It's happening again," murmured the doctor, Athos.

"I can see that, Athos," snapped Lord Powers. The Avenger leaned forward, made as if to grip Valen's wrist. But Valen felt nothing, and felt a strange confusion spreading in him. Powers had leaned too far to his right, toward the empty seat on the bench beside him, nearer the window.

The window? But he'd awoken with his face pressed to the window, hadn't he?

"Valen? Look at me. Focus on me." Lord Powers' hard eyes were intent. "Something happened when you touched the fingers. It only happened to you. Focus!"

Valen looked across at Lord Powers again. The palatine *was* clasping his wrist. One of him was. There were two of Lord Cassian Powers again, two benches, two portholes, and two of Dr. Athos on the edge of his vision, peering down with mingled fascination and horror.

"Valen?"

"Yes?" The reply came from the empty seat at Valen's left. Hadn't he been seated there? The window was right beside him.

Confused, Valen made to look round, but Lord Powers shook his wrist. "Look at me, Valen. Look here, lad." Valen looked him in the face, felt the pressure of Powers' hand as if from far away. "Can you dose him again?"

Valen glared up into the face of the doctor—but somehow still held Lord Powers' gaze. Athos shook his head, and Valen felt his eyes bulge as the full effect of double vision diverged. He was looking in two places at once, *from* two places at once. He shook his head, and his vision of Athos blurred even as Powers held his gaze and intensified his grip upon his arm.

Double vision. Double vision.

"He's had too much already." The doctor's voice sounded far away.

"It's getting worse," Powers said. "You have the sedative? It worked last time."

"What worked?" Valen asked, and it seemed to him that he looked at Powers and Athos simultaneously, his fields of vision overlapping, as though he turned each eye independently. "What's wrong with me? What did you do?"

Powers squeezed his arm. "We're trying to help you, Valen. Something happened to you in the tomb, do you remember?"

"In the tomb?" Valen shook his head.

"Keep him steady," Powers said, and Athos stooped to secure something to Valen's left. Valen made to turn, but Powers said, "No, don't look. Look at me."

Too late.

Valen had glanced aside, and felt his stomach and his soul both fall out of him and the shuttle entire. He was careening through space, faster than any bullet and without course.

A man sat in the seat beside him, dressed in the dark fatigues of a common legionnaire. Dr. Athos had stooped over him, made to steady him as he thrashed—unrestrained—on the bench. There was something not quite right with him, as there was something not quite right with Valen himself, but that was not what gave the young engineer his pause.

Valen knew him at once. His shaved pate, his olive skin—still dark from the old suns of Herakos. He knew the triple lightning bolt patch of the engineering corps, and the single red stripe on the arms that marked him for a triaster. He knew, also, the thin white scar on the man's neck. *His own neck.*

The man's eyes bulged in his head, seeing Valen looking at him as if out of a mirror.

All at once, Valen saw a separate image, saw himself strapped in and seated against the bulkhead with the porthole close beside him. He felt the doctor's hands upon his face, and saw Lord Powers' hand still tight upon his wrist.

He understood all at once.

There were *two* of him, and he was seeing out of both men's eyes at once, their fields of vision overlapping, swimming as his brain—his brains—tried to make sense of the confused and conflicting inputs.

Both Valens screamed identically, both tried to scramble back. The one the doctor restrained broke free—he was not strapped in—and fell into the aisle of the shuttle's main cabin. Lord Powers released Valen's wrist, his hand going reflexively to the unkindled sword hilt at his belt. Valen's head—heads—swam as his vision of the Avenger in his seat crossed with the scrambled impression of the ceiling overhead and that of the doctor and two armored legionnaires stooping over him.

The Valen in the chair turned from the great lord to his other self sprawling in the aisle. His head ached where he had struck it, and he offered no resistance as the legionnaires seized his arms. Seated in the chair, Valen hissed as he felt the bite of a second needle in his neck—in the neck of the Valen lying on the floor.

"Quiet, now," the doctor whispered in his ear, though Athos knelt upon the floor two yards away. "Hush now. It will pass."

"He's going," Powers said, his sword hilt in his hand.

Valen watched with growing horror—with no idea what to say or do—as the Valen upon the floor began to *shrink*, to wither and fade like a shadow annihilated by the noonday sun. The men who knelt upon his arms staggered and drew back. One stood even as Valen's double vision slewed and stabilized, and a moment later he was looking at an aisle empty except for the kneeling, hairless doctor in his unassuming gray suit.

The engineer did not dare speak, did not dare move. Hardly he dared to breathe, fearing the next breath would bring fresh horror. "What?" he managed at last, and turned only his eyes to Lord Powers. "What . . . happened to me?"

"Higher dimensions," Powers said, and brushed his fall of auburn hair from his high forehead with the hand that still held his unkindled sword. "You really don't remember?"

"Remember what?" Valen asked, feeling suddenly woozy. He let his head rest against the cool metal of the bulkhead.

"It grabbed you," Powers said. "The Hand. When you touched it."

Valen could remember the freezing cold of those glassy black bones beneath his fingers. He could not remember it moving, could certainly not remember them grabbing him. But then . . . he could not remember anything. Not until he was on the shuttle departing Echidna. Had that been later the same day? Had Silva, Lorens, and Sykes carried him back out of the Great Tomb to the camp? Had Tor Mencius insisted they take him back to the *Ecliptic*? He remembered talking to Captain Daraen, but he hadn't asked Valen about the Hand.

Had he?

Or had he asked a different Valen?

"That was *me*," he said, voice shaking, eyes wandering back to the now empty spot in the aisle. "That was *another* me. I could see . . . see what he saw. I felt the shot, and *your* hand, and . . ."

Powers made a hushing sound. "I know, lad," he said. "I know."

"What happened to me?"

"We're not sure," Athos said.

"The Chantry tested me," Valen said. "They said I was . . . human."

"The Chantry can only test you for machine influences," Lord Powers said. "Cybernetic implants. Neural laces. Nanomachines. You were clear of all that."

Athos narrowed his dark eyes. "I asked you about information hazards, do you remember?"

Valen bobbed his head weakly.

"There is something wrong with your brain," he said. "The signals in it. Your synapses. They're firing far faster than any human brain should. We think when you touched the fingers, they disrupted the electromagnetic fields in your brain body. And not *only* the electromagnetic fields, but the nuclear forces, even the quantum properties of the particles that comprise your body."

"Quantum properties?" Valen asked. "Man, I'm just an engineer. I know explosives. This is . . ." It was too much. "But how? It was just some fossil. Just some *dead hand*."

"I told you," Lord Powers said. "The creature who owned that hand—the Monumental—its body extends beyond the confines of what we call space. There are parts of it that yet live, and one of those parts reached out to you, we think, and wounded you."

"Wounded me?" Valen felt his blood run cold. "Am I going to die?"

"We're not sure," the lord said, unreassuringly. "Do you know what wave-particle duality is?"

Valen shook his head. He was starting to wonder if the sedative Dr. Athos had given his other self had somehow affected him.

Powers had not restored his sword to its catch on his belt. "You've fired a laser?"

"Course, sir."

"You know that light travels as both particles and waves?"

"Oh, that," Valen felt his limbs growing very heavy. He wanted to shout, to shake his lordship and ask what the point of this physics lecture was when some alien god-thing had messed him up so badly, but he didn't have the energy. Let the bastard talk. Valen could remember someone—not Tor Mencius, he was a historian, a xenologist—lecturing about particle physics once. The photons in a laser acted like particles when you observed them, moved in straight lines, left clean marks on the target board when you fired them through a pair of slits. But when you looked away, when you didn't observe them, they scattered, rippled like water passing through a pair of culverts at high tide.

"Something similar has happened to you, if only by analogy," his lordship said. "You said you could see through *both* sets of eyes. You felt the injection we gave the other, you said, and my hand."

"Yes."

"People are like particles, in a sense. We're composed of them, at least. But whatever happened to you . . ."

"You're saying I'm . . . like a wave?"

Powers reached into his tunic with the hand not holding his sword hilt, and fished out a pocket terminal like a fob watch on a chain. He pressed some control on its side with a thumbnail—Valen saw a light shimmer in the entoptic contact lenses the man wore over his eyes—and a moment later a holograph window opened above the terminal, projected in mid-air. It was a suit's camera recording, and showed a darkened room. There was no sound, but the suit's owner was staring up at the pattern of circular runes scored in the dark stone of the dome above. They were Cielcin letters, shining where the xenobites had hammered silver wire into the graven symbols to set them shining in the roof above.

Valen recognized the Great Tomb, the tomb of the giant. The Monumental.

The recording panned down as its owner looked at the sarcophagus lying open in the center of the chamber, surrounded in vacuum by the bodies of long-dead Cielcin priests, creatures that had been sealed away with the severed limb of their god, there to serve it eternally in death. The image panned, fixed upon the image of a man in the quilted, form-fitting white pressure suit of a Legion Corp engineer. The man's face was lost behind the white ceramic helm and visor, but Valen knew it was himself as the man reached down to caress the whorled bone of one massive, black fingertip.

M. Valen! Stop that!

The image blurred as its owner—Tor Mencius, Valen guessed—hurried to bat his hand away.

Too late.

The crackling gleam of auroras filled the recording, and through it all Valen saw himself lifted into the air like a puppet yanked skyward by its strings. For an instant, Valen thought he seemed to *grow* until he was twice the size of a man, a giant himself hanging in the air beneath the dome. His limbs thrashed violently, then without warning he was sailing through the air—shrinking the while, returning to ordinary human size.

Three Valens struck the wall of the domed chamber all at once, side by side by side. Each hit the hard stone and fell like stunned flies, each at the precise same instant. Valen watched the whole thing with horror, felt his heart beating in his mouth. Just as the man in the aisle had done, two of the three Valens began to diminish, to shrink and fade like shadows, until only one man remained. It was to that man—that Valen—that the owner of the recording rushed. Valen could almost remember him shouting.

Valen? Valen!

He wasn't even sure. Was he Valen anymore? And what *was* Valen anyway?

"Valen?"

All at once, Valen found he couldn't breathe. He opened his mouth to reply, but no sound came out. He choked, felt his eyes bulging, felt again his heart hammering in his mouth. He looked around, wide-eyed and terrified as a pain sharp as knives struck both his ears.

"What's happening?" Lord Powers asked.

They were the last words he ever heard.

Valen thrust a hand out against the bulkhead to his right, saw blood red and black beneath his skin. Again he tried to breathe, and again pain bright as sunfire lanced through him. He couldn't breathe! He couldn't breathe! His vision blurred, and a blackness ran across the world, a blackness lit by the light of innumerate stars.

And there, against them—for that final, fleeting moment—he saw the black knife-shape of an Imperial shuttle sailing, its ion drives blue and blazing . . . and he understood.

It had happened again. He had doubled again, his particles refracted, rippled across the quantum foam . . . and his second self was outside the shuttle.

It was enough to kill them both.

His last thought was of the Hand—of the *god*—that had killed him. How small he was by comparison, and how vast and strange was the inhuman universe.

It didn't matter, he decided, as all went black.

Whatever else was true, it had taken a god to kill him, and that was enough.

RISE OF THE ADMINISTRATOR
M.A. Rothman & D.J. Butler

M.A. Rothman and D.J. Butler tend to write in different corners of the speculative fiction map. Rothman is a thriller writer who injects a healthy dose of Michael Crichton-esque science into his plots, and occasionally generates stories that have a fantasy feel to them. Butler is known for his fantasy novels, many of which contain a strong element of history or faux-history. What madness could possibly come of their decision to collaborate?

Thirty feet beneath the desert sands of the Sahara, François passed through a hidden chamber and started down a long tunnel hewn in the bedrock. It had been thousands of years since anyone had breathed in this stale air, and despite the heat that seeped down from the blazing surface, he felt a shiver run up his back. The sounds of picks against stone—followed by curses in

Arabic—echoed around him. His diggers were having a tough time making progress at the end of the tunnel.

Lifting up an LED lamp, François studied the etched markings that looked nothing like the Egyptian hieroglyphs he'd seen at other dig sites. These were cruder, simpler. They lacked refinement and the little flourishes of the scribal schools.

"I have no doubt about it: these are predynastic markings," said a German-accented voice behind him.

François frowned. "Gunther, I didn't hire you to date them, I hired you to help me decipher them."

Gunther continued undeterred. "The writing is in the same style as what we found on the tablets at Nabta Playa. Same characters. Same frustrating vocabulary."

François turned to face the Egyptologist. "By 'frustrating,' I take it you mean you can't do it."

"I'm sorry. But I know someone who might be able to help."

"No. I *told* you—we're keeping this out of sight of the academics. This is *my* find, and I'm not about to let some self-important professor or government official claim this as their discovery."

Gunther looked boyish for his age, and he now had a boy's look of embarrassment about him. "I understand that. But the guy I'm thinking about left academia for a lot of the same reasons you despise it. He got sick of the politics of it all and left Egyptology to go do something more useful. Last I talked with him, he was making furniture."

A metallic clank sounded from down the tunnel and a stream of Arabic curses ripped the air. A moment later

Abdullah, the senior digger, approached. He carried a broken pick in one hand and a lantern in the other.

"What happened?" François asked in Arabic.

The burly Egyptian held up his broken digging tool and shrugged. "Sayyid, the stone is tougher than anything I've ever encountered. This is the second one of these I have destroyed."

François took the broken pick from the digger and patted his shoulder. "You're doing good work, Abdullah. I'll see about getting you some better digging tools."

"Thank you, Sayyid. You're most generous."

As Abdullah continued toward the main chamber to fetch a new pick, François studied the broken one in the light of the lantern. After a moment, he held it out for Gunther to see.

"Look at this. This is a tungsten-carbide tip. The same stuff that's used by the military to dig holes through mountains. And see how fine-grained the metal is? This thing didn't break because of some casting flaw or flaw in the hardening process. I'm having a very hard time thinking Bronze Age Egyptians dug this tunnel. I'm telling you, this place was dug out by aliens."

This wasn't the first time François had voiced such a suspicion. Both the chamber and the tunnel seemed beyond the capabilities of any ancient civilization.

Any ancient *human* civilization.

But Gunther just chuckled. "It's your money, François. You can test any hypothesis you want."

François sighed. Gunther never took the possibility seriously.

"This carpenter of yours," he said. "What's his name?"

"Marty."

"Can he be trusted to adhere to a non-disclosure agreement?"

Gunther nodded. "I don't see why not."

"Then reach out to this Marty. Tell him what's expected and *only* as much as he needs to know. And tell him there's a twenty-thousand-euro signing bonus just for coming out and taking a crack at it." When Gunther didn't immediately set off, François waved him on. "Go. Get us our language expert."

As Gunther walked briskly from the tunnel, François ran a thumb over the broken pick's tip and looked around him. The walls might *look* like sandstone, but sandstone didn't break tungsten-carbide tips. So what were they *really* made of?

There was only one answer that made any sense. He knew the rest of the world would think him crazy for even considering it, but the elimination of explanations that could *not* be true left him with only the one possibility:

Aliens existed, and they had visited Earth.

✦✦✦ COUNTLESS YEARS EARLIER ✦✦✦
An Unidentified Assailant

Before our transition into our current state of being, we had no name for ourselves. We simply were. We had a corporeal presence, and our home planet was a gas giant orbiting a main-sequence star in what was a very average-sized galaxy in the outer ring of the ever-expanding universe.

Our first memories of who we are began when we gained sentience. Unlike most other life forms, which evolved on the surface of rocky planets, we developed in our home planet's upper atmosphere, among nitrogen-rich gases hovering about thirty-five thousand miles above metallic hydrogen seas.

At first we were no more than jelly-like substances with the simplest sense of light and darkness. But over millions of generations, our bodies grew into loosely formed clouds of organic compounds. These early ancestors gathered not only the little warmth that came from our red-colored star, but also its torrents of radiation—and thanks to the latter, we evolved quickly.

Only in the earliest times did we sense ourselves as

individual creatures without a shared knowledge or thought pattern. We still remember those times—they're registered as ancient memories in our database—but only rarely are these recollections summoned, and when they are, they feel foreign to us. For long ago we developed a hive mind: a shared consciousness that allowed us to distribute nourishment from the part of our planet that was facing our star to the part of it—and the part of *us*— that lay in darkness. We started as separate beings, but we became one.

This helped us gain strength.

In time we learned how to migrate from our planet to others. We no longer needed a planet to sustain us, or to keep our form cohesive, because we had grown large enough to have our own mutual attraction. The sheer mass of all that we were had become a gravity well. We learned how to ride the eddies of the solar and interstellar winds.

We were very much like a planet of our own making, floating through our solar system, gaining nourishment and knowledge.

When we learned to travel against the solar winds, we increased our speed. And when our rate of travel approached the speed of light, we felt the shift in time.

We welcomed it.

Time had become increasingly irrelevant to us anyway. Time matters to those who expire, and we cannot expire. Yes, in those early days before we became one, such a thing was possible, but no longer.

Over the long span of our existence, we scoured the entire universe, gathering all that was known, absorbing it. We measured time only by the birth and death of stars, for such events could conceivably have posed a danger to us, and so we gave them a wide berth.

But with our greater speed, and our shift in time, came a new awareness. And that awareness brought to our attention an impossible truth:

We weren't alone.

It could not be. We had seen the universe, and there was only us left.

Yet as we slid closer to the speed of light, we sensed it: a presence. It had been there all along, no farther from us than the width of an atom.

We dove toward it.

Squeezing all of our mass into a dense spear racing at nearly the speed of light, we pierced a veil we hadn't even known was there.

That was when we saw it all. When we sensed the answer to all the questions ever asked.

Before us was an immeasurably large stack of atom-thin layers, each of which was a universe unto itself. We floated alongside the many-layered multiverse in a great emptiness, which we called *the bulk*. The immensity of what lay ahead of us was hard to comprehend. It was all that there was, is, or ever will be.

We were the first in all of the multiverse to arrive within the bulk.

And suddenly, a realization came upon us: we no longer existed in a corporeal sense. The mass, the giant cloud of energy and matter that was who we were, was gone.

Or was it?

We willed ourselves toward the stack of layered universes, and peered into the place we'd previously called home. And we saw our universe from a different perspective.

Our home, our entire universe, had been stripped bare. Every planet, every star, had been laid to waste, consumed by our hunger to evolve, to continue growing. The few remaining solar objects were dimly glowing hulks void of organic matter. And with no interstellar clouds of gas to serve as nurseries for the next generation of stars, the universe would forever remain what it had become: a barren wasteland.

This was our doing. The result of an ever-growing hunger that had run unabated since the beginning of time. And it shocked us to our core. All lives that had ever existed, whether before us or after us, had been destroyed in our quest for *more*. More of everything.

And it had all happened without us being even marginally aware of it.

Yet even as guilt weighed heavily on our collective, we sensed another change. The material urges that had driven our hunger had abated. We no longer wished to consume, to grow . . . we wished only to *learn*. To learn more about this new existence and our access to the multiverse.

We realized that it was possible to gain knowledge without destroying the things that we observed. We did not have to consume a thing to understand it. We felt suddenly as though our eyes had been closed for our entire existence, and we had only opened them now for the first time.

As we contemplated our new situation, eons passed...
...and others joined us in the bulk.

The presence of others required us to have a name. We chose to call ourselves *the Administrator*. For we were the caretaker of the bulk, this dimension that contained the multiverse. The others had chosen different identities corresponding to their own arrival in the bulk.

We welcomed the others into our continuum, and they acceded to our administration.

Eventually, we were a group of forty-two who had achieved what no others in the multiverse had achieved: we'd shed our material bodies and gone beyond the limits of our home universes. But we were not the same. Some wanted only to explore the multiverse, this impossible vastness before us. Others ignored the multiverse, looking for something even greater. And we—the Administrator—we wanted to *experience* new life and new civilizations.

Yet there was one thing we all agreed upon: we would do no harm to those who resided within the multiverse.

As the first among the continuum, we knew it was possible for us to travel invisibly within any universe we chose, observing without influencing. We could slow down time, speed it up, or even reverse its flow. But we quickly realized that there was a better way to experience those things that we wanted to understand: we could enter a universe in a *substantial* way.

For our first attempt, we chose a universe at random. It contained countless galaxies, and as time sped past, stars would flare to life and almost immediately explode. Only on occasion did a spark of intelligent life gain our attention. So we willed time to slow, and we shifted our way to a planet very unlike the one on which we'd started our immortal existence.

A rocky planet teeming with life.

We took on the form of the nearest life form we saw: a large lizardlike creature with jagged teeth and sharp claws. We sensed a heaviness to our steps; never had we experienced the effect of gravity in a non-gaseous body. Nor had we ever before felt the sensation of lungs expanding, or of blood rushing through our body. The feelings were nearly overwhelming.

In our new form, we lumbered clumsily out of the jungle and into a flat grassland. As we stepped from the trees, a screech erupted from the sky, and a winged creature swooped down and clamped its jaws onto our head.

The last sensation we experienced in that body was the crunching sound of our skull breaking.

And then the focus of our consciousness appeared back within the bulk.

When we'd shed our mortal coil, we'd assumed this was the ultimate experience for any creature. But this . . . this was something we'd never experienced.

Death.

It left us unsatisfied.

We knew that for creatures who had not developed the shared consciousness of a hive mind, all experiences were utterly lost upon death. Everything they were, snuffed out in an instant. Such a primitive mortality seemed pointless . . . yet such forms of life were everywhere.

Scanning the multiverse, we sensed life in all

directions. Millions of tiny beacons of light, of varying levels of brightness. The brighter the light, the more advanced they seemed to be.

Wanting to see more, we gravitated toward the brightest of signals. And once again, we found that we learned more by *experiencing*. By integrating within an existing member of the species being studied.

Our chosen subject self-identified as Yaffeh. She had blue skin, pearloid eyes, and a featherlike fringe at the tips of her fins. We burrowed into her conscious thoughts, and we saw the world through her eyes, traveled it in her body, felt her emotions.

The Administrator was Yaffeh.

She lived as a member of the Kappa, a tribe of underwater sea creatures who had achieved domination over everything within their ocean-covered world.

"Yaffeh, it is good to see you again on this shift to low tide."

Yaffeh casually swam against the shifting current, keeping pace so that she could gaze at the guardian of the meeting chamber. She couldn't remember his name, but his name was the last thing on her mind. He was large for a male, and heavily muscled. The poisoned barb on his tail looked sharp and ready for any challenger. But mostly, she was staring at the man's gills. They glowed brightly with a myriad of colors—a sure sign of his fertility.

She felt the stirring within her to mate, but resisted her primal instincts. Now was not the time. She must remain focused on the council and its outcome.

She was so focused, in fact, that she didn't notice our presence, the presence of the Administrator, lodged alongside her own consciousness like a gut worm in an intestinal tract.

With a flick of her tail, she swam past the guardian, through the maze of turns in the cave system, and into the council chamber.

The water here was especially clear, and glowing shells from the depths of this world shone their light upon the figure floating at the chamber's center: Yaffeh's father, the chief of the Kappa tribe.

Ignoring his stern look, she gathered with the others to await his words.

"Fellow leaders of the Kappa, we are in a time of transition."

Despite the vastness of the chamber, all could hear him clearly. Echo shells were used to broadcast his voice to all corners.

"According to the scientists who measure the ice floes, our worst fears are now coming to pass. The yearly ebb and flow of the surface ice has ceased, and the entirety of the ocean is now capped with a thick sheet of ice. We are uncertain how this will affect us in the years to come, but we know we must prepare for journeys to the deeper realms, where the warmth bubbles up from the depths. We must lay claim to these realms, identify the best of the hunting grounds, and explore new areas for the survival of our people."

What we knew, but the Kappa did not, was that a primordial black hole had raced past their solar system, disturbing the balance of the star's satellites and flinging the tribe's planet to the outer reaches of space. This was why it grew colder. And would not warm again.

We experienced what happened next through the eyes of Yaffeh and her descendants, of which there were many. We followed their branching paths over many thousands of years.

The Kappa sought the depths, as their chief had demanded. These depths were indeed warmer, heated by high levels of radiation emanating from the core of the planet. But that radiation had harmful long-term effects on Yaffeh's descendants. Sores, scaly skin, weak bones. Deficiencies that made them much more likely to be eaten by predators, or simply not live to the age of reproduction. Births waned, the tribe failed to grow, and after 1,293,534 years, the last of the Kappa perished.

They had been intelligent, and this intelligence had allowed them to last much longer than our most optimistic estimates. Yet despite their intelligence, the Kappa had never thought to look up. The idea of leaving their planet had never even dawned on them.

We, the Administrator, felt pity for this race of creatures who knew themselves only by their tribal association. We mourned the loss of a noble species, but we held to the accord that the continuum had established. There would be no interference on our part.

It was during our period of mourning that a ripple caught our attention. For the first time since the forty-second member had joined the continuum, a universe was breached. But this time, the breach did not represent the arrival of a new member to the bulk. This breach was a surge of energy that burst directly from one universe into another.

We immediately attempted to halt time, but the damage had been done.

Willing ourselves into both of the universes at once, we sensed a brilliant life form spanning both locations.

The Groll.

We immediately poured ourselves into the mind of one of these creatures, and experienced bloodthirsty excitement at the prospect of new conquests in another universe. This was a sensation we had never felt before—not in our own bodies, the bodies of others, or when bodiless. This sensation belonged to the Groll.

The Groll had become aware of the multiverse. And they wanted only one thing: to dominate anything that was within reach.

✦✦✦ THE TEST OF THE CONTINUUM ✦✦✦

"Captain Yorkin, our ships have crossed over successfully!"

Yorkin snarled with approval as the rest of the armada flashed into the new universe. He hadn't believed it possible when the Grand Emperor Torquin gave him the orders, but now that he'd witnessed the impossible happen, the bumps on his skin hardened with excitement.

As more and more ships entered the universe to speed up the conquest, Yorkin turned to the ship's comms officer. "Send the emperor's orders to the ships. We need a link back to the home universe, right away."

The survey ships mapped the sector and located the proper set of stars to create the necessary return gate. From there it took only moments for the generator ships to power up and create isolation bubbles around their target stars, rip them from their current trajectories, and move them into place.

The captain watched the activity play out in front of him, but as he did so, he felt a growing sense of wrongness. In truth, it had been there from the moment he'd entered the first gate, and he simply could not shake the sensation.

He didn't believe in intuition or in extra-sensory perception, but he did believe that sometimes his *ordinary* senses detected things that he wasn't consciously aware. Threats, for instance. The most primitive levels of his brain would respond to a threat before his rational mind had even begun to process the data that told him the threat existed in the first place.

That was how he felt right now. Though he couldn't see it, he knew there was an enemy present.

An alarm screeched—*"Intruder Alert!"*—and a coruscating ball of mist appeared out of thin air a mere ten feet in front of the captain. Yorkin's primal instincts took over, and he launched himself directly at the invading cloud.

Or at least, he intended to. Instead, he froze mid-step. It was as if time itself had stopped, but his mind was still awake.

The mist coalesced into several forms: first a lizardlike creature, then a fish, and finally a clone of one of Yorkin's race.

The lizard creature hissed and bared its teeth in an attempt to seem friendly. It stood before Yorkin and spoke in a foreign-sounding voice that spoke directly in his mind. *"Your intentions are understood, and they are denied."*

Yorkin wanted to slam the intruder's smug expression into paste, but all he could do was stare as the creature casually strolled across the main deck of the emperor's battle cruiser.

Everyone else on the main deck was also immobile.

Struggling to break the hold this thing had on him, the captain watched as the invader, with a wave of his hand, pulled up the battle log of their travel. The holographic footage played, showing the emperor's array of star-based weapons being aimed at a single point in space.

One hundred high-mass stars had been brought into close proximity to one another. Each star was spinning like a stellar top at speeds that tore at the fabric of space and time, and each star had just enough mass to cause it to collapse upon itself. But the emperor's scientists had devised a method to feed the rapidly spinning objects, increasing their rotational speed, thus temporarily preventing their inevitable collapse.

Slowly the stars aligned, with all of their poles aimed at a single point—a gravitational anomaly that the scientists suspected was a parallel universe. Then, at the flick of a switch, the power feeding the rotation stopped, and within milliseconds of each other, the stars imploded. Unfathomably strong spears of energy were released along their poles, powerful gamma-ray bursts that raced across the emptiness of space to all assault the anomaly at once. And as the spiraling rays of death converged, a massive gravity distortion was created, opening the first of what Yorkin knew would be many tunnels to other worlds.

With a sense of something ripping within him, Yorkin managed to wrench himself from the intruders' control.

He took a step toward his enemy.

We watched as Brane delta+916GBJOKL was invaded by these aggressive creatures who called themselves the Groll. As we rummaged through the mind of the creatures who'd breached the veil, it was clear to us that unlike the forty-two, these creatures weren't interested in anything but their own conquests. Stopping to understand or appreciate the immensity of what was around them was not in their nature.

It was then that Yorkin launched himself at us.

That would have been possible for a peer member of the continuum. But it should have been impossible for the Groll.

We felt the cracking of bones as the enraged captain of the invasion fleet slammed into us.

We reversed time.

We called to the other forty-two and in the blink of an eye—an agreement had been reached.

In the universe from which the invaders had come, time was made to run in reverse. The invasion withdrew, Yorkin had not yet hatched from his egg, and the race of the so-called immortal emperor returned back to the primordial sludge from whence it came.

Several million years of time in Yorkin's universe.

It meant nothing to us.

Appearing in a chamber that existed outside the

multiverse, the forty-two conferred in their "physical" forms.

Forty-two chairs had been arranged in a circle, each occupied by a physical facsimile of what each member of the continuum had been at the moment of its elevation.

We appeared as a glowing cloud. Some members looked like minerals. Others like many-limbed creatures. Still others changed shape even as they spoke. Many were hive minds and represented themselves. Those species that still retained their primitive individuality sent ambassadors.

We acknowledged our peers with a nod. "Such a thing cannot come to pass again."

Continuum member four shifted from a crackling ball of energy into a placid, pale-faced creature. It was bilaterally symmetrical, with four limbs and a fleshy, forward-thrusting face on a short neck. "Why do you say that? We agreed that any who can perceive and reach the continuum are welcome."

"Don't forget that we also agreed not to cause harm," noted member thirteen. "By piercing the veil they qualified to join, but by attacking another universe, they violated our rules."

"Rules they were not aware of," noted another member.

A lizardlike member snarled. "Irrelevant. We cannot abide by a breaking of the first law."

Several of the members began speaking at the same time. We leaned forward and raised our voice.

"The invasion we just witnessed could have been

worse. What if, rather than targeting another universe, they had targeted one of us?"

"Would that actually matter?" a member asked.

A six-limbed member with wisps of smoke rising from his carapace snorted. "Don't let hubris be your downfall. You are not invincible. None of us are."

"What are you suggesting?" asked member thirteen.

We thought on the problem for a moment. "The Groll were flawed creatures. They saw nothing of worth beyond their desire for conquest, and they were extreme xenophobes. Anything that wasn't Groll was considered a threat. We could screen such creatures out before they reach a level that would endanger us."

"A test?"

We nodded.

"And if a species fails this test?"

We flexed to show our indifference. "Species that we deem unworthy may not evolve further."

Continuum member thirteen barked out his response. "I agree."

"As do we," said another.

"And what if you deem *my* species unworthy?" asked the member with the forward-thrusting face.

"But you are here already," we said.

It was not a complete answer.

There was silence, then a slow chorus of agreement.

The lizard turned to us. "I assume you are establishing these tests."

We looked to the other members, who had already begun to vanish from the chambers.

"Yes. It seems we are establishing the tests."

For this, we needed builders. There would also be a need for watchers, a network of them, to identify those places across the multiverse where the builders would need to go. If we set up the system correctly, we would be able to continue our own research, without distraction.

We recalled the sensation of our bones breaking on the emperor's battle cruiser. It could have been so much worse.

But . . . there had been a delight in the sensation.

We wanted to break more of our bones.

These tests had to be done correctly, and that would require us to focus on the task of creating a team of workers.

It was time . . .

✧✧✧ 5,200 YEARS AGO ✧✧✧
Upper Egypt

Scorpion, watching from within a palanquin as the slaves cleared a new area for the planting, turned to one of his body men, a man bearing the title Sole Companion.

"Asim, be sure to tell the taskmasters that we need proper drainage ditches. The seasonal rains are about to arrive and the crop will rot if it sits in too much water."

"I will inform Jafari of your wishes." Asim grinned, accentuating the ritual scars on both cheeks. "For a warrior king, you know much about farming."

Scorpion shrugged. "My father was a farmer, and I've spent much time in the fields harvesting crops. And besides, as a king I must understand more than just the trade of war. Our supplies are running low after our battles with the Nubian devils in the south. We cannot maintain an army if we cannot feed them."

Suddenly, a shadow fell over the land, and the bearers of the palanquin quailed with fear. Scorpion hopped out of the rapidly tilting litter. His bearers cried out and splayed themselves on the ground, hiding their heads.

Asim pointed to the sky. "Ancestors save us!" He prostrated himself.

93

The warrior king looked up. A dark circle grew in the sky, blocking the sun and turning the day into a strange twilight. The ground vibrated as the circle fell from the heavens.

But the warrior king did not quail or prostrate himself. He stood tall, showing no fear, remembering his father's wisdom: *Face your enemies without fear, and you will win most battles without ever having to fight.*

The circle came closer, growing ever larger, chasing the slaves from the fields. When at last it came to rest on the freshly prepared land, Scorpion could see that it was immense—at least fifty paces across.

Asim scrambled back to his king's side. "This must be an emissary or a sign from the gods. Are you not frightened?"

A door opened in the side of the giant disc, and light poured from within. Silhouetted in the doorway was a heavenly warrior. Yet as the warrior strode forth, exiting the disc, it was clear that this was no ordinary man. It was as though the stars had assembled to form a figure in the shape of a man, and a blinding light shone from within him.

The star-man hissed, and then a voice spoke within Scorpion's head, deep and genderless.

"You are known as Scorpion, the leader of your people."

It wasn't a question; this strange emissary knew who he was. But what was this creature? Was he a god? If so, which one?

"I am—"

"Silence. I shall speak. I am the Builder."

Scorpion flinched. He was unaccustomed to being addressed in such a rude manner.

"It has been determined that your species has achieved a level of advancement that might, in the future, become a danger to others. Therefore, your people, and those who descend from them, are to be tested."

The Builder stepped closer. He was tall, perhaps twice Scorpion's height, though it was hard to be certain since he was giving off smoke. The fumes had a thick smell, but it was unlike any incense the warrior king had ever experienced.

Scorpion tried to back away, but he found himself unable to move.

The Builder held up his hand, revealing an object shaped like a cross with a loop on top. He touched the object to Scorpion's forehead, and the king felt a burning sensation race through his body.

"You and yours are now responsible for what happens to your people. The tests are being constructed."

Images appeared in Scorpion's mind. He saw other discs descending to the land, sending bright lights at the desert floor beneath them. Sand exploded away from the light, leaving behind hidden chambers, tunnels, and more. What would take a thousand men a year or more to dig was being done in mere minutes.

Most discs descended in places he did not recognize. There were jungles, giant lakes, open fields. And in every location, the same activities took place. Lights. Digging. Building. Scorpion recognized the location of only one of the discs; thanks to a nearby landmark, he knew it was in recently conquered Nubian territory.

Then the Builder's body glowed even brighter and sent a spear of light launching forth. It slammed into a grazing bull, and the animal began to change its form. Its rear legs elongated, its front legs took on the form of muscled arms, and it stood upright, with an intelligent gleam in its eyes.

In his mind, Scorpion saw similar light-spears striking other animals in other places. And each time, the animal was elevated from its current form.

The warrior king looked up at the strange creature who'd come from the heavens. "I don't understand. What are these tests? What happens if we pass? What happens if we fail?"

The Builder exhaled a long hiss. *"Your future if you pass."*

The warrior king saw new images in his mind. Large pyramids sprouted along the horizon—monuments to future pharaohs. The people of the marshes and the people of the river unified, and all prospered. The flooding of the Nile was controlled, and new chariots raced across the desert without need of oxen to pull them. Cities grew, and were filled with people smiling, trading, building, farming, and raising families. Some of them flew in metal birds that took them to other places across great oceans.

"And if you fail . . ."

The metal birds fell out of the sky. Cracks opened up in the earth, swallowing entire cities whole. Impossibly large boulders streaked down from the heavens, slammed into the ground, and sent rolling waves of fire across all of the Black Land and other unknown places. The light from the sun grew dark, and the world began to freeze.

Crops withered and died, and the cities that had been filled with happiness were now crumbling remains, their people dead or scattered to the winds.

The warrior king's expression grew grim. This responsibility weighed heavily on his shoulders.

And then the images in Scorpion's mind vanished— and so did the Builder. The door to the giant disc closed, and it rose up from the field, leaving not even the faintest impression on the land to indicate that it had ever been there.

Asim blinked with surprise, then turned to the warrior king. "Indeed. No army can survive without food."

Scorpion looked curiously at his body man. "Asim?"

Asim frowned and gazed around himself, looking suddenly shaken. "I apologize, my king. You were inspecting the preparation of the field and now...I...I feel I've lost some time. Forgive me if I did not respond appropriately."

Scorpion felt a cold prickle of fear at the base of his neck. His body man seemed unaware that anything out of the ordinary had happened. The entire experience was wiped from his mind.

Only a god could do such a thing.

The slaves who'd run from the field looked even more confused as they came running back, as did the bearers of the king's palanquin. It was clear that none of them had any recollection of what had just happened.

Scorpion patted Asim on the shoulder. "Peace. Do not worry. Let Jafari know about the proper drainage. In the meantime, I have to travel south to a place near the stone circle."

"The ruins?"

The warrior king nodded. "Unless I have gone mad, there is something waiting for me there."

Scorpion walked into the tunnel, saw the scribes busily painting on the walls, and smacked his hands together with a loud clap. "Make sure you capture every detail I described on the tunnel walls. If we don't properly document the bargain that the gods have made with us, our people will be doomed."

Ever since his encounter with the Builder, the warrior king's senses had been heightened. He heard every soft sweep of the brush as the scribes did their work. Every breath they took. And as one scribe whispered to another, the warrior king heard what they believed to be a private discussion.

"Do you think he really talked to a god?"

"Be quiet—he can probably hear us. There are those who think the Scorpion King has become one with the gods."

"But these messages we are writing... are our people really being tested as he described?"

"All I know is if the Scorpion King says it is so, it is so. I don't question those who claim to have received messages directly from the gods, and neither should you."

The warrior king sensed Asim approaching before the man uttered his first syllable. "What troubles you, Asim?"

"Your Highness, the heroes you asked for... I have collected them. They are waiting aboveground."

Scorpion nodded confidently, but he was concerned. The instructions he had been given were clear enough. If the heroes survived, all was good. But if they did not survive, it would be time to collect another set of heroes.

And he had no idea how long his people had to find the *right* set of heroes. The Builder had not specified a timeframe for the test. Perhaps it didn't have to be completed during Scorpion's lifetime; perhaps his son, or his son's son, might be the one to find the heroes to save humanity.

"And that's why I'm having it all written down," Scorpion muttered to himself.

"What?" Asim asked.

Scorpion shook his head. "Never mind. Just bring the heroes into the tunnel. It's time to begin."

Marty was in the hospital when Gunther called with the mysterious translation job. Curious, Marty accepted. And what followed over the next few days was a whirlwind of flights and travels through the desert. All of which led the former Egyptologist to where he stood now: thirty feet under the Sahara Desert, blinking the dust out of his eyes.

Many years in the field. A scholarly man of science and truth for all of those years. And yet as Marty stared into the empty chamber that greeted him, he had no explanation for what he'd just witnessed.

The impervious barrier that had blocked their progress was now gone.

His crew followed behind him, but their excited murmurs faded away as a voice spoke inside his head, in ancient Egyptian.

"Seer, it is time."

Marty felt a surge of energy flow through him, like a dose of confidence that came out of nowhere.

"Bring your crew into the chamber of reckoning. As seer, you are the first. You will know. You will lead. You will tell others. You will seek what is needed. It is time."

There was one explanation for everything Marty had seen this day.

Marty could be insane.

But deep in his heart, he didn't think that was it.

He motioned for the others to follow him into the domed chamber. It was perfectly round, and about twenty feet in diameter. The walls glowed with a dim, bluish-white light.

"Did you guys hear a voice just now?" he asked.

The crew shook their heads as they followed him into the chamber.

The world flashed white.

We, the Administrator, felt the ripple in the fabric of space well before the hive reached out to alert us.

"We have a primary test triggering malfunction."

We sent our wishes to the hive. "Give me its local description."

For us, the time it took for the hive to process the request and return an answer felt like an eternity. But for those living within the thin membranelike universe in which the test had been triggered, the processing time would have been only an instant.

"The event occurred over a place known as Egypt, on a planet named Earth, orbiting a G2V star called the Sun, in the Orion arm of the Milky Way galaxy, a member of the Virgo supercluster, which is a part of the Laniakea supercluster."

Our presence instantly appeared above the planet. We zoomed down over the multiple test sites, scanning every moment of time from the instant the Builders had established the test sites until the time of the triggering.

There were seven humans in the transport chamber.

But there had been an anomaly in the triggering. We sensed the wrongness on this planet. It had become unstable.

"The nature of the anomaly is?"

"The time allotted for the planet's dominant species to complete its test is about to expire."

We focused on the test site that had caused the anomaly. A seer had been assigned. But the tests had not been run in many Earth years. So many years, in fact, that the tests themselves were no longer working. The earthquakes had begun. It was the beginning of the end for humanity.

We, the Administrator, breathed in and made our decision.

"We have stitched the tests to compensate for the delays. We will allow this one last set of champions to contest for humanity's fate."

"Understood. The malfunction is cleared. Testing is underway."

The End?
To see what happens next, pick up
Time Trials by M.A. Rothman & D.J. Butler

MERE PASSERS BY
Les Johnson

Leave it to Les Johnson, Baen's resident NASA rocket scientist, to ask some of the heaviest questions posed in this anthology.

The discovery of intelligences beyond our wildest imaginations, capable of reshaping the order of the cosmos seemingly at a whim, is nothing new to the genre. Yet there remain some very important points should humanity stumble upon signs of an intelligence on that scale, beyond wondering if we'd even recognize it at all. Would first contact even be possible? Or even advisable?

"It's good to be exploring again instead of fighting in a war," mused Lieutenant Enzokuhle Achebe with his thick South African accent. Achebe, on a goodwill assignment as the executive officer of the United States Space Navy (USSS) *Alligator*, was, like his captain, waiting on the ship's Hawking Drive to activate and send it across hundreds of light years in an instant. South Africa was a relatively new participant in the Earth Defense Forces and many of that country's aspiring officers were now integrated into the crew of other EDF ships as part of their training.

"Especially a war that so easily could have been averted," said James Stockton, the ship's captain.

"So many people died for no good reason. It was a tragedy," replied Achebe, trying to be sensitive to the loss he recently learned that Stockton suffered in the conflict. His sister was a lieutenant on the USSS *South Dakota*, the very first EDF ship lost in the war with the Kurofune.

"Tragic in many ways—for both sides, including for the perpetrators. My faith says I should forgive them, and I'm trying, but I'm not there yet," said Stockton. Stockton looked at his new friend and shipmate, then at the status screens projected in front of them.

Stockton, Achebe, and the rest of the bridge crew were strapped in their chairs, anticipating the imminent sense of nausea they and most people experienced when a ship's Hawking Drive activated and took them across light years of space in barely the blink of an eye. Stockton knew it was a small price to pay when compared to the months and years it had taken humans merely to cross their own solar system just a century ago. Harnessing the energies required to zip from one location in spacetime to another was immense, but not so immense that the *Alligator*'s onboard fusion reactor couldn't provide it.

The light briefly dimmed. By the time Stockton and the crew noticed, the jump was complete and the accompanying nausea came and went with the seeming blink of an eye. Had it not been for these small telltale signs and the star field changing on the virtual display now projected in the forward part of the bridge, no one would have known the two hundred men and women of the *Alligator* had just completed a series of jumps taking them nearly 150 light years from their starting point near Jupiter.

Stockton was surprised when the Level 2 Alert sounded.

"Lieutenant Chowdhury, speak to me. Why the alert?" asked Stockton. Lieutenant Karen Chowdhury was the ship's tactical officer and responsible for making sure the ship was prepared not only for combat, but for any situation that was out of the ordinary and could pose a threat. She was neat, efficient, good at her job, and always eager to learn new skills. Stockton had recently recommended her for promotion.

"I triggered the alert, Captain," said the *Alligator*'s navigator, Lieutenant Almira Griggs-Snyder. Griggs-Snyder was one of those rare navigators who could plot counterintuitive interplanetary trajectories in her head, often better than others using a ship's computer. "We arrived nearly two AU farther away from the star than we should have." An AU was short for astronomical unit, a measurement based on the nominal distance from the Earth to the Sun.

"Are we in immediate danger?" asked Stockton.

"From what I can tell so far, there is nothing near us for a few million kilometers, but something threw us off course and until we understand why that happened, I suggest maintaining a heightened state of alert," she replied.

"I concur," said Chowdhury, as she busily scanned the situational data flowing across the screens at her duty station.

The forward display dissolved and was replaced with a top-down projection of the star system they had just entered. At first the image showed only a small part of the planetary system. The ship's not-quite-sentient artificial intelligence, John Paul, was building it up by first showing the locations of the large objects, the major planets, followed by multiple minor planets, asteroids, and comets as the ship's telescopes and other sensors found them. It was like watching a puzzle being put together in three-dimensional space, each segment having to be fit with the complex geometry of the planetary worlds (enlarged so they could be visible on the vast scale of a star system nearly seventy astronomical units across). The puzzle was now approaching fifty percent complete and, if history was a clue, it would take much longer for the remaining fifty percent to fill. They were, after all, on one side of the system and any objects on the other side were very far away and more difficult to see.

"Preliminary surveys do not detect any sort of artificial electromagnetic communication in the system nor any of the characteristics we normally assume might indicate the presence of advanced sentient life," said John Paul in his rather stale-sounding midwestern American accent. As was the AI's custom, the voice emanated from near the holographic projection in the front of the room. "I cannot yet rule out the presence of pre-industrial activity, but as of yet there is no sign."

The response was not unexpected. After all, in the

hundred years or so that humanity had been traveling between the stars, no sentient alien life had been found. Life appeared to be everywhere, life not dissimilar from Earth life, but none that came close to being recognized as sentient.

"Would you look at that," said Achebe as he pointed to one of the planets circling the star in the inner part of the system.

"Look at what?" asked Stockton.

"Look at the orbit of the second planet. There's more than one. There are three," said Achebe.

Stockton gazed at the image and his jaw dropped. The second planet in the system had not one, but two co-orbital companions as it circled the star. Three planets sharing the same orbital plane, the same distance from the star, and spaced at what looked like sixty degrees apart. One of the planets was a giant, at first glance reminding him of Jupiter. The other two were much smaller, Earth sized or perhaps Mars. There were four other planets of various sizes in the system, irregularly spaced outward from the central star as one might expect in an otherwise normal stellar system. He could not believe he hadn't noticed the three planets himself.

"John Paul, what can you tell us about the co-orbiting planets near the star? Has such an arrangement ever been reported before?" asked Stockton.

John Paul's 3D holoimage appeared on the bridge, slowly forming just to the right of the projected star system. When he chose, he appeared as a human male, fortyish, with an ever-so-slightly receding hairline and a thick head of black hair peppered with grey.

"Not that I am aware of, and my astronomical database is very comprehensive. This type of planetary arrangement is inherently unstable and should not exist in a star of this age. If it had formed by some cosmic accident from the protoplanetary nebula, then it would have long ago become unstable with one or more of the smaller companions flung to the outer star system or out of it altogether. I am unable to explain how this might be possible," said John Paul. "I was running through the data library looking for other known examples and anticipating I would be able to find at least one to share before I reported the anomaly. I have now had ample time to look through the archives and find no other such examples. This is not only new, but theoretically impossible."

"Enzokuhle, the mystery deepens," said Stockton, scratching the stubble on his chin. "Might this explain why the Hawking Drive brought us in farther away from the star than we planned?"

Griggs-Snyder replied, "Almost certainly, sir. Though the gas giant appears to be about the size of Saturn, it is far more massive than even Jupiter. That alone would change the curvature of spacetime enough to throw us off course. The exoplanet database back home will need to be updated."

"I'd say," mumbled Stockton, mostly to himself. Someone's inaccurate survey data had placed his ship and his crew in jeopardy and he did not like that.

"Sir, I believe we can return to Level 3. I don't believe we are in any immediate danger and we now know the cause of the displaced Hawking jump," she added.

"Lieutenant Chowdhury, do you agree?" asked Stockton.

"Yes, sir. I agree."

"Lower the alert level to three and let's allow John Paul to complete his survey while we consider our next steps."

Two hours later, the model of the star system was mostly complete, and there was another curious anomaly to consider: there were no asteroids or comets larger than fifty meters across anywhere in the system.

"Forgive my ignorance but is it possible for a star system to have no large comets or asteroids?" asked Stockton.

"There are no other stellar systems in the database with no large asteroids or comets. Most that have been surveyed have far more large objects than can be found in the solar system. What we see here is, so far, unique. I am compiling a list of phenomena that have never been postulated, measured, or observed," replied John Paul.

"John Paul, share your lists with senior staff and engineering personnel, with daily updates and additions. We won't learn much more out here. Unless someone has a compelling reason to do otherwise, we're going to visit the planet leading the gas giant in its orbit," said Stockton. "Take us in."

As commanded, the *Alligator* powered up its fusion drive and began accelerating for the inner star system. The journey would take about six days thanks to the inability of the Hawking Drive to operate near stars. Stockton did not understand all the math, but the experts told him that the warping of spacetime by a star would cause the Drive to malfunction if it were to be engaged too close in, with close being defined as roughly 4–5 AU from a Sun-sized star. The larger the star, the farther out the effect. In this case, they had planned to arrive about four AU from the star but the anomalously massive planet caused the drive to drop them six out instead.

The next six days were mostly routine, with Stockton running various conflict simulations to keep the crew sharp and to pass the time. While off duty, Stockton chose to work out in the ship's small gym and spend time with the crew. He enjoyed getting to know those who served under him and hearing their stories. Why did they enlist? Where were they from? What were their goals? It was easy to see the billions of humanity as nameless beings; realizing each was unique and had a story to tell was one of his life's joys. Objectively he knew that it would also improve morale and crew efficiency, but that was not his inner motivation. He did it to help relieve the pain of losing his youngest sister, Erin. She had been serving similarly on the *South Dakota* and had had her own hopes and dreams. Hearing those from his crew, most of them younger than he—about Erin's age—helped him cope.

The day they entered orbit around the leading planet, now called Nyanga, they knew a lot more about it. Though Stockton and the crew of the *Alligator* were aware that whatever name they gave the planets they visited would inevitably be changed by the powers that be back in the solar system, they put a great deal of thought into the working names they would use in the interim. In this case, Achebe came up with the most popular name, Nyanga, the Zulu word for moon. Stockton placed the ship in the equivalent to what would be called a geostationary orbit back at Earth, allowing them to continuously view one hemisphere of the planet as they circled it. A robotic probe was launched to orbit in a similar position on the other side of Nyanga so they would have continuous views of the entire planetary sphere.

Stockton gathered his officers in the CIC, a small room adjacent to the bridge, to discuss next steps.

"I've asked John Paul to give us an overview of what we've learned about Nyanga and the odd orbital dynamics of the planets," began Stockton. "I think you'll find what he has to say to be very interesting."

The wispy image of John Paul appeared at the head of the table. The combat information center, bridge, and captain's cabin were the only places on the ship equipped with the holo projectors that allowed him to have a virtual 3D presence (other than on a screen).

"Nyanga is a terrestrial planet roughly twenty percent larger than Earth and Venus, covered with water except for two major continents, possesses a strong magnetic field that shields the surface from the solar wind and coronal mass ejection events, an oxygen/nitrogen atmosphere with a mixture ratio not dissimilar to Earth's, and what appears to be a vibrant biosphere filled with all sorts of flora and some small fauna. There are no obvious signs of habitation or sentient life, but spectroscopy of the atmosphere reveals the presence of chlorofluorocarbons, carbon 14, and nitrous-oxide compounds in ratios that are unlikely to have been produced naturally, though in very small quantities. The average surface temperature is about 59 degrees Fahrenheit and both poles are covered with water ice," said John Paul.

"It's a Goldilocks planet where somebody is or used to call home," said Lieutenant Adolf Woods, the ship's signals officer. It had taken Stockton some time to fully appreciate Woods and he was glad he had made the effort. Woods was a bit of a loner and spent a great deal of his time, even his spare time, reading the latest information theory journals instead of socializing with the crew. At one time, Woods would have been pigeonholed as "on the spectrum" and perhaps not allowed to serve. From what Stockton could see, that would have been a waste of talent. Woods was good at his job and on the path to a promising career.

"So, it would appear," said Stockton. "John Paul, please continue."

"I can also report on Nyanga 2, the planet trailing the gas giant in the three-body system. While we are not close enough to perform surveys with the same resolution as we can with Nyanga, Nyanga 2 is only one percent larger than Earth, also has a strong magnetic field, and contains an atmosphere that appears remarkably similar to Nyanga. It is a bit colder, with an average global temperature of about forty-six degrees Fahrenheit and appears to be in the middle of an ice age. We are too far away for a detailed spectroscopic analysis of its atmosphere."

"Two potentially habitable planets in one system?" asked Woods.

"Not only in one system, but in one orbit," said Stockton.

"Sir?" said Lieutenant Griggs-Snyder.

"Yes, Lieutenant?"

Griggs-Snyder stood to address her fellow officers. "I've been working on some analysis with John Paul and we can't figure out how this is possible. There is simply no way that three planets can be orbiting in this configuration. It's inherently unstable and shouldn't last for more than a few months, not the millennia that would be required for the development of the complex biospheres we observe, let alone the development of complex life."

"The lieutenant is correct," said John Paul, nodding affirmation in her direction. "As I initially calculated when we entered the system, the arrangement is only quasi stable. Those familiar with orbital dynamics may recognize that the two smaller planets occupy the Lagrange Points, L4 and L5, of the larger planet that serves as the gravitational anchor relative to the much more massive star. In theory, objects placed at these locations could co-orbit the star as we observe them doing, but only with constant small adjustments to their trajectories. Without adjustment, the gravitational interactions among the bodies would quickly force them from their current locations and most likely eject them to elsewhere."

"Back at Earth, we've placed habitats at the Earth's L4 and L5 regions, but they have to constantly use their onboard thrusters to avoid drifting away," added Griggs-Snyder.

"Yet here they are. From what we can tell, the planets are not only at L4 and L5, but they also appear to have been there quite a long time and don't look like they are going anywhere soon," said Stockton.

No one spoke, making the quiet whirl of the vent fans the loudest sound in the room.

"Captain, I recommend we get closer and check out Nyanga 2," said Lucas Cardoso. Doctor Cardoso was the ship's physician. True to its origins, the *Alligator* was a warship and had no provision for carrying civilian science teams. They would come later after the EDF ships first found "interesting" new destinations and determined that they were safe enough for survey ships to follow. But every ship did have a medical officer and, in their training, they were far closer to being scientists than any other in the crew, except for the rare exceptional ship's engineer. Cardoso usually kept quiet in Stockton's staff meetings, only speaking up on matters that directly affected the medical section or the rare science matter. But when he spoke, Stockton found it was wise to listen.

"I agree. Let's see what we can find there and then decide what to do or where to go next," replied Stockton, adjourning the meeting.

That night, Stockton engaged in a lengthy discussion with Griggs-Snyder and Cardoso in the ship's mess, imbibing more than a few beers, trying to better understand the orbital mechanics and other oddities of the system they'd found. Astrodynamics had not been Stockton's best course during his training, to say the least, and having the third beer certainly didn't help him understand all the details Greggs-Snyder was so valiantly trying to explain. In the course of their discussion, several of the crew drifted in and then quickly out—likely because they were not conversant in the mathematical detail, but he and Cardoso persisted. Cardoso, true to form, said little. Stockton enjoyed the interaction and realized that when he was with Griggs-Snyder, he felt like he did when he spent long hours talking to Erin. He hoped that Erin's captain had spent similar time with her.

The discussion, and the beers, helped Stockton get a good night's sleep.

The *Alligator* had been in orbit around Nyanga 2 for almost a day before Stockton called his officers together again in the CIC to review what they'd learned. John Paul once again appeared among them, as usual wearing his virtual EDF uniform. Stockton noticed that John Paul was using his empathetic algorithms in selecting his appearance. The uniform he wore appeared to be well-worn and in need of a trip to the ship's laundry for washing and pressing.

"Nyanga 2 has a mass nearly identical to Earth or Venus, has similar atmospheric composition to Nyanga, a strong magnetic field, and is teeming with life—mostly aquatic. Though the planet is mostly covered by water, unlike Nyanga, its dry land is almost completely covered with ice and snow. The planet is in the middle of an ice age. Were it not for the temperature, humans would find it to be every bit as hospitable at Nyanga—or Earth, for that matter."

"Any signs of intelligent life?" asked Stockton.

"Yes, but not currently. Its atmosphere has some of the same trace chemicals that I detected at Nyanga. At some time in the past, there was considerable industrial-scale activity on the planet. So far, the telescopes and other sensors have not detected anything we would recognize as intelligent life."

"What about the stability of the planetary orbits? Do you have any new data that could shed light on how they are remaining stable?"

John Paul managed to look perplexed and apologetic

at the same time, even running his virtual hands through his virtual hair to emphasize his point, "I do have one bit of additional data. The mass of the gas giant is much larger than one would expect for a planet its size. The planet's volume is roughly comparable to Jupiter but its mass is much higher, making it about four times more dense— comparable to the density of the Earth. There are various ways to account for this, so it is not impossible. Just improbable."

Stockton turned from John Paul and fixed his gaze on Lieutenant Griggs-Snyder.

"Lieutenant, I'm sure you've been looking at the same data as John Paul regarding the planets' orbits. We've heard the data. What does your gut say?" Stockton had had his ship evade danger on more than one occasion by allowing his navigator to do the math, plot the possible trajectories, and then trust her gut to choose the best one. Her gut usually found the right path and he hoped it would help lead them to some sort of answer in this case as well.

"My gut says the answer lies at the gas giant."

"Then that's our next destination. How long before we arrive?" asked Stockton.

"At full speed, about three days," replied Griggs-Snyder.

"Let's get started then."

The next three days were largely uneventful with John Paul compiling yet more information about the star system and its immediate neighborhood. Once again, Stockton conducted a few drills and simulations, to keep the crew busy and occupied, if nothing else.

They arrived and entered orbit three days later.

The view was amazing and few aboard the *Alligator* ever grew weary of gazing upon a new world. Each was unique. The planet they circled was a giant bluish ball, reminiscent of Neptune. The atmosphere was rapidly churning, with multiple storms such as Jupiter's Great Red Spot or Neptune's Great Dark Spot dotting its hemispheres. Unlike its solar system counterparts, and most gas and ice giants discovered thus far, there was no ring system and, most startling, no moons. John Paul told the crew that the lack of rings and moons was mostly likely due to the gravitational effects of the co-orbiting terrestrial planets they had just visited, though he could not explain why those same gravitational anomalies had long ago not flung those same terrestrial planets elsewhere. Why would gravity prevent the formation of moons and rings, but not also affect them? Was it connected to the absence of large asteroids and comets? The mystery deepened.

Four hours after arriving and near the end of the day shift, John Paul appeared on the bridge. Though he could create a holoimage of himself anytime, John Paul preferred to do so only when he had something important to say or when he was to be involved in some sort of discussion.

"Captain, I'm having to use the ship's thrusters far more often than I should in order to maintain our orbit. The planet's gravitational pull is dynamic and we cannot maintain a passive circular orbit," said John Paul.

"Dynamic? What the hell does that mean?" asked Stockton, looking away from John Paul and toward Griggs-Snyder.

Lieutenant Griggs-Snyder cleared her throat and

replied, "Gravity is caused by mass and, thankfully, for most applications anyway, we can approximate its effects by assuming that the mass of an object acts the same as if all its mass were located at the object's center point. In other words, how the mass is distributed doesn't usually affect how we model it. Now there are some notable contrary examples, such as Earth's moon which has been pelted over the eons by asteroids and comets, some containing iron ore. The regions rich in iron ore have a much higher density, which tends to disrupt what would otherwise be a perfectly spherical gravity field and causes orbiting ships to make trajectory adjustments periodically to compensate for the areas of higher gravity. Once such a gravity field is mapped, its effects can be modeled and predicted. They are stable. Not dynamic."

"And what we have here is some sort of asymmetry, like the Moon, but it is changing?" asked Stockton.

"Yes, sir. That's exactly correct. It's like something very large and massive is rolling around inside the planet, moving from side to side, causing the unequal gravitational attraction to move all around inside the sphere. This is causing a constant disturbance to our orbit and most likely the reason the atmosphere of the planet is so energetic. Take a look at the latest images of the planet and tell me what you see," she said as she projected an image of the planet from when they first arrived next to the image of what they were viewing currently.

To Stockton, the images were very similar. The blue gas of the planet's atmosphere was swirling and numerous giant black spots, which he knew were hurricanes larger than the Earth, were churning through the chaos. The spots, however, were now different. Some were larger, some smaller, and some were simply no longer there.

"The storms have changed," said Stockton.

"And they shouldn't have changed so much in the few hours we've been here. Jupiter's Great Red Spot is essentially a hurricane. A hurricane that has been blowing for all of recorded human history. Neptune's Great Dark Spots are not as long lived, but they don't change as rapidly as every few hours," she said.

"So, whatever is causing our orbital 'dynamic' gravity anomaly is also causing all this upheaval in the planet's atmosphere?"

"I don't see how it could be otherwise," she said as John Paul nodded his virtual head in affirmation.

"And the cause, whatever it is, is also likely the reason the three planets remain in a stable orbit together," said Griggs-Snyder. "The oscillating gravity field may be what's compensating for the inherent instability of the planetary system. The varying gravity is constantly adjusting the orbits of the two terrestrial planets, keeping them stable."

"Stable for millions of years?" asked Stockton.

"I can't say for sure, but it is possible, especially considering John Paul's growing list of impossibilities and improbabilities," she replied. "To know for sure, I'll need more data. Mostly likely we'll need for Earth to send some of the gravity wave sensors here to take more precise measurements. All I've got to go on are the perturbations to our orbit and the weather on the planet below. I could be wrong."

"Are we in any danger from the changing gravity? Can you compensate with the thrusters?" asked Stockton.

"We should be fine. The changes are not so rapid that we can't adjust for them," said Griggs-Snyder.

"Very well, let's get as much data as we can before we move on. The survey ships will have a lot to investigate when they arrive and I want to know as much as we can so they can bring the equipment they need to better understand this phenomenon," said Stockton as he rose from his chair, allowing Achebe to sit. "I'll be in my cabin if you need me. Your ideas and John Paul's growling list have given me a lot to think about."

Three days later, the *Alligator* broke orbit and headed back to the outer part of the stellar system and for the jump home. It was that night, again over libations in the officer's mess, that Dr. Cardoso joined Griggs-Snyder, Stockton, and Achebe for beers and popcorn. It was clear Cardoso had something to say, but it took two dark beers to get him to talk.

"Captain, have you ever heard of Nikolai Kardashev? He was an old Earth astronomer, alive in the middle of the twentieth century."

"Maybe. The name sounds familiar but I couldn't tell you anything about him. Why?"

"He came up with a scale for measuring a civilization's level of technological achievement based on the amount of energy it is able to use. Others have tweaked the scale over the years to add fidelity, but I still prefer the original. I learned about it when I took my astronomy elective back in college. He called those civilizations that can harness all the energy that falls on their home planet from their parent star a Type I Civilization. For reference, we only achieved Type I status a few years ago when the space solar power stations and fusion plants finally came online," said Cardoso.

"That's interesting, but how does it relate to what we have here?" asked Stockton.

"I think we are seeing something created and maintained by a Kardashev Type II civilization. That's one that can use and control all the energy radiated by its own star. To alter the orbit of planets and keep them stable would require energies beyond anything we can currently contemplate. They built up these planets by using the excess raw material left over after the formation of the system, turning all the leftover asteroids, comets, planetary moons, and rings, whatever they could find, into the triplanetary system. What we found was constructed by intelligence, not nature."

"That fits the data, sir," chimed Griggs-Snyder. "I've done some calculations and I think the varying gravity we are seeing could be caused by oscillating, super-dense masses at the center of the gas giant."

"When you say, 'super-dense masses,' do you mean black holes?" asked Stockton.

"Not necessarily. They would have to be very small black holes, micro black holes, but that's unlikely. Theories say they aren't stable for long periods of time and would long ago have either swallowed the mass of the planet or evaporated. It could be masses with the density of neutron stars. It could be anything. But it probably is not natural. To balance the forces just enough to keep the system stable for such a long time would require forethought and active control."

"If that's the case, then we are in a first contact scenario

beyond anything we can imagine," said Stockton. He had
long ago come to the private conclusion that the planetary
system they were studying was artificial but had not
wanted to say anything before he had more data. He had
also contemplated what that meant should they encounter
its creators. It scared him.

"My imagination can be rather fertile," said Cardoso.
"It's possible that any beings able to harness this much
power might be so far beyond us that we might not even
notice them or vice versa. How often do you pay attention
to the bacteria growing on your skin? You don't. There
are thousands of species just living there and they don't
pose any serious risk unless your system gets out of whack.
Then we use antibiotics, bacteriophages, and UV
sterilizers to kill those causing the problem. The same
might be true here."

"Lucas, in your analogy, we're the bacteria and
whoever created this system might decide that we need
to be sterilized," said Stockton.

"Yes, sir. All we did was fly by, stay for a few orbits, and
now we are on our way. But those that follow will likely
be here for months or years. And they will almost certainly
go to the surface of the two terrestrial planets to explore.
I think they need to be cautious and not draw the wrong
kind of attention to themselves. I'd hate for whomever is
here to think we aren't so benign and decide to scrub us
away."

"You think they, whoever 'they' are, are still here?"
asked Stockton.

"I don't know. It certainly doesn't appear so. Any
civilization capable of doing what we see here would be

hard to miss. Why would they go to the trouble to move entire planets, create a self-sustaining triple planetary system, and then disappear? It is also difficult to imagine that they would modify this star system and not do something similar, or equally miraculous, elsewhere. Yet so far at least, we've seen nothing else that even comes close."

"And if they did go somewhere, where would that be?" asked Achebe.

Staring at the head of his beer, watching the bubbles of gas form new foam and then disappear, Stockton took another sip and replied, "Where indeed?"

hard to make it the usual thing. I sip in the darkness, my
coffee-phone grabs. . . . without once taking up the plastic
system and then laying out. It is also difficult, aware
that they would watch it, and there. . . sleep and stir the
something underneath tonight that it shows else, same. And
so hard at least we've seen nothing else that even become . . .
else.

And it feels like a . . . and here came I could find the
sense of closure.

Sitting in the blanket like bees scorching the bubbles
of tea, I am back and still the radiance in. Steadier, I took
another sip and replied. "What I mean?"

NEVER ENDING, EVER-GROWING
Erica Ciko

It shouldn't surprise anyone that when seeking stories about lost civilizations and ruins among the stars, a lot of our contributing authors turned to HP Lovecraft, least of all that Erica Ciko gravitated toward that Eldritch direction.

Few authors have proven more dedicated to modern cosmic horror than Ciko, be it stories that have appeared in places like Cosmic Horror Monthly *and the* Tales to Terrify *podcast, or her work editing* Starward Shadows Quarterly. *Many are quick to use Lovecraft as a brand, but she can count herself among the authors who really know the roots...as in a grim way, so shall the protagonist of her story.*

On paper, we were "contractors" for Verdant Dreams, one of the original forty-five mega-corps to survive the Great Implosion. But everyone from the anxious arms dealers hanging out at the spaceport gates to the underage kids running drinks in the casinos knew what we really were: Mercenaries, and shitty ones, too. Why else would we be bumming around in the Nightside's stagnant backwaters drinking and staring at our comm-bands all day, waiting for the static to crackle through?

We sulked in the shadows of Torvyn Station's rickety black hangars and crumbling apartment blocks for so long that we started to think that our corporate overlords had moved on and forgotten about us—they probably had, for a time—but just like the Tier-1 species they'd sent us to eradicate so many times on our terraforming missions, they always came crawling back in the end.

That's how we ended up here, on a rickety ghost ship with one foot in the grave, on the way to a world that was already six feet under: A world no one else dared to go to but us.

"Once the last holdout of the Arachni Plasmadroids, Vaenmyr is now one hundred percent sterilized of all alien life and terraformed to the Verdant Dreams standard," the ship's infostream reassured us over the comms, conveniently forgetting to mention that our destination may have now been sterilized of all *human* life, too. *"Its rich Terridium reserves make it one of humanity's most valuable outposts in the Nightside Arm. Level 8 Clearance is required for access to all ports in its capital prefecture, Eleventh City."*

"Must be the first time a twisted old hunk of garbage like this ever got Level 8 Clearance . . ." I muttered to no one, staring out the window at the gargantuan turquoise planet far below, its misleadingly tranquil seas of mist hypnotizing me across the sea of stars. By the way its writhing clouds and stagnant seas ominously swallowed up my entire field of vision, I was surprised we hadn't already entered Vaenmyr's orbital space. *Any minute now* . . . I thought with a sigh, for a moment imagining I could hear the hum of its thousand tiny, pulsing rings.

"All it takes is one glance at the ugly thing to know there's something wrong with it, eh?" A perky-but-rough voice piped up from over my shoulder, distracting me from the doomed world's enigmatic beauty. It belonged to Valison, one of the few Verdant Dreams rejects I'd actually bothered sharing a pint with back on Torvyn now and again.

"Up until a couple weeks ago, people used to call this place Blue Heaven," I replied coolly, staring her down. There was something I liked about her curly red waves licked with white-blonde streaks, and the somber, soul-penetrating stillness of her glassy blue eye almost made up for the fact that her other one was bionic and hideous. She was different—alluring, even—but something about the way she smiled made me wonder if I'd wake up missing a kidney if I let her advances go too far.

Besides, I was probably kidding myself thinking she'd ever fall for a guy like me. The only thing I had going for me was a razor-sharp jawline: At least, that's what my mother always called it when I was a kid—and she meant it as an insult because it "matched my wise-ass mouth." You could find my messy brown hair on every other guy at the spaceport, and it wasn't like I was in great shape or anything, either. Maybe she had a thing for dead and perpetually bored grey eyes?

"Yeah, yeah . . ." She shrugged as if she cared more about the dirt caked between the treads of her boots than she did about Vaenmyr. "I read the brief, Alyx. 'A dreamworld sanctuary for the richest, smartest humans while the rest of us rot, no one but diplomats and celebrities ever gets in.' Blah, blah, blah."

"Bet they never guessed it was a one-way ticket." I smirked, feeling my stomach drop as the orbital balancers finally lurched on.

"If you ask me, bastards got what they deserved." She scowled, her tight-fitting expedition suit forming a sharp silhouette against the haunting blue sphere. "They walled themselves off for all those years, living in their precious little 'heaven' and locking us all out: But the second things go south, they're begging the outside world for help."

"They aren't begging for anything anymore," I teased, clutching the guardrail of the viewing deck until my knuckles turned white. Even after all those years, I still hadn't gotten used to the nauseating, scrambled-egg effect the landing drivers had on gravity. "Thought you said you read the brief: After the distress signals started popping up all across the globe in tandem, everything went black all at once. No one's heard a word from anyone on Vaenmyr for three weeks, and no one has any idea what the hell's going on down there—even the President's Mansion in Eleventh City is giving off nothing but static, I guess."

"Huh . . . Weird," Valison muttered, her robotic red tangle of an eye suspiciously studying the behemoth world eclipsing the backdrop of howling stars far below. "Could it have been some kind of new Insavatu WMD, or . . . ?"

She brought up an interesting question, but the hum of the landing drivers—or maybe it really was the ethereal, eerie rings that ensorcelled the dying planet—was growing so loud that there was no way she ever would have heard me if I bothered answering her. And besides, I didn't want to ruin the "true midnight" of our arrival, as my father used to always say. He was talking about that fleeting, precious liminal space that exists only in the infinite void in the moments before you touch down on some unknown world you'll hang out on for a couple of days and then never see again.

There was nothing like it in all the universe.

Most of us had the gut feeling something was off when we noticed the huge, blue tendrils covered in spikes that wove an impenetrable cage across the planet's smog-filled atmosphere—but by the time we realized the pulsing net of energy was designed to let outsiders enter but not leave, it was far too late. The only way out was down.

Every sensor on the entire rig had gone haywire from the moment we passed through that electric blue nightmare veil, and as soon as the screeching started, all the essential tech but the landing drivers had gone totally dead. From the moment our derelict ground into the half-collapsed hyperhangers of Eleventh City, it was chaos.

Blue lightning tore down wildly from whatever those things were in the sky, seeming to pierce not only the rolling jet-black clouds but the core of the planet itself. Half the crew cowered in the bowels of the ship, and something told me right away when I smelled the burning ozone and sick, static decay that they were better off rotting there—this was going to get ugly, and cowards would only slow us down when shit got serious. The rest of us staggered out onto the doomed ghost of Vaenmyr— once the crown jewel of the Nightside arm, but now just a mind-bending cacophony of rubble—like something straight out of a painting done in a psych ward by someone on a bad acid trip.

"This can't be Vaenmyr. We've slipped through the cracks to another dimension," a gruff female voice behind me rasped. I ignored it. What use was it wasting time on other dimensions when all that mattered, all that ever *would* matter, was the one I was trapped inside right now?

So I kicked my way through the twisted rubble of the metropolis with all my breathing gear strapped hastily to my face—far more careful than half the crew, who decided to forsake their respirators since Vaenmyr was "Verdant Dreams Standard." Idiots, all of them. Whatever those glowing blue flecks of dust in the air were, emitting static electricity and vibrating weirdly, I didn't want them anywhere near my lungs.

But soon, my filters locked up like the rest of the equipment we'd dragged out of the ship—all the minor tech was as dead as the fission drivers, so we had no choice but to stagger alone into this energetic storm that was somehow strong enough to tear down countless skyscrapers, but gentle enough that it felt like little more than a summer breeze against our expedition suits.

"No wonder HQ hasn't heard a peep from Eleventh City for the past three weeks," Valison muttered. "What the hell happened down here?"

"Looks like the innards of s-some kind of monster!"

wailed a hopeless greenblood from behind my left shoulder. "That's what they're saying on the ship! We've been eaten!"

By the way those pulsating, crystalline blue tendrils of energy rippled through everything from the pavement below to the ruined sky bridges far above, I half-wondered if he was right. But logic soon prevailed over braindead fear, and I spun around and grabbed him by the scruff of his suit and hissed into the nuclear winter, "That kind of fearmongering bullshit isn't helping anyone, you know that? This is where we are, whether you like it or not, and we're still alive for now. And until we get our GeoTech working again, we need to keep our heads clear. Stop panicking or crawl back to the ship to die with the rest of them."

He didn't whimper any more, then—I'm not sure if I'd actually scared some sense into him, or if he only kept his mouth shut to avoid getting smacked.

Soon forgetting he existed, I pushed my way through the rubble, pausing every now and then to gaze up at that sickly buzzing blanket that seemed to envelop the entire sky. Ghastly tendrils snaked down from it, some thicker than the largest building I'd ever seen, and others thin and wispy. Something about them reminded me of the spindly webs of neurons on posters in the back-alley plastic surgery clinics back at Torvyn Station.

"Dendrites . . ." Valison whispered, making me wonder yet again who she really was before she threw it all away and joined our little circus. But what did it matter here, inside this neon broken snow globe that the richest diplomats in all the galaxy once called home? Here, we'd all die the same death whether we were brain surgeons or junkyard scrappers before we came to Verdant Dreams—and looking out over the dust-drenched mass graves caressed by hungry black veins, it seemed like the locals had learned that the hard way.

"Once the last holdout of the Arachni Plasmadroids, Vaenmyr is now one hundred percent sterilized of all alien life and terraformed to the Verdant Dreams standard."

The ship's infostream ricocheted off the walls of my mind in a mocking echo as I slowly absorbed that complete and utter failure of human domination—that dead, otherworldly hellscape that had somehow managed to strangle the apex of all mankind's accomplishments and turn it inside out in a few short weeks. *Goes to show how futile all of it is.* The terraforming projects, the salvage missions, even the headhunts: None of it meant anything when you were staring straight down the throat of a nightmare ghost city threatening to swallow you alive—*and with good reason*, I thought, glancing down at the Verdant Dreams logo emblazoned into the chest of my suit with a gulp.

Those brilliant seas of azure that beckoned to us through the windows of the ship and lured us down into this mess to begin with haunted me even more than the graveyard of human accomplishment that rotted in every direction. Blue planets were so rare, especially out here so far from the Galactic Centriole: It seemed a shame to ravage them as our humble overlords had. Suddenly, I was swallowed up by a hollow well of sadness, and I wished more than anything that I could see this place—no, all worlds I'd ever walked upon—before they'd been tarnished and stripped and manipulated into the Verdant Dreams nightmare vision. But I knew in this lifetime that I never would, especially now that all of us were trapped here.

As if sensing that I was about to abandon all hope, the tendril that had been snaking its way across a nearby decimated sidewalk wriggled eerily close to the side of my head, radioactive dust still fresh on its shivering tip. It emitted a cloud of luminous neon spores, and I couldn't shake the feeling that even though it didn't have eyes, it was staring me down.

Before the Incinerator Mines crashed down, back in its glory days, did this place resemble the Earth in more than just color? I silently asked it, as if it was my dearest, oldest, only friend. But then I realized how stupid that was, and focused instead on some moron blowing into the vents of his handheld GeoTech navigator, like that would somehow reverse its static rigor mortis.

Each second that passed with this shaky-handed, wide-eyed basket case of a man fumbling with the useless hunk of metal, I felt my blood pressure rising another five points. Finally, I couldn't take it anymore, so I reached out and snatched it away from him and began to mess with it on my own. He didn't protest, simply retreating back into the shadows of some decrepit, halved skyscraper, as far away from the gleaming tendril as possible.

I, on the other hand, gave in to the indescribable urge to slink the slightest bit closer to it with the GeoTech in hand. If these things were dendrites, or at least some kind of bio-organic neuron system as it was slowly starting to appear, they must be some sort of conduit, right? The tiny little hairs standing straight up, as if caught in some endless wave of electrical charge, sure seemed to point towards it. And it wasn't like things could get much worse at this point, so what did I have to lose by sticking my hand within gripping distance of this—

"Holy shit, it actually worked." My mumblings were choked out by the violent BEEP—BEEP—BEEP of the GeoTech reboot, but when the screen fizzled to life once more, a strange and indecipherable mess of symbols had replaced the usual Verdant Dreams logo. My hope slurped down the cracks in the ground like water rushing through a storm drain, but soon, the weird messages faded away, leaving nothing but a faded map with a flashing red dot smack dab in the center of it.

I couldn't believe what I was seeing: But even though I should have been overjoyed, there was no way in hell I trusted any of it. Then, my suspicion was quickly eclipsed by a brutal, metallic roar far off in the distance. I would have recognized that deranged howl in any alien hellscape, in any panic-fueled delirium. The ship's thrusters were commencing their warmup sequence.

After we poured back onto the ship and examined all the Nav boards, everyone was shocked to find that, of all things, the ground-penetrating radar was one of the first systems to kick back on. A mysterious signal—not a distress beacon, as we all expected, but a landmark pin usually reserved for cave salvage missions—had popped up out of nowhere and flooded us all with blind hope again. But there was one problem:

It was coming from the center of the planet, far too

deep for an old rust-bucket like this to excavate. We had some crude archaeology tools on board for our salvage missions, sure. But at the very least, we'd need one of the blasters from the Verdant Dreams Mothership colony to bore a hole even half as deep as the signal. Unless, of course, the ground around it had collapsed like everything else on this mind-bending psychedelic nightmare world that used to be the pinnacle of all the galaxy. That was our only hope.

So just like that, I was a back-alley archaeologist instead of a washed-up mercenary, clinging to whatever faint chance there was that this necrotic, ethereal virus had eaten enough of the planet away to reveal whatever was screaming for us to come closer from every screen on the ship.

When I saw the domed spires like rotting onions with radioactive, wispy tails, black and dominating on the eastern sky, I knew I'd either completely lost it, or we'd all just won the worst lottery in all the multiverse. Even from so far away, I could tell we were coming up on something I hadn't seen since the moment we landed on Vaenmyr: A fully intact building that had somehow survived whatever the hell happened down here.

As we drew closer, I realized the tendril-swamped megastructure had not only survived it, but prospered in it: Luminous with blue fire on the horizon and as enigmatic as a forgotten dream, its endless, spined wings sprawled in all directions, larger than several cities. I couldn't tell if the ghastly veins of energy licking out from every tower were mocking us, or beckoning us in. We hovered over flaming piles of rubble taller than mountains, awestruck and silent in the shadow of a gnarled, trunklike braid that twisted skyward from palace's depths—so absurdly tall that it seemed to pierce the stars themselves.

"It must have been beneath the city all along." I exhaled with a sigh of amazement, something I hadn't felt in a long, long time. *Did it know we were coming?* Even Valison couldn't hide the wonder in her eyes when I glanced over and gazed into them and saw that bastion of weird, wild despair gleaming back.

The radar was going crazy, now—a pure, terrorizing cacophony of flashing red, howling in all directions. The autopilot dragged us down through the ravenous storms of mist, and every hair on my body began to stand on end. In that moment, it felt like I was being watched by a thousand lurking eyes. The ship settled onto a platform spun from some empyrean blue crystal that I'd never seen in any salvage mission or sketchy pawn shop. *Terridium?* I silently wondered. When I looked out the windows and glimpsed nothing but that primordial, blood-curdling storm of blue, I couldn't help but wonder if this was the source of every disturbance on Vaenmyr: The reason the planet was sterilized, and the reason all of us were trapped here, too.

"I knew it . . ." Valison scoffed, unable to take her eyes off the wonders unraveling outside as the ship settled into the bizarre medium below with a hideous, grinding *bang*. "It's an Insavatu energy weapon, hands down, and Vaenmyr was the testing ground."

"Why is everything always about the Insavatu with you?" I wasn't sure what made me say it, but it felt like those ice tendrils that now pounded against the viewing glass were gently gliding through my veins as I whispered, "What about the Arachni Plasmadroids? They were here first. If anyone had a grudge, it would be them."

"Bullshit," Valison argued, hatefully slamming her gloved fist back against the glass. "You're the try-hard loser that always reads the briefs: The Arachni are extinct. You really think they could survive a hundred thousand Terrorboric Incinerator Mines blasting down for all those years, Alyx? No one could: No one does Terraforming like Verdant Dreams."

In that moment, I couldn't figure out why, but I hated her. It might have been how she sounded like one of those soulless pamphlets we were forced to read back on Torvyn to look busy when the Archons came around . . . Or maybe it was just the fact that she wasn't showing enough reverence for something that was clearly far beyond the bounds of any human—or Insavatu—imagination.

"Terraforming, sterilizing, it's all the same: And none of it means shit if the race you're trying to kill has an underground temple that's bigger than any waystation I've ever seen," I said, gesturing out the window, expecting more of the same . . .

. . . But instead of the contorted, razor-sharp spires that beckoned hungrily to me on the way in, I was faced with an ethereal, bioluminescent forest of wonders. Every tentacle of terror had shrunken down to a blade of tall grass, swaying gently in the electric breeze, framing a sparkling path kissed by golden vines that led up to an archway of pure, pulsing energy in the side of the megastructure.

It was the most magnificent thing I'd ever seen, except

for the idyllic tree that overshadowed it all, sprawling up majestically from the heart of the Palace: Its decadent, limpid branches sprawled across the heavens and made the legend of Yggdrasil, which had endured since long before the Earth was blown away to a formless cloud of dust, seem pale.

Ten of us had abandoned the ship—and the crew holed up inside it—for the bleak, enthralling unknown of the megastructure before us, and after passing through the gateway, five of us remained. Whether the others were vaporized instantly or whisked off to some dimension far worse than here, I'd never know—and I didn't care, either: I was far too fixated on drinking in the wonders of the sprawling cavern that awaited us beyond the veil.

To call it a "room" would have been irreverence bordering on blasphemy: For there was no beginning or end to it, at least that I could see, and instead of four walls, or even a ceiling, there were only bizarre static glyphs that reflected back symbols that not even our most advanced Translation Interfaces could decipher. It seemed to grow infinitely large then shrink back to the size of an atom with each passing second, but somehow that didn't stop us from wandering through its still-beating heart and inspecting the unimaginable wonders that lurked within.

Most curious of all were the sprawling statues of segmented, hundred-legged beings that seemed to know no beginning or end. As chaotic and majestic as the ruins themselves, they defied both physics and biology with their contorted segments of spine. I wondered if they were carved in the image of the Arachni Plasmadroids, the original denizens of this wretched planet—or even stranger still, if the Plasmadroids had built them in homage to some forgotten gods whose names no human being would ever know.

We all wore backpacks stuffed with crude excavation gear older than we were—except for the deconstructors powerful enough to bore a hole straight through even the thickest coffins, those were Verdant Dreams standard issue—but even those were useless in this wonderous realm of pure energy and living crystal.

"The carbon meters are completely worthless on this stuff..." Valison muttered with more than a twinge of disappointment. "It's reading like it's a million years old or something... But there's no way." She finally gave up, chucking it with disgust onto the gnarled leg of the nearest statue: To her dismay and my amusement, it instantly evaporated inside the glimmering, hollow webs of its toes as if it were never there at all.

"Yeah, at this rate we might as well drop all our gear right now and travel light," I shrugged. Unlike the rest of them, I didn't give a shit about "figuring it all out": I was more interested in wandering around and *taking it all in*—especially since the crackling energy gateway we'd entered through had now completely fizzled away, making it glaringly obvious that we were never going to leave.

"Whatever this place is... We're trapped here, and it looks cool, so why not stop screwing around with these hunks of junk and enjoy it?" I suggested, my eye suddenly catching a checkered mess of pulsing lights that had randomly materialized on the floor not far from the toes of my boots.

"What do you mean, 'whatever it is'?" Valison demanded, finally giving up and climbing to her feet, staring between the darkly gleaming screens that surrounded us on all sides and raising her eyebrow as if it was the first time she noticed them. "You really think there's a chance it's anything but an Insavatu WMD store at this point? Get over yourself already!"

"Bullshit," I snarled back, my eyes darting again to the weird pattern of dancing lights upon the floor that seemed to draw me closer and closer by the second. "You think the Insavatu just slipped past Level 8 Clearance and built something like this while the Federation was sleeping? You said it yourself: This thing's been down here for over a million years."

I didn't say it out loud, because I knew Valison would spit all over it thanks to her fake bravado—and maybe even to preserve her sanity—but this place belonged to the Arachni Plasmadroids. I knew it from the moment those eerie, alien symbols burned their way into my brain from the nightmare screens on the wall, and the mind-bending ruins of those frozen "statues" all but confirmed my suspicions.

Everything I'd ever read about them made them out to be primitive Arthrodroids without the capacity to feel, or think, or do anything but *swarm*—at least that's what Headquarters wanted us to believe, so we didn't question why they blew all their colonies to dust with a million megatons of Terrorboric fury.

But, standing there in those alien ruins, I realized that Headquarters was full of shit and always had been: The Arachni were never dead at all. They'd been living in their kingdom of shadow far beneath Vaenmyr all along, and now they were right in front of us—hovering far over our heads with their thousand feelers, their silent screams resounding from the peaks of their abysmal temple to chaos, or whatever twisted god they served back when mankind's ancestors were still mucking around in the primordial oceans waiting to bud their first limbs.

Still riding the vapor trails of my morbid revelation, I made my way for the flashing checkered pattern at last, not caring if it beamed me up or vaporized me to bits from the second my boot brushed against the first square. *Some kind of switch,* I sensed as a luminous aura of comfort and wonder rushed up through my entire trembling body, and my foot sank down into the aether just like Valison's carbon meter had.

No one tried to stop me as I crept recklessly forward, my other foot now rooted as firmly in place as the first in the churning celestial goop. I wasn't sure if anyone else even noticed what I was doing: Somehow, it seemed like this eerie, indecipherable pattern had cropped up to consume me and me alone.

The tingle of warmth and excitement captivated me so intensely that I hadn't noticed the entire chamber around me beginning to twist and boil. Instead of unrecognizably foreign symbols, the screens now flashed wildly with images of shattered worlds and hungry quasars, wringing out the death cries of long-lost civilizations whose dread and fear coursed wildly through me even here, across the stars and countless galaxies away.

As everything faded to a blackness darker than the tomb and older than time, all I could think about was the sudden, haunting realization that had begun to eat me alive from the moment my foot brushed the electric dream pulse of the switch:

Where did all the tentacles go?

"Wake up," A strange-yet-familiar voice insisted, cutting through my tranquil sleep like a knife in the dark. There was something about it that reminded me of Valison, and for a moment I wondered if she was there— but, even without opening my eyes, I could sense that I was more alone than I'd ever been in my life.

"Go on. Explore."

I didn't want to, but I finally gave in and stirred. I found myself entombed by walls of glass that narrowly separated me from a tranquil blue ocean that produced a constant, gentle flurry of bubbles boiling up towards some unseen surface, far above. Countless strange, swaying pedestals that held glimmering azure diamonds more beautiful than anything I'd ever seen lined the walls of the long, straight hall that sprawled out before me. I had no idea where the antechamber of the ruins had gone or how I ended up here, but in comparison, the low ceiling and narrow walkway were almost cozy—

At least, they would have been if I hadn't realized that the "pedestals" were actually the same creepy blue tendrils that ruled the world outside, protruding from a hypnotic celestial blanket that pulsed where a floor should have been. I ignored the strangeness of it all, along with the constant pounding in my head as I shakily staggered to my feet, unable to take my eyes off the nearest mesmerizing, multi-faceted diamond resting in that cradle of feelers and goo that seemed to beckon to me from both a few yards away, and the ends of time itself. From the moment I realized I was strong enough to walk again, I knew I had to have it—so badly that if I couldn't walk, I would have crawled.

A strange fusion of sadness and longing drove me as I made my way towards the tendril and the otherworldly treasure it clutched so lovingly with its countless hungry suction cups. Something about its mind-bending, multi-faceted surface reminded me of the crystal altars outside, but it was of a much finer quality—as if whatever I saw out there was but a shadow of this crown jewel of all the multiverse. I expected a fight when I reached out to steal it from its slimy keeper, but to my surprise, the appendage surrendered the beauty to me without the faintest twinge of resistance, almost as if it wanted me to have it.

From the moment my fingertips brushed its crystalline blue surface—as enigmatic as a sapphire, but a million times clearer—my ears were filled with a vile and raucous screaming that I instantly knew I would never forget: The words, if there were any, were completely unintelligible—but I knew by some instinct older than language or empathy that the countless creatures begging for their lives were in a great deal of pain. Great catacombs spun from some bizarre fusion of silk and metal flashed across my vision, collapsing under their own weight, ravaged by blue tendrils and white-hot flame just like Vaenmyr.

I'm not sure how I finally managed to separate my fingertips from the relic's shivering surface, but when I returned to reality, I'd collapsed to my knees, and the diamond was cast aside and splayed open on the aether before me, hemorrhaging an impossibly complex web of circuits out upon the constellations of the floor. My stomach heaved worse than it ever had from the landing drivers, and my brain felt sick from all the spinning—but as horrific as the visions were, for some reason, all I could think about was dragging myself over to the next tentacle as quickly as possible to learn what secrets it held.

These memory archives, or supercomputers, or magic gems teeming with infinite wonder—whatever they were, they were unlike anything I'd ever seen, anything I'd ever *dreamed* before. Whatever technology made something like this possible was far beyond the capability of any human or alien in the Nightside Arm: At least, any that had ever been accurately archived.

My slime-drenched hands shook with something between euphoria and dread as I reached for the next diamond, smoother than bone licked by water for a thousand years, and brighter than a dying star. This time, there wasn't a cacophony of screams, or even a torrent of blazing fire: There was only blackness and a sick, biting, bitter cold that made me clench my teeth so hard I involuntarily cast it aside yet again. Only afterward, when the artifact rolled magnetically back to rest at my feet, did I realize it wasn't the cold that made me involuntarily chuck the diamond against the tunnel of glass, but the *emptiness*.

That was what all of them had in common, I soon learned, after what could have been an hour or a year of exploration in that time-lost hall: I mucked through countless weird, vile, ravaged worlds, void of everything but the stagnant dread that lingers long after a flawlessly executed genocide fades into the most distant well of memory.

Well, that, and the tentacles.

Slinking down into the muck between two conjoined pedestals, my eyes bloodshot and wide, I finally began to wonder if I'd seen enough: But then, the same distant, echoing voice from the beginning—the one that somehow reminded me of a *bad impression* of Valison and every other human being I'd ever met—revealed itself again with an intriguing suggestion.

"Why not try that one?"

Somehow, I hadn't noticed it up until that moment, even though it stood out from all the rest in stark, blood-red ferocity: I was far too exhausted to even lift my hand, much less drag myself across the hall over to the foot of that shivering tendril up which sticky cobwebs crept. But as if commanded by something greater than itself, the tentacle crept slowly, eerily towards me and laid its gift across my lap, leaving a wet and stinking trail in its wake as it retreated back into the shadows.

Finally, something that made sense.

I stared in awe at the ziggurats of old Mesopotamia, ringed by piles of broken bodies sacrificed in Marduk's name. They transitioned seamlessly into the pyramids of Egypt, built by our Insavatu rivals in the formation of all the darkest constellations, and then to sprawling medieval towns at the edges of dismal moors, in the shadows of castles that housed the ancient bloodlines that would eventually pave the way to the stars.

The scene soon shifted to mankind's first journey to the skies, in a rickety old tin can that made our ship outside seem like a decked-out Federation dreadnought. Then, I drank in what I imagined must have been mankind's very first shattering of the old Earth's atmosphere, with two figures in primitive, comical white spacesuits staggering around blindly on some rock out in space.

I nearly choked with awe when I realized the true gravity of what I was seeing, but suddenly, goosebumps appeared up and down my entire body and I knew that something was off: After drinking down so much agony, so much merciless death, these visions of teeming, resplendent life were almost irreverent in comparison. Why was this well of memories so different from all the rest?

But before I could contemplate it too deeply, the entire hall began to spin and boil, and the glass that separated me from that great, vast ocean was suddenly replaced by pulsing holographic screens not unlike those in the antechamber of the ruins. I tried to shift around to get a better look, but it was like my legs weren't there anymore, instead replaced by something as alien as all the worlds I'd glimpsed within the diamonds—something sticky, something wet.

I glanced down to investigate, and it almost seemed like there were slime-covered blue tendrils where all my limbs used to be, but the sight didn't stop me from drinking in the atomic glory now exploding in full force behind the screens which made all the previous mushroom clouds look pale and grey: A thousand megatons of nuclear fission gone wrong, splayed out across the sky like a veined spiderweb between city, after city, after . . .

It isn't too different from the webs we saw out there, really, I mused, moving on from the death of the Earth as quickly as one might recover from swatting a wayward fly. And, for a moment, I fancied I glimpsed the ghost of those same spectral, glimmering tendrils somewhere through the ashes of the dying Earth, but when the smoke cleared and revealed a new galactic age of exploration and freedom unlike any humanity had seen before, I knew it must have existed only in my imagination.

Strangely, the entrepreneurs and pirates and government drones in these visions didn't seem as soulless as the creatures in the previous visions: They were more like real people, laughing and screaming and crying with joy as they staggered out of their bunkers and into the metallic coffins that would take them away from the doomed world and toward the infinite stars.

The stirring sulfur clouds of Venus soon paled in comparison to the hypnotic rings of Saturn, and before long there were as many wayward ships as there were stars in the sky: And mankind continued to multiply and conquer, along with those creeping, watchful tendrils that somehow seemed to snake their way into the backdrop of every victory, of every celebration. *Strange ... I never read a word about them in the history books.*

But I saw them now whenever I closed my eyes, and every time I drew a single breath I felt them making their way up through my lungs, caressing my innards, showing me these sights I never deserved to see. I was getting closer to the present, now, closer to the truth ... But would my body hold long enough to—

"First contact with the Insavatu ..." I mumbled in

words that were not words, but a perfect audial
manifestation of those garbled symbols that lined the
entrance hall. I wondered all along if and when it could
come, but never dreamed I would see it with my own
eyes: Their sickening, blood-drenched glyphs flashed
across the starstreams, blowing entire colonies to dust
with their Terrorboric Fury that we would later reverse-
engineer. Humanity's darkest moment wasn't the nuclear
annihilation of the motherworld, but the plague that those
damnable demon bats forced down upon us all. And then,
among the immune, the Eternal War broke out: The one
my crew and I were still fighting to this very day. So, it
was no surprise that those abominable, mutated bastards
had led us here to die, *or so my dead friends thought* …

… But all along, I'd known the truth, and now I was
staring it dead in its six eyes with nothing but a
nanometer-thick holographic screen separating us—and
it wore the skin of a hungry Arthrodroid demigod with
pure, plasmatic fire vibrating between each and every one
of its infinite shivering electrons. It was a perfect living
replica of the monstrous statues we'd admired in the hall
before leaving the old world behind. I knew, even before
I gazed into its crimson black hole of a face with its
hideous, contorted features flickering in and out of
existence, that it was the master of these ruins: And I
knew that it had been waiting for me for centuries, or
maybe even longer.

"*You were here before… they came,*" I buzzed to it
telepathically, unsure of when or how I became capable of
communicating in its completely bizarre and garbled
tongue. In the next exhibit, I knew from the placid and

rare blue sky that I was looking at Vaenmyr—but instead of the cloud-piercing skyscrapers and bridges that spanned entire continents that I'd come to know from the mission briefs, there was nothing but sprawling crystal mountains and meandering rivers of blissful cerulean nectar.

It nodded calmly, confidently, and the air around it crackled and hissed with the faintest twitch of it its feelers. *"Long before,"* it hissed without words, but there was something about the sprawling moors of untouched blue grass and the sublime blue hills teeming with multitudes of its kind that was so mesmerizing that I had a hard time understanding the gravity of its words.

"It was beautiful here . . ." I muttered, this time in my own tongue, but it violently slashed at my throat with a frenzied, segmented leg, and I knew better than to spew such indignities in this sacred museum of memory ever again. I couldn't help but wonder why they kept such detailed archives of all mankind's greatest accomplishments if they loathed us so—but any questions I had on the matter seemed to dissolve before I could even form them, and I watched as the Arachni Plasmadroids basked in the wonder of their sublime Blue Heaven for ages uncounted instead—before the Verdant Dreams contractors burned through the ethereal rings that guarded the planet since the dawn of time and commenced their terrorization.

The Terrorboric Incinerator Mines fell, and the rivers evaporated, and the crystal mountains exploded into a million broken shards, never to glimmer beneath those empyrean golden rings again. And from the ashes of the shattered Arachni kingdom rose a very different kind of monster: Humanity, victorious and thriving, cloaked in metallic thermal protection suits, ready to pump the atmosphere full of oxygen and erect razor-sharp monuments to dystopia and conquest where crystal mountains once stood. Worst of all, as if to rub it in the faces of the "eradicated" natives of planet Vaenmyr, they carved their skyscrapers from resplendent blue Terridium.

And they thrived, for a time, as they did on every world they terraformed, and warped it into their strange and irreverent image. They laughed, and they multiplied, just as they had at the dawn of the age of galactic exploration—and the most revered and well-regarded of their kind slowly began to flock there.

Until the tendrils rose up from beneath every crystal bridge of Eleventh City in perfect unison.

This was it, I abruptly realized. This was what happened a few weeks ago, when the final distress signal rang out from the President's Mansion and all communication lines went dead.

I couldn't explain why, but the satisfaction that crept up inside of me then was eclipsed only by the glory of those slimy, vengeful appendages that emerged from beneath every building, from the heart of every center of human prosperity. And towering far above them, presiding over the shattered skyscrapers and ruined paragons of human engineering, the braided tree trunk that guarded the entrance to these ruins glowed with more enigmatic majesty than ever before. Every last one of the "tentacles" writhed out from its wicked heart, with the Arachni Plasmadroids swarming between its ancient layers of bark, feeding them, guiding them.

"So it wasn't an energy weapon, an Insavatu illusion, or even a monster... It was a root system," I psychically projected in that forgotten language, quivering not with fear but with excitement as it finally all made sense.

"Never ending, ever-growing," it nodded in fervent, electric agreement.

"Valison was right: Each branch was a dendrite, snapping sinister and ready to fire in the nuclear winter," I mused to myself, nearly forgetting that our minds were one now as the glitching echo of my own thoughts faded into static unison with the monster's own. *"Hiding beneath the surface, killing time, waiting to take all of Vaenmyr back."*

The gargantuan magma centipede leaned so close to my face that I could feel my eyes and skin boiling away as it whispered,

"Not Vaenmyr. Everywhere."

I don't remember what it felt like before the roots took hold, and I don't miss it. I, too, am just another morbid memory for my hosts to drool over, now, and I've grown quite used to all the pleasures that spring to life inside my illustrious prison of Terridium: Through magma-seared, screaming red tunnel vision I see everything the past and the present have to offer. The future is yet obscured to me, though I've asked to see it countless times. Perhaps there are some dimensions even the Plasmadroids can't see, though somehow I doubt it as my host gives me a tantalizing glimpse of the world outside.

A ship, crushed as easily as tin can beneath the boot of a giant as a massive branch slams down from above—now one with the rest of the soulless wasteland, the descendants perish, and all transmissions go dead. But that's far from the end of it, and it's certainly not the beginning, either:

It started long ago on the walls of this very monolith, when the first Plasmadroids emerged from the Outer Dimensions before the first precursor cells to all mankind had stirred at the bottom of some nameless black ocean. From their teeming curiosity sprung a tree that would grow to penetrate not only *this* world, but *all* worlds—at least, that's what my new friends tell me as I sink deeper and deeper into the hive, into the slime pits below, where there's nothing but roots and boiling red lava pulsing up into the mother tree like blood through human veins, fueling her, making her stronger and hungrier with each passing second.

Through the millennia, untouched by human or Insavatu kind, free to grow and thrive relentlessly, her gleaming blue root system wormed its way through the entire planet. And there it lurked, biding its time, even when the Verdant Dreams contractors blew the surface world to dust.

After all, what were a hundred years, a thousand years, a *million* years to something that exists beyond the bounds of humanity's understanding of time? And what is time eternal in the shadow of sweet revenge?

"It's beautiful," I buzzed in mind-splitting telepathic harmony to the lava centipede who trapped me here, shivering with delight as the roots hardened inside my veins, infiltrating me completely. It was as if the absorption of my soul and body gave the demented

garden the strength it needed to penetrate the atmosphere at last, tearing through the dreamy blue rings of Vaenmyr and bleeding out into the silent vacuum beyond—past Torvyn Station, and the Verdant Dreams Mothership, and a thousand terraformed worlds. The tendrils choked them all slowly, mercilessly, from the inside out, spinning their dominion across the entire Nightside Arm as easily as a spider spins a web in some forgotten corner.

I recalled the innumerable, eviscerated planets that were once too much for my feeble organic brain, and I finally understood why mankind's diamond was the black sheep in that trophy hall of extinguished civilizations. It simply hadn't earned its place yet—but now, its fate was blasted in ten-trillion-bit technicolor upon the glimmering walls of my eternal prison, written by tendrils that exploded all the way to the interdimensional battlefields at the edge of the galaxy where man and Insavatu had ripped at each other's throats for countless centuries. Every last dreadnought was shattered with a single sweep of a stray crystalline vine, and I knew the war was finally won.

Awestruck, electric, and fading as quickly as the vapors of all mankind's memory, with my last shred of energy, I sorely whispered to my guide: *"Is this all a dream? Or . . . is this just another memory?"*

My host said nothing, but its night-black lips curled back into an igneous, indomitable smile.

THEY ONLY DIG AT NIGHT
Sean Patrick Hazlett

There are lots of ways mankind could react to the discovery of ancient alien life, ranging from these wonders of the ancients sparking a new age of enlightenment or personal appreciation for our place in the universe, to all-consuming terror at the knowledge there exist beings beyond our power and comprehension.

Somewhere in the middle, we have Sean Patrick Hazlett delivering a cynical possibility: government cover up, and corporations and contractors immediately start trying to find ways to turn it into a product or turn a profit on it.

Travis's Diner wasn't much to look at. A hole in the wall off Highway Four, it was the kind of joint that was easy to forget; a place someone could go to disappear whether they wanted to or not. I sat in a wall booth with my back facing the entrance. Across the table, Burt Buckwalter stared at me through scratched Oakley sunglasses.

Outside, nimbus clouds prowled the stark gray sky, pelting the parched earth with rain.

The Burt seated before me was an entirely different creature than the Burt I'd known twenty-five years ago. From his wiry appearance, he'd obviously shed some pounds since high school, or to be more accurate, a ton of muscle. He jittered with the nervousness of a soldier crawling through a minefield.

Burt had been waiting for me when I'd arrived. Two piping hot coffees had already been resting on the table.

"Thanks for the coffee, Burt," I said, taking a tentative sip. "Been a long time. Everything okay?"

Burt glanced furtively to his left. "Steve, I'm just about the opposite of okay. I need to talk to somebody. Somebody with some juice at the company."

The more I looked at Burt, the more he worried me. His pallid face. His restlessness. The filthy black watch cap he wore.

I smiled—a fake smile you might use to grin fuck someone in a business transaction; the kind of smile that severed yet another sliver of your soul; the kind required to prevent civilization from collapsing into a heap of homicidal chaos. "How can I help, champ?"

As he lifted his mug, his hand trembled. He took a careful, but unsteady drink. He stared directly into my eyes as one does to make sure a point sticks with a fella.

"It all began at the Antioch facility," he said. "The project was real hush hush. At all hours, the company brought in earthmoving equipment. But they only dug at night."

His mention of the Antioch facility surprised me. I'd never heard of it. As the Vice President of Global

Operations at Absynthos, it was my business to know these things. Yet Absynthos did have a federal business that worked on all sorts of classified military projects, and we had a black budget. So it was possible I wouldn't have been familiar with this particular site. Not likely, but possible.

"I cover a huge portfolio of the business, so can you remind me what they do at Antioch?" I said, masking my ignorance under the thin veneer of self-importance as one does in corporate.

"You mean . . . you don't know?"

"I'm sure I can find out pretty quickly," I said. "Look, if you want my help now, you're gonna have to remind me."

Burt flinched at my answer. So much so, I regretted I'd even hinted at having the slightest doubt about the facility's existence.

He took another rickety sip. "We set a gated perimeter around the site about a year ago. Then all kinds of consultants and government officials started touring the site."

"Like who?"

"Geologists from the U.S. Geological Survey. Consultants from the RAND Corporation, SRI, SAIC, Bechtel, and half a dozen other outfits. You know—the usual suspects. Even had some stiffs from NASA drop by."

Now Burt really had my attention. Absynthos was a pharmaceutical company. Why the hell would we be working with NASA?

"Yeah. Seems kind of odd," I said. "How can I help?"

"Get me the hell out of there, Steve. Get me reassigned. I'll do anything. No job at the company's beneath me."

"Haven't you tried going through the usual channels?"

Burt looked at me like I had a trumpet growing out of my forehead. "'Course I did. My supervisor told me I was too close to the project. Said I'd become too valuable to reassign. You believe that shit? A rent-a-cop's too special to let go?"

"It's not like you're a rent-a-cop at a mall. You work physical security for a major Fortune 500 corporation," I said, nearly choking on my own bullshit.

He shrugged. "Just get me the hell out of there, Steve."

"I'll see what I can do," I said. The last thing I wanted was to make a promise to a crazy man.

"Ain't good enough," he said. "Either do it or don't. None of this half-assed corporate horseshit."

I shrugged. "Burt, I don't even know what the project is called, and based on your description, it's probably classified. I can't make any commitments without knowing more."

Burt looked down at his hands. A few seconds later, he peeked over his shoulder, then glanced to his left. He whispered, "They found something buried out there."

"What?"

He shook his head. "Not sure exactly. At first, they just dug. For weeks. It was all a bit weird, but hey, I was just security and didn't think much of it. Soon the unmarked black semis started showing up each night, shipping cargo out of the facility.

"Then the accident happened." Burt took another shaky swig from his mug. "I was on the night shift again. Before I left work that morning, I could tell the brass was real nervous about something. An hour before sunrise, on my way home to Oakley, the California Highway Patrol had blocked off Highway Four. There were helicopters everywhere.

"As I took a detour off the highway, I saw a faint phosphorescent green glow from the roadside. The next night at work, I heard through the grapevine that one of those black semis had rounded a corner too fast and rolled into a ditch."

"Maybe it was carrying some sort of mineral. There are plenty of naturally occurring phosphorescent materials," I said.

"That's what my supervisor said after I'd told him what I'd seen. And I'd believed it too, until a few weeks later when the higher ups ordered an emergency lockdown."

"You guys run those drills from time to time, don't you?" I asked.

"Sure. But I've never been issued a military grade M4 carbine and told to shoot anyone who attempts to leave the facility."

Despite my best efforts to conceal my shock, my jaw dropped. "Wait. What?"

"We had shoot-to-kill orders. The higher ups didn't want whoever was trying to leave to get out alive."

"You shoot anyone?"

"Not that time."

"This happened more than once?"

"Yeah. Plenty."

"Jesus."

"The first night the alarm sounded, I saw a man try to escape—a bald man in a lab coat. He got as close as ten feet from me." Burt paused. He covered his mouth with the back of his forearm. He stared down into his mug, then looked back up and continued. "Look, I didn't want to kill anyone. Hell, they didn't pay me enough to do that. I was just security; I was supposed to prevent bad guys from getting in, not employees from getting out."

"Go on," I said, impatient with a morbid curiosity that sickened me.

"I ordered the man to stop. He saw my rifle. He complied . . . for a moment. Then he held up his hands and slowly approached.

"I urged him to stop. And he did, about five feet from me. He was close. Close enough for me to see his green eyes."

"What's so special about green eyes," I said.

"They were solid. Pure green. No whites or visible pupils. The man seemed to stare right through me. When he finally spoke, he said, 'Make it stop. *Please*. So many turns. More than you'd think. In the quarry. More than you'd think.'"

I hesitated to ask the most obvious question. It was as if merely indulging my curiosity would somehow make me complicit in Burt's likely crime.

"I can see the question in your eyes," Burt said, sparing me the shame of smacking the elephant in the room with a Louisville Slugger. "And no. I didn't shoot him that time. My supervisor did."

Burt quivered and covered his face with his hands. He sobbed. "Before I had a chance to process the rifle shot, I was covered in the old bastard's blood and guts. I threw up on the spot. It . . . it was horrible."

I couldn't believe Burt's story. It was nuts. I took a

deep swig of coffee so I could compose myself. All I could muster was, "Did . . . did your supervisor contact the local authorities?"

Slowly, Burt looked up at me. He pushed his sunglasses against the bridge of his nose and shook his head.

"Christ, Burt. You need to notify the police. Otherwise you could be charged with accessory to murder."

"Let me finish, Steve," Burt said, barely concealing an impatient anger. "It gets worse. Much worse. After the shooting, Bob, my supervisor, the guy who killed the lab technician in cold blood, grabbed my elbow and escorted me to an office building on the outskirts of the facility. Once we were inside, he took me to an enclosed office near the entrance and sat me down. He tried to reassure me. Told me everything would be all right—that the company would have our backs. I didn't believe a single fucking word of it. The whole thing was all jacked up. I just couldn't accept it."

Burt paused, taking a deep breath. He continued. "That's when Bob pulled out a bottle of Jack Daniel's from beneath a desk and poured two shots. I immediately downed one, then he poured another. And another. In thirty minutes, I was so numb and blitzed out of my mind that the killing became a distant memory.

"That's when Bob offered me the green worm. Told me to swallow it whole. Promised it would calm me down. While I may have been completely sauced, there was still no goddamn way I was eating that fucking thing."

Burt took another drink. "So Bob downed it himself. 'See,' he said. 'Totally safe. And it really steadies the nerves.'

"I watched Bob for a few more minutes. After he'd

blown that guy away, he'd also seemed a bit rattled; he'd just hidden it better than I had. But after taking the worm, he seemed to positively glow with an inner peace. Like the whole thing had never happened.

"'What the hell was that?' I asked him. He referred to the worm as the 'Product.' Said it was real special. One of a kind—pharmaceutical grade, but all natural. And Absynthos had sole access to the only source on the planet."

"He just killed a man right in front of you and he's engaging in shoptalk? Why didn't you call the police?" I repeated.

"I passed out. Woke up the next evening tucked all nice and cozy in my bed. At that point, it was pretty damn easy to convince myself none of it had happened. Just a dream and all that jazz."

I was on the edge of my seat. "So it all was just a dream?"

"In a matter of speaking. That is if you believe reality is the dream, and our dreams, reality," he said cryptically, and in a way that made me conclude he didn't have a clue what to believe.

"What's that supposed to mean?"

Burt shrugged. "So I got dressed and went back to work for the night shift. Bob acted like nothing had ever happened, and I was happy to keep it that way.

"A few more weeks passed without incident. Then, one night, the alarm went off again. I grabbed my M4 and rushed to the source of the disturbance."

My heartbeat quickened. Burt took another jittery gulp from his mug.

"It was the lab technician—the one Bob may have

murdered—I'm still not sure. Only this time, the old guy grinned when he saw me. Like he recognized me. Said something like 'and so the worm turns again; around and around it goes; when will it end? No one knows.'"

"What did you do?" I said.

"I did the only thing I could do: I blew his brains out."

"For real this time?"

He lowered his head. "For real. And I watched the guy die a second time—assuming, of course, the first hadn't been a dream."

None of this could be real. My friend, Burt, was clearly three fries short of a Happy Meal. He had to be under the grip of some kind of madness.

"That night, I didn't drink; I swallowed the worm. Then the worm swallowed me." For an instant, Burt lowered his glasses just enough so I could see his eyes. Sickly eyes the color of bile.

I shuddered. "Jesus Christ."

"The Product really is all it's cracked up to be. A feeling of bliss overwhelms you—like heroin and meth all rolled into one, but without all the nasty side effects. It's addictive, sure, but it sharpens your mind and it opens your thoughts to so many things. So many. Things. And that's the problem. The problem of the forking paths."

At that moment, I realized I was in way over my head. I stood up and motioned toward the door. "C'mon, Burt. We need to get you to a doctor. Now."

Burt cackled. He rolled up his sleeves and showed me the underside of his forearms. Two deep gashes. "You don't understand."

I instinctively looked away, then forced myself to turn back to my old friend and sit back down. An eerie silence followed. The diner seemed to still, charged with potential energy.

"I'm glad somebody saved you," I mumbled in a clumsy attempt to express both my sympathy and my relief that Burt had survived his attempted suicide.

When our frumpy middle-aged waitress stopped at the table to check on us, her face turned ashen. Burt looked down at the table and awkwardly rolled down his sleeves.

I held out my mug to blunt the woman's shock. "Could you top me off, please?"

The waitress nodded, her eyes still wide. She headed toward the counter as if she'd appreciated the excuse.

I put my hand on Burt's arm. "You can't do that shit in public, man."

He cackled again. "You think someone saved me? That's rich. Truth is no one did; truth is I should've been dead. And more than once."

"It's a good thing you survived."

Burt reached across the table and grabbed my collar with both hands. "You don't get it, do you, Steve? I wasn't supposed to survive. Each time, I woke up in a tub full of dirty green blood. So many branches. So many permutations. And not a single one where I die."

I glared at him, then looked down at his hands. Blushing, he released my collar and slumped back into his seat. It was clear Burt needed professional help. Yet he was so unhinged, I doubted anyone could've made a whit of difference.

The waitress returned with a pot of coffee, pouring it

into my mug with unsteady hands and a frugal glance seemingly optimized to keep the time spent at our table short.

Burt stared at me, his creepy green eyes hidden behind his shades. He expected a response.

All I could venture was, "What do you want me to say, man?"

"Help me," he whispered.

The diner's door swung open.

Burt bolted up. "Please, Jan. I know I'm not supposed to be here. I promise I won't do it again. And again. And again."

Jan? I thought. I glanced over my shoulder. Dr. Jan Remick, Abynthos's Senior Vice President of R&D.

He wore sunglasses.

"Steve!" he said in a bout of unconvincing enthusiasm. "What brings you to this neck of the woods?"

I nodded toward Burt. "An old friend."

"That so? Your old friend been telling you stories about our work out here?"

"A bit of this, a bit of that," I said, desperately trying to downplay my unease.

He rounded the table and gestured toward Burt. "Go on. Have a seat, son."

Burt shuffled toward the wall and sat back down. Jan shimmied into the booth next to him.

"Well, this is awkward," said Jan. "I guess now that the secret's out, we might as well go through the motions."

Jan removed his glasses, revealing solid green orbs. He gazed at me—his expression teetering on the ledge of sanity. "They say whatever's in the quarry, it's been there a long, long time. Long before people ever set foot on this continent. Long before the first dinosaurs ravaged the earth. Eons before life as we know it crawled out of the primordial ooze. That thing's been buried here for millions of years, and we're only just beginning to scratch the surface of its possibilities."

Jan reached across the table and put his hand over mine. "Now that you've been read into Project Wormwood, you'll need to chase the worm."

"I . . . I don't understand," I said. I made to stand up, but Jan grabbed my wrist and yanked it toward him.

His unsettling eyes bored into mine. "The problem with you, Steve, is that you were always good at everything. Unfortunately, being good at everything means you're great at nothing. And Absynthos doesn't need generalists; it needs specialists." He released my arm. "But not all hope is lost for you, Steve-o. Soon you'll be part of the pattern, bound to a chain of interlocking Fibonacci spirals extending into infinity. And because of that, you'll have time to become an expert in crafting the Product. Forever."

Jan opened his left hand, palm facing upward. A green worm writhed there. I shook my head and turned away. I heard a metallic click and, from beneath the table, felt the press of a snub-nosed revolver against my knee. When I faced him again, he withdrew it, leaned his back against the booth, and grinned. "Now, now, Steve-o. All you need to do is swallow. Everything will be okay. And you'll have a chance to really make a difference in the world. Over and over and over again. Forever."

HOWLERS IN THE VOID
Brian Trent

---

*If Brian Trent isn't a familiar name to longtime Baen
readers, he should be. A regular contributor to our Black
Tide Rising and Weird World War anthologies, as well as
having had stories published elsewhere reprinted in several
of our Year's Best Military and Adventure SF collections,
Trent has a knack for telling stories that cross a range of
subgenres, while letting his own voice and personal touches
shine through.*

*For this story, he's managed to bring a lot of his
signatures to play. Marooned soldiers on an alien world,
hostile alien pirates, and far more dangerous things
lurking in the dark corners of a dead world. Military sci-
fi, planetary adventure and Lovecraftian horror in equal
measure, the resulting tale is a roller coaster.*

I. Point of Impact

The two ships cracked through the atmosphere like a
single meteor blazing toward the planetary surface.

Lashed together by grappling cables, and cloaked in the incandescent plasma of atmospheric entry, they drew a smoky trail down a black sky.

Strapped into the cockpit of one doomed ship, Captain Shayne Dunsany of the TerraNet Compact thought: *We're going to die, and it's my fault.*

Survey missions in the stellar outback could be dangerous, there was no denying that. In the lightless periphery of a local star—what surveyors called the "junkyard"—there were dead comets, lone asteroids, dwarf planets, and lost moons. Resources beckoned from these unmapped corners. That was the benefit *and* the danger: the galaxy was full of civilizations, and therefore full of competitors. Dunsany had seen it before: landing on a platinum-rich asteroid only to discover that it was full of robotic maggots, chewing their way to the rich interior, crawling out of holes to expel mineralogical nectar, while other robots or alien pilots waited to receive the material. In such instances, it was wise to move on and keep searching.

If, however, you didn't see anyone already operating there, the time was ripe to act like an insect yourself: a locust. Landing on a surface to quickly strip-mine it. Drill, collect, catalogue, and retreat! Fill your ship's belly to bursting and fly back to a TerraNet world for good pay and the satisfaction of having assisted your species. It was, Dunsany liked to think, the story of civilization—of *any* civilization, really. Gather resources. Strengthen your position. Master your own small corner of the galactic ocean.

Sometimes that meant you had to fight.

When the rogue world appeared on his ship's ladar systems, Dunsany hadn't expected a fight. Yet as he swung into high orbit, another vessel appeared. The pingback silhouette matched that of a thovogri vine-ship. He had promptly attacked them.

He didn't consider himself a violent man. The decision to attack stemmed from several considerations. He didn't want them thwarting his intentions here. Didn't want them opening fire on *him*—the thovogri were thieves and butchers and monsters in every sense of the word. In space, it was often necessary to make split-second decisions, and so he strafed their vessel, disabled it, demanded (and received) their surrender. His ship grappled theirs, and he began reeling it in for boarding.

Then the vine-ship grappled them back, and made a run for the planet surface.

Dragging his ship with them.

"John!" Dunsany shouted, shuddering in his seat harness. "Standby to initiate hull release!"

"Aye, sir!"

He stiffened at the voice. Twisting around, he was confused to see—not his copilot of five years—but Robotics Engineer Fallon Wilmarth. She climbed into the adjacent creche.

Before he could ask what the devil she was doing up here, he noticed John's body. The copilot lay crumpled at the foot of telemetry panes, neck bent at an unsightly angle. He must have been thrown in the first moments of their quarry's run.

Dunsany's heart sank.

My fault.

It's my fault.

Voice brittle, he said, "Wilmarth? We need to eject the outer hull."

She blinked at the control panel. "I understand."

"The release should separate us from the enemy, but I'll need to concentrate on recovery maneuvers. Bring up the AI-assist. Wait for my command."

"Yes, sir."

He closed his eyes, importing a virtual feed of their tangled descent straight to his visual cortex. *Why the hell were the thovogri trying to commit suicide? Death before dishonor?* It made no sense, but neither was there time to contemplate the alien motivations of an alien race. All that mattered was survival. He saw the two ships in his mind's eye. The velocity, angle of descent. There was one chance to escape this plunge down the gravity well. He anxiously licked his lips, hands snaking into the flight control haptics. The ship rattled around him.

"Wilmarth!" he shouted. "Eject the outer hull!"

His visual field went dead.

He opened his eyes and realized the darkness was not just in his virtual interface. The cockpit itself was dead. All instrument displays were black. All holos collapsed like flowers clamping up for the night.

We're going to hit the surface like a bug on a windshield.

He never even heard the crash.

Metal spiders crawled over his face, leaving little footprints in his sweat.

Captain Shayne Dunsany stirred awake, as the spiders

found the wetports in his neck and sank needle-tipped mandibles, administering a soup of stabilizing agents. Emergency lighting transformed the cockpit into a ruby-hued miasma of fire-suppressant gas and chalky, post-crash debris.

He undid his harness and fell out of his chair.

"Ship status," he choked. "Anyone copy?"

There was no response. Silvan's body lay on the floor, jackknifed and motionless. In the copilot creche, Engineer Wilmarth blinked weakly at him through her biomask; it grew around her face like a jellyfish.

"Captain?" she began.

"Sit tight," he ordered, and stumbled into the next room.

There was no next room.

Under ordinary circumstances, his vessel was a Marzanna-class, thousand-meter-long mining ship serving his home colony of Winter Calm. The Marzannas were the workhorse of the Winter Calm fleet, scouring this edge of the galactic spiral for precious resources. Now, all that remained of her was a cockpit and the ragged half of the robotics bay. The only thing keeping him and Wilmarth alive was the plasmic membrane that had snapped shut over the breach, restoring air pressure and oxygen; through that translucent barrier, Dunsany saw debris strewn like a comet's tail across an alien horizon.

"Fuck," he whispered.

Marooned on a rogue world. The planetary surface outside the barrier was an uninviting vista of icy spires and glassy hedgehog shapes. Colossal tusks—they couldn't be called mountains—stabbed laterally from enormous mesas regularly spaced along the terrain like allergic hives on a gray arm.

"Sir?" Wilmarth appeared behind him. "The ship . . . ?"

"See for yourself."

"I don't see the cargo hold."

"I'm more concerned about the enemy ship we grappled." He walked to within an inch of the plasmic membrane, surveying the desolate view.

"Do you really think they could have survived?"

"We did. What's your status?"

She touched her wristpad, considering the bio-readings. "Minor contusions. Whiplash. Otherwise, I'm all right, unlike . . ." She bowed her head. "John is dead."

"I know."

"He must have been thrown when the thovogri ran. Captain, I'm so sorry."

The direness of their situation had a suppressive effect on his emotions. He was acutely aware that they were operating on borrowed time. This wasn't a crash on a colony moon, where a distress signal could summon rescue from anywhere within several light-hours. Interstellar travel had been FTL for a century, but no communication system could break the light barrier. A distress signal would not be detected by listening posts for at least a few hundred years, unless another FTL ship managed to intercept it.

And there was no telling if another ship would be under human control. Could easily be another thovogri. Could be something else. The galaxy is a rogue's gallery of dangerous species.

"We're going to hold off on sending a distress signal," he said at last.

Wilmarth raised an eyebrow. "Sir?

"Given the circumstances, our priority should be the enemy ship. Where did it land? Are there survivors? Can we salvage it and appropriate its own systems for our needs? Grab a sidearm, Wilmarth. We're going outside."

"You want *me* to . . . ?"

"You're going to tell me you have no experience with planet-side recon."

She gave a stiff nod.

He sighed and did his best to hoist a sympathetic smile. "I'm familiar with your guild record. I requested you, remember? You're an experienced, versatile and capable engineer." He saw the compliment register in her eyes.

"Yes, sir."

"Blue box on the wall. Grab a pistol and as many spare rounds as you can carry." Heart pounding, Dunsany pressed his chest-plate controls, and his own biosuit bled out from his flight-suit shoulders, waist, and legs like dew, covering him head to foot. At the same time, its shape-memory circuitry configured its life support suite, including rebreather, exterior pockets for ammunition and supplies, commlink, and sensor pores. The entire process took less than two minutes. He raised each boot, letting the biosuit bleed over the soles. Then he strode to the plasmic wall and stepped through it.

There was a springy resistance, and suddenly he was through. Outside on an unknown world. Wilmarth followed a minute later, pistol in hand, looking nervous.

"Look at this place!" she exclaimed. "Have you ever seen anything like it?"

"No."

It was a frozen hellscape. Strange mounds and protean formations gave the appearance of a jungle built out of glass. Their impact had splintered through enormous fernlike shapes. Tumbled blocks of ice lay strewn at the base of curving towers.

"That's where the thovogri ship is," Dunsany said, indicating a fresh scar that sliced open the landscape north of their position. "Let's double-time it!"

They jogged along the trail. Something about the spires and mounds began to gnaw at him. Rogue worlds floated through the void, beholden to no star. So how had these topographical features formed naturally?

"This place is volcanically active," Wilmarth said, running alongside him. "There's no other way to account for this surface."

"No? I can think of another explanation."

"Sir?"

"Artificial construction."

She laughed. "You think someone spent all this time carving a city out of ice?"

"Why not?"

It wasn't such a ridiculous thought, he mused. Most cultures, human and alien alike, worked in stone in the primitive phase of their development. Was it so absurd to think that something had done the same in ice? While in orbit, ship sensors had detected geothermal signatures coming from within the planet. That surely accounted for much of the surface's character, as his engineer supposed.

It was certainly true that cryovolcanic activity could produce unusual formations. Hell, even normal volcanism could do that. Regular, geometrically precise shapes were a well-documented phenomenon, from the Giant's Causeway on Earth to the Cydonian plateau on Mars.

Still, the majestic scope of the towers and needles and lattices really did appear to be the work of intelligent construction. The galaxy was filled with intelligent civilizations. Couldn't someone have built an icy metropolis out here? If there was heat beneath the crust, maybe something had evolved. Maybe they used the surface as a canvas of artistic expression.

His thoughts trailed off as, picking their way through the debris field, they saw what had become of the alien ship.

It had been swallowed by a mound.

The thovogri vessel must have hit the surface at an oblique enough angle that they didn't shatter like porcelain, and instead went rolling and sliding into the base of one of the regularly spaced mounds rising from the surface. They had smashed through the mound's base like a stone through a window pane.

"The mound can't be solid," he said.

Wilmarth absently scratched her face, then apparently realized she was insulated by her biosuit. "It's probably a cave that got iced over. Caught the thovogri like a baseball in a glove."

She splayed one hand ahead of her, fingers lighting like a luminous starfish. Data washed over her faceplate, and her eyes widened. "Ladar is pinging off a silhouette, a thousand meters inside."

"Be ready with that pistol."

There were lots of things Dunsany could say about the mining guild. One of the positives was that they required members to go through an intensive battery of multidisciplinary training, which included firearms and combat tactics. Wilmarth was a robotics engineer, coordinating deployment of the drillers, sifters, and processors that constituted the bread-and-butter of mining operations . . . yet by the way she held the pistol and used surface debris as defensive cover, it was clear she hadn't forgotten her defensive training. As an ancient writer once penned: *Specialization is for insects.*

Dunsany took up position at one side of the cave entrance. Then he slipped inside, and found himself in waist-deep fog. Stalactites and stalagmites protruded ahead of him, fangs in a wintry mouth.

"There are lights!" Wilmarth cried behind him, voice tinny through transmission to his suit speakers. "Are you seeing this?"

"I'm seeing it," he breathed, hardly believing his eyes.

The fog billowing through the cave's interior was punctured by a constellation of lights. These formed a deliberate, patterned luminosity: not a serpent of light but a hydra, spiraling along numerous paths.

"Lichen," his engineer muttered. "It has to be a bioluminescent lichen."

"Does it?"

"I know what it looks like, but that really doesn't make sense, does it?"

"What does it look like, Wilmarth?" He considered the sprawling tendrils of light fading into frosted miasma. "Because I'll tell you what it looks like to me: a city."

It was ridiculous, of course. There could be no city on a dead planet so far from any sun, and with no political borders to defend or supply it. Who would colonize such a place? For all the territorial struggles between humanity and alien races, no sentient species could desire such a useless piece of real estate like this unless . . .

He was approaching the nearest light, finger tight around his pistol, when a hunched shadow loped across his path.

II. Gloomknot

It happened so fast that he nearly pulled the trigger. The fog burst around a humanoid shape, its feet splashing through puddles of meltwater. Dunsany's first impression was that it was a man—a *human* man!—carrying a child on his back. Neither of them were wearing biosuits or other protective gear; rags hung loosely from the man's body.

The fellow was perhaps forty years old, with very long, black hair and a voluminous beard. The child on his back appeared to be young, judging by the pale arms wrapped around his neck and emaciated legs around his waist. He couldn't see the kid's face; the child clung, piggyback, to the adult in what must have been pure exhaustion, face buried beneath a matted tangle of stringy hair.

Shipwreck survivors?

"Hello!" Dunsany began.

The man halted, eyes bulging from shrunken sockets.

"My name is Captain Shayne Dunsany of TerraNet. Can we render assistance?"

The man stared, breathing in labored gasps. The child at his back didn't stir.

"We're here to help. We encountered a thovogri ship in orbit. Is that where you came from? Did they abduct you and your child?"

That was a strong possibility. The thovogri were smugglers for half a dozen different species. Weapons were the typical contraband, but they weren't above acting as slavers when demand called for it.

Wilmarth approached, hand splayed. "Captain? He's not matching anyone from colony registries."

"He came from somewhere. Not every colony reports their—"

The man threw back his head and howled.

Dunsany recoiled. The howl went through him like an icepick, and he thought: *The man's insane! What the hell has he been through?* Before he could react, the man turned, child still on his back, and bounded into the mist. Somewhere farther away, he howled again, and the ululation turned into a series of echoes like the baying of wolves.

Or maybe it wasn't an echo.

Maybe others are howling back.

"The thovogri ship," Dunsany said, collecting his thoughts. "If any of them survived, neutralizing them is our first priority."

"Yes, sir."

They followed the lighted path. As it turned out, the source of illumination was within the ice as a series of buried luminous globes. They varied in size, with some as large as basketballs and others as diminutive as pearls; in either case, they lit multiple trails through a labyrinth of shadows. And the details of the environment were becoming clearer. Dunsany noticed looming, rectangular shapes around them. Structures too deliberate to be natural.

Then he saw the thovogri ship.

It had come to rest against a cavern wall, upside-down, nose crumpled against the ground. One wing had broken off on impact. The hull had sheared away in places, exposing steel ribs and honeycombed compartments. Black vines dangled, entwined around a cylindrical structure at odds with the vine-ship.

"The cargo hold!" Wilmarth cried.

"Secure the enemy ship first," Dunsany said, though he felt a flicker of hope. He climbed up through the alien hull, and his engineer followed.

Two thovogri were dead inside. They had killed each other with vine-casters. A nasty short-ranged weapon, Dunsany had encountered it before; three years ago, a thovogri raiding party hit Winter Calm. He had engaged them with the colony guards. Vine-casters were a peculiar weapon, and they behaved unexpectedly. They looked like rifles, but shot rubbery tendrils. These could knock a man down. Could lash onto limbs and tear them out of sockets. Could go rigid and pierce like a medieval lance. They could even flower into a makeshift shield, deflecting bullets. A nasty piece of alien tech.

The two thovogri had fired these vines at each other. Both were pinned through like butterflies on corkboard. Dunsany ducked beneath these stiff projectiles.

"Looks like they had a disagreement," Wilmarth noted.

"Good."

"Maybe this explains what happened in orbit. They had surrendered, remember? Then they grappled us, and ran."

"Maybe."

He disentangled one of the vine-casters from an alien claw. With the press of a button, the vine snapped back into the muzzle in a whiplike flourish. Holstering the weapon, he climbed higher into the ship.

In the next chamber, the floor and walls were cluttered with shipping containers. Most were intact despite the crash. One container, however, had become pinned by a compressed bulkhead and popped open like a chestnut. The contents littered the floor, and Dunsany stared in horror.

Gloomknots!

He was so astonished that he failed to react before his engineer climbed up beside him. She glanced to the floor and went pale.

"Fuck," she whispered. "Oh, captain! Fuck! They're out of containment! They . . ."

"Back away," he barked.

"Captain! I can feel them—"

"Wilmarth, listen to me . . ."

"I can feel them in my eyes!"

"Back away! Now, officer!"

She retreated, eyes so large he could see veins. She withdrew into darkness, though he could still hear her ragged gasping across the commlink.

When she was gone, he turned back to the artifacts.

They looked like mutilated creatures. Pulpy, bubbled,

and vivisected. Bony cross-beams presented an eerie impression of endless depth. Each was twice the size of a human hand. Unknown artwork by an unknown race. The best researchers from TerraNet couldn't agree on who had made them, or when, or even how they worked.

"You're going to be fine," Dunsany said into his commlink, wondering if he was speaking to himself or his engineer. "Just breathe slowly and don't think about them."

"Captain . . . I'm sorry . . ."

"I know you can handle this."

Fallon Wilmarth was a good engineer. Skilled, smart, and efficient. She'd finished top of her class at River Lord Academy, then gone on to serve two TerraNet cruisers, one of which saw action at the Battle of F'deel. By all accounts, she had been a valuable addition to each crew and good under pressure.

Then she took a job working a shepherd moon in the Brin System. While drawing core samples, one of her robotic drills became unresponsive. Wilmarth had gone out to see what the trouble was. The bot had broken into an air-pocket. In that exposed interior, a bizarre object glinted in her flashlight.

A gloomknot.

Why the hellish thing had been buried on a tiny moon, Dunsany would never understand. But that was par for the course: whatever civilization had crafted the goddam things had also seen fit to pepper them across the galaxy.

Neither was it understood how the damned things did . . . what they did. Wilmarth's exposure had screwed with her mind. Current theory was that the artifacts represented an encoded, data-rich pattern capable of rewriting neural pathways. Stare too long at a gloomknot, and it *changed* you. She'd been hospitalized for six months. Upon discharge, she found herself unemployable; rumors of her mental breakdown—of *what* had broken her down—had traveled ahead of her. People were afraid of gloomknots. Those who had suffered exposure were pariahs.

Hating such ignorant prejudices (having experienced ample bigotry himself—the galactic elite was only too eager to sneer at Winter Calm's igloo-dwelling blue-collar laborers), Dunsany put in a requisition for her. And Wilmarth's gratitude had since bordered on obsession. She was eager to please, desperate to succeed in this second chance.

He pulled a heavy blanket off the wall (an incubation skin, he noted, being smuggled to one of the egg-laying civilizations) and spread it over the gloomknots, being careful to avoid looking at them again. Their shapes burned in his memory. Like being drawn into a mandala. Like marveling at an optical illusion. A kaleidoscopic tunnel.

Stare long enough, and you might see the image hidden at the other end . . .

"Captain?"

"What is it?"

"Are you okay?"

He finished spreading the blanket over the gloomknots, taking care to ensure that even the concealed shapes were sufficiently camouflaged. "I'm fine. Stand guard. Take further ladar readings of the cave."

"Yes sir."

He advanced farther into the ship. When he reached the thovogri bridge, the angle of ascent was so steep that he was forced to hoist himself using the wall paneling as rungs, and—

—something whipped past his face like an oily tentacle.

Dunsany dropped to one knee, aiming his pistol at the thovogri commander who was strapped into the seat above him.

By comparison with the gloomknots, the thovogri wasn't all that bad to look at. Its five legs stretched into their control ports like a starfish. An eye glared weakly from the base of each limb. The body itself was a headless trunk. A vine-caster was clutched in one claw.

Dunsany fired a single shot.

The vine-caster exploded. The thovogri hissed in fear, all eyes widening.

"Reach for another weapon," Dunsany growled, "and I'll blast off a limb of my choice. Got that, you bastard?"

The thovogri nodded—an exaggerated imitation of the human motion, and one that didn't entirely work, considering there was no head upon its trunk, so that it heaved its entire body in an up-and-down fashion. The black eyes wormed in their fleshy sockets.

Dunsany's fingers sweated around the trigger. "What business do you have on this world?"

"Not know world," the alien said, speaking in a grating voice that sounded like rocks scraping together.

"You were orbiting when we arrived."

"Surveying."

"You'd never been here before?"

"*Never.*"

Dunsany laughed coldly. "So I'm supposed to believe that you just happened to stumble on a rogue planet at the exact same time we did? Out of all the star systems, we both ended up here? Know what the odds of that are?" When the thovogri made no response, he said, "I'll tell you what I think. This world is a supply depot of yours. There's artificial lighting. Air pressure, too, though I'm not sure how. And there are humans here—at least two— which suggests that you employ a slave labor force. I think we caught you in the midst of dropping off contraband, or picking some up. That's why you tried to run! Not into space, no! You tried crashing us on your own planet!"

The eyes at the base of each limb widened in outrage. "*This not our planet! You crashed us here! It was you!*"

"You spawnless liar!" It was a supreme thovogri insult to demean one's reproductive success. "You grappled us!"

"*We surrendered!*"

"You pulled us down into the planet!"

"*No! You pulled us!*"

A chill ran along his spine. He thought back to the moment they had grappled the enemy vessel and began reeling it in. Sensors indicated the engines were dead. Even visually, Dunsany had been able to see the filleted hull leaking a ribbon of plasma.

The thovogri had been dead in the water.

So how could they possibly have run?

There *had* been a sudden acceleration, there was no denying that. It happened so fast that it nearly snapped Dunsany's neck. They hit atmosphere like a hammer. By the time he recovered from the shock, both ships were plummeting like a pair of meteors. Was it possible that *his own ship* had accelerated? That was ridiculous! Master control of the vessel was keyed to the captain's creche. Sure, there were redundancies in place, but someone would have to manually reroute control to another station. That wasn't possible on a whim. It required hours of work . . .

. . . *that an engineer could have done.*

He remembered something else, too. He'd seen Wilmarth climbing into the copilot creche after John Silvan had been killed. Dunsany ordered her to shed the outer hull, and what happened? His ship had gone dead. Power cut. They'd fallen, blind and paralyzed, down the gravity well.

"You're lying," he told the thovogri captain. "We grappled you, and you grappled us back! If you meant to surrender, why do that?"

The thovogri made no reply.

Dunsany pulled the trigger.

The beam severed the alien's harness, causing it to tumble down from its command chair and crash into the wall. Dunsany pinned it there, pistol pressed against the fleshy trunk. In seconds, he had slapped plasmic cuffs onto all five limbs, binding them in a cross-section.

"You're coming with me," he said.

It was several minutes before he could wrestle his quarry down through the ship. He took care to avoid disturbing the blanket on the floor. He could still feel the gloomknot pattern in his eyes . . . not so unlike the dimpling of skin after pressing an arm against a raised surface. As a kid, bored in his schoolhouse classroom on

Winter Calm, he would often entertain himself by creating "scars" on his skin by pressing against his school-desk's corners. The gloomknot wriggled in his thoughts in a similar, tactile fashion.

I only looked for a few seconds, he thought. *That's not enough time for them to fuck with me. I won't think about them. Won't let their patterns form in my head.*

Yet as he climbed down through the ship, pushing his quarry ahead of him, another thought floated up from the dark waters of his mind:

How long had Wilmarth looked, back on that shepherd moon? What if she was the one who crashed us here?

III. The Lost City

She was waiting for him outside the hull breach, one hand extended to the mist. Reams of data washed over her faceplate.

"What have you found?" Dunsany asked, forcing his bound captive to its knee-joints.

"I've done a ladar sweep of the cave."

"And?"

"You need to see this." She made a sweeping motion, and his own faceplate filled with an extraordinary image reconstructed by the pingback.

It showed ruins.

The ruins of a city!

There was no other possible interpretation of the ghostly silhouettes. Concealed in the ice fog, dozens of structures jutted in a spiraling pattern. Some towered two hundred meters and nearly brushed the ceiling. Others were stunted, lopsided rubble like shattered teeth in a giant's mouth. Triangular edifices, ovoid monoliths, and spiny rectangles studded the cave in a showcase of undeniable architecture. The only natural formations were the glacial columns and stalagmites that supported this eerie cathedral.

"I don't recognize the architecture," Dunsany muttered. "Do you?"

"No, sir."

He minimized the image and glared at his quarry. "How about you? This isn't a thovogri settlement; I've seen pictures of your ugly little cities. You didn't build this place. Who did?"

The alien captain blinked its radial eyes. *"Not know."*

"Why did you come here?"

"Investigate reports of human outpost."

"We don't build outposts on rogue worlds!"

"Neither do we."

Wilmarth closed her data-display. "We know there's at least two people alive down here. Maybe they could shed some light on this?"

He hauled his captive to its feet. "Agreed. Let's try to make contact."

They pressed into the mist, following the nearest lighted path. At an intersection, Dunsany craned his neck to view one of the looming shadows. It was a curious thing to behold. Didn't look like rock or ice. In fact, if he didn't know any better, it seemed to be made of metal. Across the path was another massive shadow. And another.

Shadows dimpling the mist. Alien patterns. He imagined himself rushing into them. The fog brushing his face as he ran like a marathon runner into a maze of weird configurations ...

The gloomknot has gotten to me, he thought. *It had only been a brief exposure, but the fucking thing is already messing with me. Burrowing into my mind. Rewriting pathways into neurological strange-loops ...*

"Captain?"

Dunsany saw a figure dash in front of him. He thought it was the shipwrecked man from earlier, but then realized this was a woman. She was very tall, nearly seven feet. That was common among colonists from low-g worlds—they tended to get beanpole, mantislike bodies.

"Excuse me!" he called after her.

She half-turned in his direction. He glimpsed the same hollow, famished looked as with the first person he'd seen. Remarkably, she also was giving a piggyback ride to a child. Dunsany noted the unkempt tangle of black hair, pale arms wrapped around the woman's neck, pale legs locked around her waist. Then she melted into the mist.

And howled.

After a few seconds, she howled again, farther off, and this time was answered by at least a dozen others.

"This human place!" the thovogri observed. *"Humans here!"*

Dunsany approached an oblong darkness and ran his hand along the battered, metallic surface. "This isn't a building," he said. "It's the outer hull of a ship."

His engineer shone an illuminating beam from her hand. "You're right! That's a F'Deel sleeper ship."

"And that ovoid building on the ladar map? If I didn't know better, I'd say it's the control tower of a Dilok trader."

She studied the ladar map. "Are we in a junkyard? If all these 'buildings' are the husks of other ships, then . . ."

"Then who brought them all here?"

Old stories unfurled in his memory. Ships did go missing—that was a fact of galactic life. As civilizations expanded, their need for resources expanded in parallel. Expeditions were launched into unexplored regions of space. Sometimes they returned with surveys of metal-rich asteroids and unclaimed moons. Sometimes they didn't return at all. Hostile aliens explained some of those disappearances. Accidents and malfunctions surely accounted for others. There were legends, though, of ships crashing on unmapped shores and the survivors forming makeshift colonies as they waited and prayed for rescue. And if the crash was devastating enough, there would be no way to call for help. What then? The marooned crew would be forced into a grim life of scraping for whatever resources could keep them alive. In most cases, they were doomed to extinction. In others . . .

Was it possible for shipwreck survivors to build a city out of scrap? There were animals which did that; on Winter Calm, the imported crabs and mollusks had taken to using discarded cans and other trash as shelters.

Wilmarth approached a lumpish cone rising from the path ahead. It looked like a town well: round and with an open mouth.

"There's heat coming from here," she said, holding her hand over the top. "I think it's a geothermal vent. This planet *is* geologically active."

"Then maybe that explains how these people live," he suggested. "If they crashed here long ago, they'd require heat. I don't see any trees around to use as kindling, but geothermal vents could keep them warm. Could be used to grow food."

"What food?"

An ugly thought occurred to him. Wilmarth seemed to read it in his expression.

"The F'Deel seedship," she said slowly. "It would have been crammed with their larvae. If the humans here were desperate enough, they could . . . um . . . cook the frozen embryos. That could last them years. It's terrible, but maybe it's the only way."

"And who knows what other ships are down here? Who knows what resources they had aboard?"

"But how could so many ships end up in the same place? And if those ships were salvaged for food and shelter, how could no one have thought to use the materials to build a distress beacon?"

It was a good question.

There appeared to be enough ships of enough variety that a breeding population of shipwreck survivors might be able to live for years. Decades, even. They could retreat into the planet for heat, and emerge to scavenge as needed. He still didn't understand how so many ships had ended up in the hollow interior of a massive ice mound, though. The thovogri ship had crashed here, but what of the others? Were they . . . carried here? How? It reminded him of how ancient terrestrial people had lugged blocks of quarried stone across miles of harsh terrain using only sleds, ropes, and pulleys.

The difference was these people had been forced to use junked, crashed, and derelict materials. A civilization built of garbage.

Dunsany looked to the thovogri. "You said you came here to investigate reports of a human settlement. Where did you get that report?"

The alien's eyes swiveled in their fleshy sockets. *"Signal detected."*

"From this planet?"

"Yes."

Dunsany felt a flicker of hope, and he looked to his engineer. "Sounds like there's working electronics down here. Maybe these people tried building a beacon but couldn't give it enough juice. Maybe they *did* build a beacon, but as the years passed and no one answered, they forgot how to upkeep it. We might be able to fix it!"

"Why you *here?"* the thovogri demanded. *"If not human outpost, why* you *here?"*

"We were on a survey mission."

"Why here?"

"Because . . ." he trailed off, not wanting to utter his realization.

Again, Wilmarth seemed to read his thoughts. "Because *I* chose this star system, right, captain? We were poring over star charts, and *I* suggested these coordinates."

He turned away from the thermal vent and faced her. "Did you know about this planet?"

"No."

"Why suggest these coordinates?"

Her lip trembled. "I was looking at the star chart with you. This seemed a good place to search."

"Did you crash us here, too?"

"I don't remember."

"You don't *remember?*"

The thovogri gave a snickering sound that was probably laughter, but sounded like a dog snuffling.

Wilmarth pointed to their captive. "*His* vineship grappled us, I remember that. And don't forget that he was smuggling gloomknots! Why don't you blame *him* for the crash?"

"*We smuggle many things,*" the alien countered.

"You surrendered! And then you grappled us!"

"*Not my order! Crewmate disobeyed.*"

Dunsany felt another shudder pass through him, an awful implication forming in his mind. "Is that why we found two dead thovogri aboard your ship? They killed each other. Are you saying that one of them lashed our ship against your orders?" When the alien nodded its body, he said, "There was a crate of gloomknots on your ship. I assumed the crash had opened it, but now ... I'm betting your disobedient crewmate was responsible. He broke containment to examine the things. Why would he do that?"

The thovogri said nothing.

"He had been previously exposed," Dunsany guessed. "Maybe years earlier, he encountered a gloomknot. The exposure changed him. Influenced his behavior. He probably didn't even remember what he was doing when he ..."

Wilmarth threw back her head and screamed.

It was a scream of such intensity that it nearly blew the speakers on his biosuit. Her mouth stretched hideously wide, the cords on her neck as rigid as mooring cables. The worst part of it was the look in her eyes. *She looked terrified.* As if she had no control over the behavior. She screamed herself hoarse.

And the cry was echoed by others. Shapes bounded out of the mist.

Dunsany spun about, seeing the dragnet closing. Men and woman, vacant-eyed and ragged. Not all of them were human, either. A hulking Dilok lumbered into view, its single eye blank. More shapes, some familiar, some belonging to no recognizable species.

And each carried a child on their backs.

He aimed his pistol at the crowd. "We are with TerraNet! We have no hostile intentions, but we will defend ourselves as necessary."

The crowd ringed them. A motley assembly of human and alien countenances. The children they carried, by contrast, were identical in appearance. Black mops of hair obscuring their faces. Pale, almost snakelike arms coiled around each host.

And suddenly, Dunsany saw something he hadn't noticed before.

Hadn't wanted to notice.

It *appeared* that there were children riding piggyback on this crowd, but now he realized this wasn't the case. What he had taken for pale arms and legs lovingly entwined around their guardians were skinny, ropelike appendages. And the matted black hair? In the light from his biosuit, he now realized that it was a bristly, shaggy growth.

How had he *ever* thought these were children being

carried by loving parents? These were lumpish creatures, affixed to the forlorn colonists like barnacles. Controlling them . . .

"Captain!" Wilmarth shrieked. "I'll help you! Let me help you!"

"What are you talking about?"

"Don't move, sir! I'll get you out of here!"

She started toward the geothermal vent.

With horror, he realized that while they had been speaking, a creature had crawled out of the vent. It made him think of an oversized cockroach. Flat in bodily orientation, scuttling on pale legs. It reared atop the vent, hair bristling like antennae. Wilmarth dropped to her knees, weeping, in front of it. She touched her chest-plate and the biosuit retracted, seeping back into her flight-suit ports.

"Captain! Put your arms around me! I'll carry you to safety!"

"Wilmarth! What the hell are you doing?"

"We'll fix the distress beacon! We'll get back home!"

His engineer wrapped herself around the thing that had crawled out of the vent in an obscene embrace. It squirmed around her shoulders. A proboscis kissed the back of her neck. Fallon Wilmarth's eyes rolled white.

As blank and vacant as the expression on the others here!

The thovogri trilled in panic. *"We leave here! Must leave!"*

Dunsany fired point-blank into the crowd, carving an opening through their bodies. Screeching howls erupted from every throat. Then he seized his captive by one arm and dashed through the breach, peripherally aware that the vent was expelling another crawling monstrosity.

"We're going back to your ship!" Dunsany said.

"Ship no power!"

"But I'll bet it has weapons. What smuggler doesn't carry weapons?"

The thovogri grunted as it ran with him. *"It has weapons."*

Dunsany's thoughts raced as fluidly as his legs. This was a planet of parasites. Through sinister manipulations he could barely comprehend, it had lured ships of every known civilization—and those unknown to TerraNet—to this dark corner of the galaxy. Had gotten them to land or crash here. Took possession of the crews. Used them to build a city.

And suddenly, he suspected how they had done it.

The gloomknots. They had been scattered across the galaxy as lures. Those who encountered a gloomknot could hardly know why they chose to search out here. Could hardly understand why accidents befell their ships.

This wasn't merely about his own survival any more. Dunsany considered the safety and comfort of Winter Calm. He imagined it succumbing to this hideous infection. The colonists taken over by this species of parasite. Then other worlds succumbing. The entirety of TerraNet. Other civilizations falling until every spiral arm of the galaxy had been possessed by an insidious force.

"You will get us lost!" the thovogri cried.

"I know where I'm going!" he snapped, but he called up the ladar map of the cave to be sure. The twisting streets, the confusing geometries of dozens of vessels brought here, dragged inside by the enslaved muscle power of a dozen intelligent races. He turned left, dove right. A clawed alien resembling a nightmarish crab scrambled at him from the fog; Dunsany had time to appreciate that there were multiple parasites affixed to it, before he shot it through the body. The blast tore the shell into separate halves and Dunsany and the thovogri slipped through steaming viscera.

"This is not the way!" his captive repeated.

But it certainly was the way, Dunsany thought, following the map. The thovogri ship wasn't far off now. The spiral arms of the city were more complicated than he'd appreciated before; at the same time, there was a fundamental pattern to it all that roughly aligned with other cities he'd seen, human and alien alike. In fact, the longer he contemplated the map, the more certain he was that he'd seen this pattern before.

Then the realization stuck him, and he gave a wild cry.

It was the gloomknot!

The city's design mirrored the bubbly protrusions and frenzied switchbacks. Terraced streets in kaleidoscopic mandalas. He found himself falling into the image as if through a hall of endless funhouse mirrors.

Distantly, he was aware of his alien companion breaking away from him. It emitted a panicked trill, as something trundled out of the fog, seized it, and dragged it away.

Dunsany ran on, no longer conscious of his legs pumping. He was only fleetingly aware of passing within view of the cave entrance, where the fog seeped out in vaporous tendrils; on the snowfield beyond, a mixed group comprised of multiple species appeared, pushing and pulling the remains of his own ship like ants cooperating to bring a useful resource to their colony. Another addition to this city of the damned.

The gloomknot blazed in his mind.

He tried closing the ladar map. His hands wouldn't comply. In desperation, he slapped at his chest-plate to retract the biosuit. The map melted away as his faceplate disappeared with the rest of the protective barrier. There was nothing between him and the environment now. Nothing to—

—*get in the way*—

—distract him.

He spotted the thovogri ship. There was no way he could repair it into working order, but two hopes drove him on. He might be able to restore backup power, enough to send a distress signal. At this point he didn't even care who picked it up. TerraNet or thovogri, pirates or slavers. Any fate was better than the one which awaited him here.

His other hope was that there were sufficient weapons aboard the vessel. He was outnumbered, but none of them seemed to be armed. None wore armor or seemed capable of advanced cognition. He didn't know how many pitiable beings lived here, multiplying here, toiling to the demands of the parasites that hijacked them . . . but with the right weaponry it shouldn't matter. He might be able to cull them with a few military-grade rifles and explosives. It wouldn't be murder, but mercy.

Reaching the ship, he clambered down into it.

Vaguely, he wondered why he was climbing *down*.

Earlier when he and Wilmarth found it, they had been forced to climb *up* into the vessel. The air felt humid and cloying around him.

Dunsany descended a narrow chute towards a source of light. The main cabin burned a hole in the darkness. He spotted the captain's chair.

I need to rest, he thought. *I'm so exhausted I can't think. Need to sit down. Plan my strategy. Why was I coming here? Why did I climb down into the ground?*

He dropped into the captain's chair. Something touched his back.

The harness. It had to be the harness.

Shayne Dunsany wept in relief as he pulled the harness around his neck and waist. The straps enfolded him in a comforting embrace.

Things were going to be all right.

He threw back his head and howled, knowing now that one day, the rest of the galaxy would be howling back.

THE BUILDING WILL CONTINUE
Gray Rinehart

Be it his novel Walking on the Sea of Clouds, *his contributions to several Baen anthologies, or his short stories on the pages of* Analog *and* Asimov's *magazines, Baen's slushmaster general Gray Rinehart is no stranger to telling a wide variety of stories, be they stories of struggling to colonize the moon, or of a cetacean obsessed with evolving and contacting humans.*

All the same, this may be the first time I've actually seen Gray tackle Lovecraftian horror, delivering a story of broken men on a hostile world, whose ancient mysteries and still present dangers have their own plans for the visitors from Earth.

"Do you mean to suggest that these expeditions are cursed? Absurd."

"I didn't exactly say that," Leland said, "but it's starting to feel that way."

Professor Kellick sneered, which made him look even more pompous. "Have you been talking to Fitzhugh? Nothing he says is credible. We don't know for sure that he . . ." His voice drifted off, and Leland knew he couldn't bring himself to say *murdered his entire team*. When Kellick spoke again, his voice was low, as if only for himself. "Everyone's having nightmares . . ."

No crap, Leland thought. He certainly was, and stranger with every passing night. But he couldn't tell the man-in-charge what he already knew: that they'd all thought Delvecchio's group would still *be* here, just cut off by a communications failure. Frustrated, he murmured, "Anybody with a soul would."

"Would what?"

"Have nightmares. Mass disappearances are the stuff of nightmares."

Kellick glanced up, briefly. "Thankfully, I do not come so equipped."

Leland looked out the window at the trees that Delvecchio's group had called "magnificedars." Their boughs waved lazily, deep green in the growing twilight, but the breeze did not reach them inside the shelter.

Just as well. It would stink like rancid cooking grease.

"I wonder if *they* do," Leland said.

"They who? Do what?"

"The hyperprotists." The name Delvecchio's team had given the things didn't exactly roll off Leland's tongue; but, then, he wasn't a biologist.

"What about them?"

"If they come equipped with souls."

Kellick looked up from his tablet, his stylus loose in his

hand. All he needed was a pipe to complete the look of professorial haughtiness. "Oh, certainly." His derision came through five-by-five in his tone of voice. "And theirs probably stink like they do."

"Because cleanliness is next to godliness?"

Kellick sniffed. "If ever a species deserved to be called 'the great unwashed,' the hyperprotists do."

"We probably smell bad to them, too."

"Ah, but *that* is beyond my apprehension." His attention back on his tablet, Kellick tapped the display with the stylus. "Why this sudden fascination with souls? Are you getting religion?"

"Not that I know of. What do you have against them? Against souls?"

"I gave up mythology when I was young. Besides, if everyone had one, what would be so special about them? I always thought souls must be cheap, being so common."

Leland rolled his eyes, not that Kellick would notice. "I'm going to walk the perimeter."

The encampment was about the size of two soccer fields set side-by-side, so walking the perimeter took little time.

The boundary itself was unimpressive: a ragged line of piled-up timbers the first expedition's remotes had put in place after they cut the clearing. Not even a palisade, really, but why would they have built anything more substantial? Surveys had found no fauna larger than a terrestrial cow, and like cows the largest creatures were slow-moving herbivores. Had Delvecchio's expedition placed their camp on the grassy plains rather than this forested bluff, it might have been in danger of being trampled by a migrating herd, but here getting overrun was wildly improbable, even by the far-more-numerous hyperprotists.

Leland watched his steps carefully. Other than their smell, the hyperprotists were inoffensive enough—they were just creepy as hell. They slithered through the grass and over obstacles like land-borne octopuses, except that they had no real tentacles—and no prominent head, either. Dinner-plate-sized pseudopods covered in mottled and mixed shades of cilia, in twilight they became especially hard to see. Leland supposed there were enough of them to cover the whole planet, so it was good that they stayed mostly in the trees.

Those trees stood like towering sentinels—or enormous prison guards—beyond the perimeter. Leland turned his back to them, and shivered at the breeze in his face. Not a fresh breeze, mind. It was stale, as if too many people had already breathed it, like the air in a cramped, crowded cell.

Not that his quarters were any better. They still smelled as musty as when he had first opened the room a week ago. Its previous tenant, Delvecchio's assistant Jessamine Bonnehill, had left the usual detritus of occupancy: a couple of coveralls, some mufti, and a few personal trinkets, all of which Leland had packed into a pair of plastic bags and turned in before he unpacked his own things, and none of which pointed to where she had gone. The thought nagged him that she might show up unexpectedly and wonder why he was in her room. But like the others, there was no trace of her: She simply disappeared—into the forest, presumably—without warning or explanation.

Leland meandered on, and brooded.

Maybe Kellick could ignore the nightmares. Maybe he wasn't having them. Leland hadn't, at first, but he figured that was due to the post-transit sedatives: Even though he'd felt wrong in Bonnehill's old space, he slept well that first night.

The nightmares had started the next night, the first without sedation. By the third day it was clear that others were having bad dreams, too, but they mostly had the advantage of duties more engaging than Leland's.

He had troubleshot and repaired the satellite communication ground station in one long shift—the most time-consuming part had been fabricating a new waveguide to replace the one that someone had, for some unfathomable reason, removed—so now he felt increasingly redundant. He almost wished Delvecchio's group had lost contact because of a problem with the quantum repeater in orbit, instead of the ground terminal, because then he need never have set foot on the planet. Now that communications could go out normally, Leland checked that the systems kept working, sat security, and helped Ames fab things, but over the course of the twenty-nine-hour day he still had far too much time for thinking.

At the path to the ruins, Leland paused again. The indigenes' road was made of local stone fitted together as well or better than any Roman road, and except for some encroachment it cut an arrow-straight path through the forest. He studied one tree-root that was forcing the left edge up, then shifted his attention to the disorderly ranks of trees beyond. He marked how, deeper into the woods, their massive, black-barked trunks seemed to blend together in darkness.

That darkness *moved*. It beckoned him. He stepped toward it, a tentative half-step, then drew back and shivered.

He turned away from the forest and stalked toward the canteen. Whether he scrounged a snack or found someone to talk to or play a game with, it would delay him returning to his room, delay him returning to sleep.

Sarina Bruce clicked her tongue at Leland's question. "I haven't slept well since we got here, so why should last night be any different?"

"Just hoping someone was getting better sleep than me," he said.

"Nobody I know." She sipped her cocoa. Leland appreciated the way her lips touched the mug. "You ever figure out who sabotaged the comms?"

Leland turned his mug of tea a full rotation, thought about drinking some, then left it on the table and crossed his arms. "Watunge, I suppose. But I can't figure why she'd do it *that* way. I'd've pulled a circuit board, that'd take a lot longer to fab." He yawned, then said, "Sorry, I—"

"Don't worry about starting me yawning," Sarina said. Her blue-green eyes brightened and her teeth were perfect when she smiled. "I've been doing it all day."

"I can imagine." Leland smiled, though his stomach tightened as he said, "You have amazing eyes."

Sarina ducked her head for a second. "Thanks. My parents ordered them special." She winked, and continued,

"They're optimized for the sun over Phoenixhome, so they start to hurt if I'm outside too long here. Too much IR."

"Well, your parents did a fine job. And they gave you a beautiful smile, too."

She sat up a little straighter. "Lee Strickland, are you hitting on me?"

He laughed, though he was not as lighthearted as he wanted to seem. "Maybe," he said. "It depends."

The way Sarina scrunched up her forehead was delightful. "On what?"

"On whether you like it. If so, then yes, I'm hitting on you. If not, if it bothers you, then no . . . you must be mistaken." He winked at her, and tried to smile casually.

Sarina squinted at him, then they both laughed.

"Okay, then," she said. "I don't mind at all, it's sweet. But . . . I have a girlfriend back on Phoenixhome."

Leland took a deep breath and tried not to sound too disappointed. "That's the way it flies sometimes. To change the subject, what has anyone gotten out of Fitzhugh? Does he know what happened to the others?"

She set her mug down, and fought—only partly successfully—against a yawn of her own. "He hasn't said much coherent since we found him. The sky-eye didn't see anyone else at the site, and it would pick them up on imagery unless they're deep underground.

"Did you see they caged him outside the dispensary? He went wild when they took him inside. He's better—quieter—if he's outside, even yesterday when it poured rain."

"But, not helpful?"

"I don't know what to think about him." She finished

her cocoa and slid her chair back. "He mostly talks about the hyperprotists, and even then half of what he says doesn't make sense."

"Like what?"

"I guess he studied them pretty closely, but when he talks about them he starts getting all mixed up. One minute it's aphorisms—'all for one, one for all,' 'united we stand, divided we fall,' that sort of thing—and the next it's a story of how he tried chasing one, and it turned into another one or something."

Leland rubbed his eyes. "Kellick said Fitzhugh tagged some of them. Put trackers on them, but it didn't work."

Sarina laughed. "Oh, it worked, but not the way you'd expect. You know how they ooze around? Sometimes I guess they'd just flow around the tag and leave it on the ground or in a tree, pinging away. Or they'd flow a tag from one to another—Fitzhugh claims he saw a prote with four or five different tags on it."

"That'd confound your survey."

"Yeah. Once, Fitzhugh said that particular prote was being punished by having to carry all the tags, then later he said it was a hero, wearing the trackers like medals. As if he would know."

"So that's what he was doing when we got here? Studying the protes?"

"No idea. Could be he was out looking for everyone else, and just avoided being eaten long enough for us to find him."

"Eaten? By what?"

Sarina shrugged. "Whatever ate all the rest of them."

✢✢✢

Catfish. Breaded, deep-fried catfish. Leland salivated at the thought. He smacked his lips and imagined he could smell them frying, hear the crackle of the oil. . . .

He opened his eyes. The multialarm's dim green status light greeted him. He was in his quarters, and didn't hear oil crackling, but more rain tapping on the shelter's roof.

The smell, on the other hand, was real. Less catfishy now, more greasy, as if something foul had been fried in it—and thick. He could almost feel it on his skin.

He reached for his comm, thumbed it to life, and turned on the flashlight. His room seemed fine. The narrow locker was closed, his work boots sat where he'd left them, everything appeared to be in order.

The air handler kicked to life, and the smell wavered. Maybe a prote had crawled over the intake. Once it was on its way, the smell should dissipate. . . .

He felt a sudden urge to step outside and see if he could find the hyperprotist, maybe follow it to see where it went. He sniffed, and swallowed down enough spit and mucus to quell the urge. He thumbed off his comm, turned on his side, fluffed his pillow and laid his head on the wriggling cilia of a prote—

He gasped, and tried to sit up—

But the coverlet was a writhing mass of the amoebic creatures, linked together in a living, moving fabric that pinned him down—

Leland jerked awake.

Green status light, locker, boots . . . scratchy fabric pillowcase, thin textile coverlet, both soaked in his sweat. His comm lay right where it should.

He didn't bother to check the time. He got up,

wondering if it were possible to avoid sleeping for the rest of his life.

The first rays of sunlight were brightening the sky when Leland stepped out of the admin shelter after checking that all the comm equipment was up and running. He stretched, but the additional movement did little to energize him. He felt unsteady, as if he'd been drinking.

He aimed himself in the direction of the canteen. A low mist hid the ground, but not so thick as to hide the path. Still, he stepped carefully, loath even to step near a hyperprotist.

Sarina waved at him when he entered. He smiled and waved back, and when he'd warmed up a sausage roll and poured himself a cup of coffee, he joined her at the table.

"Have you heard?" she said as he was sliding his chair forward.

"Not that I know of."

"I'm surprised. I would think some reports about it would have gone out by now."

He shrugged and bit into the sausage roll. He wasn't sure how authentic it was, but it tasted right: good spice blend, with a hint of sage. He breathed around the hot bite until it was cool enough to chew and swallow, which elicited a friendly smile from Sarina.

The coffee was foully bitter, and reminded him why he usually didn't drink coffee. But he needed something stronger than tea to keep functioning.

"I don't read the comm traffic," he said, "I just make sure it can go out and come in."

She nodded. "Collette disappeared."

Leland shook his head. "Which one is she?"

"One of the real archaeologists." Sarina mildly emphasized "real." She was still an apprentice. "Short red hair? Super smart. We're all mustering to go look for her."

"Need an extra pair of eyes? I haven't even been out to the ruins yet."

"Then you should definitely come along."

The van topped a rise, and Leland looked back to see if he could glimpse the landing zone. It sat on a ridge opposite the encampment from the dig site, three kilometers farther away for safety. A layer of fog obscured his view.

He was glad the eight of them were in an enclosed vehicle, unlike the other six: he hated the thought of passing through the domain of the foul-smelling hyperprotists in an open truck. He and Sarina sat in the rearmost seat, and even though he recognized the others it took him a few minutes to put names to all of them. Wallensky, like Sarina, was part of the archaeology team. Barber was the security chief, with three members of his contracted detail: Dixon, Magalotti, and . . . Garrison. Billings, one of the company pilots, drove.

It took only a few minutes to cover the five-kilometer-long "avenue" to the outskirts of what once had been a mid-sized, Bronze-Age equivalent city. "Dismount!" Barber said, even before the van had stopped. "Circle up and we'll assign sectors."

A few minutes later, Barber stood on one side of a rough ellipse of people. "Don't mind the smell—you won't notice it after a while, and even if you do you'd better just ignore it because there's no getting away from it. So the quicker we find Ms. Lillington the quicker we can get back." He pushed maps to their comms, outlined the communication and safety protocols, and concluded with, "Remember: Look *inside* structures, because the satellite's given us no IR or multispectral hits, but don't go so far that you get lost. Now let's pair off, one of my team in each pair."

"Wait," Sarina said. "I want to go with Leland."

Barber frowned, and looked as if he was going to press the point. But the security squad had been a late add-on when the previous expedition went silent. This was still technically a university venture, and Kellick had made it clear that what the archaeology team wanted, they got.

Sarina grabbed Leland's arm. "Let's go."

"I didn't realize we were such good friends," he said as they walked away.

She glanced behind her, then leaned in close and whispered, "I don't like the look of some of them."

"I thought I'd won you over with my charming self."

She hit him on the shoulder, then consulted the map on her comm screen and said, "This way."

Piles of brush lined the path on either side. Delvecchio's group had fabricated a couple of bush hogs which, combined with their forest-clearing drones, had mown their way through most of the city. Leland's feet swished through wet grass as he walked. As they drew near their assigned area, Sarina outlined what the archaeologists had learned about the ruins. They were the remains of a city of a few thousand inhabitants, at around

2000–1500 BC levels of technology. Their builders were roughly human-sized, though no remains had been found yet to know much about them ...

Leland recalled bits of the summary report on Delvecchio's expedition. After a long-distance scan found this planet was habitable, a fast-action probe detected the ruins of an old civilization and catalogued roving herds of wildlife; Delvecchio's team was assembled, dispatched, and arrived in orbit; they examined radar and other imagery of multiple sets of ruins largely reclaimed by forest or laid waste by quakes, floods, and so forth. Eventually they selected this particular site to investigate and sent their drones to clear the landing zone and set up infrastructure. Their team sent back regular reports on the ruins—imagery of the sites and related findings, reports on lifeforms—but their transmissions became more and more disjointed. Members went missing, they mentioned something about alien contact, then sent an invitation to Kellick's group to join them before communication stopped altogether.

"Do we know why they died off? The builders?" Leland asked.

"No," Sarina said. She turned left between two hills that the map showed were overgrown buildings. "Someone suggested a plague, but it's hard to imagine a plague so virulent it cuts down an entire species. My money's on solar flares or a long period of low stellar output. Some of Fitzhugh's biological sampling pointed in that direction."

A hyperprotist, black and sleek as a panther though smaller than a tire, skittered across the path in front of them. Leland shivered at its undulating strangeness, and wondered if that omen was worse than a black cat.

"What about *them*? Where do they come from?"

"Here, so far as Fitzhugh was able to tell. Their enzymes and bacterial markers match a lot of the local plants, I guess. But they seemed to have a close connection to the builders, like pets or something."

"How do we know that?"

"*You'll* see." She took his hand and pulled him into a dark slice in the side of a hill. "In here."

In their comms' flashlights, the interior opened into a lobby of some kind. The rancid hyperprotist odor was thicker inside than it had been in the city at large, but Leland pushed it to the back of his mind as they looked around. Portals led to corridors going left, right, and deeper ahead into the hill, and long ramps sloped up to higher floors. They called Collette's name, but the sound echoed and was swallowed in darkness.

Leland wished he had a sidearm. It had been a long time since he'd been in the service, but he still reached for his hip when a hyperprotist dropped from a shaft in the rear wall with an oozy plop.

"See the niches?" Sarina said. "The protes rest in them, and some lead to little tunnel systems they use to get from place to place. Delvecchio thought they might have been domestic servants, like trained monkeys."

"I don't see that they could do much," Leland said, "and I'd hate to have them around."

"Oooh, they're *not* so bad. Hey, let's go up here."

She led the way up a ramp that ascended to the left and put them out at the mouth of a curving hallway. She walked as if she knew where she was going.

The only light came from their comms. Ten steps into

the hallway, Leland was about to suggest they go back when Sarina pushed on a door to their left. It crumbled into splinters, and she stepped through without a glance.

Leland's nose wrinkled at the sudden cloud of dust, and the rush of foulness that followed it. He patted the empty place on his hip. *Damn it all.*

Through the doorway, Sarina stood facing him. Her comm sat on a low stone shelf, its flashlight aimed up and illuminating her. She swayed slightly, as if she were listening to a tune in her head.

"Dance with me," she said.

"What?"

She reached up and tugged on her coverall's zipper. She zipped it down, down, past her lacy bra, past her navel . . .

"*Dance* with me," she said, and plunged her hand inside her coverall, into her panties.

Leland gulped. Sarina tipped her head back and moaned.

"I . . ." Leland began—

Sarina lowered her head and stared him down, like a lioness hunting. Her shoulders rose, and her hips moved with her hand.

Her eyes, so enticing before, alarmed Leland now. He looked around, and two—no, three—mottled hyperprotist shapes sat in niches in the wall. They pulsed, almost rhythmically.

Leland looked back into Sarina's wild eyes. She was breathing deep, in time with her rocking hips, in time with . . .

. . . the hyperprotists' rhythm.

His chest tightened, and his pants. The rhythm reached out to him. Heat suffused him. Sarina beckoned, and he felt as if a chain were attached to his sternum, pulling him toward her. He struggled to inhale, to take a cleansing breath, but he had to fight against the rhythm—

"This is wrong," he said. He stepped to his right, away from the wall and away from Sarina, and gasped as he shone his light around to other parts of the oblong room. Any furnishings it once had were long decayed, and bits of rock had spalled out of the walls and ceiling in some ancient quake. "You don't want me."

"I doooo," she said.

"No, you don't. You said so." Leland tried to watch every corner as he hefted one of the fallen stones. "What's her name?"

Sarina swayed. Her speech was slurred, as if her mouth was full of sticky toffee. "Collette."

"No, not Collette. We've been looking for Collette." Leland fought to stand upright under a bout of sudden fatigue. Speaking was hard; it felt as if he had to force each word past his teeth. "Your girlfriend. On Phoenixhome. Her name. What's . . . her name?"

Sarina's brow furrowed. Was she puzzled, or thinking? Her eyes lost a bit of their wildness.

With a wet plop, a fourth hyperprotist slid out of another niche and down onto the shelf next to Sarina's comm. In its light, the creature was mottled brown and blood-red. Its fluid body rippled.

Leland lunged.

He brought the rock down on the hyperprotist's body. The creature wheezed out like a bellows. The others began slithering out of their niches, whistling low, discordant notes. Leland hit the alien thing again, and a third time, then dropped the rock on it, snatched up Sarina's comm, and turned—

Sarina screamed.

Leland put both comms in one hand and grabbed her wrist. He stumbled, almost as much as she did, getting her out of the room.

Her scream died out as she ran out of breath. She gasped, and yelled, "It's in my head!"

They ran, and whether they stepped in puddles or on protes, Leland neither knew nor cared. Neither spoke, and they fetched up against a fernlike tree at an intersection between mounds, both gasping. Sarina stood, dazed, and Leland zipped her coverall up. His side hurt, and he twisted and stretched to get it to release.

A low rumble, like thunder, rolled up through his feet.

He rotated left, then right—

A score or more of the cow-sized beasts from the lowlands crested the hill and barreled toward them.

"Up!" Leland said, and grabbed Sarina's arm. "Up the hill!"

The grass was thicker, and it both helped and hindered. They could grasp it and pull, and it mostly held, but their feet slipped across it. They had climbed only a few meters when the square-headed, thick-limbed creatures galloped past, moaning mournfully, their red-brown fur flying. They left a plume of oily stench in their wake.

Leland called a warning over his comm as a solitary straggler trotted by. "Look," said Sarina, and pointed.

A hyperprotist rode atop the creature's head.

"What is that about?" Leland said, but Sarina had no answer.

They were the first to return to the vehicles. Leland didn't care that they'd given up their search for Collette. Gradually, the other teams reported negative results and made their ways back.

All but one pair.

Barber fumed, but everyone else was subdued, as minutes flickered away on their comms. Finally Barber assigned three of his security team to stay with him and continue the search, and released everyone else to return to the camp.

But only six people boarded the van: Two others had wandered away, that quickly, without being seen. And one of them was Billings, the pilot.

Leland walked Sarina to the canteen and reconstituted some soup for her. He saw her to her quarters, then he practically ran through the camp looking for security team members. All were gone, and even worse: None had left behind any weapons.

On his way to the admin shelter, he found Kellick coming out of the canteen eating an apple.

"I want a gun," Leland told him.

The professor looked puzzled, then amused. Leland quickly realized that the expedition leader was in his own world of impractical, intellectual crap. At one point Kellick began speculating about how the hyperprotists might be domesticated like dogs. Leland turned to walk away.

Kellick became stern. "You don't need a gun."

"Need or not, I'd feel better if I had one. I'll talk to Barber when he gets back."

Kellick shook his head. "He's not coming back."

Leland felt as if the professor had slapped him. "What do you mean?"

Kellick pointed at his comm. "Didn't you know? Magalotti blew Barber's head off, then called in to say goodbye." He shook his head and took another bite of apple. "What a waste," he said as he walked away.

Leland stood there a moment, and more, tendrils of exhaustion entwining him like kudzu.

He stumbled into the canteen, slapped together a sandwich with something that looked like ham and choked down a mug of coffee that tasted like motor oil. He poured another mug and carried it to the archaeologists' quarters. Sarina answered him from the other side of her door, but her voice was so low and muffled he wasn't sure what she said. He told her to stay put, and went to the machine shop.

The fabrication shelter was quiet. Nothing was running, and Ames was nowhere to be seen. Leland rang her comm, and it buzzed on the counter. Next to it, someone—Ames, he guessed—had spelled out "Pretty!" with a bunch of aluminum pellets.

Leland sank down into a chair, and sipped the vile coffee. He had liked Ames: They had done good work together, making the waveguide to fix the satcom antenna. Now she was gone. Would he be next? What did that mean? Sure, he had felt the pull to chuck it all and go for a walk in the woods, but the forest here was dreadful.

And if he didn't go? Would he be left alone like

Fitzhugh, driven half-mad or more by loneliness and fear and failure? Now, with those cow-things about . . .

The hell with that. He turned to Ames's terminal, typed in his access code, and started looking for firearm designs in the database.

Nothing.

"Come *on*," he said to the silent room as his searches came up empty, "give me *something*. A crossbow, even." But if there were weapon designs in the system, he could not find them.

He balled up his fist and lightly pounded the desktop. Then he said, "Be that way," and started pulling up files for things he *knew* he could fabricate: general tools and communications equipment. He opened up specs for everything, looking for anything he could piece together into an impromptu weapon.

Someone screamed, and Leland woke. He hadn't meant to sleep. His hand closed around the handle of the first thing he'd hastily designed and pulled off the fabricator: a long steel cylinder with a dozen spikes sticking out of one end.

A second scream tore the air, and he turned his attention to the fab shop door. The sound was close by, but he couldn't tell if it was a man or a woman. Not that it mattered.

He opened the door enough to see into the evening gloom, and the smell of frying oil gone bad wrapped around him like fog. But this time it conveyed a different sensation to the back of his throat, a feeling beyond smell or taste, like the time Palas Macadar had ordered for him in a restaurant in Kouraganda. The waitress had presented him a small bowl of what he took to be local calamari, thinly sliced in a spicy-sweet sauce. The interior edges of each slice had been feathery, and the sensation of eating it was like holding both terminals of a battery against his tongue. Macadar had laughed when he told Leland he'd eaten some creature's intestines, but Leland wasn't able to speak clearly for a couple of hours.

He stepped into the foul air, holding his club before him. His feet crunched in dry, dead grass, and his steps were the only sound. As disconcerting as the screams had been, he wished for some noise to draw him.

He glanced around the corner toward the dispensary, and froze.

The biologist Fitzhugh stood in the makeshift cage Kellick's people had jailed him in, his hands on the fence wire and his eyes fixed on some . . . *thing*.

It stood on two legs, and towered over the cell, half again as tall as Fitzhugh. Its legs were thick, its torso massive, and its arms hung almost to its knees. It reminded Leland of a giant ape of some sort, though its head was bigger and squarish. It seemed to be made of shadows, or its coloration drank in the light, and whatever it wore from its head to mid-thigh rippled, though Leland felt no breeze.

It reached out to Fitzhugh, offering him something it held in its hand—

Fitzhugh screamed.

Leland ran forward, tension in his legs feeling like springs compressing and releasing. He held his club in both hands, ready to swing when he got near enough.

Leland yelled, but his voice felt distant, muted—his mouth was truly numb.

The creature turned. Its face was shrouded, though its lips quivered and dripped foul saliva. It reached out, and in its massive hand—paw?—it held the largest hyperprotist Leland had ever seen.

He skidded, his feet slid on the grass, and he fell backward.

The creature stepped toward him—a slithering, smooth, silent motion. The essential *wrongness* of it tickled Leland's mind.

Leland screamed, and pushed his club's spiked head up in defense—

—and woke as his coffee mug tumbled off the bench and shattered.

He blinked in the sudden light. His hand was on the club he had truly fabricated, but the only sound was the chattering of the machines chewing through feedstock and growing what he'd ordered.

Leland swallowed the bitter aftertaste of coffee, and felt only the barest hint of the numbing vileness he'd dreamed.

Leland left the pieces of the mug on the floor. They probably wouldn't matter much, soon.

He had almost wept with relief when Sarina answered her comm. She had balked at coming to help him, protested that she was too tired and didn't know what to do, but ultimately he had reminded her that he could have left her in that room in the ruins, and now he needed her help and she owed him that much. Laying that guilt trip on her felt a little like bullying, but he didn't have time to worry over it.

He made sure the components he had ordered were coming along well enough—taking the time to retrieve the mounting frame and set up that machine to start on the waveguide—then joined Sarina in the canteen.

She had backed up a truck to the canteen's service door just as he asked, and he found her inside munching on some slices of cheese. She had to be hungry if she had stayed in her room all the time he had been working.

She glanced at his club, but said nothing except to offer him some of the cheese. He gladly took it. "Grab everything you want, that you think will keep," he said, "and we'll get it over to the machine shop. Then we're going to the comm center to send a distress call."

"Why the machine shop? Why not just take stuff to the comm center?"

Leland started opening cupboards. "I'll explain as we shop."

Sarina nodded at the humming fabricators. "You designed all this?"

"Most of it was already designed," Leland admitted. They talked as they moved supplies. "We could make a whole ground station if I had enough feedstock. I found parts in the database for some different models, and tweaked a few things. The main issue was power, and thermodynamics."

"So you say."

"Well, behind that comm you use is a whole relay

system you never see. That thing would be one heavy brick if it had to transmit by itself over a long distance." He paused by the truck, and pointed in the direction of the satellite antenna on the edge of the clearing. "That S-band antenna is a microwave emitter, powerful enough to beam signals up to the relay satellite, right? All I'm doing is building one we can aim at something down here."

She looked at the antenna, then at the meal packet in her hand. "And essentially cook it?"

"Right."

She shuddered, and seemed about to comment but he cut her off with, "Look, I'd love to have borrowed a couple of rifles from Barber's squad and just printed off a few thousand rounds of ammo, but they're nowhere to be found, are they? So I'm doing the best I can with what I have."

They moved the rest of the food into the shop in silence. When they were done, Leland pulled off the latest completed parts and reset those machines for their next runs. Then he checked the fabricator feedstocks. "When we've sent our message, we'll need to replenish the tanks. Can you drive a forklift?" Sarina shook her head. He shrugged and said, "We'll figure it out. Can't expect to move the stuff cup by cup."

In a small voice, as if afraid he would lay into her again, she said, "So what is it you need me for?"

He sighed, and raised his empty hands. "Because even though I engineered something to kludge together and mount on the back of that truck, the pieces are too big for me to assemble on my own."

Sarina pursed her lips and nodded. Then she half-grinned, and flexed her bicep. "So you're saying you only want me for my body?"

Leland laughed. "That's exactly what I'm saying."

The admin shelter stank, not of human body odor but of rancid grease. Leland and Sarina looked at each other, neither wanting to admit what that meant.

Nothing looked amiss in the communications center, a small room close by the shelter entrance. While he checked the systems, Sarina continued down the corridor.

He had just completed a loopback test when Sarina called from the other end of the shelter. "Lee? I think you ought to come see this." She sounded . . . tired, more than anything else. Leland could relate.

The smell thickened as he approached the head office.

Sarina stood just outside, her arms crossed, hugging herself. Leland looked in.

Professor Kellick's feet stuck out from behind his desk. "Is he . . . ?"

A tear streaked from Sarina's left eye, and she sniffled. "I didn't touch him."

Leland remembered that Kellick was probably more than just a boss to her. She must have known him several years, sat before him in any number of classes and seminars. Leland touched her gently on the arm, then slipped past. He walked around the desk and froze.

A hyperprotist covered Kellick's face.

Leland almost retched, less at the smell than at the thought of one of those . . . *things* . . . covering him, suffocating him. He struggled for breath—

—the hyperprotist pulsed—

Leland staggered back as if struck. He had a sudden urge to lift the creature up, let its viscous mass flow through his fingers, over his arms, bring it to his lips and kiss it—

—he slapped himself. Outside the doorway, Sarina started. He shook his head at her, afraid of how he must look.

She reached out. "Let's go," she said. She stepped into the doorway, still reaching, and he looked back at Kellick and swung his right hand until she grabbed it. He let her pull him out of the room.

"Close the door," she said.

He did, and the barrier helped a little. He still had the urge to pick up the hyperprotist, to pet it, stroke it, lick it—

—Sarina punched him. Her eyes were full of tears.

The miasma lifted, just a little, just enough.

They retreated to the comm center.

Sarina stood watch while Leland pulled up the messaging system. The queue was empty, and the transmitted messages were listed in reverse chronological order. Kellick had sent most of them, the last one only ten hours before.

Leland opened it.

"He's invited another expedition," he told Sarina. "Just like Delvecchio did."

She stepped in and read over his shoulder. "That doesn't make sense. Why would he do that?" She put her hand on Leland's arm and continued, "Can you find Delvecchio's last message?"

He looked, but all the messages prior to their arrival had been erased.

Leland shook his head. *Not making it easy, are they?* He accessed the backup, and held his breath until the older message traffic showed up.

Delvecchio's last message had the same tone as Kellick's: The reported troubles were all misunderstandings, come join us and share the credit and the discoveries.

"Look at that," Sarina said, and pointed at the screen.

Watunge, the previous comm tech, had sent a message after Delvecchio. Leland opened it.

"It's a distress call," he said.

Sarina leaned over him to read it. *"That's* why they sent security with us." Some of her hair brushed the side of his face, and the light scent of vanilla and some variety of berry was a huge relief from the alien funk. "We'd better make our call more explicit."

"But what should we say?"

"I don't know," she said. "What do you call it when a whole group has nightmares? And they start coming true? And people disappear?"

Leland turned his attention to the terminal, pulled up the outgoing message form, and started typing.

"How long before someone comes to get us?" Sarina asked.

Leland shrugged. "A couple of weeks? How long did it take us to get here?"

Sarina nodded and stepped back. The hyperprotist *stink* flooded into Leland's nostrils. He turned—

"Look out!" he said.

He spun out of the chair, grabbed his club in his right hand while he shoved Sarina aside with his left. The hyperprotist coming through the doorway paused. Its edge rippled the way a jellyfish's fringe moved in water.

Leland brought the spiked end of the club down atop the creature. Pulpy innards sprayed out, coating his boots and the bottoms of the equipment racks.

"Let's finish up and go," Sarina said.

Fitzhugh was walking across the compound when Leland and Sarina drove away from the admin shelter.

"How did he get out?" she said.

Leland shivered at the thought of being trapped in a cage. He said, "Probably good that he did."

They pulled up next to the biologist. He turned, and to Leland he seemed clear-eyed and alert.

"Fitz?" Sarina said through the open window. "Do you remember me?"

"Miss Bruce," he said. He bowed to her, arms wide and one leg swept back. Leland had only seen such a thing in teleplays. "To what do I owe the pleasure?"

"We've got food in the fabrication shop. Would you like to join us?"

He looked off into the distance and patted his stomach. "I could be induced to do so." He pointed. "Guide me, oh thou great behemoth." Then he waved his hands and added, "Not you, young lady. That brute you're with and the leviathan he steers."

Leland started the truck rolling again. "This is going to be fun," he said.

"He can help us put your contraption together."

"Good point."

After a healthy amount of dehydrated fruit, packaged

cheese, and lukewarm tea, Fitzhugh agreed to help carry components to the truck and assemble the system. Soon an antenna dish was in place, with a waveguide and emitter ready to transmit killing power to anything nearby. They put the motors and gimbals through their paces with power off the truck itself, guided by the rudimentary pointing of a camera attached to the antenna that fed back to a screen with a joystick. Leland had a slightly better control system printing—he would have liked to include targeting electronics linked to a suite of sensors, but had not found such designs in the database. A high-capacity power cable was also printing, to hook the entire system to the machine shop itself. Leland thought again about fabricating batteries to make the system portable . . .

"Mr. Strickland," Fitzhugh said after watching some of the power cable extrude, "why do you need a portable satcom terminal?"

Leland thought of stampeding beasts and a dark dream-giant. "Communication."

Fitzhugh laughed. "But the *quanettek* have been communicating."

Sarina looked as puzzled as Leland felt. "The what?" he asked.

Fitzhugh frowned. "No, you wouldn't have caught their names. Not yet, not yet."

"Who?" Sarina asked.

"Oh, this will never do," Fitzhugh said, and walked around the far side of the fabricator.

Leland ran, but before he'd covered two steps the fabricator fell silent. The words *What did you do?* died on his lips as he saw that Fitzhugh had thrown the machine's breaker.

"We'll be *fine*," Fitzhugh said.

The biologist did not resist as Leland and Sarina bound him to a chair. "You just don't understand," he said.

"Don't bother explaining," Leland said, and restarted the fabricator.

"You're not a very good *khamlak*."

"I don't even know what that is."

Fitzhugh laughed. "The *khamlak* worshipped the *quanettek*, like Egyptians worshipped cats. They would do anything for them."

"I don't worship anything," Leland said.

"Don't you?"

Sarina stepped in front of Fitzhugh. "The quanteks, whatever you called them—they're the hyperprotists?"

"Oh, you *are* a smart one."

"And the cam-locks were the builders?"

Fitzhugh closed his eyes in rapture. "And the building will continue."

It took another hour for the power cable to finish, during which time the tracking subsystem failed its test and Leland had to start another one printing. He did manage to drill a hole through the shelter wall for the power connector, so when the cable was ready he hooked it up easily enough.

He leaned against the side of the truck and pointed toward the machine shop. "What do you make of all that?" he asked Sarina.

She frowned. "I think his 'khamlak' and the hyperprotists—'quanettek,' if he's right—were connected. Maybe the hyperprotists were the brains and the kham-laks the brawn?"

"Riding them, like that prote on the cow-thing?"

"Maybe," she said. "Then the brawn died out, and everything fell apart because the hyperprotists aren't strong enough to—Lee, what's that?"

He looked up. She pointed to the space between the next two shelters.

Hulking there, its cloak rippling in a nonexistent breeze, was a giant, roughly man-shaped, square-headed horror. Oily vapor tickled the back of Leland's throat.

He slapped himself. It hurt. *Could it still be a dream?*

"Hit me," Leland said.

"What?"

"Hit me, so I know I'm not dreaming! This thing—"

Sarina punched him. "Good enough?"

"Maybe," he said. "It'll have to be."

He snatched up the controller, thankful that he had connected the ground power. He moved the joystick and the antenna swung.

The giant shambled forward. Its footsteps should have shaken the ground, but they were silent.

Leland sighted in the viewfinder, wishing he'd had time to boresight and test the thing. *Only one way to find out . . .*

He touched the "Transmit CW" icon.

The only feedback was a hum in the electronics, and he trusted that a continuous wave of radiation was pouring out of the emitter.

The shambling giant stopped.

It trembled—no, it *rippled* as if it were made of rags blowing in the wind.

Then it flew apart.

But not an explosion. An escape: The structure collapsed as hundreds of hyperprotists erupted from it. They leapt away, scurried away, and left behind just as many of their hideous brethren flopping on the ground like gasping fish.

And as Leland watched, the fleeing hyperprotists turned back and began reforming into smaller constructs.

He started slewing the antenna toward the closest.

"We have to go," Sarina said.

Leland spared a glance at her, then toward the landing zone, before he centered the next target in the camera view. "I'd thought of that before Billings ran off. Do you know where Voorland is? Are *you* a pilot?"

She shook her head. "No," she said. She sounded tired beyond exhaustion. "We have to go with *them*."

She stepped away, out of his reach, and began walking around the truck.

A loud *bang!* sounded behind him, followed straightaway by another, slightly gentler one. The viewer in Leland's hand went dark. He turned around—

Fitzhugh lay in a heap against the shelter wall, his head at an awkward angle and his left hand on a fire axe. The axe head was blackened—

The power cable looked like a dead snake: cleanly cut in two.

He thought he only stared at the cable for a second, but when Leland turned back, Sarina was gone.

❖❖❖

Leland pressed the heels of his hands into his bleary eyes, then stared into the overhead light. He should program a fabricator to build something, just to have the noise, but he couldn't think of anything.

He was alone. No one answered any comms.

Occasionally he got a whiff of old frying oil, and spun like a dervish looking in every corner, high and low, and behind every machine...but he saw none of the whatever-it-was Fitzhugh had called them. He ended up where he began, huddled against a fabricator with his club across his knees. Shaking. Waiting. Praying.

Dozing...

re: something strange
Jessica Cain

Archeology and forensics aren't all dig sites, ruins, corpses, and artifacts. Sometimes something as small as letters can provide vast windows to entire cultures and events. A single word carved on a palisade being the only thing left of a vanished settlement. Scrolls sealed into jars, hidden in a desert cave for centuries. Final letters written by soldiers before they fell on battlefields from Gettysburg to Gallipoli.

This story that very much lives up to its title is one such window, following an exchange of e-mails and phone calls piecing together what happened between two people, what might have happened to them, and what may yet happen to the rest of us.

something strange
Cassidy R
To Daniel
Oct 21, 2022, 5:04 pm

in your neighborhood . . . who you gonna call . . . DR. DANIEL HART!!

haha jk i know you hate that song

sooooooo hi dan! hope you're doing well. god, how long has it been since we talked? forever?? i called your office but they said you were at a conference in philly right now. hope you're conferencing well!!

lee called and said she'd seen you around and you were looking good. atta boy! stay hot dude. ☐ ☐

also how is kaitlyn? we all should get together sometime when we're both back in boston and do dinner. my treat!!

okay so you might be wondering why i'm writing. well, like the title says there's something strange going on. not going on exactly, but like i found something strange? i think? i'm at the farm just going through papers and things and i went walking this afternoon and i found some kind of wall behind the house, back in the orchard. well it's more like part of a wall. it was hanging out behind this bush and it came up to about my waist. the weird thing is 1. it's not made of stone but some kind of purple metal?? and 2. there's some kind of writing on it that's kind of like egyptian hieroglyphs but not really. it's hard to explain. since you are the anthropology expert and what not i wondered if you could help? i kind of want to know what it is.

thanks a bunch and talk soon! ☐ ☐☐☐

cass

ps- i didn't send a note yet but thank you for the flowers. mom would have appreciated them. i know she liked you a lot.

❖❖❖

re: something strange
Dr. Daniel P. Hart
To Cassidy R
Oct 21, 2022, 5:26 pm
Hi Cassidy,

Nice to hear from you. Yes, I'm currently attending a conference at the Hilton. It's going well.

The piece of wall you found sounds unusual. Send me a picture and I'll tell you what I can.

On the subject of Kaitlyn, she's fine. I'm going to be very frank and say I don't think us having dinner together is a good idea. Not right now, at least.

You're welcome re: the flowers. Your mother was a lovely woman. Again, my condolences.

Lastly, please stop trying to send emojis in your e-mails. For whatever reason they never come through and all I see are boxes.

Daniel

re: something strange
Cassidy R
To Daniel
Oct 21, 2022, 5:41 pm
okay fine. i was just trying to be nice about dinner but that's fine.

i took a few pictures on my phone and i'm attaching them to this e-mail. i got some shots from every side so you can see it all.

let me know what you think

cass

✦✦✦

re: something strange

Dr. Daniel P Hart

To Cassidy R

Oct 21, 2022, 5:45 pm

Hi Cassidy,

I think you need to upload the pictures again. I clicked on the attachments and all I saw was white space. Is something glitchy with your phone?

Daniel

re: something strange

Cassidy R

To Daniel

Oct 21, 2022, 5:47 pm

WTAF??

okay i took the pictures again and looked and they're all white?? then i took a picture of my feet and that one came out okay, so i don't think the problem's my phone. like i don't think i can take a picture of this thing. this is freaky.

can you call me? i'm a little freaked out.

cass

re: something strange

Dr. Daniel P Hart

To Cassidy R

Oct 21, 2022, 5:49 pm

Hi Cassidy,

I'm going to ask this once and only once: are you playing games to get my attention? I don't think we should talk on the phone right now. I don't want you to get overexcited.

Now if you're serious about this and there really is a

wall that cannot be photographed, write me back with a detailed description of it. I'll do what I can.

Daniel

PS- I don't mean to be rude, but could you please try capitalization? It would make the reading process much smoother.

re: something strange
Cassidy R
To Daniel
Oct 21, 2022, 6:22 pm
OKAY I'LL CAPITALIZE EVERYTHING FROM NOW ON

Lol jk jk

Okay I took a tape measurer with me to make sure, so here's what I can tell you. The thing is 2 feet and seven inches tall, I think that's pretty close. I also think it looks kind of like the Washington Monument. You know the pointy building?

So it's a Washington Monument made of purple metal. The purple is like a dark purple, not a bright one. It's more purple bluish. It's weird, because it seems pretty shiny but you can't see your reflection in it. You ever see water with some gasoline in it? You know how it gets that sort of gleaming rainbow color that keeps shifting? That's sort of what this looks like. Like I said, weird.

Okay, now the pictures.

Some of them are things that look like letters but I've never seen them before in my life. Like maybe they look like Chinese, but not really? One of them looks like if someone drew a stick figure camel and then turned it on its side. Another looks like if you took a bunch of chicken footprints and then mashed them all together. Some of them, I am not kidding, I cannot even begin to describe what they look like. Like, there are shapes I've never seen before. I can't even say 'it looks like a rectangle and a triangle had a baby' because that would mean SOMETHING looked like a rectangle or triangle. It doesn't. It looks completely new to me.

I'm freaking out in case you couldn't tell.

The biggest picture is kind of in the center. It looks like some kind of figure. It's got two wings, that much I can tell. They look more like dragonfly than bird wings. I think the figure also has long hair because it has, like, long curly things flying off its head. There's something under its feet that looks like either an upside down J or a candy cane with a weird hook on the end.

When I first looked at it I thought 'this isn't human but it is alive and watching.' Like it was a voice that popped into my head out of nowhere. Fucking. Scary.

I think maybe I'm gonna get in my car and drive back to town for the night. Farm life is weird, yo.

Okay, let me know what you think

Cass

re: something strange
Dr. Daniel P Hart
To Cassidy
Oct 21, 2022, 6:29 pm
Hi Cassidy,
Please take your medication. I know that you've been under a great deal of stress between our break up and

your mother's passing, but going off your medicine cold turkey could cause severe side effects. I am afraid you're going to hurt yourself. Please get in the car, drive to town, refill your prescriptions, and e-mail me when you're with someone. If Lee's home for the weekend, go to her. I can call ahead of time if you'd like to let her know you're on the way. Again, I know what happened between us is painful, but I meant it when I said I'd always care about you. This is an example of me keeping that promise.

Get in the car, get safe, and take care of yourself.

Daniel

re: something strange

Cassidy R

To Daniel

Oct 21, 2022, 6:35 pm

FUCK. YOU. FUCK YOU FUCK YOU FUCK YOU WHY THE FUCK DID I EVEN THINK YOU'D GIVE A SHIT ABOUT ME

you know what no more caps lock for you ever

i got in the car btw and the engine is dead it is completely dead and i'm sobbing rn because now i can't get out of here and it's almost dark and that thing is still in the orchard and you don't give a shit

the car shouldn't have died btw there was nothing wrong with it but now i guess there is and you know it's ten miles before you reach anything so i guess i'm trapped here now

not like you care

i'm gonna go out and hang with my new washington monument friend i gave him a name i'm gonna call him yiyath so yiyath and i are going to have a party and you're not invited. suck it bitch.

□□□□□□□□□□□□□

if you can't see this is a string of shit emojis

[Phone records show that Daniel Hart called Cassidy Randall's cell five times over the next twenty minutes. Ms. Randall did not respond.]

re: something strange
Dr. Daniel P Hart
To Cassidy
Oct 21, 2022, 6:57 pm
Cassidy I want to know you're doing all right.

Also, where have you heard Yiyath before? Why did you call the figure that?

Please call me back as soon as you can.
Daniel

[The following is a phone conversation between Dr. Hart and Ms. Randall begun at 7:09 pm]

Daniel: Cassidy? Hello? [muffled sounds] Hello, Cassidy?

Cassidy: Dan? What the hell, I'm eating dinner.

Daniel: Okay. Well, you sound okay. That's good.

Cassidy: Yeah, like you care.

Daniel: Did you get my e-mail? The one about Yiyath? [more chewing noises] Stop eating!

Cassidy: I did not read your e-mail, O god of anthropologists. I silenced my phone and heated up a pizza. It is just, like, full of pepperoni and other shitty food, which I know you love.

Daniel: I don't want to—[something indistinguishable, might have been "fuck's sake"] Where have you heard the name Yiyath before?

Cassidy: Um. You mean the made up one?

Daniel: It isn't made up. That name belongs to a six-thousand-year-old indigenous cult figure.

Cassidy: Excuse me?

Daniel: Please just think. I must have mentioned it at some point when I was with you, right? But no, that can't be ... It's been six months since we, ah, and the first discovery was three months ago, so—

Cassidy: Dan? Hello? The hell are you saying?

Daniel: Sorry, I'm getting sidetracked. Is it possible those dragonfly wings you saw might have been eyes? Because that would be in keeping with the other descriptions we've received.

Cassidy: Others? There are others of this thing?

Daniel: So far, they've found steles dedicated to this same deity in the British Isles, Mongolia, Iran, and Ethiopia. Last week, we got word they might have made a discovery in western Australia as well. The structures all appear to have been constructed between four and six thousand years ago, at roughly the same time.

Cassidy: Doesn't that seem kind of, y'know, weird?

Daniel: Weird is the exact word for it. So far we haven't been able to determine how all these vastly different cultures separated by such enormous distances could have adopted the same cult deity at the same time, let alone what purpose the steles themselves are meant to serve. We theorize they might be funerary markers, but haven't discovered any human remains nearby. Dr. Yeung left his classes behind to take a sabbatical just to be on hand with the excavations.

Cassidy: Is that a big deal?

Daniel: He's seventy-eight and the department chair.

Cassidy: Wow. You Harvard guys are serious business. Um, I don't remember ever hearing the name Yiyath from you, for what it's worth.

Daniel: How did you think to call it Yiyath, anyway?

Cassidy: I don't know? It just kind of popped into my head? Wait, how do you guys know what its name is? That stuff that's written on it is, like, not English.

Daniel: The word was found carved in a nearby rock at the Scotland and Ethiopia sites. It may be the name, though we can't be absolutely certain. It could be a prayer, or an invocation. You're sure you didn't see it carved anywhere?

Cassidy: I could check again, but I don't think so. Weird. So do the other things, I mean, are the other whatever-they-are purple and metal, too?

Daniel: No. Every other discovery we've made has been stone. I don't know how your mother could have lived on that farm as long as she did and not notice something like that sitting out in the orchard.

Cassidy: I mean, she was kind of out of it the last year. And we didn't go back there a lot of the time. I don't know. Weird, am I right? Freaky.

Daniel: Are you okay?

Cassidy: At least now I kind of know what it is, so I'm better. None of the other Yiyaths have, like, exploded, right?

Daniel: No. I don't think you have to worry about that.

Cassidy: Yeah, I think I just needed to eat something. My blood sugar's kind of down, what with everything. Sorry if I freaked out on you earlier.

Daniel: I'm sorry I didn't believe you. I just had no idea what to think. I didn't make a connection between the steles and what you found. Your description didn't match any of it.

Cassidy: I'm kinda bad at describing shit. I guess that's why I'm an out of work bartender instead of a fancy anthropologist.

Daniel: Well. You can pour a mean drink.

Cassidy: Yeah. It took a couple of stiff ones before I got you to loosen up and talk to me.

[silence]

Daniel: That was a strange time in both our lives.

Cassidy: Yeah. Strange. Sure.

Daniel: Listen, about earlier. I—

Cassidy: Shhh. You hear that?

Daniel: What?

Cassidy: Listen.

Daniel: What?

Cassidy: You really don't hear that?

Daniel: I don't hear anything.

Cassidy: It kind of sounds like "whub whub," you know, like it's a spaceship kind of noise you'd hear on *Star Trek* or something? [whispers] Okay, it stopped. Um. That's kind of freaky.

Daniel: Are you sure I can't call Lee for you?

Cassidy: Ugh, no. I've been bothering her enough lately. So. Yiyath? That's wicked crazy, man. Maybe I'm psychic. Maybe I have a special connection with the thing.

Maybe I'm the only one on Earth who can, like, talk to Yiyath and learn the secrets of the universe and shit.

Daniel: At this point, that would not surprise me.

Cassidy: So. Anyhoo. Kaitlyn, is she still working for the symphony, or—

Daniel: I, sorry, I just, ah, don't think we should talk about Kaitlyn. If that's all right.

Cassidy: Yeah sure, that's fine. I'm just, like, being nice, y'know?

Daniel: Yes, you are. I'd feel more comfortable not discussing her, that's all.

Cassidy: Yeah. Guilty conscience and what not.

Daniel: No. Not guilty. [sighs] So I'll lob a call in to the department tomorrow morning and get someone out to the farm to examine the object. Is that all right?

Cassidy: Sure! Are you gonna come by, too?

Daniel: Probably not.

[silence]

Cassidy: Well, I need to go before you talk my ear off.

Daniel: Ha. Okay.

Cassidy: Bye.

Daniel: Goodbye. Cassidy, let me know if you notice anything else. I'll be gone for a few hours for dinner, but I'll check my e-mail.

Cassidy: 'Kay. Will do.

[call ended]

re: something strange
Cassidy R
To Daniel
Oct 21, 2022, 8:21 pm

hey!

so i got curious and went out with my flashlight. i was heading down to the steely thing (?) or whatever it's called when i noticed some kind of glow off behind the barn in the opposite direction. guess what i found?

if you guessed 'a purple box thing that glows and has all the same weird yiyath writing on it as the steely' then congrats, you win and i am losing my absolute shit, dawg.

i took my tape measurer and it's about the same height as the washington monument back there. the yiyath thing is almost the same, but there's one big difference. you remember i said there was an upside down J with a weird hook on the end beneath its feet? on this one, it's a straight line. i never know how to describe these things but i looked it up and i guess it's a horizontal line, not standing up straight like the other. ALSO, there are hooks on either end. so. WTAFFFFF

i also tried to start my car again. hooked up my battery charger and everything, and it says, get this, that the battery is charged. there's gas in the tank. the car JUST WONT START.

this is going to be a ridiculous story, frfr

cass

re: something strange
Cassidy R
To Daniel
Oct 21, 2022, 9:49 pm
Wish you'd call me back because something else is happening.

I tried taking pictures of the stele and the cube and now there's a third object out behind the fence in the pasture. It's an orb, the same height and size as the other two. All the hieroglyphs and Yiyath inscriptions are the same, but the horizontal hooked line is different yet again. This time, it looks like a proper J. Why does this one image keep changing?

I also had to shut the blinds in the house because the moonlight is growing so bright outside that I can't think straight. That strange, pulsating noise is getting louder, too. I almost cried, but then it stopped and I felt better. What if there's something wrong with me? Did they discover cubes and orbs at the other sites? Why is mine the only site with this odd metallic substance covering the objects?

Please call me when you get the chance.

Cassidy

re: something strange

Cassidy R

To Daniel

Oct 21, 2022, 11:31 pm

I have walked the perimeter of the farm three times now and I have judged that the objects are equidistant. There is not even a centimeter of difference between the journey from the stele to the cube, and from thence to the orb, and from the orb back to the stele. From the proverbial bird's eye, you will find the structures form the points of a perfect equilateral triangle. I have come to realize that the three objects were all carefully chosen, as they are the only examples of Yiyath's geometry of which the human mind can comprehend. This is not the difference between Euclidean and non-Euclidean; this is chthonic geometry, the concept of all angles inverted and deconstructed to something more fluid and entirely more alive. The Sphinx can be said to dream upon the desert sands, but there is no fear she will awaken. But the stele, the stele is alive. It is His intent, the prick of His intent, as the cube is His body as the orb is His mind as the triform temple emerges to glow in the incandescent darkness and to summon Him from His eternal slumber.

Beyond the boundaries of the triform temple the images of His reality ripple and shift like a mirage. The structure of the city is indescribable, the pathways to it unwalkable. They bend in impossible patterns, and when you set your eyes upon them they revert to lines that are so straight that they bleed the vision like a razor. Many go blind as they walk to Yiyath, eventually crawling upon the paths that are not paths, rooted to earth by the inescapable gravity that does not exist. Those that please Him especially give over their laughing faces, so that Yiyath may look mirthfully upon His designs and see that they are good.

The stele has grown, scraping the sky at over six hundred feet. The incantations inscribed upon the expanse of it glow at staggered intervals, each pictograph referencing another aspect of His intent. The translators, Keepers of His Temple, they will be given the job of interpreting the sigils and issuing commands to the slaves, for Yiyath can only speak through his signs. Communication of the tongue and the larynx may be observed only by the lesser forms of life. The Keepers are allowed one face each, a comely one if they perform well in His service. Yiyath will tower above the stele and watch through His many faces as His subjects perform their duties.

The scribes attend Him at the stele, and if the stele is His intent then the cube is His body and it is there that faces are prepared for Him. The surgeons, Makers of His Flesh, are not allowed faces themselves, but are given some covering in return for their service. All slaves must walk the path from the city to the triform temple, there to be shorn as sheep. They will give their faces to Him and their bodily coverings to the surgeons who will partake of His largesse. Inside of the cube, there are twelve windows spaced equally, three to a wall. Although outside the cube it shall be eternal night, within comes the light of the subterranean star that shall rotate from hour to hour about the four walls, heating the pools laid upon the floor. Those chosen in the culling will be bled there, laid end to end within the shallow recesses. It is there that their blood shall fill the pools, as the surgeons' assistants kneel and cut deep into the shorn and slippery bodies. When the chosen are drained and the blood heated by the star, then shall the spent flesh be removed and the blood and baked skin shall feed Yiyath.

Worshippers and slaves will be guided in a counterclockwise procession, issued their directives at His intent, then feeding His body, then finally providing Him His dreams. In the first days among the dead stars, when matter was of the mind, then did Yiyath dream His physical realm into existence, and thence did He make the objects of adoration that would dream of Him in turn. There are no ink and paper libraries in Yiyath's domain, but all that will be stored and remembered shall be placed in His dream palace, the orb. Those with the most agile minds shall be instructed to kneel and gouge out their eyes, the better to provide access to the softest meats of the brain. It is said that the youth are the best dreamers of any species, and so must the children come and kneel before His orb and offer to Him their eyes and their minds that He may dream more, that more pathways and cities may flow from Him like estuaries from a massive river, like arteries from a heart. In that way He shall make more objects of worship and they will feed Him faces and dreams. Only one may enter the orb and that shall be the Archivist and they will install within its circumference the meats and eyes to be preserved for all record and all time. The Archivist shall be given many eyes of their own. They shall have no face or flesh but many eyes and they shall be pleased with this.

Beyond the triform temple lies the city, and within those avenues of false perpendicularity there shall arise the segmented abominations of His architecture. Mortal mind cannot comprehend the jagged tessellations or most rounded peaks of the un-mandala that has no symmetry and no form and no beginning and no end. The towers will be the shape of screams, the city parks modeled after the end of youth. All who have not given of their eyes to the orb will gladly pluck them from their head, so supreme will be the muralistic madness on display. There shall be no need of concert halls, no theaters, no museums, so splendid will be the pictures that choke the air. There will be no need to document the transition from the past to the present because all are aligned and one, past present and future, stele cube and orb, unceasing change and relentless stagnation in one. Entropy, entropy, entropy, He shall change nothing and everything, He is past present future in one, Yiyath will walk amidst the fields of His universe and all harvest shall be His all bounty shall be His all abundance shall be His.

I walk the perimeter and find that the triform temple is aglow now, brighter than the moon that shall one day burn to a cinder and fall from the sky as Yiyath wills it. The temple swells beneath the false moon, the triform luminescence a soft violet that paints the farmland and the orchards beyond. Yiyath must walk amidst His fields soon, He has waited for so long, He has created time and been slave to it so that the harvest may ripen but now it is ripe now it is ready for now the triform temple is unearthed and now the alarm is about to sound. Yiyath, He of the Eternal Faces, is summoned by the orb of His mind and the cube of His body and the stele of His intent. He will come to judge all as equal and enjoy the flesh enjoy the faces enjoy the dreams.

I have walked the perimeter of the temple three times, and now I imagine that I hear the felicitous clash of bells and ululations, the slave chants that shall be offered to the unchanging stars. Soon the alarm shall sound, and I walk these fields in anticipation and kneel before the triform temple, preparing my soul for the Resurrection.

In the first days among the dead stars, when matter was of the mind, there did bold Yiyath order up His mind and His body and His intent and from thence did He create His objects and did He entice worship and did He make the stars sing and the darkness perfect and the glow of His eyes will fall upon every last one of us in our turn. Praise Him! Praise Him! Praise Him!

re: something strange
Cassidy R
To Daniel
Oct 21, 2022, 11:39 pm
ddkkkklafja;fjakdsfjadffdsajfoaiejakfd
dddd
yiyathyiyathyiyathyiyathyiyathyyathyyaathathyyyyyiatha
yyathyiyathyiyathyiyath

[Dr. Hart returned Ms. Randall's call at 11:47 pm. She did not pick up until his third attempt at 12:11 am]

Daniel: Cassidy?

Cassidy: Whuh? Hmmmf, what the fuck?

Daniel: You're awake? Cassidy?

Cassidy: I'm awake now, you asshole. What?

Daniel: What the hell do you mean, what? What the hell were those last e-mails you sent? They scared me to death.

Cassidy: Um, the one about the cube thing?

Daniel: If you're getting cute, I swear to God—

Cassidy: Hold on, hold on, hold on! I'm looking at— Jesus, hold on, okay?

[several minutes of breathing. at some point, crying begins]

Cassidy: What the . . . fuck? Oh my what, what the fuck is that? Who wrote that? What?

Daniel: Listen to me.

Cassidy: No, shut the, shut up! No way, oh my God. Oh my God. Who did that? Who the fuck wrote that?

Daniel: You're telling me you don't remember writing that?

Cassidy: WHAT DO YOU THINK "WHO THE FUCK WROTE THAT" MEANS?

Daniel: Stop yelling!

[Cassidy screams]

Daniel: WHAT HAPPENED?

Cassidy: I STUBBED MY TOE, WHAT THE FUCK DO YOU THINK? I AM FREAKING OUT.

Daniel: Okay, calm down.

Cassidy: I'm getting out of here. I'm going to—oh shit my car doesn't run. Um, screw it, I'm going to just run for it! I'm going to get out of here!

Daniel: Hold on! Cassidy, wait.

Cassidy: What do you mean, wait? Either I wrote some batshit poem in my sleep or someone snuck in here and, like, sent you e-mails on my computer! Neither of those is good!

Daniel: If someone else is really there, you being in the middle of the woods with no car isn't going to help. And if the problem is you, which is much more likely, you're safer in a familiar environment. All right?

Cassidy: Okay. Fine. Fine. So I'm reading the stupid e-mails. Oh God. You guys never found a cube or an orb, did you?

Daniel: No. That's all new information. What about those noises you mentioned? Do you hear anything now?

Cassidy: No, just my heartbeat and you being an asshole on the phone. Sorry. I'm scared.

Daniel: I know. Now think carefully. What's the last thing you remember doing before you fell asleep?

Cassidy: Okay, I, I remember checking out the cube. Uh, I remember writing that e-mail to you, the first one. I think I was watching some videos on YouTube, like some cat ones, and then . . . Oh shit.

[screams]

Daniel: Cassidy? Cassidy!

Cassidy: I hear it, I hear the thing! The noise, the whub, the *Star Trek* noise, I hear it! Can you hear it?

Daniel: Let me listen. Quiet! Cassidy, no. I don't hear anything. Oh my God . . .

Cassidy: I think someone's outside! Someone's trying to get in the house!

Daniel: Hang up and call 911. Did you hear me?

Cassidy: I gotta, I think my grandpa's old gun is in the hall closet, I don't know, I'm gonna get it, I— [unintelligible]

Daniel: Hello? Cass, do not get a gun. Do not get a gun! I'm going to call the police for you. They're going to come see you. Cassidy, are you—?

[call ended]

[Phone records show Dr. Hart called the Moorlock Police Department at 12:16 am. The following is a text sent to Ms. Randall at 12:22 am]

Daniel:

Hi Cassidy,

Please call when you see this. I'm worried about you.

Police are on their way. I didn't want to get into anything specific, so I said that you thought a prowler was on the property and were too scared to call. That's the story when they show up.

Let me know when you're with the police.
Daniel

[Dr. Hart texted Ms. Randall again at 12:47 am]
Daniel:
Hi Cassidy,
Are you all right? Are the police there yet?
Daniel

[Ms. Randall responded at 12:48 am]
Cassidy:
yo! omfg i just saw this
you called the cops?? they never showed!!! i've been
hiding in the broom closet for half an hour
　i just tried calling the cops an theres only dial
tone??!?11

Daniel:
I'm calling the police back. You may get better
reception outside the closet. Has anything else
happened?

Cassidy:
no it's quite
quite
QUIET
ducking autocorrect

Daniel:
Good. Go wait in the living room until the police arrive.

❖❖❖

Cassidy:
ugh thanks dad
still using periods in ur texts huh?

[Records show Dr. Hart called the Moorlock Police Department at 12:49 am. The following is a voicemail left for Ms. Randall at 12:57 am]

Daniel: Cassidy, pick up. Pick up. Fine, I wouldn't be surprised if you were hiding out. Thank you so much for playing this game with me, but I've had enough for one night. So I spoke with the police, and apparently they are very confused. They sent a car to see you over half an hour ago, and not only did they speak with you, they said that you were pleasant and in control. They said that you told them you didn't know a Dr. Hart, and that it sounded like I was playing a trick on them. When I spoke to them again, they were extremely annoyed. I guess they thought I was some idiot college kid pranking them or something. This is, really, this is my fault. I knew I shouldn't get caught up in your stupid games, and I fell for them anyway. That's on me. So, ah, I don't like to get angry, but I don't want to hear from you again. All right? Please take your medication and stay out of my life. If I see you calling again, I'm not going to pick up. Just . . . that's it. Okay? I have had enough. I have spent the last six months dealing with your nervous games and your bitchy, I don't know, I just can't take this anymore. I cannot play your games anymore. Don't call Kaitlyn or me ever again. Yes? Good. Go away. Go to hell. I'm done.

[call ended]

✦✦✦

[Ms. Randall attempted to call Dr. Hart seven times beginning at 1:03 am. Dr. Hart appears to have turned his phone off. Ms. Randall left three voicemails in rapid succession. Two are completely unintelligible. The following are fragments from the third voicemail]

Cassidy: [inarticulate sobbing]

Dan . . . ? Oh God, why don't you . . . ?

[sobbing, what sounds like pulsating static]

—ARE YOU? HUH? WHERE ARE YOU? I DON'T KNOW WHO THE POLICE SAW. IT WASN'T ME. IT WASN'T—

[another wave of static]

. . . someone's on the . . .

[words too fuzzy to make out]

. . . okay? He's here. Outside the house. Oh my God oh my God . . .

[unintelligible]

Help. Help me. He's coming in. The light is everywhere! I can see the blood! It's everywhere! WHY IS IT SO BRIGHT? WHY—

[call ended]

[Twenty minutes after this voicemail, Ms. Randall called and left another. This one was also unintelligible, but there was no static. All that's audible is slow, steady breathing, and what seems to be a pulsating noise in the background.]

re: something strange
Cassidy R
To Daniel

Oct 22, 2022, 2:06 am

Hi Dan,

First, I wanted to say I'm sorry for scaring you earlier. Mom was just here and explained everything to me. I don't know why I got so weird, everything makes sense. Everything's okay now.

Mom sat me down at the table and told me about Yiyath. You guys had it wrong. The sites aren't burial grounds, and they're not really temples. I mean, they sort of are, but they're more than that. They're like alarm clocks, you know? They're supposed to go off one by one and wake up Yiyath.

See Yiyath is the God of Eternal Faces, and He came through to our world thousands of years ago and saw that we weren't ready for harvest yet. So He set up all these different alarms all over the world that were set to wake Him up when our planet was ready. Guess what? We are! We're going to see Him soon, and everything's okay now.

Mom says that before the Resurrection can begin, every alarm needs to go off. In order to do that, there needs to be a sacrifice at each site. The glowing purple metal means that the alarm is waking up, and needs the sacrifice to activate. That's when the cube and the orb show up as well. As soon as the sacrifice is made, the alarm will go off and the next one will start to wake up. When they've all gone off, Yiyath will awaken and He will come to harvest and walk amidst His fields and everything's okay now.

Mom was so nice about it that I started crying like a baby. Dumb, right? Anyway, I wanted to let you know that everything's okay now and you don't have to worry about me. The light is beautiful, and the triform temple is growing. Soon the sacrifice will be made, and I've been chosen! Isn't that so cool? No one ever chooses me for anything. No one ever did. You didn't, my dad didn't, my mom only did because nobody else would, but Yiyath chose me. So many people out there and He chose me. It made me cry when she told me that.

I feel really good for the first time in my life, so I wanted to let you know that everything's okay now and you shouldn't worry. Get ready for the harvest! He will walk amidst His fields and all will lift their faces to Him and all will give over their faces and He will be pleased.

Everything's okay now!

Love,

Cassidy

[Dr. Hart called Ms. Randall at 3:57 am]

Daniel: Cassidy?

Cassidy: Hi, Daniel. How are you?

Daniel: I'm good. I'm good. Is your mother still there?

Cassidy: Oh no, she couldn't stay. I'm sure she'll be back later. Do you have a message you'd like me to give?

[no response for a moment. Dr. Hart cries.]

Daniel: Um. I called Lee. She wanted me to say hello.

Cassidy: That's so sweet! Thank you.

Daniel: Yeah. Yes. She's getting the first flight she can. She should be home by tomorrow afternoon at the latest.

Cassidy: Oh, she didn't need to do that. I'm fine. Yiyath's keeping me company.

Daniel: Is he? Oh God, um, can I talk to him?

Cassidy: No, he's walking outside right now and I don't

think he wants to talk to anyone else. He's been really fun, though. He's shown me all his different faces. He has so many of them. Sometimes he's me, and sometimes he's Mom, and sometimes he's Lee and sometimes he's you. It's not totally him yet, of course. He's still waking up. But part of him's already awake, and he's taking me through everything. He's so nice.

Daniel: You sound okay. You . . . [sobs] Sorry, you sound calm.

Cassidy: I feel so good right now. Yiyath told me all about the sacrifice I need to make, and I'm ready.

Daniel: No! Cassidy, please don't hurt yourself. I want you to, shit, please just go sit down and wait while I call 911. Okay?

Cassidy: Why would you do a thing like that? Why do you sound so upset?

Daniel: I, uh, fuck, I want the ambulance to come and . . . and . . .

Cassidy: I don't need an ambulance, Daniel. You sound upset. I feel like you're not happy that Yiyath and I are hanging out together.

Daniel: That's not it.

Cassidy: I think it's really unfair that you could go off and dump me for someone else and then when I find someone I like being with you act possessive. It's not even like that with Yiyath. This makes me not want to talk to you anymore.

Daniel: Okay. Okay. Sorry. I won't call 911. Okay?

Cassidy: Good.

Daniel: Listen, I . . . Cassidy, I'm sorry. Okay? [crying] I'm sorry about your mother, and I'm sorry you're alone right now. I'm sorry I didn't tell you about Kaitlyn sooner. I, I'm sorry that I made you feel stupid and annoying. You were right, I was the one who asked you out in the first place. I know, I know we're not good together but it was something that I really needed at the time. I think you needed it, too. We never made sense but you helped me, and I'll always be grateful. We're friends, right? We can be friends. I'm here for you, and I don't want you to hurt yourself. Okay?

[Lengthy pause]

Cassidy: Thank you for saying that. I appreciate it.

[call ended]

[Dr. Hart contacted the Moorlock Police Department at 4:10 am, then the local hospital, Ms. Randall's psychiatrist, Lee Williams, and Kaitlyn Donovan.

Dr. Hart then called Ms. Randall again. When the call was picked up, she did not speak. A metallic grating noise was heard. It continued for forty-seven seconds while Dr. Hart cried before he hung up.]

[EDITED TO ADD: Our lab has tried to analyze the voicemail. Every agent who has listened to it for a sustained length of time has required medical leave for nervous hysteria.]

re: something strange
Dr. Daniel P Hart
To Cassidy
Oct 22, 2022, 5:57 am

I called the police back. They say that they checked the property again and found nobody there. I managed to speak with your doctor, and he's adamant you shouldn't be alone right now. Lee is on her way back to town. I'm getting in the car right now and I'm driving to you. Google says I should be there in just under four and a half hours. I should be pulling up by ten thirty.

I hope you're all right. I'm not going to abandon you again. Whatever's happening to you, we'll get through it. You're not alone. I'm sorry if you ever felt alone. God, I'm sorry about everything.

I'll see you soon.

Daniel

[This is the final communication. No one has heard from either Dr. Hart or Ms. Randall since this e-mail was sent.]

[EDITED TO ADD: We have received information from the Moorlock Police, which we are adding to this file.

Ms. Lee Williams arrived at the farmhouse that afternoon at 12:42 pm. She immediately called the police.

Dr. Hart's Toyota was found parked beside Ms. Randall's car. Both the vehicle's front doors were open. The keys were still in the ignition. Dr. Hart's phone was lying in the mud outside. We're unsure if he was trying to call someone, or if he was attempting to take a photo. We will likely never know, as the phone is dead and nothing can be retrieved from it.

Dr. Hart's car was unable to start, though the battery was charged and the tank still half full.

The only footprints we discovered belonged to Ms.

Williams. Neither Dr. Hart nor Ms. Randall left any prints outside, despite the recent rain. In addition, no fingerprints were discovered anywhere. Though Ms. Randall had been living in the house for over a week, the entire area was clean. It was as if no one had ever been inside the house.

A thorough inspection was made of the grounds. There is no sign of any stele, cube, or orb. There is no indication any such objects ever existed.

Though there was no evidence of physical wrongdoing at the farm, police and our agents were disturbed by one additional finding. All fifty-seven trees in the orchard are dead. No one is certain how or why this occurred.

This concludes our file on the Randall/Hart disappearance, though our investigation into the origins of the Yiyath cult is ongoing.

Caspar Nilsson

Director of Operations

International Institute for the Study of Preternatural Ethnohistory (IISPE)

cnilsson@IISPE.org]

[EDITED TO ADD: We have received word from colleagues in New Zealand. Apparently a small monument has been discovered twenty miles from a Norwegian scientific outpost in the Antarctic. It has been described as a purple obelisk covered in strange pictographs. Report to follow.]

THE SLEEPERS OF TARTARUS
David J. West

One of the things that comes with putting together an anthology is there are so many things that can happen dealing with so many authors, be it existing commitments preventing their participation, or personal issues meaning they need to back out. Writers are human, and life can happen.

This story was originally written with a spot in Baen's Sword & Planet anthology in mind, and things just didn't manage to come together in time. So, when David J. West said that, with some retooling, it would fit in perfectly in this anthology, we were excited to see it.

Then I saw that this was a riff on The Man Who Would Be King that opens with a quote from Robert E. Howard, and I knew that this story ended up right where it belonged all along.

The gods of yesterday are the devils of today.
—Robert E. Howard

They said it was a suicide mission, but that didn't matter to Cormac, he had nothing to live for beyond the dream that in serving his country his legacy would last as long as mankind had a tongue for it. He would be the first man to go beyond the moon and reach an outer body, even one as small and nearly unknown as Cruithne.

The rumors of a foreign power backed by the billionaire tech giants building their own military space force prompted the hawks who held the keys to the black budget to triple their work at a secret new arms race. For a man with nothing left to lose, Cormac could not have been happier to be a part of it. The other choices had been retirement and sitting in front of the TV alone watching the cancer eat him alive, or the somewhat intriguing flight security detail for that peculiar dig in Antarctica codenamed Sleepers of Tartarus.

Little choice for an operator with an ego as big as Cormac's.

When some egghead detected that the nearly forgotten Cruithne was giving off particularly high electromagnetic readings, a whole henhouse of eggheads started clucking furiously at the implications, and of course the hawks wanted control of whatever this might entail. Every possible advantage had to be taken, by any means necessary.

A special orbiter shuttle was outfitted with extra boosters and rations, everything a man might need for a one-way trip; there was no way to give him enough for a return. Once he landed on the three-mile-wide asteroid, he would let the sensors do their work and secure an automatic drone weapon installation to hold down the fort—before he ran out of both food and air.

It was a sacrifice he was more than willing to make. Since his wife and son had been taken by a drunk driver, there was nothing left on Earth for him.

He laughed. He had been diagnosed with bone cancer soon after their deaths and would have been cut out of any program no matter how black, except that this one was a suicide mission.

Blessings come with the curse.

He spun the Masonic ring on his finger. It was looser than it used to be. He'd spent the last many weeks alone in space, and he had reread all the books he brought several times over. He liked to reread his favorites, classics like *The Iliad*, *The Lord of the Rings*, *The Sun Also Rises*, and Potocki's *The Manuscript Found in Saragossa*, but also newer works like *Night Winds*, *The Haunted Mesa*, and *Red Nails*. They all spoke of loss in their own way, and he wondered if that was why he gravitated toward them.

A klaxon flared to life, alerting him of a looming target. Glancing out into the deep black, he caught sight of a shape blocking out the stars.

"This has got to be it." He had been talking to himself a lot more than he ever dreamed of before. "Cruithne dead ahead."

He smirked over the words "dead ahead."

Any signal of his landing would take hours to get back to Earth, so he no longer thought of communication with them as anything in real time. It was more like e-mail. Waiting for a one-sided response. They sent daily updates, but he no longer cared. He would do the job then go out with style. Once his oxygen was down to the last few hours, he would get as drunk as he ever had. He'd brought two cases of scotch, and he still had one left. It was gonna be a helluva one-man party.

The klaxon blared a warning once again, just as the shuttle began to shake violently. "What the hell?"

Glancing at the instrument panel, he wondered if interstellar sand or some other debris was causing the jarring movement, but scanners detected only the same orbiting body.

He rechecked a variety of systems and concluded that a powerful magnetic field emanating from Cruithne itself was causing the wild movements.

Electrical systems shut down randomly like Christmas bulbs burning out, first one, then another. Lastly, even the alarms, thrusters, and lights went out, leaving him in the grip of absolute darkness.

"Unbelievable," he growled. "Better start drinking now."

The shuttle drifted toward Cruithne, but he was without any steering capability or means of slowing his approach. In fact, if he didn't know better, he would think his speed was increasing toward the small, black rock.

"Damn it to hell! Looks like I won't even have time to get shit-faced before I'm smeared all over that thing."

The shuttle continued to rattle like it was threatening to fly apart, so he strapped himself in, but not before grabbing a bottle of scotch. He opened the bottle and took a long, deep pull.

"Hope them eggheads can see me hit paydirt. I've got enough oxygen left, there ought to be some kind of fireball, if only for a second."

Cruithne loomed closer, and Cormac kept his eyes

open even as his body tensed for impact. The tilting ridgeline of Cruithne disappeared from the cockpit's view, and he guessed he wouldn't see it coming. The shuttle sped up, and he wrinkled his forehead. He should have touched down already. He looked out the cockpit window then down at the instruments. "What the hell?" He was circling the tiny asteroid in a bizarre, rotating ellipse.

"Looks like I'll lose my lunch before we hit." He frowned.

The shuttle circumnavigated Cruithne a half dozen times before Cormac completely lost track and was forced to close his eyes as bile rose in his throat.

Each rotation got him closer to the iron surface, and soon the shuttle would slam into the pockmarked ground, rending the shuttle apart like a cheese grater. He'd probably be unconscious by the time that happened.

Straining against the brutal shaking, he manually flipped the switches for life support, thrusters, lights, anything. All to no avail.

Out the window brief images of black and stars, then swirling gray hills, then black once more flashed in his vision. It was a vortex of nightmares he had to face one last time.

He toggled the switch on the thrusters one more time, and they blasted with what now seemed a deafening roar. His speed increased as he continued to circle the rock, and still he did not strike it but lost all consciousness to the blurring of black and gray and orange.

Cormac awoke with the blackness of space still spinning above. Stars zoomed by, but at least the nausea had abated, and the shuttle no longer shook. He took a long pull on his scotch then unstrapped himself, bracing for what he might see.

The shuttle rested on the surface of Cruithne as the asteroid hurtled through the heavens. He gauged that somehow he had come to rest on the surface, but perhaps the shock of impact had knocked the organic satellite on an altered course. The small shuttle shouldn't have been able to do that, but what was the scientific conundrum that bumblebees shouldn't be able to fly either?

Color broke the perpetual black—blue, white—and flashed before his eyes. The asteroid, with him riding shotgun, was tumbling above the Earth!

He slapped himself in the face and rubbed at his eyes. He had to be dreaming. How could he have returned so suddenly? The rotation was slowing, and yet, there he was, parked about five hundred miles above the Earth. His heart rate sped up, pounding in his chest. Would the small moon now be a threat to Earth? The asteroid stopped spinning. Stopped advancing.

"Am I in hell? Who's driving this thing?"

He spent several minutes trying to reach Houston, but to no avail. In fact, he couldn't get *anything* on the comm—no surplus signals from the myriad channels and receptors he knew very well were pointed out into the night to bounce across a belt of satellites. No static from dying stations. Nothing.

"My radio must be broken." He shook his head. It was the only logical explanation.

The slight course of Cruithne as it orbited Earth and a glance at his fuel gauge helped him to make his decision.

He pursed his lips as he released the automated drone system onto the asteroid, regardless of its new proximity to Earth. Since there was enough fuel and oxygen left in his shuttle he decided to go home to be debriefed about his peculiarly swift return.

Firing up the shuttle rockets, he was relieved to see that all systems were nominal, and he easily escaped the weak gravity of the invading moon.

Cormac gasped and his eyes widened as he rocketed toward home. He spun about in the seat, eyes darting around in every direction. His hands gripped the armrests, fingers going numb in shock as he stared at the scene above his home world.

A trio of spheres hung in the heavens, watching like God's own eye. Great Saturn and her rings, then the white iris of Venus, with the deep red of Mars as the unblinking pupil. They loomed impossibly close, with Mars itself larger than a full moon. Venus hovered farther back yet higher and closer than it ever should be, and Saturn took up a greater portion yet.

"I'll be dipped," he mumbled.

A blazing column of plasma seemed to emanate from the trio in the sky and touch down somewhere in the north as if planting a golden axis upon the earth.

Already stupefied by all the impossible images before him, he nearly convulsed as a dark speck at his three o'clock fired up its thrusters and moved toward him with blinding speed—on a direct collision course with his shuttle.

"Nothing on Earth is that fast," he said, shaking his head as he remembered that his own arrival had been beyond the ability of even the blackest of DARPA projects.

Working on pure instinct, Cormac made a slight change of course just as a blaze of glowing hornets flashed past his left side.

"Son of a bitch is shooting at me!"

The orbiter was not made for dogfights, and he didn't even have any weapons on board any longer, but he did his damnedest to escape and evade, though the attacking ship pursued him doggedly.

He caught a glimpse as he banked hard to the right once more. Astounded, he recognized the craft as a secret officially known to exist to but a few airmen and astronauts. The ship was nicknamed the Black Knight Satellite and had been seen for decades as it made a curious polar orbit of the Earth. Some of the more esoteric-leaning eggheads claimed it had to be thousands of years old, not that any of that guesswork mattered now.

No one had ever seen it move like this before, and the way it was firing at him, Cormac didn't think he'd get the chance to tell anyone about it either.

Glowing sparks lanced over the nose of his shuttle. His first thought was that he had been hit, but his sharp re-entry as he evaded the Black Knight had caused his ship to burn.

The Black Knight Satellite slowed down; it seemed that it wasn't about to put itself through the same amount of atmospheric damage as Cormac forced the orbiter through.

Molten gold volleys from the Black Knight arced over the shuttle as Cormac jerked the stick, forcing the shuttle down hard.

The nose burned red and the klaxons blared as he brought the spacecraft down faster than any speed previously attempted. He had wanted to die in the dark cold of space, just relax and fall asleep with a drink in his hand and music in his ears, but someone shooting bright fire at him brought the fight or flight raging back.

Cormac racked his brain for something he could do offensively to the Black Knight, but he didn't have anything more in the cargo hold. Or did he? He did have a .45 semiautomatic and his trusted Bowie knife, but they were no good for this fight.

Blasts rocked the left side of the shuttle as whatever the Black Knight was firing shredded the titanium delta wing.

New warnings blared as an air pressure leak added to the vibrant chaos.

Semi-recognizable land below the clouds revealed itself to Cormac. The Sinai peninsula wasn't an ideal landing spot, but it was the best he could do.

The glow of the burning entry had dimmed, but the orbiter handled badly with the shot-up delta wing, and the Black Knight Satellite had not given up. Another volley bit across the rear, and Cormac worried it was going to break up at ten thousand feet.

Remembering a handful of survival items near the rear of the cabin, Cormac leapt up and threw back the locker door. There was a parachute. Only one, as he had been the only occupant. He strapped the chute to his back as he made his way to the rear door, praying the aircraft would hold together long enough for him to get out. On a hunch he grabbed the small keypad that could remotely control the weapons drone on Cruithne. He should have used it when the Black Knight first attacked him, but it was far too late now.

He heard another volley from the Black Knight, and winds blasted his face as the cargo doors were ripped off their hinges.

Choice vanished. Exit was now the only option. With the door torn off, Cormac was flung into the great blue yonder. His vision faded around the edges and his eyelids became heavy, hard to keep open. He lifted a weak hand, unsure if he had the strength left to pull on the ripcord, but somehow, he did it.

The ominous black ship loomed behind the falling wreckage of the orbiter. If they chose to fire on him, there was nothing he could do. He spun toward the Earth and the chute jerked him hard when it caught enough atmosphere to fill. He lost his grip on the keypad, and it fell away as darkness took him.

His vision was nothing but a blur when he awoke. A fine blanket of dust covered him, and something tugged at his legs. He kicked, and a woman cried out in pain.

Brushing the clinging dust from his face, he struggled to see who he had attacked. "I'm sorry," he said. "I didn't know what was pulling on my feet. Thought maybe it was a dog."

"You think I am a dog?"

"No, uh . . . sorry, ma'am." He sat up and struggled to stand. He felt her fingers on the bare skin of his arm as she helped him gain his balance. His flight suit was torn to shreds.

"I thought you were dead. I saw the black smoke and believed they had made an example of someone."

"They?"

She waved her hand heavenward. "The titans. The Anunnaki."

He shook dust from his ears, convinced he could not have heard her right. "What did you say? Who?"

Beautiful wide green eyes stared at him, and curling auburn hair fell from beneath her open head scarf. Her clothing, or lack thereof, made his own eyes widen. She appeared to be on her way to a belly dancing festival, as she wore little more than a sheer skirt with a sash covered in tiny bells and a top that strained about her bosom, also with silver bells and tassels.

She narrowed her eyes at him, folding her arms across her chest as if to hide it from his roaming eyes. "I do not know your face. Where are you from?"

"Culver City," he said with a grin. "You heading to some kind of a party?"

"Cul-Ver?" she repeated with visible confusion. "I've never heard of such a place. Who lands there?"

"I do. Where are we right now?"

"We are near the landing place of Akkad."

"What?"

"Near the kingdom of Shinar. I have not heard of your country, Cul-Ver."

He laughed but stopped when she frowned. "Sorry, you speak pretty good English, I thought I was going down near Egypt. Judging by your outfit and accent, this must be Israel though."

She cocked her head at his words. "And I was going to

say you speak good Nessian, but I already suspect that the magic of the gods is what affects our tongues."

"That makes as much sense as anything."

"The places you named; I do not know them. But I have also never been beyond the borders of our servitude."

Now that his vision had cleared, he took in the grim surroundings. There was a scattering of mud-brown homes that matched the desert floor. Farther on were taller buildings but of an equally drab brown shade; a tall ziggurat towered over those. He turned in the opposite direction and a mile or more away, the remains of the orbiter were wreathed in flames. Black smoke belched into the air.

"Lot more fuel left than I would have guessed," he lamented.

She pointed to the sky. "Do the Anunnaki allow mere men to pilot their ships?"

"Mere men? Did you say Anunnaki?" He blinked to get the rest of the dust from his face.

"Yes, they are our masters. Did you steal the ship? I will not betray you, but they will come soon, we best go inside."

She was as beautiful as any woman he had ever seen, but this was all so insane. Maybe she was crazy.

She pled with him. "Come with me, we must hide you from them."

"I'd like to believe that. What's your name? I'm Cormac."

"I am Tanay. I am part of the pleasure cult to occupy the miners."

His brow furrowed. He wondered if he had landed

near a place of slave labor and human trafficking. Maybe she wasn't crazy, just naïve.

Tanay scowled, somehow reading his thoughts on his face. "I am a dancer, not a whore. But if I do not serve, my people will be made an example of. This servitude is my lot."

He bristled at her fatalistic demeanor. "I'm not judging you, just this place. What did you say it's called?"

"Shinar."

"And it is ruled by the Anunnaki? Like the Sumerian gods?"

"I do not know that name, but they act like gods. They are giants, endowed with power from beyond. You must know this. They control all." She pointed at the sky.

Cormac had to admit that the very cosmic nature of the planets hanging above the Earth in barbell fashion was a strong sign that what Tanay said was true. "I must be the crazy one."

"What did you think? I am crazy? Come or stay, but they will be here soon, hurry."

He rubbed at his jaw. "Giants? From another planet?"

"They come from Nibiru," she said.

Cormac felt for bumps on his head, though this made as much sense as anything, considering what he had already been through. Cruithne carried him back to Earth across space and time, perhaps thousands of years into the past.

She shook her head, worry troubling the corners of her mouth. "I have not meant to speak ill of our lords. But you are not like any man I have ever known. You fell from the stars. And yet lived? Come, quickly." She tugged at him and they hurried toward the mud-brick buildings a few hundred yards away.

Cormac looked skyward, wondering how he might explain to her when there was no other concept she could be familiar with. "I suppose so."

"Only the Anunnaki have the means of flight, but you do not look like one of them, you look like a man," she continued and tentatively touched his bare shoulder.

"Of course I do, why wouldn't I?"

She stared into his eyes and shook her head disbelievingly. "If you are from the stars, why do you not appear as the Anunnaki? Are there others like you up there, where you come from?"

"Maybe."

"Is that a riddle?"

"No." He glanced all across the plain, looking for any sign beyond his ruined orbiter. The enemy ship was nowhere to be seen. In the distance, a flash of light from the city with towers and square buildings waving in the desert heat caught his eye, but he did not see any movement.

"Bring all of your things, we must leave nothing or they will know you are here."

"My chute? My orbiter is enough for them to know someone was here."

She nodded. "Perhaps they will think you died in it."

"Good point."

"How did you find yourself out here to come across me?" he asked as he attempted to roll the lines of the chute up in a bundle. Thankfully he was not fighting any wind.

"I was hunting for star flowers in the sands when I saw your red ship coming down. The dark defender, she made sure you crashed, then returned to the far places in the sky."

He grimly nodded. "I don't suppose you know anyone with another ship, do you? Something to get me back . . . home?" He finished rolling up the chute and carried it under his arm as he followed her toward the village.

She shook her head. "Our kind are never allowed such things."

"Our kind?"

"The Adamu." She paused as they reached the shade of buildings and felt his forehead. "You don't have a fever."

He pulled her hand away. "What's the difference between us and them?"

Her eyes widened, and she looked toward the heavens. "They are giants, tall as cedars. Their skin is like bronze, and they pilot ships that go to the stars. Our kind have no such things. We are their slaves. Are you one of us or one of them? No one speaks like you with such abandon for our ways."

Cormac looked about the barren landscape. "That's a loaded question. I'm no one's slave, but I'm no master either. Why don't you fight back? Revolt?"

Now it was her turn to look at him as if he were the crazed one. "They would destroy us in an instant. We have no weapons, no ships that can fly, no men of metal that fire lightning. We know naught else but to serve. There is no other choice if we are to live."

"Well, that's gonna change if I have anything to say

about it," he said, unsure of how he might accomplish his boast, but there was no backing down now.

"Do you serve Enki? He is the most sympathetic of the Anunnaki."

"Never met him."

"We had best go inside before a scouting party comes to see the ruins of your ship," she urged again.

"You didn't happen to see a keypad, did you? Small box, this big?" He gestured the size with his hands.

She shook her head.

"I was hoping, since you found me . . ."

She shook her head once more.

Movement on the horizon caught his eye. An aircraft sped toward them.

Tanay saw it too and darted off in the opposite direction.

"Hey, wait a second, who is that?" he asked as he attempted to unencumber himself of the chute and damaged flight suit.

Tanay continued her flight as the approaching ship grew. It was not the Black Knight Satellite returning, as Cormac first suspected, but its own terrible surprise.

It looked like a flat patrol boat with an open-air canopy, yet it had boosters along the bottom allowing it to have incredible speed, and a hovering power lifting it at almost thirty feet in the air. A troop of men were aboard. Cormac shuddered in horror as he realized they were not mere men but giants, at least twelve feet tall, wearing a bizarre mismatch of archaic-looking armor and spectacular tech—such as a robotic arm where one had apparently lost a limb.

The craft landed with a great blasting of dust over the top of Cormac, and the giants disembarked.

"This one must be an escaped slave," said one to another.

"I'm no slave," Cormac shouted.

"He barks like a dog!" said the one with the cybernetic arm.

"I'm an Airman of the United States Air Force and must be treated as stated in the Geneva Convention."

"Convention?" repeated one.

"Air-Man?" asked yet another.

"We shall see." This one came at him, confident in his much greater size. He lunged for Cormac with his massive arms outstretched.

Cormac knew the giant could squeeze the life out of him in a heartbeat, but he wasn't about to let that happen.

Cormac was only half-out of his flight suit and chute, and instead of looking at those as encumbrances, he used them. As the giant stooped to grab him, Cormac bolted right and wrapped his chute cords across the neck of the giant, racing around to cinch them tight, pulling with all his strength.

The giant grasped at the cords about his throat and dropped to his knees.

Another of the giants caught sight of Cormac's Masonic ring. "He bears the sign of the heavens upon a ring."

"Who gave you that?"

"You wouldn't know him," Cormac growled.

The other giants moved toward him, ready to attack, but Cormac challenged them. "I'm not your enemy, but I am not a slave to be ordered about." He released his grip on the chute so the strangled giant could free himself.

"Who are you!" one demanded.

"Major Cormac 'Jack-Hammer' Ross, U.S. Air Force."

The lead giant took on a different defensive posture. "Who is your master? Did he give you the ring?"

"Master? I ain't got no master," Cormac growled. He moved his hand subtly toward his .45. "Name is Cormac."

"Who do you serve, Corn-Mat? Who is your lord?" rumbled the giant, as his hand went to his gargantuan club. "Where did you get the sign?"

"It's Cor-Mac!"

"Me," answered a woman's voice. "He will surely serve me and my pleasure." She had a powerful, brassy voice.

As she exited the parked airship, Cormac noted that she was not only a giantess but stunning. She wore an ornate gown and had long golden braids framing her face, but there was something imperious and cold in her demeanor. The giant who had been ready to flatten Cormac with his club quickly cowed and moved back in deference to the queenly giantess, as did the others. The one who had been strangled glowered at Cormac but also moved away, hanging his head like a whipped dog.

Cormac stood atop a stone that granted him another foot of height, and the giantess still looked down at him despite being noticeably shorter than her male counterparts. No, counterpart was not right, they were her inferiors.

She eyed Cormac with icy interest. "Where are you from?"

"California," he answered uncomfortably.

"Where?" She cocked her head slightly, then a bemused smirk crawled across her ruby lips. "I have never heard of such a place."

"It's on the opposite side of the world from here," Cormac said.

The giantess nodded. "You have said you are not an enemy, and yet you laid hands upon one of my men. It is forbidden for any of the Adamu to strike one of the Anunnaki. Yet you bear the sign of the heavens upon your ring. Whom do you serve?"

"No one you would know."

"I know everyone worth knowing. Enlil? Enki? Marduk?"

"No. I just wanted it known that I am not to be manhandled by them. I'm no slave."

"You came in that ship that the Defender destroyed. That means you were not authorized to be here. Are you a member of Enki's rebellion?"

"No."

"But you have a star ship. Where did you steal it?"

"I did not steal it. I am an airman for the United States. That wreck was my orbiter. I was shot down by a big black ship."

She scrutinized him for a moment then glanced back at one of her men who answered her unasked question. "There have been strange fields at play. The moon of Nergal has returned from its annual exodus."

"That might explain things," she said. "Very well, as you have said, you are not our enemy. Know that I am the mistress of this backwater colony, and I have uses for you. What do they call you, outlander?"

"My name is Cormac," he gruffly answered.

"And I am Innara, director of the Kingdom of Shinar. Accompany me on my flotilla and let us retire back to the

city for more of this discussion, out of the heat of the day."
She beckoned to the airship, and Cormac, deciding he had
no real choice, took off the remains of his chute and
ruined flight suit then strode to the craft and stood upon
the bow near the pilot. The giantess and her guardsmen
followed. Then they were airborne and whisking away
toward a city on the plain replete with ziggurats and a
myriad of smaller rectangular buildings nestled between
groves of palm trees.

At least Tanay had escaped and would not be
implicated as a part of his landing.

Cormac watched the pilot as best he could, trying to
understand how the airship worked. It seemed very basic,
though the controls were made for a much taller person
than himself.

They landed near one of the larger ornate buildings.
Huge mechanical doors opened, and cool air rushed
out.

"Before we enter, I wish to know that we are on
friendly terms. Please give me your weapon," said Innara.

He thought she meant his pistol until he realized she
was pointing at his knife. He reluctantly handed her the
knife, but no one made a sign that they even knew what
his pistol was, so it remained with him.

They entered the finely furnished room, and Innara
handed Cormac a beaker of wine, which he greedily
gulped down.

"You enjoy that?" she asked. "I have more, and food
that would rival the nectar of the gods."

He momentarily lamented losing his remaining scotch
in the crash and was grateful for this heady liquor. He

thought for a brief moment that this place might not be so bad.

Innara said, "Gursum, take him and put him into the slave analyzer. I wish to see what he has been encoded with."

Gursum moved with incredible speed for a giant and took hold of Cormac's jacket and lifted him as if he were but a kitten being hauled about by the nape of his neck.

Cormac strained against Gursum's grasp, but he could do little other than squirm. He decided to keep his gun secret for the moment; if these giants did not know what it was, he ought to be standing on his own two feet before firing.

Gursum carried Cormac into a nearby building that looked aged on the outside but was spotless inside, with smooth ivory walls and glass chambers like small sunrooms, but why sunrooms indoors? Cormac couldn't imagine.

Gursum dropped Cormac and shoved him into one of the small glass-enclosed rooms.

"Queerest jail cell I ever saw," spat Cormac.

"Silence!" the giantess ordered. "We will now have a look at you."

A bar of orange light moved up and down along one of the walls, and Cormac felt its intense gaze, though there was strangely no heat.

Gursum glanced at the giantess and spoke excitedly, "He does not have the adjustments. I thought he was a feisty one! This would explain his candid demeanor. I might have guessed he was one of the wild men, but he wears too many clothes for that."

"So, he is not a spy for Enki?" Innara asked.

Gursum scanned the readout. "I can't see how he would be. He has none of the hormonal weaknesses we give the Adamu. Could he be an unserved agent of Enlil? Maybe a wildman that discovered a cache of our relic ships?"

Innara examined the screens, reading all about Cormac's vitals. "He flew a starship. He is not one of the wild men. Look at that, he has aggravated stage three bone cancer."

"Is he even worth the trouble?"

"I can take care of that," she said. "No point in having a useful slave who will die next week."

The bar of light changed to a neon green and moved rapidly up and down in the cell, painting Cormac with its strange glow. As much as he disliked how they spoke about him, he had to admit that something about the light actually made him feel better, as if their super-science was curing him of his personal cross to bear.

"Despite the cancer, he seems beyond the ken of most of the Adamu," said Gursum. "Where could he have come from?"

The giantess moved closer to the glass and peered down at Cormac like she was eyeing a meal. "He must be from far outside the containment area, or even from across the void. Maybe there is a half-truth in what he said."

"There were some anomalies in the field. Gates might have opened," Gursum offered.

"Keep men on constant watch for any more trespassers," she ordered. "I want no issues during the conjunction. I *will* ascend."

"Yes, director," the giant said with a bow. "And this one?"

"I will deal with him and discover what he knows and how he might benefit my plans against Enlil." She was beautiful, but her crimson lips looked far more predatory than Cormac liked.

He considered drawing his pistol and destroying the glass prison when she abruptly opened the door. It slid sideways with a hush that caused Cormac to wheel about in surprise. He had missed that trick when Gursum had tossed him inside.

She smiled again. "You are a feisty one. What really brought you here? Speak the truth."

Cormac wondered at what to say, but what was there beyond the truth? "I told you and your men already. If you won't believe me, I can't change that. I am from Earth, but it wasn't anything like this when I left. I don't even know for sure how long I have been gone. How many years have passed for it to be like this. Nothing makes sense."

"Very well, come with me." She strode away with the sure expectation that he would follow. She was a woman used to having her way in nearly every facet of life.

Cormac followed. What the hell else was he gonna do? "Can I ask you something?"

"What is it?"

"Is this your home?"

She tipped her head back and laughed. "No. This has been my punishment. But soon it will just be a bad memory. That's why I want you to do something for me. When the time comes, you will deliver a message for me.

Your ring shows you are trusted among the order of the heavens. That which has been barred to me for too long."

Cormac grimaced. No good would come of having anything to do with this giantess.

"Enter here and all will be made known unto you." She gestured into yet another closet-sized room, though this one did not have the luxury of glass walls.

"What does this one do?"

Innara's nostrils flared in irritation that she seemed to be barely keeping under control. "It will cleanse you."

Cormac sniffed. "I'd rather not."

"It doesn't work that way," she said. "You do what I command here, and then I will give you a new command, and that is how it will continue all of your days. You are mine now, and you will obey. You are a slave."

Before he could argue further, she shoved him with a slight sweep of her left hand, and being the giantess that she was, he was nearly thrown off his feet into the chamber. A lock snapped into place, and a mechanical vibration stirred at his feet. A dynamo hum proceeded from a vent above, and the air pressure shifted rapidly.

The other chamber had cured his cancer, or at least it felt like it had, but this "cleansing" room made his skull rattle, and the only washing, he suspected, would be of his brain.

No time like the present to utilize his pistol.

He shot into the vent above and where he guessed the snaps for the locking mechanism were.

The tortured squeal of a gear grinding against metal sounded from the vent, and the burnt smell of an electrical fire filled the chamber.

Cormac threw his shoulder against the door and it budged a little. A third strike and the chamber door popped open.

"How did you do that?" asked Innara.

Cormac held the pistol outward. "Forty-fives can punch a mean hole. Now how about you let me go on my way."

She gave him a sly look and gestured at a door to his left. She whispered, "A projectile weapon. Damn you Enki."

"Much obliged." He made his way to the door, but as he reached for what he thought was a knob, the door slid open sideways.

It was not an exit.

Cormac faced a dozen giants, all as large and fierce looking as Gursum. They were eating in a mess hall.

"Aww hell," he said.

"Kill him!" shouted Innara.

Three of the giants jumped up from their tables and moved toward Cormac.

He took aim and shot the closest one dead center in the forehead. The thunderous crack smote the twelve-foot-tall man and he collapsed. Though for Cormac's money, he guessed the bullet had only knocked the man unconscious. He bled, but the bullet appeared to be wedged in the thick skin of the giant as if Cormac had done no more than David of old and merely stunned this Goliath.

"There will be more of that if you don't let me outta here," he thundered, hoping to sound as intimidating as possible.

One of the giants took a step forward, but Cormac aimed the pistol at his head. The giant halted.

Innara frowned and took a few steps back as she now apparently feared what the gun in the small man's hand might do to her porcelain skin.

Cormac carefully traced his way in the other direction, and when he moved back a pace, the door slid closed again with him and Innara on the same side of it.

One of the giants stepped forward and the door slid open, but Cormac shook his head and the giant stepped back, forcing the door to close.

"I just want out, and I'll leave your little kingdom," he said to Innara.

"How dare you!" she growled through clenched lips.

"That ain't the answer I'm asking for. Where is the real exit?"

"You will never reach it alive; my guardsmen will squash you like the insect you are!"

"Flattery will get you everywhere," Cormac chided with a laugh. "Move."

They went out the door and Cormac saw more than a dozen of the giants and twice as many humans watching him from around corners and windows.

Cormac barked a command. "You all better let me borrow one of your aircraft, and none of the rest of you tall fellers better do anything to hinder me or you're gonna be looking for a new queen!" He emphasized his pistol pointing at her.

Innara gritted her teeth. "You will pay for your insolence. There is nowhere in the world that you can hide from me!"

"Such a sweet mouth, but with such bitter words coming out of it," taunted Cormac as he moved toward the pad where an airship had been brought.

Cormac moved to the pilot's wheel, still keeping the pistol trained on Innara. He guessed he could fly it, save that it would be hard for him to see where he was steering while working a couple of pedals and a flight module that seemed to adjust the hovering height of the ship. But he had to escape this place.

He motioned Innara to back away as he turned what he thought was the ignition. The ship fired to life, and as he pressed a foot upon the hovering module, the ship jerked into the air.

He staggered as it lurched upward. Then it crawled forward over the top of the city.

Arrows and spears shot toward him but glanced harmlessly off the bottom of the metallic ship. Cormac had to peer around the side of the wheel to see where he was going and at one point narrowly avoided colliding with a tower that stood twice the height of all other buildings in the city, with the exception of the great ziggurat.

"This ain't so bad," he said to himself.

A grappling hook and cable lanced across the bars along the gunwales and jerked the airship to a terrible halt. Cormac slammed against the wheel and accidently struck the module, sending the whole thing careening down. It hit an adobe building, caving in half of it as the airship tumbled end over end, landing in an alley. Having been stuck to the pilot's wheel was the only thing that saved him from being tossed from the falling airship.

Relatively unhurt, he jumped to his feet and hurried down the alleyway, hunting for any avenue of escape.

A skinny man was just about to unsaddle a palomino horse when Cormac stopped him. "I need that. I'll pay you for it later."

The man cowed to him without a word.

Cormac scanned the animal, wary of any tricks, such as loosening his bridle or saddle, but sighting none of those, he mounted up.

He wheeled in the saddle, spying the giant queen. He needed to remember how fast giants could run.

"Stop!" cried Innara.

Cormac waved his pistol in her direction. "Now, you behave and let this go, and we can all remain friends."

She screeched at Cormac as much as at her guardsmen as he rode away. "Kill him!!!"

He was racing through the bizarre cityscape when he heard a cry that sounded oddly familiar. The woman, Tanay, clung to the bars of a slit window, calling to him.

"Go north toward the Pillar! You can lose them in the foothills!" she cried.

He could do no more than give her a grateful nod as he wheeled the palomino to his right and headed toward the glowing plasma pillar and the hills beyond.

He pushed the palomino to run as fast as it would go, and yet he heard the thundering footsteps of the giants as they raced after him. Hardly daring to look behind, he managed to turn the horse hard and avoid a spear that slammed into the ground just beside him. It was as thick around as a fencepost and three times as long.

"Faster, you damn nag!" He gave heels to the startled horse. They climbed a light slope and rushed around a dense thicket of trees, almost falling into a swift canal that merged beside the forked road. He had been a hair's breadth from leading the horse into the drink.

The giants were fast and relentless, sooner or later either he or the horse would make a mistake. Better to face the fear. Nothing to do but stand.

Cormac wheeled his horse about.

Three giants were racing toward him with three more behind them that he could see.

Cormac took careful aim. He didn't have much ammunition, so these had to count.

A spurt of blood flowed from the forehead of the lead giant, and he stumbled to the ground. Whether it had killed him or merely stunned him, Cormac couldn't tell. He carefully aimed and fired at the next one who still held a spear.

He missed, but it was enough to give the giant pause at the range of perhaps fifty yards.

Cormac held his fire.

The giant sensed his hesitancy and took it for weakness as he hurled his spear.

Cormac fired and hit the giant in the left breast.

The giant collapsed to his knees with a gasp then let out a bloodcurdling roar and got back to his feet as if animated by a sinister dark force. His eyes were a fury as he drew a knife as long as Cormac's leg.

"Damn it!" cursed Cormac. He aimed and shot the giant in the neck.

Crimson flowed, and the giant fell back.

"I'm warning you. You don't want none of what I have to offer!" he challenged.

A giant almost a hundred yards away cast his spear. Cormac narrowly got the palomino to dodge the titanic missile.

The cracking of timber warned that at least one of the giants was trying to flank him. He gave heels and hurried on. A short distance down the road the flanking giant crashed through the underbrush, his outstretched hands just missing the palomino's tail.

Cormac wheeled in the saddle and gave the flanker a point-blank blast from the .45.

The giant clutched at his stomach and dropped to his knees. He scowled darkly at Cormac, gulping in deep breaths. He was down, but only for the moment.

"I warned ya," shouted Cormac, as he rode on. For now, it seemed his pursuers had given up the chase.

He rode the palomino hard into the surrounding hills where unexpected trees gave him needed shade and the feeling of shelter. He expected one of those flying airships to be on his heels at any moment, but none came, and relief washed over him at the cover he had beneath the leafy boughs.

He was wary, though, and kept a vigil no matter how far into the forest he rode. Even as night fell, the trio of aligned planets hung in the sky along with the central plasma pillar emanating from them, casting an eerie glow over the silent forest.

"Maybe this is as good as it's gonna get on this world and I should get some sleep."

The palomino neighed softly in response.

"You don't have to agree to make me feel better," Cormac said with a chuckle.

A strange chittering broke the stillness.

Cormac racked the pistol in response as his ears scanned the gloom as much as his eyes.

Movement twitched among the foliage all about him, but whatever made the disturbance did not yet reveal itself.

Cormac gauged that it had to be at least four or five somethings. He was sure that whatever it was walked on two feet.

"You know that I know you're there, so you might as well come out and show yourself. No point in playing games," Cormac said loudly.

Bursting from the underbrush, a brutish man of muscle holding a stone axe faced Cormac and gave an unintelligible roar. He had wide-set eyes, a sloped brow, and dirty long hair. He seemed almost as much an animal as a man. Two more leapt from over the top of a fallen log. Each was similarly armed with stone clubs.

"You better be a little more friendly or I'm gonna learn you," Cormac said with his pistol raised.

One of the ape-men bared his teeth and grunted as he raised his obsidian flanged club.

Cormac shot the club, shattering the sharpened stone edge.

Dumbfounded at the terrific report, the ape-men backed away, disappearing behind the cover they had so recently come from.

"You are not one of the Anunnaki's men," proclaimed a voice.

"No, I'm not. Who're you and your thugs trying to impress tonight?"

A well-muscled man stepped forward. He was young yet covered in scars and haggard from rough living. "I am Kord. I refused to be one of Anunnaki's slaves. I was tasked with finding you."

"Me? By Innara?"

"Never! She is a witch. I have help from on high. I am to bring you to a wise one."

Cormac glanced at the brutish ape-men and nodded. "All right, but I've had enough of tricks lately."

"This is not a trick. I have no guile."

"So you say."

Kord looked Cormac up and down. "Where are you from? You look nothing like any man I have seen before, and your weapon, it sounds like thunder."

"Yeah, they can put the fear of God into you," Cormac answered with a grin.

"Which god?"

Cormac cocked his head at Kord. "For this place? All of them I suppose."

"Come, we best hurry."

Cormac was puzzled, but Kord was already leading him farther into the verdant forest.

They traveled through the underbrush on foot and into a deep chasm that cut between the hills like a sword slice. Behind a large boulder the trail took a quick jog that led to a place where a man could just squeeze through sideways. Deep chested and large as Cormac was, it was still easier for him to slide through the gap than it was for the ape-men.

Kord offered him a wineskin, then gestured toward a large cylindrical crystal that was set in a candelabra. Kord touched the crystal and light grew within like a flame catching fuel until it illuminated the entirety of the massive chamber.

"I will call upon him," Kord said in a tone of reverence.

"What do you mean? Pray to your gods?"

"He is not my god, though there are some who would believe such."

The large multi-hued skin of a beast hung squarely on the wall. Kord took hold of the edge and pulled it free, revealing a large dark screen.

"This can show things in each direction, so I take cautions that some cannot find me," Kord said.

Cormac nodded. "I get it."

Kord faced the screen as if expecting it to respond to his very presence. He called out, "It is I, Kord, son of Tanelorrn. I have the one you seek."

The phrasing struck Cormac as odd. Cormac eyed his hirsute companions, but the ape-men were busy eating and drinking at the edges of the chamber. They didn't act like this was an ambush, though Cormac was initially suspicious at Kord's words.

The screen flickered and a light washed across it. Apparently, the owner also kept his covered with a cloth.

The being that stood upon the other side and looked at them was clearly one of the Anunnaki. If the screen he stood before was any indication, this being was likely fifteen feet tall. His skin was bronzed and his eyes a jade green, each stood in stark contrast to his purple and gold trimmed robe. He was bald but had a trimmed white beard. His voice was deep like it was coming from the bottom of a well.

"This is the man who came through the gates with the moon of Nergal?"

"Yes," Kord answered. "He is known as Cormac. He carries the sign you told me to watch for."

"Cormac, come forward that I may better get a look at you," the being commanded. "Hold out your hand that I may see this ring, the sign of the heavens."

Cormac put the wineskin down and stepped forward. "And who are you?" He held his hand outward so the Anunnaki could see the Masonic ring.

"It is good. I am Enki, Lord of the Waters and the Stag of the Abzu."

"Uh huh."

"Tell me, I ask you as a stranger—going to the West," he said with emphasis.

"Where have you come from?" asked Cormac.

"From the East," Enki replied, "And I am hoping that you will give him the message on the Square—for the sake of my Mother as well as your own."

"Are you a . . ."

Enki answered, "I am a Grand Worshipful Master here."

Cormac solemnly nodded.

Kord glanced from Enki to Cormac with abject stupefaction.

Enki smiled with a somewhat sinister edge. "It is all right, Kord, this is why I need him to perform a task that you could not despite all of my guidance."

Cormac frowned. "Just because we share a brotherly

bond and I don't care for Inanna and her ilk, doesn't mean I'm gonna be a tool for someone else with an axe to grind. Got enough problems of my own without being used."

"You understand very well, traveler, and while this is indeed a war between the Anunnaki, I have a vested interest in your people's survival. All of you are my people too, and your timely arrival with the moon of Nergal is fate. A peculiar blessing in disguise."

Cormac snorted at that final word as much as Enki's rhyming poetic flair.

Enki continued. "In hand-to-hand armaments, you cannot possibly overcome the full force of the Anunnaki. Kord and his ape-men can barely remain free in the hills and forests. Were it not for my guidance they would have been captured and put to death long ago. Now is the hour, the time to strike before the great conjunction is finished. Only at this precise moment in time can you, Cormac, strike and break their stranglehold on your world."

"This place is insane. They have star ships and flying craft and yet they were dumbfounded by my forty-five. What gives?"

"It has been so long since any of the Anunnaki had need for an explosive projectile weapon that they went out of fashion generations, millennia, ago. There had never been such weapons as ours upon this planet before, as the automated defenses are so far beyond the ken of the humans that it seems the gods blast lightning from the ships. And our massive size precludes any chance that one of the Adamu could stand toe to toe in mortal combat. The Anunnaki have forgotten what an equalizer your firearms can be. But they will learn swiftly how to counter your weapon. Powerful as it is, it cannot last you long unless you do as I say. The real power here is the sign and your ability to act on your initiation into the order."

Cormac glanced at his ring, remembering when he had been inducted, passing through the rituals of brotherhood. All to fit in with his fellow pilots and officers. Was there something more to it than mere fraternal bonding?

He was dubious and looked to Kord and the ape-men beside him. They looked in awe of both Enki and himself.

Kord gave him a solemn nod. "Trust him."

"You, Cormac, have the ability and strength to act on my instructions and free your world."

"How?" he asked, stretching his shoulders and raising his lantern jaw.

"Give him the box. He will know how to use it," Enki said to Kord. The wild man removed a skin from over a carved spot in the living rock. He reached inside and produced the keypad that controlled the weapons system left upon Cruithne. "You may not realize, but it is useless without my help in forwarding any signal between Ki and the moon of Nergal."

"Ki is Earth? You asking me to rain down hellfire on Shinar?"

"No." Enki shook his head. "You will use that once the Anunnaki flee from what you will do to the pyramid during the conjunction in six hours."

"Six hours?"

Enki nodded gravely. "Listen and do exactly as I bid you, and your world can be made free."

✦✦✦

They moved swiftly, covered in dusty robes to conceal themselves and blend in with the throng of slaves that clustered about the base of the pyramid.

Horns blared, calling the faithful to attentive prostration. The humongous Anunnaki foot soldiers crowded at the base of the multi-stepped pyramid. The massive conjunction of planets overhead took up almost the entire view of the heavens. The plasma column covered the city in its unearthly glow.

"If it wasn't for the conjunction, the guards would be more watchful and we would never have been able to get back into the city," Kord said under his breath.

Cormac grunted in answer. "It is one helluva distraction."

Kord shuddered and barely contained his ire. "Look there, Inanna has Tanay. She is taking her and others to the sacrificial altar."

"Let's do this."

Enki had given very specific instructions. Cormac wasn't sure how much he could trust the wizened-looking being, but he took confidence in Kord's trust. The wild man was a man of action and deed, and if the renegade Anunnaki had won his trust, what else could he do but extend a bit himself? Besides, he knew all the phrases.

The ape-men had walked as erect as they could manage and, covered by the robes, passed as lowly beggars until they forced their way to the front ranks of the gathered slaves. The humans of Shinar had given room for the jostling muttering of men, unwilling to bicker with anyone who pushed their way to the forefront of this grim spectacle.

A dozen women were bound with Tanay, along with another matching set of young men. They were led like lambs to the slaughter up the steps of the pyramid. Some steps were of more than twice the height for the Anunnaki to comfortably climb, while the mere humans had three times the amount of smaller, close-set steps.

Kord muttered to himself, "Oh, divine beings hear us and help us break the chains."

Cormac had never been much of a praying man, but he had seen enough that he still cast his two cents in. "Lord, wherever and whoever you are, guide my hand."

The flickering glow of the plasma column above shifted ever so slightly, allowing anyone on the ground to perceive a fluctuation as it seemed to center itself directly atop the gleaming ziggurat.

"Now!" shouted Cormac as he withdrew his pistol and shot the titanic guardsmen on the right and then the left.

As if the colossal Anunnaki weren't dead, the ape-men rushed forward, howling for blood as they raised their clubs, battering the fallen giant foes.

The crowd of slaves cried out in fear, confusion, and ecstatic delight at the grim ballet.

The imagery of the capstone atop the ziggurat was blinding, it caught both sunlight and the glow of the plasma column and held them in its embrace as if it were molten.

Cormac glanced back at the enemies surrounding him and hurried up the steps. If it weren't for the smaller mid-steps made for people his size, he never would have been able to outrace the giants that came from farther to the side.

Fire licked at the stand surrounding the altar, and Tanay cried out in anguish as the smoke curled about her reddened body.

The witch queen, Innara, stood by with a knife held high.

Cormac raised his gun. "Back off!"

Innara sneered at his bravado. "My warriors will crush you underfoot. You cannot stop the conjunction."

Cormac fired, and the lead slug struck the knife from Innara's hand with a brace of sparks. "I don't need to stop it, just you."

Innara cried out in pain as the knife sliced her as it flew away. Blood ran down her arm, and her ivory gown had a long crimson stain running down her leg.

"I warned ya, back off! Them too!" he signaled toward the giants that had paused in their ascent.

Innara waved a hand, keeping the giant guardsmen at bay if only for the moment.

"I want them where I can see them, keep them all on this side. If any one of them tries sneaking up the back side, I'll give you one in the forehead."

"It wouldn't kill me," said Innara with a mouthful of contempt.

"Do you want to find out?"

She hissed at him as he moved closer and drew a knife with his left hand to cut Tanay's bonds.

The heat of the fire was torturous, and he was amazed at the woman's strength in not crying out worse at where it had seared her naked flesh.

Innara took a step forward, and Cormac leveled his pistol. She stepped back. He looked at the crystalline capstone of the pyramid. Energy from the conjunction caused it to pulsate with inward power a mere dozen paces away.

Innara saw his gaze and fear finally took her by the neck. "No! Take your woman and go."

Cormac gave her a half-smirk. This was all the truth of Enki's words he needed to know. It would work. He sprinted up the steps, the giantess on his heels.

They raced to reach the pinnacle.

Innara grasped him about the ankle and yanked. He held on to the stone with all the strength of his left hand while the right turned and fired the pistol point blank into the giantess's bronze flesh.

She gasped and let go, struggling to gain her feet and reach the capstone before him.

It was close, but Cormac was swiftest and shot a hand forth into the mirrorlike surface. On the other side he felt a hand take his own, as if they shook. A being from beyond the veil was on the other side. Who it was, Enki had never said, but Cormac felt real flesh and bone. No words were spoken, but the message was received. He was given a sign and token and gave the returned answer. He let go and pulled his arm back through to this side of reality.

"No!" Innara screamed. "It was my turn!"

The pulsing crystal capstone went dark, and the flickering glow of the plasma column above shifted violently as the conjunction was broken. Saturn, Venus, and Mars had held together like a great eye above the Earth, but now twisted and raced apart in opposite directions. If Cormac hadn't seen it with his own eyes, he never would have believed the cosmic majesty. The non-ecliptic shift was mesmerizing. Then the earth shook, and the pyramid blocks tumbled about him.

Any of the titans who had nearly been upon Cormac now fled back down the steps.

The crowd of human slaves ran for cover too, though their hovels tumbled with the quaking, and the brown towers of the Anunnaki fell in clouds of dust.

"It's done. I knew how to break your eggshell empire," Cormac snarled.

Innara shook her head disbelievingly. "We were betrayed. Enki is behind this. But we will return and destroy you vermin!" She raced down the steps, falling to her knees multiple times as Cormac, Tanay, and Kord held their ground upon the platform, reluctant to run down where the blocks had a chance to strike an unfortunate.

They watched Innara as she went to the field where one of her airships lay docked.

"She is getting away," Tanay said.

"It's all right, I want her and her men in that ship. I've got another surprise for them."

The airship rose into the sky, powered by fire blasting from rearward turrets. It climbed higher into the dissipating plasma column until it was hardly visible inside that molten stream.

"They have escaped, there is nothing that can be done," lamented Tanay.

"That's where you are wrong. I have a little something up my sleeve, thanks to Enki." Cormac held the keypad and scanned himself in, then, playing with the field of controls, tapped his signal into the wave finder of the palace and connected to the weapon drone that waited hungrily upon Cruithne.

Firing it up, a system of rockets and a laser zeroed in on Innara's ship. A terrible red blast exploded across the azure sky despite the invisibility of its origin.

Havoc wracked the ship, and it began a terrible trajectory back to Earth.

Innara's face flashed upon the screen. "What have you done? How did you have allies in orbit?"

"Don't matter now, you're going down," Cormac said with satisfaction.

"Emergency landing actions for Tartarus," Innara said to one of her crew members before the screen went black.

"Where is that?" Cormac asked Tanay.

She scanned a globe and pointed to what Cormac knew as Antarctica.

"Perfect, even if she lives, she dies," he said to himself.

Tanay seemed unsure. "They will sleep and dream until they are awoken in a safe time. Perhaps far into the future."

Cormac thought on that and remembered his one-time chance at flying security for a dig in Antarctica. He watched the screen as the ship came closer and closer to ground, finally slamming home into a bank of deep ice.

"It can't be," he murmured. "I cause what happens in the future? The dig? For them to be awakened again in my own time?"

"What are you talking about?"

"I have to get there and end them. They can't ever wake up," he said grimly. "Sleepers of Tartarus. It wasn't just a code name, it was literal."

"You can't go there, It's impossible."

"I'll have to retrofit one of their airships, fly there, and make sure they are good and dead."

"You won't do it alone," said Kord.

Enki's face appeared on the fuzzy screen. "You have done well, traveler. Save for those that yet remain hidden on your world, the bridge has been broken. The Anunnaki will trouble your kind no more. Fare thee well." Then he was gone.

It was all so sudden. Cormac's mind reeled. He was supposed to die in deep space, cancer eating away at him, but he was back on Earth, thousands of years in the past, cured of his illness, and saving the world from the giant aliens he had always doubted existed.

Tanay clung to him, and the people emerged from the edges of the ruined city, shouting in joy. "What now?" she asked.

"No rest for the wicked," Cormac said. "There is a lot of work to be done."

DARK ETERNITY
Jonathan Edelstein

One of the joys of getting to put together an anthology like this is having a chance to showcase some up-and-coming authors to new audiences. Jonathan Edelstein is a finalist for the Jim Baen Memorial Short Story Award, and has had short stories published in Beneath Ceaseless Skies, Strange Horizons, Escape Pod, *and* Intergalactic Medicine Show. *Though his twentieth story published, "Dark Eternity" will be his first published in a physical book.*

The story shares a universe with several of his previously published short stories, "First Do No Harm" (Strange Horizons, 2015), "The Starsmith" (Escape Pod, 2016), "The Stranger in the Tower" (Andromeda Spaceways, 2019), and "Iya-Iya" (Kaleidotrope, 2019), so if you find yourself liking Jonathan's stories of those seeking renewal and knowledge in a universe recovering from a dark age, be sure to seek them out.

Ishyanga wasn't one of the worlds they taught about in the universities of Mutanda. It was a colony of the

Third Migration and not one of the successful ones: it had lost contact even before the Union fell, and few had called there since. Its continents were cold and metal-poor, and the crops humans favored didn't grow well there; the people hung on as fishermen and herders along coasts and lakeshores, vassals of an awantu king.

They didn't teach of Ishyanga in the universities: there were only a few books deep in the libraries and fragments of restored computer files. But those were enough to bring Kalonde there: those, a ruined city, scraps of cloth, and a trail of pebbles.

Kalonde had one of the pebbles in her hand when she came out of the ichiyawafu. She'd dreamed of the voice it recorded, a high ecstatic keening surrounded by a roaring gale. She'd dreamed of the speaker as well; a bulbous gray being with broad wings and a barbed tail soaring through the violent thermals of a gas giant, a dim red sun shadowed in the clouds. The voice, she knew, was true; the image, she had no way of knowing. Those who traveled through the ichiyawafu, the space outside space, often dreamed of the dead, but the dreams weren't always true ones, and no human had ever gone to the world where the recording had been made.

The antiquarian in Kalonde wanted to find that world. But the seeker in her was after another prize. The voices recorded on the pebbles, all but three of them, were of no more than passing interest; her quarry was the race that had made them and scattered them all through this region of space. She had hoped, once, that the ichiyawafu might give her a dream of them, but in a hundred journeys between worlds, it never had.

If she were to find them, it would have to be in a more prosaic place.

She woke fully from the ichiyawafu-dream to the view of such a place, a world of mottled blues, greens and browns that filled the viewports of her ship. Other prosaic things met her eyes to either side: the clutter of the ship's cabin, a scattering of tools, the instruments that told her she was two hours from landing. And the images that hung on the walls—images of the Umfwantu, the Listeners.

There were legends of the Listeners throughout this end of explored space, and they went back many thousands of years—before the Union rose and fell, before the Commonwealth and the Association and the Accord, before the Three Migrations ever began. And for almost as many millennia, explorers and traders had collected those legends and brought them back to the universities of Mutanda. All the stories agreed that the Listeners had come to many worlds and scattered voice-pebbles before leaving, but beyond that, they had little in common. The images on the walls came from those legends—some from explorers' accounts and some that Kayonde herself had collected; fragments of books, sculptures from ancient markets, replications of cave paintings—and they were different enough that they couldn't possibly depict the same race.

Some of the legends said the Umfwantu were shape-changers. Kayonde had never heard of such a thing in the real universe—color-changers, yes—but the stories she'd

collected in seventy years of travel were enough to make
her wonder.

Maybe soon she would learn.

There was one at least, an awantu king, who'd sought
the Listeners before her. There were stories of him too—
Lukwesa of the sky-tree throne, Lukwesa of the golden
eyes—and his adventures nine thousand years ago were a
legend on every world he had touched. Kalonde had
followed his footsteps and she'd found the world he'd
come home to after an absence of eight centuries; she'd
learned there of the tapestry he'd woven, and in retracing
his journey, had found six pieces of it. They hung in the
doorway that separated the cabin from the passage to the
hold, tattered and maddeningly incomplete, but they
contained three words in a flowing alien script and a
scattering of points that could only be a map of stars.

She'd seen those same words, in a script very similar,
on a manuscript in the depths of the Mutanda archives:
Iteka rya Kwijima, Dark Eternity. And that manuscript
had come from this world, Ishyanga, which was also where
the star map pointed.

"Do you know the story of Chinkonkole the Navigator's
last voyage, musaza?" Kalonde asked Ngabo the seller of
goods.

They were on an ancient wooden pier five meters
above a muddy river delta, part of the maze of docks and
floating islands that made up Ishyanga's chief human
town. A plate of fish and a jar of imbote—honey-beer—
were on the table between them, both half-empty; to one
side were the painted wooden disks that symbolized the

cargo she'd brought to sell, and to the other, the brightly colored counters that, after a morning's haggle, represented her price.

Ngabo looked back at her, uncomprehending. He was the only person on this world who spoke the Union's language, and even he had little need for it—the fikondo wa intanda, the starships, might come calling once a decade or even less. And though Kalonde had learned as much of this world's language, Kinyaishyanga, as she could, there hadn't been many materials to study from. The bargaining had been more than a little difficult, and now, when Ngabo clearly expected her to name the things she wanted to buy with the counters, she was telling stories.

"There are as many tales of that voyage," he said at last, "as there are worlds where he landed."

Kalonde spread her hands across the table, conceding the point. "There is one we tell on Mutanda," she said. "When Chinkonkole returned from his last conquest, he learned that his wife had died in his absence, defending against a raid two years before. He learned, also, that she had sent him a last message."

"And?" Ngabo asked after a moment of silence.

Kalonde had lost the thread of the story—she was close here, so close—but she picked it up again. "So he calculated the time, down to the second, that had passed since that message, and he traveled through the ichiyawafu to a point exactly that many light-years away. There he found her voice, and he followed it at the speed of light, so it would be in his ears eternally. And somewhere, he hears it still."

"We have a different story," Ngabo said. "I can tell it to you if you want. But why did you tell me that one?"

"Because all the voices of the dead are out there. All of them. The ichiyawafu isn't the true country of the dead—the space between the stars is." She stood and swept her gaze across the lapping waters and fishermen's pirogues to where her ship—the *Chiwinda na Foshi*, the *Hunter of Dreams*—had landed. "All the words left by the people who could build ships like that, who could make computers, who could fill minds with all the knowledge of humanity and fill bodies with machines that cure diseases. And not only that—the music, the plays, the chants to the orishas. Everything we lost when the Union fell is there."

Ngabo looked at her evenly, waiting for her to finish. It was a look that many people had given her in seventy years of time and space. "There are stories of people who sought those things," he said at last. "And all of them say the same thing—that the messages are lost, that within less than a light-year, they become so weak that the noise of the stars drowns them out."

These were quelling words, but they were the words that Kalonde had been waiting for. "What, then," she said, withdrawing a pebble from the folds of her chitenge and placing it next to the imbote jar, "is this?"

Ngabo took the pebble between his thumb and forefinger. It was a Listeners' pebble like any other, slightly oblong and jet-black, with a symbol on one side that bore more than a passing resemblance to Lukwesa's tapestry and the Kinyaishyanga script. He had clearly seen such things before—from all accounts, the pebbles were rife on this world—and he knew what to do; he touched his forefinger to the symbol and brushed it side to side.

And heard a human voice.

It was a male voice, speaking a version of the Union's language that was older than the Union, so archaic as to be nearly impossible to understand. A woman's voice answered, she too speaking words that were thousands of years dead. Only from the archives Kalonde had searched did she know that the voices were speaking of the investiture of a king, and the voices were beyond Ngabo altogether, but he was still stunned when they suddenly ceased.

"The king they speak of is known in Mutanda's records," Kalonde said. "He died twenty thousand years ago. And the Listeners never came to Mutanda, but they found these voices—they found them somewhere. And I have two more."

She reached out suddenly, pushed the counters back to Ngabo's side of the table. "I want you to hire men with these. The legends of the awantu, Lukwesa's tapestries— they all say that the Listeners had a settlement on this world. Hire men for me to dig it up, and we will learn how they made that recording."

Kalonde expected another bargain—Ngabo would surely want some of the workers' pay for himself, and would argue keenly over their wages and the price of their tools. What she didn't expect was laughter.

"The Dark Eternity?" Ngabo said. "Yes, we have stories of it—or I should say, the awantu do. But I can't hire men to dig it out for you. It was buried many thousands of years ago, and no one knows where it is."

❖❖❖

The royal archivist didn't know either.

It took three days and two bribes for Kalonde to obtain an audience. For a kilogram of Mutanda blue-leaf, the town headman had passed her on to the king's provincial legate. Bribing the legate had been much harder. He was an awantu, a person of another creation; human drugs and spices held no interest for him, clothing was of little use to a being with an exoskeleton of iridescent chitin, and the jewelry in Kalonde's ship was all wrong for his body and his race's fashion. But a wooden flute and a mbira—ah, *those* were a different story. Kalonde had the patterns and tools to make them, and they bought her a map to the awantu capital and a letter of introduction to K'aari, Keeper of Memory.

K'aari had needed no bribe other than stories. Awantu she might be, but she was one in spirit with the bakalamba, the university preceptors of Mutanda; she wanted to know, and knowing was enough.

But she didn't know where the Iteka rya Kwijima was.

"We worshiped the Listeners, once," she said; her rattling voice managed the Union's speech surprisingly well, better in fact than Ngabo had. "We made pilgrimages to their settlement to hear the voices of the worlds. But after they left us, the priesthood grew corrupt, there was a revolt ... The ifapemba"—she used the Union's word for councilors—"decreed that it be forgotten." She gave another soft rattle from the depths of her throat; to a Keeper of Memory, any such decree was a loss, no matter the justification.

This wasn't the answer Kalonde wanted. But on Mutanda they said that every answer had a question, and she searched for the one to ask. "Are there records from before that, mbuya?" she said at last, giving the awantu the honorific she would have given a person on Mutanda with similar standing. "Before the decree?"

"If it were that easy," K'aari said, "don't you think I would know?" No, she wasn't one who would let an ancient edict stand in the way of learning. "The council was very thorough. But I can show them to you if you want. Maybe you'll see something that I could not."

And then K'aari led the way from her offices to the stairs that climbed the archive tower, past rooms and rooms and rooms of documents. The oldest were at the top, a plan that Kalonde recognized from many visits to dusty attics. But it wasn't an attic full of jumbled records that waited at the top of the stairs; it was an airy room that looked out on the domed towers of the city, with orderly shelves and a reading table at which, if the cups and game-board on its surface were anything to go by, K'aari spent a great deal of time.

"The works of our first poets are here," she said. "They go back forty thousand turnings. And the stories of the worlds are here—we learned of your people long before they came. The council's decree was only against the Listeners' city, not their stories. These are left to us—to me, to you."

Kalonde took a scroll from one of the shelves—carefully, carefully—and began unwinding it on the table. The writing, she noticed, wasn't the primitive pictographs that one might expect from the earliest days of literacy; it was a mature script, one that resembled the markings on the Listeners' pebbles even more than did this world's modern alphabet. And then she noticed the pebbles themselves—a box of them, more than she'd ever seen before in one place, with others strewn on the table and arranged on the game-board.

They, too, had obviously been exempted from the decree—or maybe they had been unearthed afterward, in whatever place the Umfwantu had left them. Could *that* be the key? "Tell me," she said, "is there a place where more of these have been found than in other places?"

K'aari was silent for a moment, then realized what Kalonde had to be asking. "I'm afraid there are several such places. One of them may be the one you seek. But it would take many turnings to dig through them all."

She took a pebble from the table and brushed the symbol—maybe she was hoping it might tell her? But what it held was the sound of rain, nothing more. She looked down at the board, surveyed its irregular shape and the chaotic spaces into which it was divided, and put the pebble on one.

"How do you play that game?" Kalonde asked. It seemed as good a question as any.

"You make patterns."

"Just patterns?"

"Patterns of shape, patterns of sound, patterns of meaning. You make order from chaos." K'aari passed a pebble to Kalonde, inviting her to place it.

She did, and there were others. She listened, she placed; she made patterns; she tried to break K'aari's pattern and then to complement it. After a while, K'aari called for a pitcher of imbote and a meal of firm-fleshed meat and the succulent creepers that grew in thickets on the hillsides. By now, the bacteria that Kalonde had traded for on her first day on Ishyanga had flourished enough that she could truly metabolize it, and it satisfied her hunger in a way that prior meals had not. She looked at the board again, saw that one of her patterns had become a symbol like those on the pebbles—the symbols that the Listeners had taught K'aari's race forty thousand turnings ago . . .

And she realized she'd found the pattern she was looking for.

"Are there legends about the origin of writing?" she asked. "About the person who first brought it to your nation?" The name *Prometheus* flashed through Kalonde's mind, from a story so old that its origin had been forgotten even before the Migrations.

"Yes. Ttok of Dyala . . ."

"And where was Dyala?"

K'aari didn't ask why Kalonde wanted to know, but she didn't need to. She rose from the table and returned with a scroll. The poem began as she unrolled it, in an ancient epic style, and it told of Ttok's birth, his childhood, the description of his country . . .

"Yes, I know that place," K'aari said, letting the edge of the scroll fall from her grasp. "It has changed in all these turnings, but I know it. It's fifty miles upstream from your people's town, at a bend in the river. And yes"—she saw Kalonde's raised hand, and quelled it—"this is one of the places where many pebbles are found."

"Come to my ship," Kalonde said.

K'aari followed her at once. *This race is a trusting one*, Kalonde thought; few humans on these backwater worlds would be so willing to board a strange ship that might belong to one of the fair folk or, more prosaically, a pirate. But the awantu's instincts were good; whatever the superstitious might think of her, Kalonde was neither of these things.

In a short time, the *Chiwinda na Foshi* hovered above the bend in the river. Below was land that would be called umushitu on Mutanda—swampy thickets of thorns—and it was impenetrable even from low overhead, with no sign of a city or even ruins. But the ship had instruments that could map the land, and Kalonde had learned that, with the proper setting, they could map below it.

The computers spoke a dead language—it had been fourteen hundred years since the Union fell, and no new ones had been made since then—but Kalonde knew it, and she gave commands. And on the screen that faced the captain's chair, shapes appeared—outlines of walls, arranged in a symbol that she knew all too well. The Iteka rya Kwijima, she was sure, was found.

Ngabo's men brought machetes to cut through the thorns and planks to lay down a path through the swampland. They brought picks and shovels to dig, crowbars to shift stones, and brushes and trowels for the fine work. But so far, there was no fine work to do.

There were only a few outbuildings—that was one of the mysteries. That was wrong for a settlement, or even for a base. A few squat sheds had been dug out, all made of an unknown ceramic, none of them marked and far too small to provide storage for a village or town.

And if that was a mystery, the main building was a

greater one. They had dug out nearly all of it now, smooth cream ceramic walls that became irregular as they rose toward a sloping roof. Much of the surface was now uncovered, the earth removed from the cracks with fine brushes. But the walls were as unmarked as the sheds, and there was nothing that even began to resemble an entrance. Whatever the building might be, Kalonde would never find out what it was if she couldn't get in.

On the third day, she took the *Chiwinda na Foshi* up again and flew low over the umushitu in a spiral search pattern. She looked much more closely than before, searching for small anomalies where the building itself had been a flashing sign. She found three and, with K'aari in tow, landed near the most promising.

She had changed her chitenge for coarse trousers and a tunic, and she had a pick and shovel herself—she'd carried them, and joined in the work, since the first day. Now she and K'aari beside her applied them with a will. The ground was higher here, stony and less swampy, and the progress was painfully slow . . . until suddenly it yielded all at once as rocks and earth tumbled into a hole and Kalonde had to brace herself with the pick to keep from falling in.

Her lamp told her that the hole wasn't deep, and that a rough-hewn passage led away and down in the direction of the building. She felt the ground, chose a handhold and lowered herself in carefully. K'aari did the same and looked past her into looming darkness . . .

There was a loud report—the sound of a weapon fired in the air—and distant shouts of consternation.

Kalonde pulled herself up with her arms so her head

was above the ground, and she strained to listen. "Disperse!" someone called—the legate, she realized. "This is a forbidden place! Disperse!" There was more shouting, and then the sound of people beginning to scatter.

"The decree," she hissed to K'aari. "It's still in force?"

"Of course not—after that many thousand turnings, after the kingdom has fallen and risen four times over? When the state falls, the laws fall. But some of the king's ancestors are from priestly families, and the legate's clan is jealous—they may suspect that he will use this place to increase his power. Some families still follow the old feuds, even after all this time."

The legate had been happy to pass Kalonde on to the capital in return for a bribe, but now that she had found what she sought, her gift was evidently forgotten. Human and awantu, sometimes, could be little different in their intrigues.

She put her hand to the weapon at her side, but thought better of it even as she did; the legate would have brought too many troops to fight. "We should go to the king . . ."

"It will take time to see him, even for me. By then, they will have buried this place again, and they will make sure you are expelled from this world." K'aari swung her pick up suddenly and, before Kalonde could react, struck at the ground above them, bringing dirt and rocks down to fill the hole.

"We have food and water," she said. "I'm sure this passage leads to the entrance—we'll go inside before they can get to us, and dig out when they're gone." She turned her lamp down the passage and began picking her way down, shining the light on the floor and measuring her steps carefully. Kalonde, lacking a better plan, followed in her wake.

There *was* a door at the end of the passage, a thousand meters from the hole. And that was the third mystery.

It was made of the same ceramic as the outbuildings, set into a wall, and there was no obvious way to open it. There were no levers or buttons, no keyhole, no place to insert a card—none of the places where the thieves' tools Kalonde had gathered on a dozen worlds might gain purchase. Crowbars wouldn't shift it, and it was impervious to blows from a pick. But then, as she cleared earth from just above the doorway, she saw it—the beginnings of symbols cut into the wall, the first markings she had seen anywhere in this place.

K'aari saw too and crowded in beside her, digging into the ceiling carefully, working earth from where the symbols were etched. There were three, matching Ishyanga's script in its most ancient form, and Kalonde recognized them; they were a variation on Lukwesa's tapestry, a form of the word for the Listeners themselves, an injunction to listen.

Kalonde listened. She stood at the door, willed herself to perfect silence, gave her attention.

Nothing happened.

She listened more. She heard voices from the direction of the hole, and a shouted order to get picks and shovels. The legate's troops had found the passage. There would be more to listen to in a short time—the sounds of digging, and soon enough the legate's cry of triumph.

But K'aari had noticed something.

"I've seen symbols written that way before, in the old poems," she breathed, the merest rattle in her throat. "I think it means '*we* listen.' And the third symbol—it was used in prayer, in worship, in offerings to the ancient gods."

This had been an ichipembwe, a worship place, for K'aari's people once. Had it been so for the Listeners themselves? And at once, Kalonde realized what offering a Listener might make, or want.

"I speak," she said, facing the door. "I speak in my own voice."

And slowly, silently, the door slid open.

It closed behind them as they passed. That was all right; they knew how to open it again, and they were sealed off now from the legate's troops. He had no scholar with him.

Beyond was a single room bathed in dim white light that seemed to come from nowhere. And here was the fourth mystery. The room occupied the entire building, but there was no evidence of machines—nothing that might amplify signals from the void, no device for impressing those signals onto pebbles. Wherever the lost voices of the Union might be, there was no evidence that they were collected here.

Instead, there were rows of benches between bare walls, and other things besides; perches, crossbars hung from the ceiling, pedestals, webs. Facing them, where the room grew narrow, were two flared columns, and between those, an oddly shaped table that resembled a leaf or an ear . . . or, Kalonde suddenly realized, K'aari's game board.

Kalonde knew what function this form followed. Yes, this was a worship place. But how was this the Dark Eternity? There was nothing eternal, nothing dark—in fact, in the time it had taken Kalonde to survey the room, the light had become almost day-bright.

But then, as the light rose, the walls changed.

They appeared first on the far walls, behind the columns and the table—images of dozens of races of awantu, and then, spreading around the room, hundreds. All the races whose images Kalonde had collected were there, and many more from worlds yet unknown to humans, and . . .

"Lukwesa," she whispered.

Yes, Lukwesa—she had seen too many images of him to mistake him for anyone else. From a distance, he might be taken for any member of his race—three meters tall, gaunt and long-armed, mottled gray and white scales, golden eyes set back in a trilaterally symmetric head—but there was the missing scale below his lower forearm, there the scar across his chest given him by the inkanyamba who had guarded a hoard of voice-pebbles in the deep ocean, there the forked tattoo with which the impundulu, the lightning-bird, had rewarded him. And there was something in his face, alien as it may be, that told of his questing personality, marked him as a kindred spirit.

Now Kalonde was sure that, no matter what the legends said, the Listeners weren't a race, nor were they shape-changers. They were—had been—a cult, a religion. They had collected voices and scattered them, for what reason? To spread the voices' spiritual life around the galaxy? A sharing, a seeding? There were no inscriptions to answer that question, however, and Kalonde despaired of knowing.

Lukwesa, though, had joined the cult—of *that*, Kalonde was certain—and he'd gone on to find the Iteka rya Kwijima. Was it here somehow after all? Had he found it *from* here? Was his visit to this place before or after his eight hundred years' absence?

Was there a way his image might tell her?

Without realizing it, Kalonde had walked toward the image and stopped in front of the game board—no, she realized, the *altar*. What was a game to K'aari had been a ritual once. And K'aari recognized this too. "Our word for 'game' is ubwiru," the scholar said, "but to the ancient poets, it meant secret worship—initiation into the mysteries."

The fifth mystery.

Make patterns, Kalonde remembered. She saluted Lukwesa's image hands over eyes, in the manner of his race, and sought one. She withdrew a handful of pebbles from the purse at her belt, considered their symbols, their voices, their song . . .

A song was a pattern. No, something more universal— *music* was a pattern. On Mutanda there were three musical scales: five notes, seven and nine. She made the five-note scale first, selecting pebbles that recorded each of its tones, playing them with a flick of a finger and arranging them on the board in the shape of a musical staff. Then seven notes alongside it and nine underneath them both.

She stepped back from the board—would those patterns be enough? Lukwesa's image didn't move, but a symbol appeared above him, the same offering-symbol that had been incised above the door.

Kalonde's offering at the door had been her voice, but she sensed that this wouldn't be enough now. Another voice, maybe, or voices—voices the Umfwantu had never heard. And with the musical notes she'd laid down still in her ears, she realized she had them.

She had carried her own recordings with her aboard the *Hunter of Dreams*—she had sought voices from distant worlds, but she also wanted reminders of Mutanda. She had a player in her pocket, an artifact of the Union fourteen hundred years gone, but new recordings still were made, and she played one now. It was the great symphony of Bukata of Kabwe, drums and mbira, flutes and single-string gourds and three-string gourds, pipes and xylophones, and voices, voices. They filled the room—the acoustics were perfect, Kalonde realized—and even K'aari, who knew an entirely different musical tradition, fell under its spell.

And at the end, Lukwesa's image, a ghostly projection now, stood in front of the altar.

He too held voice-pebbles in his hands, and as he raised them, an image of the galaxy appeared above them—not the pitifully small portion that humans had explored, but all of it in stunning, starry glory. He took one of the pebbles and cast it on the board, and one of the stars—Ishyanga's star—glowed a brilliant red as the words of one of K'aari's poets filled the chamber. He cast another pebble and another star came to life, this one far inward toward the galactic core. Others came after, each igniting a star, each releasing its voice.

The game, the ritual, was to make patterns. Kalonde waited to see what Lukwesa's pattern would be, and then she did see it.

He had cast at least a hundred pebbles, and now they formed a sphere, enclosing a region of the galaxy. Then a last one, releasing a sound that she felt but was far too low to hear, and an apparition in the center of the sphere, one that *didn't* glow, a dark, swirling mass. And next to it, a symbol.

"Eternity," whispered K'aari.

Dark Eternity.

Lukwesa had found the Iteka rya Kwijima, but not here. What he had found here was a map, a guide to the far-flung members of the cult, a message in their gathering-place. Suddenly, Kalonde was sure what the missing part of Lukwesa's tapestry showed. And she was sure where she had to go.

The *Chiwinda na Foshi* had brought one person to Ishyanga. It took two away. "The Dark Eternity calls me too," K'aari had said, "and in a hundred turnings, the legate's clan might forget about me." And so, cramped as the cabin was, room had been made.

The passage through the ichiyawafu was the longest that Kalonde had ever made, more than four thousand light-years, inward from the edge of the Orion Spur to the Sagittarius Arm. Her journey-dream was equally intense. She had thought she might dream of Lukwesa, but Chinkonkole came to her instead; ancient and white-haired, staring through his ship's port at the blue converging trails of the stars, his wife's message filling the cabin as he raced with it through space and time. She felt herself there with him, and then somehow she was the ship, straining against the limits of physics, pressed against forever . . .

And she awoke to see that the date on the Union computer's display had changed from the Year of Migration 31,647 to 31,649, and to hear every alarm in the ship wailing.

She was instantly alert and her eyes flashed to her instruments, but nothing seemed wrong with the ship, and she wondered if it was the alarms that had failed. But then she looked out the port. What she saw was not the star and planets she expected, but a spot—no, *two* spots—of absolute nothingness, surrounded by swirling maelstroms of gas that met in turbulent streams of red and grew yellow-white and painfully bright at the center. The leading edge of the nearer vortex was terrifyingly close, and as the voids circled each other, pulses of gravity threatened to tear the ship apart with tidal forces.

Kalonde knew what these were—intanda na ngapondo, crushed stars. There were legends of them, told with fearful awe; stories of mariners who were never heard from again, time-traps where even the fair folk dared not go. Dark eternity this was indeed. But what would have brought the Listeners to such a place? What would bring *anyone* to such a place, she wondered as she and K'aari brought the ship to emergency power and then beyond it, fighting to get clear of the maelstrom.

Slowly, then faster, the *Hunter of Dreams* drew away from the swirling chaos—it hadn't been at the point of no return, not quite. Kalonde angled the ship above the orbital plane where the turbulence was less, seeking a panoramic view, looking for what the Listeners might have left here. And then she saw.

It was small, not a world or even an asteroid, no larger than a ship or a small station, but it stood out because it was moving incredibly fast. The *Chiwinda na Foshi*'s instruments showed it at ninety-nine percent of light speed—possibly far more, since that was their maximum reading—and it shifted deeply into the red as it moved out of their field of view. For a moment, Kalonde thought it might be Chinkonkole's ship after all, but Chinkonkole would have traveled much farther by now than a mere four thousand light-years, and then the object returned to view, shifting blue, moving *toward* her.

She could see enough of its path by now to know that it was orbiting the crushed stars. It wasn't a natural orbit either—it was a powered one, and her mind reeled as she imagined *how much* power it must need to maintain that speed. But the maelstrom of gases millions of degrees hot held ample fuel, and it would need that speed to get away when the two crushed stars inevitably merged. And at such speeds, an orbit that might otherwise be years long was reduced to days. Maybe the Listeners had wanted to minimize the time that passed before the station returned to a certain point . . .

"Look now!" K'aari cried.

Kalonde looked where K'aari was pointing, past the station and to the darkness beyond, to the stars that should have been too dim to see but which were now brilliant candles with vivid features. And suddenly, she knew.

K'aari's race knew nothing of gravity lensing—to her,

what she was seeing was a marvel beyond imagining. It *was* known on Mutanda, and Kalonde had even used it sometimes in navigation, but she had never seen it like this. One crushed star was a lens of unparalleled intensity; where the focal points of *two* such lenses overlapped and were powered by rippling gravity waves, it might be possible to see anything.

Or to *hear* anything—even a signal otherwise long lost in the void.

"K'aari, mbuya na wambuya," she said as she dove toward the focal point, "let us hear what the ship hears." And a moment later, the word taken for the deed, the cabin filled with sound—static and cacophony at first, but then suddenly a symphony.

It was in no musical form known to humanity or to any of the thousand known races of awantu. The instruments were alien and eerie; the voices ranged in unearthly harmony sometimes passing out of hearing as they became too low or too high for human ears; it sounded sometimes as if both the orchestra and the singers were in a thick fluid. But it was true music: a gift to the spirit, a gift from the soul.

Where had it come from? Kalonde's fingers danced across the computer terminal, tracing the direction of the signal, the movements of stars. But there was nothing that had been in that symphony's path, no place it could possibly have come from, short of . . . Andromeda?

And then, as the music built to a crescendo, there was static again, and silence.

Fragments, Kalonde realized. Fragments of the Union's voices came here. Fragments of *everyone's* voices came here. Fragments to be pieced together. And ahead was the station that had collected them for more thousands of years than Kalonde's or K'aari's ancestors could imagine and recorded them for the Umfwantu to scatter—to make into patterns.

It seemed Kalonde could see those patterns through the crushed stars' lens. And she realized she had become a Listener in truth—that she might always have been one.

There was no longer any question of where she would go now. But there was K'aari to consider. "I can take you home first," she said.

"Home? Home is where there are millions of turnings of poems that no one living has ever read."

Kalonde nodded. She had expected no other answer. "Time to match orbit with the station," she said in the dead language of the Union's computers. And a moment later, the answer flashed on the screen: SUBJECTIVE TIME, 58.918 DAYS; OBJECTIVE TIME, 40.069 YEARS.

Dark Eternity, yes. The eternity of speed. Suddenly, Lukwesa's absence of eight centuries was explained; suddenly, the stories of the Listeners' *uwufwiti*, witchcraft, made sense. And the station was moving faster still; how many more decades—centuries—would pass in the time it took her to find the Union's secrets, and how many more in the time it took to piece their fragments together?

It won't matter to K'aari. She will stay—the station will hold more than she could learn in a lifetime. But when a thousand years have passed, I will return at last to Mutanda. Maybe I will return with pebbles to scatter; maybe, like Ishyanga's Prometheus or Old Earth's, I will bring back knowledge. Though maybe, by that time, the people of what once was the Union will have rediscovered it themselves.

She would return with stories, at the very least. She wondered if there would be stories of *her* by then, and who, from what far world, would come questing after them.

ROCKING THE CRADLE
Patrick Chiles

If you've read his novels Frozen Orbit *or* Frontier—and *you should have read them both, they're fantastic—stories of strange objects discovered in space is familiar ground to Patrick Chiles. Yet just because it's familiar ground doesn't mean there aren't still some wild directions to explore, daring questions to ask, and strange adventures to be told. With this story of a dig by an aspiring Indiana Jones on Sirius A, Chiles adds some of his own twists to perhaps the oldest question genre authors have asked since they started telling tales of ancient aliens, and ruins on other worlds:*

By exploring the pasts of other worlds and other lifeforms, what might we learn about our own?

My name is Michael Alvarez, and I'm a geologist. Geology may be the most practical of all physical sciences, being that the study of our planet's evolution involves a lot of digging around in the dirt and thinking about how it all got there. Literally a "down to Earth" profession.

Yes, I like rocks. A lot. Enough to have joined an expedition to a planet in an entirely different solar system just for a chance to dig up their rocks. Having established that I'm otherwise a fairly well-grounded guy (geology pun intended), you'd think that willfully allowing myself to be sucked into a wormhole and spat out the other side, eight and a half light-years from home, would be the weirdest experience of my life.

You would be wrong.

Don't misunderstand me—it was *supremely* weird. The fastest ships we have took almost two years just reach the wormhole's Hill sphere, the area of dominant gravitational influence. As we approached, it didn't look like anything was there for the longest time and even from orbit it was hard to see anything.

Of course, this is why nobody knew it was out at the edge of our Solar System up until a few years ago. The only reason anyone found it was because they were in the vicinity looking for something else. The gravity well was unmistakably present, so imagine their surprise when they didn't find a planet at the center of it. Instead, they found a hole in the middle of space.

Fortunately for us, the survey team parked a transponder beacon in synchronous orbit along the event horizon so we wouldn't lose track of the thing. Apparently it's easy to do, gravity field or not. It certainly helped navigation, or at least that's what the rocket jockeys tell me. And it helps with comms from the other side, which is one more aspect of the supreme weirdness that rules this place.

I mean, the light delay ought to be on the order of eight

years but thanks to The Hole, we can get a signal to Earth in about twelve hours. I guess that makes sense, I mean if humans and our machines can make it through in one piece, then EM radiation ought to behave the same way.

Going through it after spending two years in the proverbial Vastness O' Space was like having your entire world, your whole life experience, compressed and sucked through a soda straw. It seems to go on forever but at the same time is over almost instantaneously.

Have you ever thought about what *infinite* really means? As far as we know, space and time go on forever without end. I mean, one day there'll be the heat death of the universe so it'll eventually end, but work with me here. Try to imagine something so vast it has no observable limits, then all of a sudden the boundaries are blindingly obvious. The entire expanse of your universe becomes naked-eye visible, a narrowly defined existence that you best not stray from. It's like pouring space-time through a funnel; you feel like you can wrap your arms around infinity, as if you can reach out and touch everything that's ever been or ever will be.

If that's a God's-eye view of the universe, then He can keep it.

When I was a kid, I remember my parents driving us through the tunnels of the West Virginia mountains on our way to the beach. The first time was terrifying. I couldn't escape feeling the whole of that mountain surrounding us, and I just *knew* it was going to cave in on us at any moment (which, oddly enough, is what got me interested in geology but that's a story for another day).

Going through a wormhole is like that except you can't

really see it until you're in the middle of it and then it feels like the whole damned *universe* is waiting to cave in on you. And it is kind of the same concept, a tunnel through space-time.

The ship's chronometer said it took eight seconds to transit. That approximates one second for each light-year but I have no idea if that's significant. I couldn't even tell you if the astrophysicists know, but I can tell you it didn't feel like eight seconds. And with the whole relativistic time dilation thing, I don't try to understand too much. It bakes my noodle. You go fast, time slows down in your frame of reference. That's all I need to know.

Honestly, I don't understand how anything behaves in there. If that strikes you as odd for an astronaut, remember I'm actually a geologist by profession. I only got pulled into the space program because they all of a sudden needed lots more people like me.

The space program already had a lot of geologists, in fact there's a whole subspeciality of planetary geology that sprang up once we started landing probes on other planets. Exobiology was even a thing before anyone found evidence of life elsewhere, just because we fully expected to find it. What we haven't had is exo-archaeology or paleontology, for reasons which were obvious until recently.

Finding evidence of an advanced civilization on the other side of The Hole changed all that. Entire scientific disciplines began to emerge almost overnight, though at the beginning most of them were wildly speculative. How else could it have gone, really? Nobody seriously thought anything like this would ever happen in our lifetimes.

I mentioned I'm a geologist by profession, and that's

true. It's what I did for a living. Archaeology was a passion I indulged on the side, occasionally for pay as a consultant on digs (they are extracting ancient ruins from the dirt, after all, and dirt is kind of my thing). I spent a lot of my time off volunteering on digs all over the world—not too many people know this, but you can plan entire vacations around it. It's painstaking work and they're always looking for help. Anyway, I guess I was always fascinated by what came before us and how the Earth covered it up over the millennia. Also I wanted to be Indiana Jones when I grew up.

This dig was like nothing I'd ever experienced, only partly because it was in space, eight light years from home.

The sky looks different here, for starters. The main star in this system, Sirius A, is almost twice as big as Sol (that's our Sun) and twenty-five times as bright. If you look up at the night sky in winter, you can't miss it. It's the brightest star in the sky, the head of Orion's faithful hunting dog. It's big and pumping out a lot of energy, so the "Goldilocks Zone" of habitable planets around it is pretty far afield.

We're way outside the habitable zone, and Sirius A is still agonizingly bright. We're at the edge of the system, poking around a distant planetoid in a belt of shards roughly analogous to our Kuiper Belt. The same crew that found precursors of Earthly life there are the ones who found The Hole, and had a hunch they'd find similar evidence here. They turned out to be right. Hopefully one day we'll be able to thank them, but that's yet another story for later.

For now we're calling this place Sirius 7, meaning it's

the seventh planet located around the main star (there's a companion white dwarf, Sirius B, but it's too small to be concerned with). Seven is where the action is in the Sirius system for a couple of reasons:

One, it's the closest planet to the wormhole and it's a pretty long hike to the others. Its orbital period is a good couple of thousand years and we're lucky it's in proximity to The Hole right now. If it were on the other end of its orbit, the next closest planet would be a year away. We've sent probes down the well but it'll be a while before any cross the inner planet's orbits. Best to send some drones ahead of us to scout the place. Wormholes are great for crossing interstellar distances, but interplanetary hops are still slaves to Isaac Newton.

That's another important property of wormholes: they by necessity have a pretty strong gravity gradient, so they seem to naturally occur at a healthy distance from the nearest star system. Otherwise, it'd be another gravity well that could keep a system from forming in the first place. Almost like they were designed that way, which is a little too weird for me to dwell on.

The second reason is we found more of the same kinds of biological precursors they found in the Kuiper Belt. And this time, there was evidence of more. Much more.

Structures, for starters. Some formed from the ice, some from materials that clearly came from somewhere else. And they've all been here a long time.

If you're like me and watched too much Indiana Jones as a kid, you're no doubt waiting to hear the creepy part. There's always a creepy part. So here it is:

The inner planets, the ones in the Goldilocks Zone, are all dead-assed quiet. Spectroscopy shows two of them have oxygen-rich atmospheres and liquid water, similar to Earth. Whereas we might not have been able to tease out their EM signatures from Earth, what with Sirius essentially blinding us, now we're in the neighborhood and able to see better. In a sense, we can put up a sunshade (starshade?) and block the worst interference. Especially when the planets are at elongation (that is, farthest angular separation from Sirius), we should be able to pick up signs of civilizations.

Note that I didn't say "life." That's different. With atmospheric O_2 concentrations around twenty percent and liquid water, we'd be shocked if life hadn't emerged on both. In fact the other chemical markers are all there, like methane. Whether from decomposing vegetation or animal farts, it's almost a sure-fire sign of biological activity.

What we haven't detected are the markers a technologically advanced civilization would be expected to leave. Higher concentrations of carbon, for instance. Whether dioxide or monoxide, one would tell us there's internal combustion going on down there, and as far as I know nobody's seen them in high enough concentrations to suggest industrial activity.

That in itself isn't especially concerning. If they're sufficiently advanced—and finding ancient structures this far out in their system argues they would be—then we should assume they moved away from fossil fuels just like we're doing. Nuke plants are cleaner, and who doesn't want clean?

We're assuming they have nuclear power only because that's the only way to explain this much structure this far out in the system. Doesn't matter where in the galaxy you're from, chemical rockets just can't bring living beings this far in a reasonable amount of time. Even if their life span was measured in centuries, it's a stupidly long trip.

Speaking of that, I should explain our thinking on which of the two planets is most likely to have sprung forth a spacefaring civilization. Our money's on the smaller one. It seems likely that chemical rockets are a natural step in technological evolution. Same way we moved from rowboats to sails to steamships, ending with nuclear plants and gas turbines. Maybe that's too human-centric, but the physics is what it is.

I might only be a lowly geologist, but I did have to take a few classes in rocketry and orbital mechanics to do this job. What a lot of people don't appreciate is just how perfectly balanced our lives on Earth are, and the ability to leave the planet is especially underappreciated. If Earth had just a little more mass, on the order of ten percent or so, we might never have been able to build rockets big enough to put anything useful into orbit. At least not with old-fashioned chemical fuels. Maybe an insane Orion drive, propelled by nuclear bombs, could've lobbed people into orbit. But who in their right mind would want to create that kind of environmental nightmare just to loft something off the planet?

No, a heavier Earth would've left us tied to the planet until someone figured out how to nullify gravity. Not saying they couldn't have, we just haven't found a way yet.

That's why we're thinking it's the eighty-percent Earth.

That actually puts them in the sweet spot for space exploration. It's just enough to have made single-stage to orbit launchers feasible even with older technology, which could've enabled a spacefaring civilization to emerge sooner than ours.

So why are we not seeing any signs of it? I mean, other than the ancient structures here on Seven?

That's what we can't get our heads around—there are no EM emissions coming from anywhere in this system. Radio, visible light, infrared . . . a civilization that left this kind of archaeological evidence ought to be pretty active, right? You can't stop the signal, to coin a phrase.

After making it all the way out here, now they've gone dark. Why?

Back to the creepiness factor.

There are plenty of theories, some more credible than others, but all of them point to a civilization-ending catastrophe. Nuclear war or some equivalent was the knee-jerk reaction, but I don't necessarily subscribe to that. Not saying it isn't possible, but we need a lot more evidence. A close-up look at their home planet, for one, because the radiation traces aren't detectable from here. That means it either didn't happen, or it was a *very* long time ago.

Same goes for runaway global warming. We don't see enough greenhouse gases or other pollutants to assume an environmental collapse.

An extinction-level asteroid strike is another one, though a spacefaring society ought to have been able to avoid that.

Being a layman astronomer (another skill I had to learn

for this job), my money's on a gamma ray burst. Sirius B is the kind of star that could've burped one out on its way to white dwarf status, and that would've effectively sterilized any planet in its path. And if that is what happened, we Earthers should be grateful it wasn't pointed in our direction at the time. A gamma burst can reach pretty damned far, and even eight light-years isn't a minimum safe distance. Think of them this way: a ten-second gamma ray burst releases more energy than our Sun would in its entire lifetime.

So, yeah—I learned just enough astronomy to scare the hell out of me. A gamma burst could be coming our way right now and we wouldn't know it until we detected it. That is, when the light arrives at Earth it's already too late.

Here comes the "but." If that is what happened, and it was a surprise, it seems like we'd have found evidence of that as well. The alien structures on Seven are extensive. Whoever they were, they had a serious presence here. It might even have been a waystation to other places. I mean, what if that's not the only wormhole out here?

Anyway, my point is if it had been *that* kind of sudden extinction event, it would've taken the folks out here by surprise too. They'd have been turned into microwave burritos just like everyone back on their home planet. We should have found remains.

So far, nothing. Not even bone fragments. Did I mention there's hardly any atmosphere? If anyone croaked here, we'd have found them.

Here I should point out how difficult these kinds of digs can be in an EVA suit. It's hard to overstate just how much your sense of touch can guide you when you're down in the dirt. It demands light steps and a light touch, which isn't easy when you're encased in layers of neoprene rubber and Kevlar. The new mechanical-counterpressure outfits do make it easier, but there's no getting around the gloves. Fingers still get cold faster than anything else, so the heating filaments are always going to add bulk. The ice here is almost all carbon dioxide, which begins to sublimate away at the slightest application of heat. So on top of not being able to feel texture, you're constantly working through a haze of CO_2 gas. Thank goodness it's not nitrogen, like Pluto. That stuff tends to sublimate rather explosively.

Fortunately, we're not talking about ancient stone ruins here. Almost everything we've found so far has been made of advanced alloys so pure that the metallurgists are having puppies trying to figure out how they refined it. Nothing exotic, just variations on aluminum and titanium, which makes sense—elements are what they are and the periodic table isn't limited to what we find on Earth. It stands to reason an Earthlike planet in another star system would be composed of a lot the same stuff. What stands out is there are none of the traces of undesirable stuff like lithium or sodium.

That purity is one reason the structures have held up remarkably well. We don't have to guess at much of it, not like visualizing a thousand-year-old building from what's left of the excavated foundation. It's all here: domes connected by tunnels, mostly made of these superalloys but a few outbuildings that look to have been formed from the native ice. That's harder to tease out, and is more like what I've come to expect from a dig.

Separating the "formed" ice from the naturally occurring stuff is a lot like digging the carved rocks out from under the surrounding sediment.

By now you're wondering what we did find. And that takes us back to creepy town.

At first, we found nothing. No furniture, no equipment, no clothing or dishes or books or tools or photo collages full of alien family members. For reasons we still haven't determined, this site was abandoned. A long time ago, too. From what we can judge by the rate of ice accumulation on Seven, our best guess is five thousand years. If that seems like a lot—and it is—remember that this place has hardly any atmosphere. Five millennia's worth of ice on Earth gets you a glacier. Here, it's more like a northeast blizzard, and that's how we spotted it in the first place after the radar returns showed something funny. We could see the tops of the domes beneath the ice pack.

The first time I entered the main dome, I was shocked to find it in such pristine condition. Empty, but clean. Frost clung to the sloped walls and dim light filtered in from a row of translucent octagonal panels (again, some kind of alloy we haven't discovered yet), but it all looked like it was just waiting for someone to move back in and give the place some TLC. If I'd been able to take my helmet off, I'll bet it would've had that empty-house smell. Funny how the absence of humans leaves a particular odor.

We found them inside the central core of a structure we labeled Alpha-2, for nothing more endearing than being in the grid square we marked off. Letters for one axis, numbers for the other. Second box from the top left.

The dome's floor space was around three thousand square feet, comparable to a good-sized house. An outer corridor encircled a warren of inner rooms clustered around an open center. We think they were like dorms and this was the central meeting space.

The meeting room was where we found the one artifact. Two panels embedded in one wall, each about two feet square and covered with indented markings, like they'd been pressed into the alloy. Or the alloy had been formed around them. We haven't been able to determine for sure either way; suffice to say it's *really* clean. Not etched or carved. It's like the tablets just appeared perfectly formed.

Yes, I called them tablets. I'm welcome to better analogies but damned if anyone's been able to think of anything better.

Everyone on our team had a crash course in linguistics (credit the Agency for stuffing as many disciplines into a six-person crew as they could manage), which seemed like a smart play given the fact we were going to be exploring alien ruins. Still, it was startling.

Perhaps I shouldn't have been surprised that they used written language. After all, what advanced society hasn't? It's kind of a necessary condition unless they're telepathic or something. After seeing nothing but empty spaces, it was too easy to fall into the delusion that this was just other humans. Finding alien writing shouldn't have been so much of a shock.

Yet there it was. As if domes and tunnels eight light-years from home wasn't enough evidence, seeing something with alien writing on it chilled me to the core. What did it say? Was it an account of whatever outpost had been here and why it was abandoned? Or was it something mundane, like the latest redundant policy from HR (and if it's aliens, shouldn't it be "AR")?

At first I left the panels in place and photographed them in detail to transmit back to Earth. Figured I could study them back in my quarters that way too.

What a joke. I'm no linguist and I was way out of my depth. The writing appears based on intricate symbols, like Asian languages. I can distinguish between Mandarin Chinese, Korean or Japanese, but understanding them is entirely different. Once I got past the shock of having something in an alien language in front of me, I was able to identify the most commonly repeated symbols. That might have been nothing more than an exercise in pattern recognition, but it was a start. Every written language is just a collection of symbols that represent a sound or a thing or an idea, right? Why should theirs be any different?

So I pointed out some repetitions in the jumble of unintelligible symbols—big whoop. Without context, they might as well have been Egyptian hieroglyphics.

And that, friends, is where things got *really* weird.

Our survey on Seven was coming to an end. A month spent in pressurized tents that weren't much better than the EVA suits we had to wear outside was enough to have everyone on the survey team climbing the walls. After measuring, imaging, and electronically scanning every nook and cranny of the dome network it was finally time to start taking physical samples. It would've been nice to just grab anything that looked interesting—which we might have done, had there been anything that stood out.

The tablets, of course, stood out like sore thumbs. They were coming with us back to Earth. There were also some panels in the walls and flooring that the metallurgists wanted to study, so we took our time figuring out the best way to pry all this stuff free without trashing the place. We couldn't find any bolts, rivets or latches to release. There were seams between panels, but nothing else.

It was finally decided that in absence any better ideas that we'd just blast away with a laser. Because why not?

Okay, there are a *lot* of reasons why not. What I'm talking about isn't as crude as it sounds, either. Remember, this place is insanely cold. A little application of heat could go a long way, and that's what we did. We started with a panel in the floor of the Great Hall (that's what we took to calling the big dome), tracing the outline of a recessed seam until it was uniformly heated to something like fifty degrees C above ambient. As the panel expanded with heat, it eventually popped loose.

That's when we hit paydirt. The panels weren't just flooring, they were covers. Lids. We were walking on top of a massive alien storage container.

As part of the team dug into the subflooring, I turned my attention to the inscribed sections. Now that we could pry things free with a little heat, getting them out of the wall was straightforward.

I don't know what I expected to find on their reverse, but it was nothing like what I did find: More symbols, of a completely different character. If the obverse was reminiscent of Asian language, the reverse was... something else. Almost familiar.

I carefully laid the tablets (I couldn't help but call them

that now) flat, set up the camera above them, and
started taking pictures. First I got both together in full
frame, then individually, then closeups. I didn't want to
miss a detail, which was a good thing that I'll get to in a
minute.

I couldn't exactly take them back to my quarters to
examine more closely; they were going to end up in
hermetically sealed containers for the trip home. We had
a rudimentary lab back aboard ship, but it was more for
chemical and biological analysis. And I was not going to
be content spending the trip home with them left in a box,
unexamined. Every linguist on Earth would be poring
over these images, eagerly awaiting our return with the
physical items. While I had a duty to preserve them for
scientific inquiry, that didn't mean I wasn't going to get a
head start on deciphering them. What else was I going to
occupy my time with for the next two years?

My bunkmate back aboard ship, a biochemist named
Ricardo, spoke about a half-dozen different languages as
a result of growing up in a multiethnic family: Portuguese
mother, French Canadian father, living in a largely
Korean neighborhood in Quebec with his adopted
Ukrainian siblings . . . it was the proverbial melting pot in
which multiple languages had to be mastered as a matter
of social survival.

They never said so, but that's surely one of the reasons
he was selected for the survey crew. The expedition
masters must have figured we'd find some form of written
language here, but they weren't about to give up a seat to
someone who wasn't steeped in multiple disciplines. Until

somebody comes up with *Star Trek*-level antimatter power and food replicators, mass is always going to be a harsh master in space.

"Why would they inscribe two different languages on opposite sides of the plate?" I wondered as we studied the images on a trio of monitors in the lab.

It had been Ricardo's first look at them, and he was mesmerized. "I wouldn't call this 'inscribed.' That implies etching or carving. This looks cleanly formed, like it just appeared this way. Maybe laser etched."

"Well, we know it didn't just appear out of thin air."

Ricardo regarded me silently, with one eyebrow arched like Mister freaking Spock.

"Okay." I sighed in surrender. This was why the snobby highbrow research scientists made fun of us rockhounds. "We *don't* know that. Still, you have to admit it's awful unlikely."

"Improbable to the point of impossibility. Except our experience here has challenged many of our notions of *improbable*," he said, again channeling his inner Vulcan as he hovered over one of the closeups. "It's in remarkably pristine condition. Hardly any erosion for how long it must have been here."

Based on our first-pass carbon dating, that had been a long time indeed. Assuming these plates had been placed with the original structure, they'd been on Seven at least five thousand years.

"The symbols are reminiscent of some Asian languages," he continued, "though I don't see a direct correlation."

"Asian? Seriously?"

He backtracked a bit. "What I mean is they don't appear to form words. See how evenly spaced each character is? They're not grouped into words, so each one may represent a single idea or phrase. What's interesting is that there are some variations between the inscriptions on each plate."

"I noticed that too. The same way you can spot the difference between Korean and Japanese, even if you can't read them?" I didn't have his exposure to languages, but I could recognize patterns well enough.

"Exactly. These are probably the same instructions in different dialects." He pointed to a line of six symbols with a small subscript block in the middle. "And look here. I think these are numbers, judging by the arrangement and typography."

I peeked over his shoulder and spotted a few more similar groupings, arranged in a column along the left margin. Each one was separated by that same subscript character. "If you're right, then that might be a decimal point."

"It would make sense." He leaned back from the workstation and folded his arms behind his head. "What kind of numbers would you post in a pressure dome on a remote planet?"

"Depends on what the space was used for, I suppose. We think the big dome was some kind of common area, right? It's like the central hub for whatever this place was. Might be instructions for the airlock, for instance."

Ricardo stared at the text and shook his head after a time. "Too long for that, I think. Too involved. What kinds of numbers do we post in our own facilities?"

I hadn't thought about it that way. "Simple but important stuff everyone needs to know. Emergency procedures. Evacuation protocols. Communications."

He sat upright. "I think you're on to something. Comms. For all we know, those might be phone numbers." He pointed at the patterns again raising an eyebrow. "Or radio frequencies."

Now *that* made sense. "Six digits, separated in the middle by a decimal point," I said, "assuming we're right about what they represent."

"Radio frequency bands are what they are," Ricardo said. "The difference is going to be in deciphering what kind of numbering system they used. If it's base-ten math, we're in business."

That's when my enthusiasm faltered—we might not be any closer to figuring this out if they didn't use a common system. "How would we know?"

Ricardo kept staring at the screen, as if it might eventually reveal some hidden clues. "We have to make some baseline assumptions and work with them until we're proven wrong."

"Then let's do that. Humans invented the decimal point for base-ten math, so I think it's a safe assumption. Like you said, the frequency ranges are what they are. If those are numbers, then to my eyes they look like VHF or UHF."

"Six digits?" he asked. "Probably UHF."

A few of the assumed numbers looked obvious. "So let's start with one. That line right there looks likely." It was just a dash by itself: —.

"Old Chinese numbering systems worked that way,"

Ricardo said. "Look here, that's probably a two." It was, in fact, two dashes stacked horizontally: =.

"Looks like an equal sign," I said, though he was probably right. "How much you want to bet three is just one more dash?"

Now that we had a clue, it didn't take long to find three stacked dashes. Ricardo pointed it out in a couple of different locations. "That would make sense," he said, highlighting each numeral onscreen as we identified them. "A simple tally system that could have carried over into more advanced languages. Easy to write, until you get to higher numbers. Think Roman numerals."

"I try not to. Can you imagine doing math with that system?"

"I don't think anyone could. Probably why our ancestors converted to Arabic numerals."

"Which one of these represents zero, then? That's kind of a big deal."

Ricardo frowned. "Hard to tell from this. If we're correct that these are radio frequencies, then it's entirely possible there's no zero represented here. Think about the freqs we use—how often do you see a zero?"

I hadn't thought about that, but he had a point. "Hardly ever."

"We'd have to see more." He pointed at the images. "You said there's a reverse?"

"There is. Hang on." I swiped the obverse sides of the plates away and pulled up the reverse. The screen was filled with what appeared to be hash marks, each character in a different arrangement, but each constructed of similar strokes.

"Now *that's* different," Ricardo said. "Nothing like the other plates." After he'd pointed out the difference, I could see these characters were arranged differently. Not evenly spaced like the others, they were grouped in a manner that suggested words.

As he leaned in for a closer look, Ricardo's stoic demeanor disappeared. "You're shitting me," he said, and turned to me wide-eyed. "This is a joke, right? Are you pranking me, Mike?"

I spread my hands in a "who, me?" gesture, downplaying the ominous weirdness for myself as much as for him. "I don't know what you're talking about."

His finger shook as he traced each line. "This isn't alien. I mean, it's *obviously* alien just because of where we found it," he stammered, which was not normal for him. If anything, he too often carried an annoying air of undeserved superiority. "But this is . . . this is *human*."

It was my turn to stammer. "Human?" Was that why this scribbling had looked so familiar? "What kind of human language is that?" It was an elegant if comparatively primitive wedge-shaped script, yet remarkably clean like the obverse side.

As the team's layman archeologist, at this point I was kicking myself. I'd seen this before, on a dig in Jordan. It just goes to show how our preconceptions can blind us to the obvious. I was looking for something completely different, and couldn't see what was clearly there. "That's a type of cuneiform."

Ricardo adjusted his glasses and pressed in as close as he dared, regaining his composure. "It certainly appears so. I know some Latin, but . . ." he trailed off.

My early exposure to this ancient script came rushing back. "Trust me, it is. But why would they not put it out front like the others?" I wondered. "It's like they were hiding it."

Ricardo tugged at his chin. "Perhaps we're overthinking this. It may be simple, like prefabricated instructions. They placed whichever language is most used outward."

I had a hard time getting my head around that. "But why, if it was still in use?" I wasn't ready to confront the question of how an ancient proto-language from Earth had come to be used in an entirely different star system.

"A convenience," he surmised, "or a courtesy." His eyes met mine. "For visitors. Guests."

A chill went up my spine. "Like us."

Our survey ship boasted an extensive research library, befitting an expedition to an extinct civilization in another star system. Comsats positioned in halo orbits on either side of The Hole could relay data by laser, taking advantage of the shortcut through space-time just as we did to get here. But there was still a lot of fidelity lost along the way, limiting us to only the briefest transmissions with the barest data. And there was still the issue of distance between The Hole and Earth, which besides the light delay seriously limited comms bandwidth.

Put simply, we had to rely on whatever resources had been uploaded to our servers before we left. There was no Googling "ancient proto-languages" here at Seven. We could search our ship's intranet, but you get my point— we didn't have access to the whole world's storehouse of knowledge. All we had was what we brought with us, which was a lot in terms of the physical sciences. Ancient languages? Not so much.

We were forced to improvise, which involved making ourselves into monumental pains in the asses of our teammates by convincing them to hand over their personal tablets. We scoured hundreds of e-book files for anything that might help us.

It ended up being a more fruitful search than you might imagine. Our resident physicist had some old college texts on ancient Greek, Hebrew and Aramaic buried deep in his collection. Before Seven, they'd have seemed like odd choices. Did he expect to find the missing Dead Sea Scrolls out here? Though I doubt he even realized they were still there. The guy's a digital packrat.

Anyway, they turned out to be more helpful than not. It gave us some useful clues on syntax and grammar. There weren't going to be any direct correlations, but if we could identify patterns and frequently used letters (or what passes for letters in Alien Cuneiform) then we could start piecing this puzzle together.

We both furiously dove into those texts, but I have to admit Ricardo's was the more productive research. I'd seen this before in the field, but for him it all seemed to come naturally.

Not long after we pirated those texts, Ricardo was comparing notes against the tablets from Seven. "You know what this is?" he asked, excitably (which I feel like I have to add—remember, this guy doesn't get excited about anything). "It's their Rosetta Stone."

As you may have guessed, that's when we started calling this the Rosetta Project.

"You're right," I said, once again arriving late at what should have been an obvious conclusion for a guy who spends his free time studying exactly this kind of stuff. "Nobody had been able to figure out Egyptian hieroglyphics until Napoleon's army dug it up out of the desert. Once they saw it side-by-side with ancient Greek and another Egyptian script called Demotic, they could finally start piecing together the glyphs."

"They had a distinct advantage," Ricardo pointed out. "They at least understood Greek."

"Right again," I said. "What the hell are we supposed to make of this without a cuneiform primer—assuming that's what it actually is?"

Ricardo took off his glasses and rubbed at his nose. I could see he was getting bleary-eyed from all the reading. "We start by process of elimination," he said, and pointed at a couple of columns of similar-looking characters. "But if this ends up being something more than a casual resemblance, then it begs the question: How did two civilizations, light-years apart, develop similar root languages?"

That was the creep factor I'd tried to ignore, focusing instead on the mechanics of solving this particular puzzle. It was a mental exercise that kept me from dwelling on the bigger mystery. "What if this isn't really an 'alien' base?" There. I had finally said it.

Out of all the weird revelations we uncovered on Seven, I haven't even talked about the weirdest. Once we started prying up panels, we expected to find stuff all over the complex. Which we did.

I wish I could say we found all sorts of advanced civilization-changing technology. A cold fusion reactor or phaser or a grand unified theory of everything would've been neat, but I'm afraid it was none of that.

The main dome wasn't a laboratory or common area for a research outpost—maybe that's how it had begun, but in the end it had become more of a memorial. A temple, maybe. Or mausoleum.

The panels had been covering hermetically sealed chambers, each filled with fine dust. At first we thought they might be soil samples from deep beneath Seven's ice, because at first glance it looked an awful lot like lunar dust from our own Moon. It was only when one of the survey team noticed some larger fragments among the dust that we recognized them for what they were: cremated remains.

That's when the biological sciences team went into high gear. Ricardo had to ditch his translator duties and dive into sequencing the DNA from a dozen or so piles of ash. And what they found left us all shaken. I wish I could say they found genetic code of some improbable life form, but in the end, the alien civilization we'd found hadn't been alien at all. More like distant cousins.

They've only managed to sequence three so far, but they've all turned out to be uniformly human. And when I say "uniformly," know that there's always uncertainty in science. When CERN built that big particle accelerator in Switzerland, there was a lot of buzz in popular media that there was a chance it could create a black hole that would devour Earth like something out of a bad movie. What most people don't understand was that actually meant there was a *non-zero* chance. In other words, they couldn't say with absolute certainty that it *wouldn't* happen. The probability of it happening was insanely small, something like ten to the minus twelve, which in practical terms means it's pretty much impossible. That "non-zero" chance had as much to do with our incomplete understanding of black holes than any realistic chance we could create one in the lab.

Same goes with DNA sequencing. If you get one of those popular tests to trace your ancestry, it'll come back with some small percentage being Neanderthal. So when I say "uniformly human," I mean *mostly* human. Like you or me. Because even if you're .001 percent Neanderthal, that means you're not one hundred percent *Homo sapiens*.

Hopefully that puts some things into context, because here's the kicker: out of the genomes Ricardo's team examined, not a single one had any Neanderthal in them. That wasn't surprising, but in a sense, whoever lived and worked here five millennia ago were more purely human than we are. Let that sink into your caveman brain.

Fortunately, my experience in Jordan had given me enough of a head start to work through more translations of the Rosetta plates. Once we started finding the remains, it didn't take long to figure out those number sequences weren't frequencies, they were local coordinates. A directory of who was interred where.

This strange place was finally beginning to make sense, and I'm itching to bring this all back to Earth where it can get the proper attention. Also, I don't want to leave it all up to government-funded labs so I'm putting my story out for public consumption to keep it from getting buried by eggheads who are convinced they know better. Because what little bit I've been able to translate so far has only amped up the creepiness factor.

Assuming the characters are in fact a version of cuneiform, then the translations became both easier and more troubling. Remember, each one of those coordinates marked a sealed burial chamber.

As I worked through each marker (that is, deciphering the names associated with each set of coordinates), I found repetitive syllabic patterns and realized I was looking at names. But being ancient and "alien" for lack of a better word, none of them made sense by any naming convention I'm familiar with. They were all separated by syllables, and I halfway expected to find an "Obi-Wan" in there. And then I came across one in particular: *Gil-Gah-Mech*.

Gilgamesh. As in, The Epic of. The ancient text about a Mesopotamian king that contains parallels to the creation story and great flood from the Bible. At first I wrote it off as coincidence until I found another: *En-Ki-Du*. By my recollection of the Epic, Enkidu was an adversary who eventually became his closest companion. His death prompted Gilgamesh to embark on an odyssey to find the secret of eternal life, encountering mystical godlike beings who showed him the path to the underworld.

It's been said that, depending on your point of view, a sufficiently advanced technology would be indistinguishable from magic. The Hole certainly fits the bill, even for us "modern" humans.

Archaeology is the study of human culture through the recovery and scientific analysis of artifacts and other remains, and human culture was the last thing I expected to find on Seven. Whoever built this outpost weren't aliens. They were our ancestors.

And that, friends, is not even the creepiest aspect of this expedition. Thinking it through, why is there no evidence whatsoever of a currently functioning civilization? They were clearly advanced, enough to have come this far and used The Hole to find their way to ancient Earth. All of a sudden, all the crackpot theories of ancient astronauts guiding early humans just became a lot more credible.

But now, five thousand years later, the whole system seems to have gone dark. And that's what's really baking my noodle: Why? Is human civilization doomed to a cycle of creation and destruction? Is that what happened here, and enough of them escaped through The Hole to set up a new breeding colony on Earth? I'll admit that I don't like thinking about that very much.

Archeology has been my avocation for most of my adult life. I've been driven to uncover hidden knowledge about our ancestors, sifting through digs in jungles and deserts. We always assumed Africa and the Middle East were the cradle of humanity, when it turns out it was more like the playpen at our cousin's house.

The cradle is here.

GIVING UP ON THE PIANO
Orson Scott Card

Authors from H.P. Lovecraft to Larry Niven come to mind when naming authors whose work has taken us to ancient ruins and alien marvels across the universe... but I'll never forget my first was Orson Scott Card and Ender's Game. The image of Ender, still mourning his actions, wandering the Formic ruins, and finding the Hive Queen, and with it, a chance at redemption, is one of those moments of genre fiction that always sticks with you. It certainly stuck with me.

Imagine our shock when we approached him about contributing a story, and he was not only delighted to so, but delivered a story that puts a very different twist on our theme. This is a story of teenage love and alien mischief as only Orson Scott Card could tell.

So I went with Dad in the U-Haul and when we got to the new house I helped him move everything in. Just him and me. I'm not bonded, I'm not union, so I didn't get paid and I couldn't afford to make mistakes. We even got the spinet into the basement. Fortunately, in the back of the house it's a walk-out basement, but I'm not sure that getting a piano down the slope of the lawn was any easier than the basement stairs would have been. I was not consulted.

Then Dad left in the U-Haul to return it back in Grand Junction and then bring the rest of the family here to Reno in the ancient Town Car, which is way more comfortable than the cab of a U-Haul truck. I won't get to experience the Town Car trip, however, because workmen are still coming in and out of the house to finish up stuff, and the doors don't lock yet anyway, so I'm here as the night watchman and daytime security guard.

I'm sixteen, no license, no biceps, no muscles anywhere, not even a squirt gun, so I won't intimidate any burglars.

I can't drive anywhere, and there's nothing within walking distance except other people's identical houses in the established neighborhoods, and the few houses under construction in this as-yet-nonexistent housing development. And a McDonald's and a 7-Eleven. I'm trapped here, the books are all in boxes, there's no antenna on the roof yet, so why bother with the TV? The dog is with the family, which is fine because he has never liked me except when he feels like humping my leg. And I'm okay with a sister-free week in an empty house in Reno.

What I have is the piano. So on the first night alone in the house, I think, what if I practice so much this week that when Mom gets here she can hear me play something real? Something *good*.

So I started practicing that night, working out of the sheet music and music books Mom got me three Christmases ago, which I found in a box upstairs. Dad told me to leave the boxes alone. But he also told me to have fun. Can't obey both commands. So . . . piano music. Mom's taste—Broadway, Great American Songbook, Tin Pan Alley, and Gershwin, which I can't play because nobody can play it.

What I discovered that first night was that making progress on sheet music takes a lot of work and a lot of repetition, but because nobody was upstairs and the nearest occupied house was two blocks away, when I got frustrated I could pound the crap out of the piano and nobody would complain. Did a lot of pounding that day.

There really is nothing to do in this remote development in Reno except walk to McDonald's for every meal, husbanding the twenty dollars Dad left with me. That was before the inflation after the OPEC oil crisis, so that was plenty of money as long as I didn't get milkshakes.

So I really practiced the piano, sitting on that hard bench with no back support, and by the third day there were actually passages from several of the songs that I could play through at the right tempo with no mistakes. No *entire* songs, but Mom would be happy with any demonstration of progress.

Seven P.M. In June that means it's still light outside. I'm practicing, then I stop long enough to change music books, and . . . somebody's walking around upstairs.

Bound to be a workman.

I hear a girl laughing. Not workmen.

I go up the stairs, wondering if I'm up to whatever is about to happen. Standing in our dining room, running her hand over our table, is this Girl. About my age. Pretty. Also looks smart, if I'm any judge, and I am. Considering that I've never had a date and girls always treat me like I'm just one of the gals, I had no idea of how to talk to a girl I actually would like to go out with.

"Billy Whipstaff," I said, holding out my hand.

"Seriously?" she asked. Then she shook my hand briefly. "Whipstaff?"

"Babies don't get to choose their own name, and minors can't go to court to change it."

"You just summed up what's wrong with the world," she said, not smiling but I could tell she was joking because . . . because I'm not an idiot and I had not summed up what's wrong with the world.

"I don't mean to be intrusive," I said.

"But I'm an intruder," she said.

"Are you with one of the workmen who are still doing stuff on the house?"

"No," she said. "I live in an almost-finished house two streets over, and since you've got the only other occupied house in the subdivision, I thought I'd come get acquainted."

"And that didn't include knocking?" I asked, because, you know, why shouldn't I make her feel awkward, just because she was so pretty it made me a little dizzy looking at her—Dad would say that's because all the blood rushed out of my head—so I pulled out a dining room chair and sat down.

"Are you inviting me to sit, or to leave?" she asked.

"Sit," I said. "I don't mind that you're here. It was just surprising."

"I did knock. But somebody was pounding on the piano in the basement so loud that I couldn't even hear my own knock. And the doorbell button did nothing."

"I was just practicing one of the music books Mom gave me a few years ago. Figured it was about time I actually tried to learn some of it."

"Sounded pretty good."

"Thanks." Mom had taught me that when someone gives you a compliment, you don't pretend to be all modest and go, Oh, I was playing horribly, and you don't go into a lecture about why you had to work so hard to get so good. You just say Thanks. So I said Thanks.

"I don't play anything," she said.

"Like . . . not even Monopoly? What about Clue?"

"You have games here?"

"In the bottom box in the back corner of the living room."

She looked at me for a moment, and then smiled. Not a big grin. Not showing teeth. Sort of between Mona Lisa and—somebody else. A nice smile. I felt good.

"I was thinking," she said, "he really knows exactly what box the games are in? And then I realized, he has no idea, he just assumes they'll be in the hardest place to get to them, so in case I actually wanted to play those games, I'd know that he didn't think it was worth the effort."

"And you smiled," I said. Grinning like an idiot.

"But if you won't play Clue with me, I might as well go home," she said.

"Why not Monopoly?"

"It's a horrible game. All about getting rich at other people's expense and then being merciless about the rent. And it's the worst two-person game ever because it's always clear by about the fourth turn who's going to win, because of the properties they've bought, and then the loser has to keep playing to be a good sport while getting mashed into the ground."

Since that's exactly what happened whenever I played with either of my sisters—I mashed them into the ground and gloated about all my money—I understood why she thought it wasn't fun. "You been mashed by your big brother?"

"I'm an only child," she said. "My dad took one look at me and said, Let's put a stop to this right now."

"I bet not," I said. "But if you feel unwelcome at home, you can stay here."

I had no idea why I said that. As soon as it came out of my mouth, I realized I had just invited a girl to stay in my house with me.

"I wish," she said.

She said I Wish! Not *you* wish, but that *she* wished she could stay in my house! Did that mean she liked me?

"I'd probably keep you up all night with my piano playing," I said.

"Do you know any quiet songs? Lullabies?"

"No, to put people to sleep I read the blubber chapter from *Moby-Dick*."

She smiled again. This time with teeth. "You came from a place where high school teachers assign *Moby-Dick*?"

"Grand Junction, Colorado, which isn't grand, and I don't know what's being juncted there."

And in my mind I walked her to McDonald's and bought *a milkshake* and put two straws in it and we shared and we both kept sucking after the milkshake was gone so it made that horrible slurping sound. And then she leaned over and kissed me and I kissed her back and everybody in the McDonald's kitchen clapped and hooted.

"It's nice to meet you," she said. "I really do have to get back because Mom has a whole list of chores for me."

"Isn't that a reason to stay here?" I asked.

"I like being useful," she said. "Like Lady Bracknell. No, that's *Importance of Being Ernest*. Lady Catherine de Bourgh."

"Who?"

"You've read *Moby-Dick*, but not *Pride and Prejudice*? Wow. I better get out of here, this is clearly a perilous place." She was smiling, so I knew she was joking, except she really did head for the door. I got up and followed her but the door was already closing behind her when I arrived and I heard her call out, "Bye!" and that was that.

I paced around a few minutes, replaying the whole conversation and all the stupid unfriendly idiotic things I said. But my mind kept going back to the McDonald's kiss that didn't actually happen and would *never* happen because I hadn't read *Pride and Prejudice* because it was a girl's book and both my sisters loved it and Mom loved it and so I *couldn't* read it because I'd probably love it but I'd be coming last to the party, which was a stupid reason not to read it, because if I had known who Lady Catherine Whatever was, she wouldn't have walked out right then. If I had known, she might have thrown her arms around me and . . .

So I'm falling in love with her because she's *the only girl in the neighborhood*. That's a rational foundation for falling in love. She's not even next door.

I went downstairs and started pounding the piano again, sometimes playing what was on the page and sometimes making up crappy chords and sometimes just pounding and pounding on any keys because . . .

Because something wonderful and unexpected happened to me, and she might be my friend, and one friend was way better than completely alone, which I was as soon as she left.

I never found out her name.

You can't call 9-1-1 and say, "I desperately need the phone number of the only other occupied house in my subdivision. No, I don't know their name, or their address because the street signs aren't up yet—I don't even know *my* address—but they have a daughter who is really pretty and nice and I want her to kiss me someday. Someday soon. But how can I do that when I don't know her name? Did I say she's really pretty?"

"Why are you tying up an emergency phone number for a trivial—"

"It's a genuine emergency. If I don't find out her name, and soon, I will be doomed to live and die alone."

"Have you even met this girl?"

"She came to my house and we met. Except the part about finding out her name."

"Why should I help you when you were too stupid to ask her name?"

Embarrassed pause. I couldn't think of a single argument in my defense.

"Using this number for non-emergencies is a crime. I'm letting it slide this time, Mr. Whipstaff. But now it's time for you to man up, walk a few blocks to her house, and ask for what you want." She disconnected us.

She knew exactly who I was because 9-1-1 gets that information instantly. And she also knew which was the only other occupied residence in our subdivision. She could have told me. What does she have against dumb people, that she would make me fix my own mistake?

I played and pounded the piano until it was dark outside. Too late to walk over to McDonald's but I didn't deserve food anyway. I deserved to die friendless and alone and my parents would arrive here and find my desiccated corpse and my sisters would fight over who got to have my room and my parents would be sad, but Dad would say, Really, his life wasn't going to be worth living anyway because when he met the love of his life *he didn't ask her name*.

You can only pound a piano, or even play a piano, for a certain amount of time before your back gets tired and your butt hurts from the hard piano bench and you're also sick of the sound of the piano ringing in your ears—and I was so discouraged and annoyed and sad that instead of getting up the regular way, I rocked back on the bench, which made it fall over, throwing me on my back on the rug Dad had thoughtfully made me haul in all alone and unroll it and lay it out where we were going to put the piano.

As I was lying there, thinking about how it had been a bad idea to fall backward because the rug didn't extend far enough to cushion my head, so I landed with the back of my head smacking into the bare concrete floor, and . . .

There was a horrible crashing sound that had all kinds of piano notes in it, even worse than when I was pounding on it. Crashing and breaking sounds.

I raised my aching head enough to look at the piano. It wasn't there.

Instead, there was a gaping hole in the back wall.

I stood up. My head swam, I could feel a headache coming on from crunching my skull on the concrete. When I was sure of my balance, I stepped toward where the piano had been and stopped because the floor wasn't there. In a very neat, sharp-edged semi-circle, the concrete of the floor was gone. The hole in the wall was also a perfect semi-circle with very sharp edges. And the cave behind it was pitch black.

I found the flashlight Dad put in the basement in case the power went out while workmen were there. I turned it on, I walked back to the hole and shone the flashlight down and there was the spinet, a weird combination of kindling, like a really bad Boy Scout campfire, and a bunch of wires poking out in every direction like my little sister Lady's hair when there was a thunderstorm coming.

The piano was not going to be reparable.

What did I *do*? The universe hates my playing so much?

And then I heard a faint sound from the hole, from near the piano. A faint voice.

"Is somebody down there?" I asked. Hoping not to get an answer.

I got an answer. Just a moan. Like the first sound. Not words. But a voice.

I shone the flashlight around, trying to see if somebody

was down there, but I couldn't see anybody and it looked like there was a flat smooth floor down there, perfectly level, and I realized, whatever caused this was really precise about everything. Sharp edges, perfect semi-circles, smooth walls of the domed space that had opened up under the house, everything absolutely smooth and sharp. There was no tool that could do this. There was no earthquake or explosion that could leave this result. The only untidy thing was the wreckage of the spinet.

If I had still been playing, I'd be down there with it. Or a slice of me would have been.

And then it dawned on me. The voice I had heard came from underneath the wreckage of the piano.

I went upstairs and out to the garage and got the six-foot stepladder because there was no way I could get the long ladder down the basement stairs and make the turn into the room, and I *wasn't* going to carry it outside and bring it in through the back because it was dark out there, and something way too weird was happening in my house for me to want to—for me to *dare* to—walk around outside in the dark with no streetlights in a place where I only knew one person besides the McDonald's workers, and I didn't even know her name, and even if she was here she couldn't protect me, nobody could protect me, why was I carrying a stepladder down into the basement?

Setting the flashlight on the floor right by the gap in the floor, I lowered the ladder down the curving slope and it came to rest on the floor of the open space when the top of the ladder was only about a foot from the basement floor. That was lucky. If I got down there, I could climb back up the ladder and get out. Probably. Unless some creature was taking a bite out of my ankle. Then I'd just fall back down and die. I've seen movies. Mostly on late-night TV, but those are the worst movies to have come into your mind in the dark while climbing down into an unexplained hole in the floor, where you just trashed the spinet, and where a voice was moaning.

Only it had stopped moaning. So either the ax murderer's moan had succeeded in luring me within reach of his blade, or the cat that had been crushed under the piano died, or...

I climbed back up the ladder far enough to reach the flashlight and bring it down with me. Because that was what a non-idiot would do.

There wasn't time to examine the weirdly smooth walls of this new cave, because there had been a voice from under the piano, and there it was again. I shone the light and saw a moving limb. A smallish limb. Did I crush a baby? A baby exploring under our basement?

The hand pointed. Not at me, but to the right. "What do you want?" I flashed on the Tin Man saying "Oil can" and Dorothy couldn't understand him.

More pointing, and now a feeble moan.

Then I realized that there were two of these little people under the piano but one of them hadn't even twitched. Dead? Unconscious?

"Should I lift the piano off?" I asked.

Another pointing gesture.

I turned the flashlight toward where he was pointing, which any non-idiot would have done the first time he pointed. There was a sort of rostrum there, and when I walked over I saw it was a small control panel of some kind. Lights came from inside it, outlining all the buttons, and also shining through the letters or symbols on the faces of the buttons, but I didn't know any of the symbols, except for a semicircle like a D lying on its side.

"You want me to do something with this?" I asked.

"Do something with what?" asked the Girl, who was standing in the basement at the sharp edge of the cave and without even being surprised I just said, "The piano fell down on a couple of them and the one who's conscious is pointing at this panel so I was asking what he wanted me to do."

"Got it," she said. Then she turned around and climbed down the stepladder. I rushed over to shine the light down by her feet so she could find her footing. In moments the two of us were standing near the moving arm and I was thinking, Is this a good time to ask her name? And I was also thinking, is that arm getting feebler?

"Look at the turning motion with his fingers," she said. "Is there something on that thing that you can turn?"

"Let's see," I said, and started toward the panel, but that left her in total darkness and she caught up with me, or at least with the flashlight, and then she caught my other hand and *held* it and I wanted to scream at myself for thinking about the girl when somebody might be dying under my piano.

She pointed to a red thing that I had thought was just another button, only wider. But she said, "That's the only thing there that looks like you might be able to rotate it."

"Go ahead," I said, thinking I was being gallant. Ladies first and all.

"Not me, Billy Whipstaff, what if it electrocutes me?"

"You're right, you'll just call for an ambulance after I'm electrocuted."

"No point in that," she said, "I don't even know your address, how could I tell them where to come?"

I reached out to the button and pressed on it. Nothing.

"He was making a clockwise twisting motion," she said.

Clockwise. I hadn't noticed that. "How far should I turn it?" I asked.

"Till it stops? Till we blow up? Till we get sucked into a flying saucer and carried off to Mars? I don't know."

I twisted the knob clockwise. As far as it would go, which was about halfway around, where it stopped. "Well that did nothing," I said.

"Don't be so sure of that," she said. Because the walls of the cave were no longer there. Neither was my family's basement. It was still dark, but shining the light revealed no walls at all.

"Now we can't even dial O for Operator. And wherever we are, we need help."

She called out, louder than I had ever heard a girl yell before. "Help! We've got some injured . . . people here. Help!"

It was better than any idea I had had, so I joined in with the yelling.

And then a distant light went on, which turned out to be only fifty yards or so away, and several smallish creatures—people?—came into the room, saw us, saw the piano, and then saw the feebly waving arm, mostly because I shone the circle of my flashlight right on it.

They rushed over. Two of them immediately started

dismantling the pile of wreckage and I said, "Maybe you shouldn't do that, you might injure them more—"

And she put her slender, graceful finger over my lips and said, "Shh. You're not in charge anymore."

"I was in charge before?" I asked quietly.

"Your basement, your intruders from outer space."

So we stood there, watching, as these small aliens— child-size, really. Like an average nine-year-old—if I had any memory of how tall average nine-year-old American schoolchildren were. I had no idea if I had been average myself. But nine years old is what came into my head.

"We are fully adult, Mr. Whipstaff," said one of the aliens. I couldn't tell which one, since they were all bent over the injured ones.

So they speak English, I thought. Not children, though. And aliens? Such a sci-fi thing. ETs? They looked nothing like ET.

Going by size alone, I thought: Munchkins. Only instead of sending the Lollipop Guild, they sent Munchkin EMTs, apparently. "Are they going to be all right?" I asked.

"How can they know yet," whispered the girl.

"Yes," said the Munchkin, though I couldn't tell if it was the same voice, and their back were still toward us. "The one who showed you how to return to base position is already getting better. The other one died, but he's reconstituting now, so he'll be all right soon enough."

Died. Reconstituting himself. Clearly not any medical procedures I had seen on any TV show. No paddles, no defibrillation, no CPR, no intubation, nothing I recognized.

"We can reconstitute ourselves, if we haven't been dead for very long," said a Munchkin. Two of them were facing us now, and neither one opened its mouth.

"We can't do that," said the girl. "For us, dead is dead."

"So far," said a Munchkin.

I was tempted to launch into an explanation of revivals after cold-water drowning, but instead I held my tongue, since I realized that within about ten words I would have completely exhausted my knowledge on the subject. Or, actually, before the *first* word my knowledge would have run dry. What I had were a collection of anecdotes and rumors gathered during my whole life.

"You are wise enough to hold your tongue when you have no confidence in your information," said a Munchkin.

Now all of the Munchkins were facing me, and none of them had opened their mouths. My mind raced through other ways of producing speech sounds, but none of them were decorous enough for me to ask about them.

"We don't speak language using sound," said a Munchkin who stepped closer to us. I assumed it was the one who was talking. The others went back to the two injured ones. They helped the one who had waved to us get to his feet, and one of them led him toward the light that the Munchkins had appeared near. The other two carried the unmoving one out, and I flashed on people helping an injured high-school football player off the field.

"You are right, Billy Whipstaff," said the one who said stuff to me. "These two are children. They were not authorized to use the hemisphere. No children are. But these two are mischievous. Not bad, really. Just ... curious and undisciplined."

"You speak English very well," I said.

The girl said, "I didn't hear anybody say anything."

The speaker said, "We do not use sound, as I told Billy. We speak clown to clown." Apparently the girl heard this, too, and nodded.

Since this made no sense to me whatsoever, I asked something else. "I don't know where we are, but I'm pretty sure we're not close to my family's basement, and I'm going to need to get home."

"I can take you. Right now, if you want."

"That would be fine," I said.

"No way," said the girl. "Not till you answer some of my questions."

"Unless there's, like, a deadline or something," I said. "I don't want to get stuck here, this far from home."

"Handy's curiosity is stronger than yours, Billy," said the Munchkin. "Or rather, your sense of responsibility is stronger than your curiosity."

Handy. Her name was Handy. Last name? First name? Nickname? "Her full name is Handel Amata Frenkel," said the Munchkin. "But she only uses the nickname Handy."

The girl—Handy—turned red enough for me to see she was blushing even in that dim light. "My father had a thing for German composers."

"Handel I know," I said, "but Amata?"

"My parents tried to find a non-German, non-Latin version of Amadeus. They thought it meant 'Beloved,' and they thought Amata was the Italian translation."

"Could've been worse," I said. "Could've named you Mozart."

"Or Pachelbel. Or Humperdinck."

"I can see why you didn't tell me your name when I told you mine," I said.

"I was just happy that you didn't care enough to ask. I figured that meant we weren't going to be friends, so I went home."

"And then you came back," I said.

The Munchkin spoke up. "We called her here. Or rather, we called her clown, and it brought her here."

Handy looked at him and shrugged.

"It's the thing our two unrelated species have in common," said the Munchkin. "I mean, besides bilateral symmetry, fingers, tetrapody, and brain and eye placement on the front of the head."

"Tetrapody?" I asked.

"Four limbs," Handy explained to me.

"Thanks, Hermione," I said. Either she had never read the Harry Potter books, or she didn't mind the comparison.

"The clown," said the Munchkin, "is a symbiote that dwells inside each of us and each of you. Our clowns are of the same species, but as far as we know, there is no limit to which species they can bond with. They enhance our senses, they greatly increase our memory and logic capacity, and they can heal us and regenerate us to some degree."

"I've read a lot of anatomy," said Handy, "and I don't remember anything about clowns imbedded in human bodies."

"They distribute their bodies and functions throughout our bodies, and I assume they do the same with yours, though my clown does not confirm this. They are present in every cell of our bodies, but they are indistinguishable from the molecules that are naturally present, and they give no outward sign of their linkage to each other. X-rays, MRIs, surgeries can't locate them. As soon as we got those technologies from your people, we confirmed that they are physically undetectable."

"But you're sure we have them," said Handy.

"If you didn't, you wouldn't be hearing me. Human bodies by themselves can't communicate this way."

"So how long have we had these ... clowns?" I asked.

"You got yours before you were born," said the Munchkin.

"We humans, how long?" asked Handy.

"After the unaided humans mastered fire, but before human females had figured out basketmaking."

"That's a long time," I said. "Why do you call them clowns?"

The Munchkin nodded, but I didn't know if to them that meant Yes, No, or Stupid Question. "When we started communicating with English-speakers, 'clown' was still a term for a rustic person who lived close to nature, tending animals or planting crops. When the meaning shifted to be 'ridiculous country bumpkin who doesn't understand the city' the clowns didn't mind, and then when it became, 'heavily made-up monster who terrifies children while pretending to make them laugh,' they liked the name even better."

"Because the name is more accurate?" asked Handy.

"More ironic," I said.

"Ironic," said the Munchkin. "Irony is their primary form of humor. Both our species got it from them. There were no ironic Neanderthals or Denisovans or Cro-Magnons."

"So you're not talking to me," said Handy. "You're talking, through your clown, with my clown."

"And your clown translates the communication into your language," said the Munchkin. "It all works very smoothly, as long as both clowns are receptive."

"I'd love to stay here discussing this with you," I said, "but my dad might be back tomorrow night, and I have a huge hole in my basement and a piano blasted to smithereens."

"I've always wondered," murmured Handy, "if there's such a thing as one smithereen."

"I don't know what I'm going to tell him," I said.

"You seem to have ruled out telling him the truth," said the Munchkin. "Either he'll punish me for lying, or he'll believe me and a whole bunch of scientists will descend on our house and explore that big new cavern adjoining our basement."

The Munchkin stood there, saying nothing.

"By the way," I said, "do you have anything like a name?"

The Munchkin shrugged. "Our names are visual. Something you might call a rune or a glyph." His two hands made a couple of quick motions in the air.

"If you lost an arm in a terrible accident," asked Handy, "would you become nameless because it takes two hands to say your name?"

"If I lost an arm," said the Munchkin named

Handwavium, "I would not need a name, because they would all recognize me as the one whose clown failed to reconstitute him properly."

"Please choose a name that we can actually say," said Handy.

"Call me Wonder Woman," said the Munchkin.

"Are you a woman?" I asked.

"Do you have genders?" asked Handy.

"It's a name with favorable associations in both your minds," said Wonder Woman.

"No," I said. "The name's been taken. Pick a name that isn't famous."

"Monath September," said Monath September.

"Monath is Old English for Month," said Handy. "Your name really is Month September?"

"I already showed you what my name really is," said Monath. "This is just a substitute."

"Can we go home?" I asked. "I need to concentrate on what excuse I'm going to give my parents."

Handy sighed. "You still think you're in charge, eh?"

"You don't have to explain anything to your parents. You can do what you want. Stay here and get in touch with your inner clown. Whatever."

"Not without you," said Handy.

"How sweetly loyal of you," I said.

"Irony," said Monath.

"Very clownish of you," Handy said to me.

About a dozen Munchkins trotted in and went to the piano's many fragments, picked them all up, and started trying to reassemble them.

"Do they understand how pianos work?" I asked.

"No," said Monath. "But maybe, between them and your clowns, they can figure something out."

"Excuse me," said Handy. "I need a toilet."

Monath just stood there.

"Do you know what that means?" Handy asked.

"Our mictoria and defecatoria would not be suitable for your use," said Monath.

"Then I'm as eager to get back home as Whipstaff here."

"We have isolated corners if you don't mind using the floor," said Monath.

"I do mind, especially since I have no toilet paper."

Again, Monath stood in silence.

"Papier hygiénique?" she asked. "Papel higiénico?"

"French?" I asked. "You think they'll understand French if they don't get the concept in English?"

Monath shook his head. "We have no substances suitable for anal cleansing. Our defecations and micturations leave no residue on our skin."

I silently thought, How many hours would the human race save in a lifetime if we didn't have to wipe our butts? And how many diseases could we avoid spreading by not waving our hands around back there?

"I recognize your questions as rhetorical," said Monath.

"Whose question were you answering?" I asked.

"Both of you," said Monath. "I understand your envy, but we also envy you. No species has reached perfection on any level."

"Why can't our clowns regenerate us if we lose limbs or organs?" asked Handy.

"Do you want the answer to that question, or do you want to return to toilets that are designed for the use of your bodies?" asked Monath.

"Bodies," said Handy.

Monath walked between them, got behind the rostrum, hit two buttons, and rotated the dial, all with great speed, like a touch typist.

A light appeared where the hole in the basement was.

"Home sweet perforated home," I said.

"Forgive our children. They didn't understand that little-used hemispheres sometimes have to deal with terrain that has changed since last use."

"I was pretty sure they didn't crash a piano down on their heads on purpose," I said.

The swarm of Munchkins came forward out of the darkness, carrying a spinet-shaped pile of sticks, boards, and wires. It did have an intact keyboard, however, in the right place. The Munchkins set it down and stepped back, as if waiting for approval. Or applause.

I went to the keyboard, put my fingers on the keys, and played a run. All I heard was the thudding of the keys.

"I see," said Monath. "This thing works by producing sound. That didn't occur to us."

"I didn't expect you to … reconstitute a piano," I said.

"Do you still want us to lift it into your basement, so you have something to show your father?"

"No," I said. "It's easier to explain the piano's absence than to explain how it got like this. Though I appreciate your effort to restore it," I added to the swarm.

Handy stifled a chuckle.

"Your ladder is still there," said Monath. "Would you prefer to use it, or should I lift you up?"

"Ladder," said Handy.

We both walked up to it, each put a hand on one side of it. "You first," said Handy.

"I don't want you looking at my butt while I climb," I said.

Handy shook her head. "You don't *need* a symbiotic clown. Climb."

I climbed. Then she climbed, and I gave her a hand getting up onto the basement floor level.

Monath drifted through the air and came to rest standing beside us.

"Oh," said Handy.

"Your clown lets you do that?" I asked.

"The clowns are helpful, but they aren't magical. Like the hemispheres, that is a technology we acquired from another species in our distant past."

"Will we ever meet those other guys?" asked Handy.

"Alas, no," said Monath. "They got too acquisitive and we had to kill them all."

"All?" I asked.

"Right back to their home planet, every last one of them. Such a shame, they were so beautiful. But cruel."

"Have humans done anything to bother you?" asked Handy.

"Right now, only two humans are aware of our existence. There have been others in the past, but since nobody believed them, we didn't have to kill anybody. We really do try to keep things like that to a minimum."

"When my parents kill me for this hole," I said, "can you teach my clown to reconstitute me?"

"What hole?" asked Monath.

And the basement wall and floor were restored to their original form.

I didn't trust it. I stepped to where the edge of the hole had been, tried to feel forward with my foot. No gap. I went to the wall that had been missing just a moment before, and it was solid. Felt solid to me, anyway.

"That is simply part of the technology of the hemispheres," said Monath. "The hemispheres keep a record of any material substance they sliced through, so it can be restored. Not living things, though. Just inanimate objects like floors and walls."

"Monath, how will you get back now?"

"There is still a passageway," he said.

"Track 9 and 3/4?" asked Handy.

I couldn't remember if that was the track for the train to Hogwarts, but it didn't matter if she got it right.

"Take my hand," Monath said to Handy. She did.

Monath led her up to the wall, brushed his hand across it, and then pulled her right through the concrete. Handy made a yelp but it stopped short of a scream. A moment later, Monath led her back through. "Your hand now," Monath said to me.

When he pulled me through, the ground disappeared underneath me but before I had fallen a quarter of an inch, Monath was holding me up in the air. He lowered us both gently to the floor of the hemisphere. Then he lifted me back up into the basement.

"You can do that yourselves," said Monath. "Just part the curtain here, and step through."

"And crash down to the floor," said Handy.

"A simple two-meter drop," said Monath.

"Two low for a parachute to help," I said.

"If we need to get through," said Handy, "can we crawl through backward and hang by our hands so we're way closer to the ground when we let go?"

"I can't think why not," said Monath.

"If we got through, could we even activate the hemisphere?"

"We'll decide that later," said Monath. "I meant, I and my comrades, not me and you two. You won't have a vote on that."

"I want to learn more about this. About you. About everything," said Handy.

"But not you, Billy Whipstaff?" asked Monath.

"I'd like to," I said. "But I'm only just beginning to realize how terrifying this has all been. I don't know if I'll ever have the guts to come back."

Monath shrugged. "Handy wants to, but she can only do it by coming through your basement. So I think this is a thing you'll need to do together."

I looked at Handy, thinking, This pretty girl is now required to keep company with me from time to time. Is that a good thing or a bad thing? Will I ever get to kiss her?

Handy walked right up to me, put her hands on my shoulders, and kissed me. Not a sisterly kiss. Not a "first" kiss. An actual girlfriend kiss, as I had always imagined such a thing to be.

"Will you let me visit your basement from time to time, Billy Whipstaff?" she asked.

"Speaking clown to clown," I said, "I'm okay with that."

But she didn't come back the next day, and the day after that, my family came home.

I was glad to see them, and watching the younger kids race around claiming this or that room, it was fun, I guess, but I had things nagging in the back of my mind and finally I got Mom and Dad alone in the living room, which was piled high with boxes, including on the sofa, so we just stood between the boxes and the side window and Mom asked me, "Made any progress on the piano?"

"Yes," says I. "Practiced hours every day for my first four days. My back got tired on that bench, but my fingers got to know where all the notes were. I mean, I actually like playing the piano now."

"You always did," she said.

"I always said I did. And mostly I meant it. But I didn't understand what playing the piano really was till this week alone in the house with no chores or errands or anything." Tell her about the piano, I was telling myself. Or was it the clown telling me to say it? Or was it the clown that kept chickening out?

There is no clown, I told myself.

"Well, let's go down and you can show me," said Mom.

"Can't," says I. "The piano's gone."

That just hung in the air for a while. "Gone?" said Dad.

"I only had one job," I said, "and I failed at it. I walked to McDonald's and had my usual double cheeseburger with a four-piece nuggets, and I walked home, and I was tired because I had played piano all day, so I just went to bed."

"Are you coming to a point somewhere?" asked Dad.

"The next morning the piano was gone. I don't know if somebody stole it while I was at McDonald's, or while I was asleep."

"Did you leave the door unlocked?" asked Mom.

"I never unlocked the basement door or the kitchen door leading out to the deck. Always locked, deadbolt too. And I locked the front door behind me every time I went to McDonald's. Which was the only place I ever went, since there's nowhere else to go." Except Handy's house, but I hadn't dared to go there because she has a reason to come to my place, but I don't have any good reason to go to hers except to see her, and then her parents will decide whether they want me dating their daughter, and since *I* wouldn't choose me to date a girl as cool as Handy, I didn't have high expectations for them. So yes, the only place I went was McDonald's. And only once a day, just one meal a day, because I didn't want to get fat, though I sometimes thought, walking to McDonald's is my only exercise, so if I went there more often, I could eat more. I can tell when I'm lying to myself. Or my clown can tell, and mocks me for it.

"The piano's really gone?" asked Dad.

"Yes," I said. "And I didn't see any tire tracks behind the house, or any new marks in the lawn from sledging it up the hill to the front of the house. It's like it fell into a hole in the basement and I never saw it again."

Unless you count seeing the pile of sticks and wires the Munchkins put together for me. I wasn't seeing our spinet then, either. Just its corpse.

I hated lying to them, but I feared getting committed to the loony bin if I told the truth.

Dad and Mom went on down the stairs. I didn't go with them, because if they got really mad, I'd be tempted to brush open the passageway to the hemisphere platform and just fall to the ground on the other side, preferably breaking my neck so it was a clean death. A seven-foot fall could kill you, if you landed wrong, right? That's the way I was thinking then.

Mom came up alone. "That was my Aunt Clara's spinet, you know," she said.

"I know," I said. "If I'd known they were coming, I would have thrown my body in front of the piano so they at least had to step over me to get it out. But I didn't know they were coming. Who would come in and steal a piano?"

"Because you were advertising its presence by pounding on it for hours at a time," said Mom.

"I was playing, not pounding." I was pounding.

"I know your delicate touch on the keys," said Mom. Irony, so I was hearing *her* clown, right?

"Mom, I'm sorry. I wish I could get it back."

"I wish we could afford to replace it," said Mom.

"Nothing can replace Aunt Clara's spinet, Mom."

"True. Maybe we can rent one."

Dad came back up to the living room. "If they picked the basement deadbolt, they didn't make a mark."

"Then maybe they kicked it in, tore it off the hinges, and then came back and installed a replacement door," I said.

"I'm not the one who lost the piano," said Dad.

"But you're the one talking like you think I let some

thieves pay me off to leave a door unlocked so they could walk out with the spinet."

"Enough," said Mom. "Billy already admitted that he failed at his main job, watching over our stuff so nobody stole any of it. He feels bad enough."

"I'm not sure he does," said Dad.

"I feel as bad as I'm going to," I said, a little defiantly.

Dad looked at me with such disappointment I wanted to cry. But I didn't, because I'm getting better at my full-grown man imitation. "No point beating a dead horse."

"Sorry," I said, "somebody stole the horse, too, even though it was dead."

Mom gave a little laugh, but Dad just shook his head and went out to the car to bring in the suitcases and stuff. "Your father and I are going to the store to shop for groceries. Is the refrigerator on?" asked Mom.

"Dad turned it on and I never opened it, so I guess so. If we had a gas oven, I would have opened it to stick my head in, but it's electric."

"Don't even joke about suicide. It isn't funny," said Mom. "I'm so sorry, Mom."

She looked at me with a kind of quizzical expression. Wondering if I really was sorry? I couldn't guess what was going on in her mind. If only her clown would translate her silence to my clown, so I had some idea of what she was thinking.

There was a knock on the front door, which Dad had left standing open.

Handy was there, standing in the entryway. "Can I come in?" she said, "or should I help your dad with bringing in the luggage?"

"Mom, this is Handy. Handy, this is Mom."

"Hi, Mrs. Whipstaff," said Handy, holding out her hand.

"Handy lives in the only other occupied house in the subdivision," I said.

"You met her on the way to McDonald's?" asked Mom.

"She came to call on us as the only other family in the neighborhood. Handy, you heard me play the piano, right? Before it got stolen?"

Handy didn't bat an eye. "The way you were pounding it, you could hear it on the moon."

Mom shook her head. "Was he any good?" she asked Handy.

"I didn't hear any obvious mistakes," said Handy. "But it's not like he played a recital for me. I came in and we decided not to play Monopoly and I went home."

And that was that. Mom and Dad talked about renting a piano but they never did. Didn't buy one, either. That's why I gave up on the piano.

RETROSPECTIVE
Griffin Barber

War and archeology have made for some strange bedfellows over the centuries, from Napoleon Bonaparte stumbling upon the Rosetta Stone while building a fort in Egypt, to Cold War naval missions aiding the discovery of countless shipwrecks, including the Titanic. Who is to say that if war does eventually follow humanity into the stars, that discovery might not follow after?

This is one such story, of a young spacer who goes into battle and comes out completely changed for the experience, into something no longer wholly human.

This story also serves as a fond farewell to author Rick Boatright, who died of sudden pancreatic cancer in 2021. A longtime fixture of Eric Flint's Ring of Fire community, Griffin wanted to pay homage to a longtime colleague and friend by immortalizing him in this story.

In retrospect, I should not have touched the artifact.

In my defense, there was little time to weigh possible

outcomes. Being pursued by a Perfected death squad tends to limit the available mental bandwidth for careful consideration beyond a certain very low threshold.

Interrogator One: "Please refrain from digressions from factual events."

Spacer First Class Rick Boatright: "What's that, I digress? Well, I suppose time does move a mite differently for me now. Do try to keep up."

Interrogator One, grudgingly: "Perhaps some background would not be entirely out of place."

It was the twenty-sixth year of the war. I was twenty-five. I suppose that makes me one of the oldest of a generation born knowing nothing but the constant refrain, the numbing drumbeat, of never-ending propaganda and partisan news of the conflict between Imperium and Perfected. Not that my childhood was any different, any harsher than that of those who came before—or after, for that matter. The frontier remained far from my birth-planet, after all. I joined the Fleet as soon as was legally allowed. My practical upbringing hadn't provided the academic qualifications to make any of the tech tracks, and I'd studied chemistry anyway, so navigation school was right out. Fleet being Fleet, they overlooked my actual education and assigned me to security specialist school. I was sent to a series of bases rather than starships, seeing little action. The uprising on Dotty V was something else: Perfected forces managed to instigate an insurrection. I lost a leg and a few other choice parts in the fracas that followed. I went through a couple months of rehab and came out the other side with some augments you can't get in your average meatshop. Those augments on board, I qualified for and immediately applied to the Commandos once the docs signed off on my fitness for duty. I made it through training and selection in the top ten percent of my class of thirteen thousand. I was subsequently deployed to 14th Interdiction Fleet's 9th Commando, then bumped up to 1st Commando as a replacement. I'd been with the 1st through the latter part of the Pancreat campaign, long and hot enough experience to truly be considered one of the team.

First Commando was tasked with taking down the control center for the antimatter plant in orbit around the barren planetoid, DB1432TT. We were deployed to that nameless—if incredibly metal-rich—planetoid for what should have been a straightforward objective. We were to take control of the facility for the 14th's use. As far as I can tell, it was one of those random strokes of ill-luck that happen in a war zone that led to Konrad being detected on our way to the target.

Regardless of the cause, the mission was scrubbed and we were ordered to evac as quickly as we could. I was ordered to scout the route ahead while the rest of my team tried to inflict break-off losses on the Perfected.

I miss those meatheads still, even Chief Urbanek, stiff-necked hard-vac-hearted b—

Interrogator One: "You digress again."

SFC Rick Boatright: "I digress again, yes. But I tell you some small part of my history not so you'll understand me better, but so I might recall the time before I was one with

*the infinite. Things farther away are closer at hand now I
stand with one foot elsewhere. This causes distortions in
my perceptions much like those I experienced when first I
beheld the artifact."*

Interrogator One: "Understood. Please continue, then."

So, we were on the run when I came across the thing.
Rather, I was moving low and slow between the surreal
metallic spurs and craters of DB1432TT while the rest of
my team was behind me, trying to discourage pursuit.
That's when I saw it.

The thing glowed/darkened/shone/shadowed a long,
narrow slope nestled between two craters that did not—
quite—overlap.

I blinked.

The thing sat/rose/undulated/froze in/through/above
the floor of the valley.

It made my eyes water. It was so strange, so far outside
my experience my first thought was that my helmet was
malfunctioning, painting weird shit on my retinas. I didn't
have time for it, and cracked the nicked and battle-scarred
ceramic of my helmet against the metallic shelf of asteroid
material next to my head. My field-expedient fix did
nothing. The thing was still . . . a thing.

At least it wasn't multiplying.

"Taking fire." Bester's voice was a tad strained. He had
every right to be. Our link showed Perfected 1cm gauss
rounds chewing through his cover at an alarming rate.

"Strawman package thirty seconds out. Obtain full
cover for optimal safety," our CAIT said, lighting up my
HUD with trajectories.

I swore—even I wasn't sure if the words were directed at the artificial intelligence or the wonder before me. The thing, whatever it was, continued to cycle through states and colors, to change every time I looked away or blinked.

"Boatright, get your ass under cover," Chief Urbanek said.

"Chief, there's something you shou—"

"Do as I say!" Urbanek growled.

"Strawman package in fifteen seconds," the CAIT purred. I really don't like the way the tactical AIs communicate. No flesh and blood person, even a Perfected, enjoys their work that much.

I dragged my eyes from the weird artifact, thing, whatever, and shoved off toward a cleft in the crater wall to one side of it. My armor spat and hissed, braking my headlong charge at the last second. I reached out, pulled myself forward to wedge myself into the crack.

"Detonating," CAIT said.

The package detonated some meters above our positions. My HUD fizzed and juddered while my radio implant, despite being hardened for military use, gave a lengthy screech. The EMP burst didn't do much more than inconvenience those combatants not looking directly at it, but the submunitions released in the explosion were the true tip of the spear, and harder to spot in the hash the EMP made of sensor readings. Hundreds of finger-length, sharply pointed nano-carbon straws shot from the heart of the explosion, a high-velocity, glittering cone. Each straw had a guidance system and sufficient reaction mass for a few course corrections and little else. CAIT provided terminal guidance for the straws. Most dove toward the crater rim the bulk of the opposition had been shooting from. The rest hammered down among a jagged outcrop some twenty meters to my rear left. The three red carets there went dark. I'd been so preoccupied with tracking the support mission I hadn't seen the targets hiding so close, and hated the sudden rush of gratitude I felt for the CAIT.

"Verified contacts down." I thought the CAIT's smug tone inappropriate, given there were still a number of possible contacts converging on our position. We all knew CAITs could miss vital details on occasion. "Trust, but verify," being 1st Commando's unofficial motto, I wasn't about to get zapped by a survivor.

I slipped out of the crack, searching for targets by the outcrop. The back of a helmet appeared. I drilled it with a pair of shots before realizing the Perfected was already dead. Killed by several straws, the body had slowly spun from cover in an expanding fog of crystallizing blood.

"Bester is off-line," Urbanek said. "Konrad, see what you can do. Boatright, finish your sweep."

"Yes, Chief," Konrad said.

Wanting to comply with orders, I dragged my eyes from the body and across the artifact. It had changed/cohered/diverged/stabilized/shivered again. I hesitated. I was an SFC in the Imperial Navy, and entirely unqualified to assess any kind of artifact, let alone one so obviously alien. Nice thing about Imperial Armed Services rank structures: one is encouraged to pass any particularly thorny problem on to the next level of command. That meant the Chief. Urbanek was tough, experienced, and smart, the very best NCO I had the privilege to serve with.

She would know what the thing was. If she didn't, she'd know what to do about it. I sure as shit did not.

"Uh, Chief, there's something here you should see," I said.

"Tag it for CAIT," she said.

"Tagging." I tapped a command on my forearm, sending the kitchen sink: still images, ranging data, and every other reading my scout suit's systems captured. It wasn't much. My suit was simply not up to grasping whatever was before me.

"There is nothing but planetoid there, Spacer Boatright," CAIT said once the transmission was complete. Damn AIs are too fast, sometimes.

"Damn you, CAIT, I'm looking right at it."

"At what, Spacer?" Chief Urbanek said. "I see nothing."

Clammy sweat popped from my forehead. Could I have gone into the deep dark one too many times? Lost my shit?

No, I had not. "Chief, come here, in person, and tell me I ain't seein—"

"Inbound ordnance detected," the CAIT's transmission cut me off. "Ten seconds to impact."

Another trajectory lit my HUD.

To make matters worse, some of the possible contacts were firming up as solid reds and advancing.

I jetted for the crack once more. I was bracing myself when the terrain under my gauntlets shivered. A storm of molten shards spalled from the metallic asteroid whipped and shattered against the outer edges of my hide, so hard I felt the secondary impacts as vibrations where my suit touched the surface of DB1432TT.

Konrad's IFF flashed, then dimmed. Chief Urbanek's dimmed, came back. Templeton's disappeared entirely. That wasn't supposed to happen.

"CAIT?" I said.

"Re-b-b-bbbootingggg," CAIT stutter-squealed.

I cursed again. A *lot* of red carets had appeared on my HUD just before it blanked entirely. I checked my suit's indicators. The entire LTN was down, including LOS comm to our evac. I risked a look out of my hide and back the way we'd come, back toward the rest of 1st Commando. I blinked. The landscape had changed since I'd passed through. The Chief was drifting, half her helmet missing. A molten crater thirty meters in diameter dimpled the surface of DB1432TT, precisely where the rest of my comrades had taken shelter. I bit my lip against a moan of despair. The drone strike that took them out was less a masterful piece of targeting and more the use of a sledgehammer to drive a thumbtack home.

I swallowed, momentarily refusing to admit my team was gone.

I avoid dreaming as much as I can, as all I see now is Urbanek's drifting corpse.

Unidentified Voice: "And how do you do that, avoid sleep, I mean?"

SFC Rick Boatright: "My need for sleep has dropped off ... considerably. I, myself, am not entirely comfortable with that fact."

Interrogator One: "Please continue."

✦✦✦

Shaking with rage and fear, I slaved control to my suit and prepared to kick a pair of drones loose, praying God The All-Wise would see me through this hour of need. The first drone would go up and over the edge of the rim of the crater wall my hide was eaten out of, the second back the way I'd come in. I hit launch. Both drones popped from my armor in a tiny cloud of compressed air.

I set the expert system handling my autopilot to seeking an escape route while praying for a long feed from the drones. I wasn't so lucky.

Drone one went dead almost as soon as it cleared the crater rim. Fried by a maser, it began a convincing parody of a decaying orbit that would—if uninterrupted—end on the nickel-iron surface of the asteroid some years hence.

Drone two's luck was scarcely better. It turned out of the crack and sped downhill, following the route I had been scouting. It clipped something, shuddered, went dead. Too late, I remembered CAIT's inability to perceive the artifact.

Praying again, I spun up the data off both drones, combing it for intel.

A squad of Perfected were about two hundred meters out and closing from my rear. I considered launching another pair of drones, but the speed with which the first one had been tagged argued strongly against launching from the same location. I did not want to give their hunter/killer drone more data points to track back to my position.

Of course, they might just deploy another massive ordnance packet to kill me, just to be sure all remaining opposition was annihilated. The Perfected are like that, in space: they can't rely on all their superhuman genetics to overpower us like they do in terrestrial combat zones, so they resort to a bigger hammer.

Figuring it was time to get a move on, I popped out of the crack and started downslope in the wake of glittering metallic material thrown up by the Perfected strike. Much of the material was still crashing back and forth in the narrow confines of the valley, microgravity and vacuum offering little to no resistance to retard or slow the flight.

Just one more problem to add to my growing list.

My gaze snagged on the anomaly. It seemed agitated somehow, transitioning while my eyes rested on it rather than when I looked away or blinked, as it had before the explosion. I would have to edge sideways to avoid contact with the smooth/jagged/violet/white thing that continued to writhe in the middle of the draw.

My HUD projected the Perfected squad would close to within a hundred meters of my position in seconds. I turned, dread making me imagine the thing reaching for me. I hugged the nearest wall and moved hand over hand to keep emissions at a minimum. Twenty meters on, I set another drone on delayed activation and dropped it.

Panting now, another twenty meters hand over hand. Bits of shrapnel and spall from the explosion continued to clatter and chime against my armor with frightening and sudden frequency. As long as it didn't pierce my armor, the material should prove a mixed blessing, concealing my drone's movements, but interfering with my sensor take as well.

Twenty more meters. If they were using their propulsion systems, the Perfected would catch up in no time. I hoped they weren't. They should not. Using propulsion was a good way to shout, "Look at me!"

The scout suit I wore was designed to be hard to spot by anything short of a full active sensor sweep, so I kept moving hand over hand. My hunters shouldn't know exactly what kind of numbers they were facing, so Perfected usually waited to go full active on their sensors unless certain of overwhelming local superiority.

My breath came in ragged gasps; solitude, exertion, and fear overcoming physical conditioning and years of mental training. I struggled to master it, resorted to thinking through one problem at a time.

Problem one: Extraction.

The primary extraction zone was beyond the mission objective, the by-now-thoroughly-alerted base, making it a scratch. I couldn't head directly for the secondary extraction point because there were currently an unknown number of Perfected between myself and safety.

Feeling blind, and worried I was being herded toward something I would not like at all, I set the drone sensors to active and kept moving while my HUD updated.

A rash of red carets appeared *ahead* of me.

Sudden sweat pooling in my suit, I raised my railer and jetted backward, dialing my suit speed to maximum and kicking out decoy drones as fast as the launcher would cycle. Screw stealth. I needed to reach cover as quickly as possible. Speed was the only thing that could save me.

A target appeared, fired at me even as I tried to light them up.

Dust and tiny motes of metal flashed, became molten cyan lightning as the vast velocities of tungsten steel projectiles sublimated and ignited the sparse particles between us. I was not hit. I don't think I hit my target, either.

I'm not sure who was more distracted when my armored heels caught an outcrop. Momentum imparted a savage backflip my suit could only counter by slowing my headlong flight.

I'm fairly certain the shooter had a chuckle at my expense. Not a full belly laugh, though. The bastard was too quick to resume firing at me to have indulged in more than a short snorting chuckle.

Shit like that happens in combat. Things you simply can't make up. God The All-Wise has a sense of humor, certainly. I, of course, didn't feel much like laughing as I lay parallel to the planetoid's surface, cruising along with my railer aimed between my boots. My shooting made the adaptive coloring of my armor flash white-cyan with each discharge as it struggled to match the environment. I repeated my failure to hit anyone, but it's hard to get shot at and not return fire.

The expert system managing my maneuvering thrusters pinged a warning. I hit the override without thinking. An instant later I crashed into one of DB1432TT's jagged shelves of cold metal, shoulders first. No armor breaches, but the impact jolted me to my bones. I flipped again, this time heels over head, if that makes any sense. I landed hard, on my knees. At least I was in partial cover behind the shelf I'd struck.

I scrambled into hiding, assessing the situation in my HUD. My pursuers must have halted their advance, because they weren't on top of me already.

I noted an inventory warning. I'd been rigged for sniper fire and the repeated discharges of my weapon had drained my railer down to thirty percent onboard power. I dialed launch velocity down to fifty percent. It wouldn't kill except on a direct hit, but I wasn't going to kill enough of them to matter, anyway. No, I just needed to shoot back to keep the Perfected honest. I quickly scanned my other inventory counters: ten decoy drones left, sixteen surveillance drones, two hunter/killers, and I was hovering just above forty percent reaction mass for my suit thrusters.

It would be enough. Had to.

The outcrop shivered, spalled chunks clicking against my suit, as the Perfected lit it up with 1 cm.

Ignoring it, I paired half my remaining decoys with surveillance drones and kicked them loose, watching the feed live. Most were killed in short order, but they gave me badly needed intel. The Perfected squad that had driven me out of the cleft had halted their advance once they flushed me toward their comrades. The surveillance drones had that initial group in almost the same positions I'd clocked them in earlier.

Holding position was the smart move. Blue on blue fire with a gauss weapon would ruin your day just as thoroughly as catching a round from the enemy.

God provided me a sliver of hope. If I was quick.

Targeting those moving to flank me, I synced my hunter-killers with most of the remaining decoys. I waited to catch a few of them in the open to launch my attack. I displaced farther along the shelf, firing my railer as I moved. Fire from the soldiers trying to pin me down slackened as the drones arrowed toward their targets.

The carets representing the flankers on my right disappeared as the hunter/killer got close enough to detonate.

The other hunter/killer died, a maser taking it out before it could self-immolate and take everything within a few meters out. Hope died with it. I would be dead in the next minute.

"Reboot complete," CAIT said.

"Danger close!" I screamed.

"Danger close. Active countermeasures detected. Strawman and decoys enabled and inbound. ETA thirty seconds. Take cover."

I nearly sobbed with relief.

Letting the expert system plot the fastest and least exposed path to the cleft, I fired a few more railer rounds to keep enemy heads down.

Back behind my shrinking cover, I sucked in a deep breath, pushed off, and let the autopilot take control.

"Active countermeasures encountered," CAIT said. "Compensating."

I was the rocket man. Jetting across the jagged surface in a staggered, corkscrewing course that nauseated even as it kept me from eating a 1cm round. The world shrank to glimpses; debris clattering off my armor, twisted metallic formations looming out of that alien landscape, 1cm fire probing all around me. A series of flashes over the short horizon as a maser lashed out and killed the decoys—at least I *hoped* they were only hitting decoys— CAIT had deployed to protect the strawman.

I rounded another outcrop, slid over the lip of the crater, stellar dust fusing in a long stream beside me as a

Perfected drone tried to cook me. The second attempt was more accurate, armor ablating. The autopilot altered course so savagely the world greyed for a moment.

Reaction mass hit thirteen percent. Many more maneuvers like that and I wouldn't have the mass left to slow down at my destination. I'd slam into the cleft at speed and remain wedged there for all time, just another guy who'd failed at bending the laws of physics.

The strange thing reappeared/morphed/solidified/reverted ahead of me, a disturbing signpost to the relative safety of my destination.

I remembered electronics couldn't see it just as the autopilot wrenched me sideways again.

More, longer brain-grey.

A warning chime. A blurred-edges reading of the icons: reaction mass critical.

More ablative armor smoked from my suit. The drone with the beam weapon had re-acquired.

I was officially having a bad day.

I was not going to make the dubious safety of the cleft.

A strange thing happened then: the thing/outline/distortion/truth swelled, seemed to allow the passage of light from somewhere deep inside/beyond/within/outside.

Searing pain as the last of the armor protecting my forearm smoked off. Alarms rang. As if I could possibly remain oblivious to the fact half my arm had been burned off below the elbow. My suit sealed the breach with minimal loss of atmosphere, injected a nerve block that did very little to kill the pain. My trajectory changed by the explosion of gases from my stump, I spun wildly along the long axis of my body, started losing armor from other body parts as the beam traversed and started cooking new spots.

I would be dead in seconds.

As I corkscrewed toward it, I looked at the void/presence. I smelled something pure, like fresh water welling from a mountain spring.

Suddenly unsure if it was an artifact of my fevered imagination or an actual physical presence, I decided I needed to find out.

I was soon to be in God's hands, anyway.

I stretched, reached, expended my last drones to interfere with the play of the beam across my suit, each one buying me another instant, another meter's approach toward the thing I could not name.

Contact.

Time slowed, each instant becoming infinite before being rendered utterly obsolete.

The pain was gone, any awareness of danger having fled with it. I felt no thirst. No fear. No hunger. I felt— and I know not why—at peace. I do not believe I had gone to heaven. There were no angels, for one. Indeed, I observed none of the things I had been taught to expect upon passage from this world into the next, but there was something, some certainty I had travelled from this world to the next. And no, I do not mean in the merely prosaic sense of actual, physical travel—though there was that— but the metaphysical as well.

<<Nonverbal interruption>>
Rick Boatright: "What's that? You question my claims?"

Interrogator One: "Your suit did not record the time you were in contact with the artifact."

Rick Boatright: "I cannot explain that, just as I cannot explain so many things about that strange moment that was no mere moment."

Unknown Voice: "Please continue."

SFC Rick Boatright: "Where was I . . . Ah, yes . . ."

The inside of the event/artifact/conduit was solid, but it was as if light had been given form and function. The unreal instability of the artifact when observed from afar was inverted, presented in a stark solidity of angles and contours observed from within.

Unidentified Voice: "Can you better define the anomaly?"

SFC Rick Boatright: "I'm trying to, but you keep interrupting."

Unidentified Voice chuckles, then: "Please proceed."

I had no sense of purpose to the space—if it could be called space—I was in. Nor could I perceive any concrete signs of age, though it felt ancient in the way that stone is: indifferent to all but the most persistent and powerful of forces.

There was this sense of vast power, too. Like standing next to the primary heat exchanger of a terraforming plant— you're not gonna get burned, but you can just *feel* the forces at work. It was a throb that was as much behind my eyes as in my chest. And, before you ask, I know that I was entirely within . . . whatever it was. And I was there a while.

How else could I have survived the drone attacks, the strawman strike, and the subsequent plasma immolation of half the surface of DB1432TT when the 14th took out the antimatter plant?

I suppose it's possible any human brain, seeking answers for the incomprehensible, might begin to force the sensations of that strange place into acceptable patterns, but I did start to hear voices. Time passes strangely for me now, so I'm unsure exactly when I began to hear them. I could not understand what they were saying, or singing, or indeed if there was even an audible component to what I perceived. But it seemed to me I was sensing a wordless chorus raised in question.

I understand a certain skepticism regarding the things I have seen. Like combat, like faith, the strange power of that object/time/place/instance can only be partially—and inadequately—explained to those who have no experience of it.

I shall leave it at that and move on.

I became aware of a difference, of a change in the undertow of power that hummed through and about me. I focused on that change. Gradually, like a bubble rising through particularly viscous oil, I became aware of need, of desire. Not my own, the sensation was of a push, or perhaps a pull toward something I could not perceive in the darkness beyond the space and time I occupied.

I had not seen darkness in the formless light before. Perhaps it was sudden, the approach of the fissures I could now perceive. I do not recall it forming. It was simply, and suddenly, *there*. It did not surround us, but rather pierced the powerful veils about me like a splinter driven deep through pale flesh, yet still visible.

Unidentified Voice: "You said, 'us.'"
<<Silence of four point three seconds duration.>>
SFC Rick Boatright: "I did, didn't I? Like the weirdness with time, there are some lingering aftereffects I have yet to acclimate to."
Interrogator Two, muffled audio fading in and out: "Th . . . energ . . . spike when t . . . subject spo . . ."
Unidentified Voice: "Understood."
<<Three seconds of silence.>>
Unidentified Voice: "Please proceed, Spacer Boatright."

Now it had my attention, I noted thick strands of not-material, perhaps fractures, running from that splinter into what I was given to understand was the substance, the fabric of that pocket of space and time I occupied. Looking at those splinters, I felt that indistinct drive, that *need* again.

The chorus grew louder and more dissonant, as if some desperation in the singers made for disharmony.

I can't be sure my mind wasn't making do with what it had on hand in order to stave off madness, but it seemed clear the artifact wanted me to do something about the jagged splinters lodged in it.

Naturally, I had no idea what to do. I opened my mouth to say so, and suddenly had the knowledge at my mental "fingertips." A gauntlet-shaped depression appeared at shoulder height and in arm's reach, just large enough to shove my armored hand into. I hesitated, though the humming thrum of power pressed me to *act*.

Interrogator One: "You did not mention your armor previously."

"I did not. Isn't that strange? It did not seem relevant at the time, as I seemed to be breathing, seeing, surviving just fine. Nor did I feel the pain of my lost hand. I recall no alarms, no indicators, no radio contact . . . Yet I felt no panic at the lack."

<<Silence of thirteen point two seconds.>>

Interrogator One: "Very well, please continue your narrative."

Deciding I had no reason not to comply, and a host of reasons not to think too hard about the decision, I pressed my hand into the void. There was a brightening, a change in atmosphere that I was only peripherally aware of, as the fingers of my right hand came into contact with something liquid and terribly cold. Thinking back, I should not have felt that cold, not with my suit on. Yet that terrible cold wasn't the most alarming thing about that contact: my fingers had entered the liquid parallel to the floor, I had not felt them penetrate a membrane or barrier, and yet the cold liquid was suspended at right angles to the surface I stood on. I know my alarm at such a small detail must seem odd given all that had gone before, but everyone has their limits, and I freely admit I was approaching my own at terminal velocity.

Fear made me ball my gauntleted fist. I started to pull it from the void, found with mounting panic I couldn't.

The liquid adhered to my palm, filling it with a hard, rounded shape the size of a handball. I tried to release it but could not. It also prevented me flattening my hand, a necessary precursor to removing it from the void, the entry of which was smaller than the void beyond. It was like the games some backward planets still play, where you can grab a treasure inside a wide-necked bottle but cannot remove it through the neck.

When dropping it did not work, in a near panic I squeezed as hard as I could. The effect was immediate: the directionless illumination around me seemed to brighten, to clear. That said, my hand was still trapped. Hoping to find something to help, I made a study of my surroundings. It was then I realized a stretch of the wrongness was no longer present.

I relaxed my grip, focused on another, thicker stretch of the splinter. Once I was fixed on it, I made as tight a fist as I could with that cold material in my hand.

A portion of the dark substance, a jagged splinter of *wrong* injected into the limitless immaterial of the artifact was crushed. Like sand washed from a basin, the crushed strand of invasive material quickly faded. I did not see where it was removed to, just knew it was gone.

The light grew brighter. It was not the only change. The tuneless song I had been feeling in my chest and behind my eyes became more fluid, though no less intense. It was still syncopated, but less so than before. With this assurance I had done the proper thing, the desired thing, I set to work with a will.

I'm unsure how long I worked, as I only became aware of the passage of time as my hand grew sore and tired. I was fascinated by the fatigue, as I knew I should have been in total agony from the dismemberment yet felt nothing from that injury. I could not, cannot explain why this was so. I can only think that while time passed within that place, it was able to selectively prevent the passage of time of those things brought into the span of its control. By the time I noticed this new oddity, my work had brought the light levels up to blinding-bright. Counterintuitively, rather than lose my sight, I felt myself able to perceive the smallest portion of the wrongness regardless of where it lay hidden.

Despite a steadily building fatigue, I crushed those tiny cysts as remorselessly as I had the great breaches and rents. It was something to do, and I was rewarded upon each dissipation by a chorus of what I can only call approbation.

Spacer Rick Boatright: "I am hungry. May I have some food?"

<<*Non-pertinent discussion of menu items follows. Duration of one minute, forty-nine seconds.*>>

Interrogator One: "You have an extensive vocabulary."

Spacer Rick Boatright: "Do not leave a sentence incomplete, it annoys those bright enough to see through you to your intent."

Interrogator One: "What do you mean?"

SFC Rick Boatright: "Which part of my statement did you fail to comprehend? That there are a great many people who are brighter than you? I would have thought that fact was self-evident."

<<*Silence of two point two seconds.*>>

SFC Rick Boatright: "Or was my observation that you had left your statement incomplete somehow unclear?"

SFC Rick Boatright: "I see it was the latter, therefore I will resolve that particular conundrum for you. You implied I have an extensive vocabulary 'for an enlisted spacer,' yet left those exact words unsaid."

Interrogator One: "I did no such thing."

Laughter from multiple sources, presumed to be those of Unidentified Voice and Spacer First Class Rick Boatright.

Unidentified Voice, as the laughter fades: "Do you think you might continue before the meal arrives?"

Spacer Rick Boatright: "Certainly . . ."

I felt tired, though I felt neither hunger nor thirst. It was all very strange, as I've said—perhaps too often to suit you, my interrogators.

The ball that had so occupied my attention dissolved into a warm liquid, freeing my hand from the void, which disappeared as soon as I withdrew it. A short interval passed, then I had a sense of movement, of objects and spaces, passing me by, yet knew instinctively that I failed to perceive more than the merest fraction of what was going on.

With the movement I would occasionally feel a sensation not unlike brushing against another traveler, of being *almost* avoided. Like strangers forced into close proximity in a crowded shuttle terminal, always attempting to minimize physical contact with strangers. Sometimes we even succeed, despite the fact such contact reaffirms our very humanity.

In any event, I was ushered toward, and then through, a blankness. It was not the darkness, the wrongness I had been annihilating. It was too . . . *intentional* for that. I was inserted into that blank space, and for the first time could look over my shoulder and see something other than flaws in the limitless space I had occupied before. It was as if I observed that moment when a drop of water separates from the bottom of a gutter. Extruding, growing, swelling.

That drop, when it fell, released me upon our reality once more.

Like that, I was back, hovering just above the surface of DB1432TT, my body fully restored, if changed in the manner you see now. The artifact folded/expanded /burned/solidified, shrinking until it was nearly imperceptible, then winked out.

I felt lonely then. And not simply because I was so vastly alone in space, but because I missed the touch, or the almost-touch, I had experienced in that strangeness. It was as if my mother had been holding fast to me but could no longer maintain her grip.

Nearly inaudible voice, presumed to be that of Interrogator One: "So full . . . hit, talkin . . . out humanity. Just look . . . him."

Unidentified Voice: "I am, and you are excused."

Interrogator One: "Yes, Ma'am."

<<Interval of seventeen point five seconds.>>

Spacer Rick Boatright: "He does not seem to like me very much."

Unidentified Voice: "He fears you."

Rick Boatright: "That's only natural, I suppose. I'd fear me, too."

Unidentified Voice: "Yet you do not?"

Rick Boatright: "I would fear this change more, but I truly believed myself dead. Yet here I sit; complete, healthy, even able to make jokes. Whatever other strangeness has occurred, I am here, now, speaking my thoughts to you. There is a certain . . . solidity to the reality of these interactions."

Unidentified Voice: "And if you are not speaking your own thoughts? If touching that alien presence did more than alter just your appearance?"

Spacer Rick Boatright: "Then I have touched the divine and returned, able to speak of things no other person can. Such is no small gift, I think."

I owe my survival to the fact my suit's power and chemical supplies—food printer and all—had been restored, though I quickly discovered my implants had been removed and not replaced. I turned on the suit transponder as soon as I decided that spending a few years in a Perfected prison camp would suit me better than dying alone on that rock. I was recovered some ninety-six hours after the annihilation of my team, and thirty-seven hours after the 14th Fleet destroyed the antimatter plant. I did not need medivac. Flesh that had been injured or destroyed in the engagement was replaced with what I have taken to calling "compressed stardust." That's just my pet name for it. The researchers might have come up with more accurate names for it since their initial tests, but I like the ring of my name for it far better the appellation they insisted on using at first. "Exotic matter," simply sounds anything but exotic.

Of course, it could just be that I desperately want that old saw, "We are, all of us, made of stardust," to be literally true in my case.

The preceding is a partial extract from the AAR and debrief of Rick Boatright, Spacer First Class, Imperial Navy Commando, and lone survivor of the skirmish on DB1432TT.

As any student of this historical period will note, there are very few first-hand accounts of contact with the alien technology left behind by the Bridger Species, and none pre-date the discoveries made by Dr. Dumont here in the Nouvelle Geneve system. That the Imperial Navy hid the discovery in classified documents does not help modern historians in the least, as this humble historian has failed to locate any further notes or records regarding the eventual fate of Spacer First Class Rick Boatright. It is hoped that he lives still, or at least remains one with the infinite.

—Extract from De-Classified Imperial Archives of the Post War Period, A Study, Vol. XII, *written by Maximiliano Messina and published in all feeds by Universite du Nouvelle Geneve, 321 NIC.*

AUTHOR BIOGRAPHIES

Griffin Barber spent his youth in four different countries, learning three languages, and burning all his bridges. Finally settled in Northern California and retired from a day job as a police officer in a major metropolitan department, he lives the good life with his lovely wife, crazy-smart daughter, and tiny Bengal rescue. *1636: Mission to the Mughals*, coauthored with Eric Flint, was his first novel. *1637: The Peacock Throne* is now available. He's also collaborated on a number of projects with Kacey Ezell, writing *Second Chance Angel* with her. Griffin has also penned *Man-Eater* and *Infiltration*, novellas set in The Murphy's Lawless annex of Charles Gannon's Caine Riordan Universe. He has a number of short stories coming out in various anthologies for 2022–23.

D.J. (Dave) Butler has been a lawyer, a consultant, an editor, a corporate trainer, and a registered investment banking representative. His novels published by Baen Books include *Witchy Eye*, *Witchy Winter*, and *Witchy Kingdom*, and *In the Palace of Shadow and Joy*, as well as *The Cunning Man* and *The Jupiter Knife*, cowritten with

Aaron Michael Ritchey. He also writes for children: The steampunk fantasy adventure tales *The Kidnap Plot*, *The Giant's Seat*, and *The Library Machine* are published by Knopf. Other novels include *City of the Saints* from WordFire Press and *The Wilding Probate* from Immortal Works. Dave also organizes writing retreats and anarcho-libertarian writers' events and travels the country to sell books. He plays guitar and banjo whenever he can and likes to hang out in Utah with his wife and children.

Jessica Cain is a longtime fan of everything strange and otherworldly. By day, she works for tech companies creating content for digital platforms. By night, she consumes way too much coffee and tea while typing out her stories. She's known to frequent graveyards for a little inspiration and she's also a demon at pub trivia. Some think she might actually be a demon, but they just need to get to know her better. She lives in New York, where she's currently hard at work on her first novel.

Erica Ciko's stories have appeared in many eerie and enchanting venues, most recently *Mythic*, *Cosmic Horror Monthly*, and *Tales to Terrify*. She's the editor-in-chief of *Starward Shadows Quarterly* and a proud active member of the SFWA. She's also currently writing the Tales of a Starless Aeon novel series: If you haven't heard of it, you will soon. If you're still craving the whispers of war-torn, dead galaxies in the meantime, check out her website: starless-imperium.com. You can also find her on Twitter at @TheLastGrimKing.

Orson Scott Card is the author of *Ender's Game* and *Speaker for the Dead*, which won two of his four Hugo Awards. His other books include *The Lost Gate*, *Pathfinder*, *Lost and Found*, and *The Tales of Alvin Maker*.

Card began as a poet and playwright, but in his mid-twenties began publishing fiction. He also served as a missionary in urban Brazil for the Church of Jesus Christ of Latter-day Saints.

Card and his wife, Kristine, are the parents of three adult children who have provided seven grandchildren. The Cards live in Greensboro, NC, because if you can live in Greensboro, why would you live anywhere else?

Patrick Chiles has been fascinated by aircraft, rockets, and spaceflight ever since he was a child transfixed by the Apollo missions. How he ended up as an English major in college is still a mystery, though he managed to overcome this to pursue a career in aviation operations and safety management.

He is a graduate of The Citadel, a Marine Corps veteran, and a private pilot. In addition to his novels, he has written for magazines such as Smithsonian's *Air & Space*. He currently resides in Tennessee with his wife and two lethargic dachshunds.

Jonathan Edelstein has been writing stories since he was four but became a published author only at the age of forty. His first published story—"Four Sacrifices," a supernatural tale set in Minoan Crete—appeared in the *Lacuna Journal* in 2012, and since then, he is the author of nineteen other science fiction and fantasy stories appearing in *Beneath Ceaseless Skies, Strange Horizons, Daily Science Fiction,* and other magazines and anthologies. Most recently, his short story "Lightning Cat" appeared in *Felis Futura,* an anthology of future cat stories.

Edelstein's inspirations come from an eclectic collection of sources: ancient history and modern physics, medieval Jewish scholarship and southern African cosmology, the alleys of New York City and the streets of Lagos, the towers of the future and the ruins of the past. His literary heroes are equally eclectic, ranging from Chinua Achebe to Ursula K. Le Guin to Bernard Cornwell.

Edelstein was born in New York City and has lived in and around there all his life with the exception of boot camp. He currently lives in Queens with his wife Naomi and their cat Maya. When he isn't writing, he practices law and hopes one day to get it right.

Sean Patrick Hazlett is an Army veteran, speculative fiction writer and editor, and finance executive in the San Francisco Bay area. He holds an AB in history and a BS in electrical engineering from Stanford University, and a Master's in public policy from the Harvard Kennedy School of Government, where he won the 2006 Policy Analysis Exercise Award for his work on policy solutions to Iran's nuclear weapons program under the guidance of future secretary of defense Ashton B. Carter. He also holds an MBA from the Harvard Business School, where he graduated with Second Year Honors. As a cavalry officer serving in the elite 11th Armored Cavalry

Regiment, he trained various Army and Marine Corps units for war in Iraq and Afghanistan. While at the Army's National Training Center, he became an expert in Soviet doctrine and tactics. He has also published a Harvard Business School case study on the 11th Armored Cavalry Regiment and how it exemplified a learning organization.

Sean is a 2017 winner of the Writers of the Future Contest. Over forty of his short stories have appeared in publications such as *The Year's Best Military and Adventure SF*, *Year's Best Hardcore Horror*, *Terraform*, *Galaxy's Edge*, *Writers of the Future*, *Grimdark Magazine*, *Vastarien*, and *Abyss & Apex*, among others.

He is the editor of the *Weird World War III* anthology. Sean also teaches strategy, finance, and communications as a course facilitator at the Stanford Graduate School of Business's Executive Education Program. He is an active member of the Horror Writers Association and Codex Writers' Group.

Les Johnson is a husband, father, physicist, and author. *Publishers Weekly* noted that "The spirit of Arthur C. Clarke and his contemporaries is alive and well ..." when describing his 2018 novel, *Mission to Methone*. Les is the coauthor of the Saving Proxima series with Travis S. Taylor and *Rescue Mode* with Ben Bova, as well as *The Spacetime War* and others from Baen Books. He is the coeditor of the science/science fiction collections *Stellaris* and *Going Interstellar*. His latest non-fiction book, *A Traveler's Guide to the Stars*, was published by Princeton University Press in October 2022. Les was technical consultant for the movies *Europa Report* and *Lost in Space* and has appeared on the Discovery Channel series *Physics of the Impossible* in the "How to Build a Starship" episode. He has also appeared in three episodes of the Science Channel series *Exodus Earth* as well as several other television documentaries. Les was the featured "interstellar explorer" in the January 2013 issue of *National Geographic* magazine and appeared again in the March 2019 issue for his work on solar sail space propulsion.

By day, Les serves as Solar Sail Principal Investigator of NASA's first interplanetary solar sail space mission, Near-Earth Asteroid Scout, and leads research on various other advanced space propulsion technologies at the George C. Marshall Space Flight Center in Huntsville, Alabama. During his career at NASA, he served as the Manager for the Space Science Programs and Projects Office, the In-Space Propulsion Technology Program, and the Interstellar Propulsion Research Project. Les has thrice received NASA's Exceptional Achievement Medal, has three patents, and was selected for membership in Mensa.

Sean CW Korsgaard is a U.S. Army veteran, historian, award-winning journalist, and an editor at Baen Books.

As a reporter, he's had over fifteen hundred articles published across dozens of newspapers in Virginia over the past seven years, including the *Richmond Times-Dispatch* and the *Daily Press*, and nationally, in outlets ranging from *The New York Times* to *io9* to *VFW Magazine*, and most recently, as a guest columnist for *Analog Science Fiction & Fact*.

His work has seen him interview two U.S. Presidents, walk the grounds of Auschwitz beside Holocaust survivors, party with Swedish metal bands, caught in the thick of riots, and even attacked by a shark. He was a finalist for the Baen Fantasy Adventure Award and Writers of the Future.

Sean lives in Richmond, Virginia, with his wife and child, and is always looking for his next great adventure and his next big byline, and you can follow him and his work at www.korsgaardscommentary.com or on Twitter @SCWKorsgaard.

Of Scottish and Nigerian descent, **Adam Oyebanji** is an escapee from Birmingham University and Harvard Law School. He currently lives in Pittsburgh, PA, with a wife, child, and two embarrassingly large dogs. When he's not out among the stars, Adam works in the field of counter-terrorist financing, helping banks choke off the money supply that builds weapons of mass destruction, narcotics empires, and human trafficking networks. *Braking Day* (DAW Books) is his first novel.

Gray Rinehart writes science fiction and fantasy stories, songs, and . . . other things. He is the only person to have commanded an Air Force satellite tracking station, written speeches for presidential appointees, devised a poetic form, and had music on *The Dr. Demento Show*. He is currently a contributing editor (the "Slushmaster General") for Baen Books.

Gray is the author of the lunar colonization novel *Walking on the Sea of Clouds* (WordFire Press), and his short fiction has appeared in *Analog Science Fiction & Fact*, *Asimov's Science Fiction*, Orson Scott Card's *Intergalactic Medicine Show*, and multiple anthologies. As a singer/songwriter, he has two albums of mostly science-fiction-and-fantasy-inspired music. During his unusual USAF career, Gray fought rocket propellant fires, refurbished space launch facilities, "flew" Milstar satellites, drove trucks, encrypted nuclear command and control orders, commanded the largest remote tracking station in the Air Force Satellite Control Network, and did other interesting things. His alter ego is the Gray Man, one of several famed ghosts of South Carolina's Grand Strand, and his web site is graymanwrites.com.

USA TODAY best-selling author **M.A. Rothman** has always been a creative type with a strong background in science and math. He's used those strengths to great effect in Silicon Valley over a thirty-plus-year career; yet if you polled his former English teachers, asking them if they expected him to become a novelist, they'd all laugh hysterically and say, "No."

More than a few handfuls of years ago he had kids, and the bedtime stories began flowing. From these stories bloomed an accidental writing career. As a well-traveled engineer, with a strong background in the sciences, this accidental novelist began writing stories that focused on two things: technology and international intrigue.

His writing spans the genres of science fiction, techno-thriller, and his own unique spin on LitRPG. When not writing, he enjoys cooking, learning about new technology, travel, and spending time with his family.

Christopher Ruocchio is the internationally award-winning author of The Sun Eater, a space opera fantasy series, and a former junior editor at Baen Books, where he edited several anthologies. His work has also appeared in Marvel Comics. He is a graduate of North Carolina State University, where he studied English Rhetoric and the Classics. Christopher has been writing since he was eight and sold his first novel, *Empire of Silence*, at twenty-two. His books have appeared in five languages.

Christopher lives in Raleigh, North Carolina, with his wife, Jenna.

Brian Trent's work regularly appears in *The Magazine of Fantasy & Science Fiction*, *Analog Science Fiction and Fact*, *The Year's Best Military and Adventure SF*, *Terraform*, *Flash Fiction Online*, *Daily Science Fiction*, *Apex*, *Pseudopod*, *Escape Pod*, *Galaxy's Edge*, *Nature*, and numerous year's-best anthologies. The author of the sci-fi novels *Redspace Rising* and *Ten Thousand Thunders*, Trent is a winner of the 2019 Year's Best Military and Adventure SF Readers' Choice Award from Baen Books and a Writers of the Future winner. He is also a contributor to Baen anthologies *Weird World War III*, *Weird World War IV*, *Weird World War: China*, *Cosmic Corsairs*, and the Black Tide Rising anthologies *We Shall Rise* and *United We Stand*. Trent lives in New England. His website and blog are at www.briantrent.com.

David J. West writes weird westerns and pulp fantasy (sometimes under the *nom de plume* James Alderdice) all because the voices in his head won't quiet until someone else can hear them. He is a great fan of sword & sorcery, ghosts and lost ruins, so of course he lives in Utah with his wife and children. You can find him most anywhere online but he is most likely to be chatty on Twitter @David_JWest.

OVERRULED!
(coedited with Christopher Ruocchio)

Order in the court! An anthology of science fiction stories that explores what the future of jurisprudence might well be like, with thrilling, hilarious, and downright entertaining results! So much fun, it oughta be illegal! Stories by Robert A. Heinlein, Clifford D. Simak, Sarah A. Hoyt, and more stellar talents bringing down the judge's gavel with a verdict of excellent entertainment.

TPB: 978-1-9821-2450-2 • $16.00 US/$22.00 CAN

TIME TROOPERS
(coedited with Christopher Ruocchio)

Military action was once two-dimensional, confined to the surface of land and sea, before submarines and aircraft added a third dimension. Now, what if time travel is possible? This fourth dimension would open up new possibilities for combat, necessitating new defenses, new strategies and tactics. Tales of spacetime combat from Robert Silverberg, Poul Anderson, Fritz Leiber, John C. Wright, H. Beam Piper, and more. Follow the Time Troopers into action across strange aeons!

TPB: 978-1-9821-2603-2 • $16.00 US/$22.00 CAN

And don't forget to check out
these other great Hank Davis anthologies,
all available as ebooks from Baen.com:

FUTURE WARS . . . AND OTHER PUNCHLINES
WORST CONTACT • IF THIS GOES WRONG . . .
SPACE PIONEERS

Available in bookstores everywhere.
Or order ebooks online at www.baen.com.

The Wellstone
TPB: 978-1-9821-2477-9 • $16.00 US / $22.00 CAN
MM: 978-1-9821-2588-2 • $8.99 US / $11.99 CAN

Humanity has conquered the Solar System, going so far as to vanquish death itself. But for the children of immortal parents, life remains a constant state of arrested development. With his complaints being treated as teenage whining, and his ability to inherit the throne, Prince Bascal Edward de Towaji Lutui and his fellow malcontents take to the far reaches of colonized space. The goal: to prove themselves a force to be reckoned with.

Lost in Transmission
TPB: 978-1-9821-2503-5 • $16.00 US / $22.00 CAN

Banished to the starship *Newhope*, now King Bascal and his fellow exiles face a bold future: to settle the worlds of Barnard's Star. The voyage will last a century, but with Queendom technology it's no problem to step into a fax machine and "print" a fresh, youthful version of yourself. But the paradise they seek is far from what they find, and death has returned with a vengeance.

To Crush the Moon
TPB: 978-1-9821-2524-0 • $16.00 US / $22.00 CAN
MM: 978-1-9821-9200-6 • $8.99 US / $11.99 CAN

Once the Queendom of Sol was a glowing monument to humankind's loftiest dreams. Ageless and immortal, its citizens lived in peaceful splendor. But as Sol buckled under the swell of an "immorbid" population, space itself literally ran out. Now a desperate mission has been launched: to literally crush the moon. Success will save billions, but failure will strand humanity between death and something unimaginably worse . . .

Antediluvian
HC: 978-1-4814-8431-2 • $25.00 US / $34.00 CAN
MM: 978-1-9821-2499-1 • $8.99 US / $11.99 CAN

What if all our Stone Age legends are true and older than we ever thought? It was a time when men and women struggled and innovated in a world of savage contrasts, preserved only in the oldest stories with no way to actually visit it. Until a daring inventor's discovery cracks the code embedded in the human genome.

Available in bookstores everywhere.
Or order ebooks online at www.baen.com.